# THE NEW EXODUS
## A Study of Israel in Russia

*Harold Frederic*

*ARNO PRESS & THE NEW YORK TIMES*

New York • 1970

Reprint edition 1970 by Arno Press, Inc.

Library of Congress Catalog Card No. 71-115538
ISBN 0-405-03027-4

*Russia Observed*
ISBN for complete set 0-405-03000-2

Reprinted from a copy in
the Newark Public Library

Manufactured in the United States of America

# RUSSIA OBSERVED

*Advisory Editors*

HARMON TUPPER    HARRY W. NERHOOD

# THE NEW EXODUS

ALEXANDER III

# THE

# NEW EXODUS

## A STUDY OF ISRAEL IN RUSSIA

BY

## HAROLD FREDERIC

AUTHOR OF "IN THE VALLEY," ETC.

*WITH ILLUSTRATIONS*

NEW YORK: G. P. PUTNAM'S SONS
LONDON: W. HEINEMANN
1892

To the Memory of

GEORGE JONES,

The Founder of a Great Newspaper

and

The Lifelong Champion of Good Causes,

This Volume,

Owing its existence, as it does, to the

Deep and Sympathetic Interest

With which the Horrors of the Jewish Persecution

in Russia filled his Last Days,

is reverently Dedicated.

# CONTENTS

# LIST OF ILLUSTRATIONS

# THE NEW EXODUS

## CHAPTER I

*"PARA DOMOI!"*

EDMUND BURKE confessed, over a century ago, that
he knew not the method of drawing up an indictment against a whole people. The task is no
easier now than it was in 1775. Moreover, the
world's jury, grown callous to sensation and wearied
with ever-multiplying claims upon its sympathies,
takes, in these latter times, a deal of moving.
Not even Burke risen from the dead could hold
its undivided attention for a second four days'
speech.

On the other hand, the day of the solitary and
unaided advocate is past. Mankind is far too
busy now to listen for more than the briefest
minute to any individual voice. A thousand men
toil daily to collate the facts and arguments upon
which it passes in judgment over its breakfast cup.
The story to be told in these chapters seeks only
its proper place among the great mass of accusa-
tory records that truthful observers and inquirers
for ten years back have been piling up at Russia's

A

door.   These records are in themselves an indictment—an indictment more solemn, more sweeping, more terrible than exists in written language
against any other people.   Were the waning nine-
teenth century a hundredfold more idle-minded
and indifferent than the *fin de siècle* cult would
have it, still must this indictment compel attention.

My own share in the gathering of materials is
represented by a long and painstaking journey
through Russia, both within and outside the Pale,
for the most part under the guidance of practical
men who were able to ensure to me the minimum
of wasted time.   The tour was made without official
assistance, and, I am happy to believe, escaped
official notice.   This fact prevented my making
personal studies of the Czar's domesticity, of M.
Pobiedonostseff's piety, of General Ignatieff's
urbanity, and of other similarly fascinating features
of polite Russia, concerning which so much has been
written.   The Russia I saw was not polite.   It was a
Russia which had never done anything more than
promise sometime to get civilised, and now for ten
years had openly surrendered itself to the engulf-
ing return wave of barbarism.   It was a Russia of
dark and hopeless ignorance, of drunken incompetency, of frank and even smiling contempt for
everything of thought and word and deed that we
call honesty.   I saw it in cottages, in fields, in
churches, camps, and market-places—and everywhere, depressing as the picture was, it furnished
the background to a still more sinister scene, that

of a whole race being hunted from its homes, despoiled of its possessions, hounded by the Cossack and plundered by the *tchinovnik*, and all unpitied by any one.

To attempt to deal in any satisfactory way with the whole question of the Jewish persecution in Russia is like setting out to write an Encyclopædia Britannica. The subject is so vast that its bulk fairly frightens one. To tell merely what is being done—what has happened since March of 1891—would require the space of many volumes, and the labour of as many men as there are scores of towns, villages, and hamlets in a section of country stretching from the Baltic to the Black Sea, and containing a population of fifty millions of people. The most industrious gleaning cannot hope to gather the thousandth part of the past twelve months' tragic facts. The scope of the figures staggers the imagination. More families, for example, have been affected by this new and savage enforcement of Ignatieff's May laws and the added ukases than were called upon to mourn the loss or wounding of relatives on either side during the great American civil war. Yet even a comparison of this kind fails to convey an adequate idea of the host of human beings involved in this brutal and wanton persecution.

How much more difficult must seem the task, then, of striving to explain this strange and monstrous excrescence upon the history of our century. To comprehend the position of the Jew in Russia

one must study the Russian, and get to understand the curious qualities and absence of qualities
which make him, although nominally master, in
reality the intellectual and material serf of all
the strangers within his gates—Germans, Jews,
Tartars, Finns, Poles, Armenians alike. One must
realise, further, that in this present barbaric
attempt of the Russian to drive out one of the
groups of people who know more than he does,
there lies both the whole long story of the effort
to civilise Russia, and the final admission that
the effort has failed and is abandoned. Truly, a
complex subject!

And in starting upon an examination of this
tangled and far-reaching web of race hatreds,
dynastic ambitions, and religious strifes, it cannot
be too clearly kept in mind that this raid upon
the Jews is only one phase of a vast national
movement. All things conspired to point to the
unhappy Jew as the one to begin upon. It will be
the turn of the German next. Even now the air
is filled with ugly suggestions as to the confiscation of German factories and industrial plants, and
new laws are actually coming into force which will
compel foreigners to choose between naturalisa-
tion and flight. The Finns are already under
the harrow. The fact that their autonomy was
sacredly pledged to them under the Grand Ducal
Crown never mattered for a moment. The pledge
was simply broken—snapped over the Imperial
knee like a dry twig. A hundred solemn pro-

mises, to which had been given the weight of
Ministerial seals and Imperial signatures, were as
calmly tossed on the dust-heap when it was
desired to drive the Jews from Moscow. Good
faith has no meaning in Russia. No assurance, no
pledge, no law will avail for an instant to save the
German and English properties in Russia, once
the Ministerial hand is lifted to seize them.

Upon the banners of the advance guard in this
prodigious national movement might well be in-
scribed Aksakoff's famous words, "*Para domoi!*"
("It is time to go home"). The phrase at the
moment thrilled Moscow with new Pan-Slavic
raptures. It has come to be, if not the spoken
watchword, at least the tacit motto of rank and
file as well as leaders.

We talk glibly enough of Pan-Slavism, but
rarely define it, even to our own minds. To
most persons it signifies in a vague way something about grabbing Bulgaria and Roumelia whenever the next war with Turkey comes, and
meanwhile subsidising spies and agitators in the
Balkans. In reality Pan-Slavism signifies something incalculably broader and more important to
the rest of the world. A big book could be
written—nay, the next generation will have many
big books written—upon its meaning. When
Aksakoff called out "*Para domoi!*" every Russian knew him to mean that it was time to give
over the pretence of apeing Western Europe;
that it was time to throw to the winds the effort

to appear civilised; that it was time to turn the clock back again to the starting-point of Peter the Great, to undo all that his German successors had done in imitation of Occidental models, to frankly relapse into Slavonic barbarism.

One must go to Moscow to comprehend the strength of this feeling and the tremendous fascination it has for the Russian mind. A dozen years ago it seemed to be the exclusive property of a small though influential group of reactionary thinkers—the Aksakoffs, Katkoff, Ignatieff, and others less well known to European fame. To-day it literally possesses the nation. Those of the educated Russian classes who are too intelligent to be really moved by it, are precisely the ones who most vigorously simulate being under its sway. The feeling is quite akin to that of the child who, having laboriously sat out the long hours of a church service in tight boots and a stiff shirt collar, returns home to tear off these hateful bonds and roll barefooted and collarless in the hay. The Russian is captivated with the thought of ceasing to pretend to be civilised. His is the longing of the young Indian brave at the mission-school to get back again into the breech-clout—to exchange the school-desk and books for forest glades and the chase.

We of the outside world have no notion whatever of the lengths to which this reaction has already gone in matters affecting not merely the Jewish population, but the whole social structure

of Russia. Few, for example, realise that on
July 1 of last year corporal punishment was re-
established in Russia. The horrors of the knout
used to be dilated upon in every book about
Russia. No collection of instruments of torture is
complete without one of those terrible bunches of
leathern thongs, their ends knotted in balls of lead,
and curious visitors look at them with as much
sense of strangeness as if they came from the
Papal Palace at Avignon or the old Binnenhof in
The Hague. It is indeed only thirty years ago
since it disappeared in Russia, when the Liberator
Czar remodelled the judicial system of his country.
It is perhaps too much to say that the knout has
come back. Such beatings as I have heard of
have been with rods. From this to the knout is
but a short backward step. If the latter is itself
restored, it will appear in company with so many
other savage revivals of pre-liberation days that
its return will be scarcely noted.

In the same way the old landlord magistrate
has come into existence again. After the serfs
had been emancipated it became necessary to
provide decent legal machinery for the trying of
minor cases. Up to that time the "owners of
souls" had dealt with petty offences and disputes
after their own sweet will, punishing, fining,
maiming, killing, quite as they pleased, and with
only the barest forms of law. Alexander II, in
September of 1862, eighteen months after the
emancipation, established by decree a system of

minor jurisdiction, presided over in each district by a justice of the peace (*Mirovoi Sudya*), who passed upon all cases involving not more than 500 roubles ($330), and who, in criminal cases, was bound by an explicit criminal code. Alexander III, on July 1 of last year, 1891, abolished all the justices of peace outside St. Petersburg, Moscow, and a few other large cities, and returned to the old system of Nicholas. Instead of the justice of the peace, there is now a *Natchalnik* of the *Zemstvo*—that is to say, a landlord who has time and needs the place, and who is elected by the landed gentry of the district. This is the gentleman who, during this last awful winter of famine and pestilence, has so ably muddled or obstructed the efforts of the central authorities and the Red Cross Society toward popular relief. Of only one or two of these *Natchalniks* has any good word been spoken by those who have been studying the famine districts. More often they are alluded to as rough despots or hopelessly stupid fools. Occasionally we hear of one like M. Dementieff, *Natchalnik* in Samara, who late last autumn got together 300,000 roubles on the pretext of relieving the suffering in his district, and coolly left the country with the entire sum. It is to these officials that the power of ordering corporal punishment at will has been restored.

This is only one of scores of similar revivals, showing on every side the governing desire to get Russia back again into her Asiatic shell.

The signs of this reaction force themselves upon the attention at every corner in inner Russia. Gentlemen and officers who fifteen years ago affected rationalism in religion, and left the demonstrative part of the Church ceremonial to the monks and the moujiks, now ostentatiously halt before every shrine and church edifice to bow and cross themselves. The pilgrimages to holy places have swollen enormously in volume, and embrace now a well-to-do element which under the last reign they never knew. If this were accompanied by any spiritual awakening inside the Church, or even an increased activity in theological discussion, it would invite more respectful comment. But nothing is more certain than that there has been no spiritual or other awakening. The Russian Orthodox Church—of which something will be said later on—is spiritually and mentally as dry and barren as a sandbank. It exists solely in forms and ceremonies for the intelligent, and in fetiches for the unintelligent. This augmented observance of the ceremonies, everywhere noted by on-lookers, indicates merely a general consciousness that the Church is playing a part in this grand national retrograde movement.

Another indication, perhaps even more significant, is found in the immense proportional increase of books printed in the Russian language. Booksellers who formerly kept a few Russian works, and devoted most of their shelf space to French, German, and even English literature, now see the

conditions quite reversed. The new Russian
generation is far less inclined to reading of any
sort than was that which flourished under the
Liberator Czar, and is also far less well educated, in
the better sense of the word. Scholars, students
and booksellers, with whom I talked in a half-
dozen widely separated large towns, all told the
same tale : the demand for serious works was
yearly diminishing, and the younger Russians were
not learning languages as their fathers did. The
principal display in every window and on every
counter is of pamphlet translations from Zola,
Belot, Richepin, Gaboriau, and other modern
French novelists. Next to these in importance
come imported editions of these same books in
their original French. The literature of strictly
native production seems to be almost wholly confined to pamphlets.* No one talks of a visible
successor to Turgenieff, Dostoieffsky or Tolstoi.

Even in the army curious effects of this ruling

---

* A critic, writing to the New York *Nation* under date of
October 3, 1891, took exception to my earlier statements upon this
subject, and quoted the St. Petersburg *Knizhny Viestnik* (a
publishers' organ) to show that of the 4358 works published in
Russia during 1890 only 10 per cent. were translations. One may
prove anything under the sun by Russian statistics. I sent copies
of this criticism to student friends in both St. Petersburg and Kieff.
The replies were that I was absolutely right ; that the vast majority
of the books on philology (455), medical science (372), political
science (337), &c. &c., were either text-books or obscure pamphlets ;
and that M. Struve, the Russian Minister at Washington, had
publicly described the intellectual and literary decadence of Russia
in terms much more sweeping than mine.

idea that "it is time to go home" are observable.
The soldiers — stout, deep-chested, docile, and
hardy-looking fellows—are fast getting out of the
stiff, pipe-clay routine which the other Czars, in
their passion for imitating the German model,
insisted on. If there were any geniuses among
the military leaders of Russia, they would doubtless have invented before this a series of original
Asiatic formations to answer as substitutes for the
corps, division, regiment, and squadron borrowed
from the hated Teuton. Unhappily, this flight is
beyond their intellectual level. They must still
have a Guards Corps in St. Petersburg as in Berlin,
and use a German manual of arms. But both
officers and soldiers are already a long distance
away from the standard of discipline that was enforced a dozen years ago. The officers in their
uniforms do not scruple to pay open court to the
*cocottes* in the public gardens of St. Petersburg,
Moscow, and Kieff. They sit with them at the
supper tables in the open air, buy wine for them,
quarrel with one another for the privilege of their
society, and drive away in *droschkis* with them,
all without the slightest thought of concealment
—and all in full uniform! The private soldiers
no longer try to stand erect or carry themselves like warriors. They slouch along at an
easy, round-shouldered gait, hands in pockets,
and it is a mere matter of taste and convenience
whether they salute a passing officer or not. Only a
few months ago the case was reported of a young

Russian officer who drew his revolver and shot dead a private soldier who failed to salute him.

A sympathetic Russian explained to me this laxity of discipline which I noted on every side among the soldiers by saying that formerly they were drilled a great deal in all sorts of precise, dry-as-dust German formalities, but this did not suit the spirit of the Slav, and so now that was all abandoned and reliance was placed solely on " moral discipline."

Thus, evidences of the reaction might be multiplied and extended into practically every department of Russian existence. But the sequel will of necessity deal with this subject in detail.

The essential point is that the overwhelming mass of Russians, educated, half-educated, and ignorant alike, are for the moment enlisted under the banner of reaction. If there are dissenters, they hold their peace, sneering in private, but openly throwing up their caps for the march backward. All those who have the intelligence to see what folly it is, joined with the courage to speak their minds, are in Siberia or in exile. So far as public opinion is visible in Russia, it is unanimous. Everybody professes to be in favour of Russia for the Russians, and to be quite satisfied with the measures adopted and foreshadowed to make that policy good.

This absence of criticism is a fatal bar to any general awakening on the subject. The value of any set of ideas, if they are persistently promul-

gated and may not be debated, will naturally
establish itself in the public mind—all the more if
that public mind is inherently indolent and limited.
Thus, Moscow and inner Russia generally has
come to believe that the Western civilisation—the
civilisation of Germany, France, England, and
America—is absolutely corrupt and diseased, and
must, from its own rottenness, very soon break
down altogether. They ascribe to it nameless
abominations, of which Western Europe has hardly
so much as an abstract idea. And their editors
and spokesmen profess continually the conviction
that, when these wretched and effete nations of
the West shall have collapsed and perished in their
own putridity, the pure and untarnished Slavonic
race will inherit and regenerate the earth. The
wildest of these frantic teachings takes root somewhere. The broad notion at the back of them—that
the Russian race can do great and wonderful things
by itself, that it has not thus far done them because
its energies have been directed in mistaken
channels, and that it is high time now to turn back
and begin again *à la Slav naturel*—has taken
possession of the popular mind.

Of course this popular mind is a very childish
affair. Indeed, the temptation continually arises
to find parallels for all things Russian in the
fantasies and queer aberrations of childhood. The
Slavic brain is nothing if not juvenile. It is
invincibly optimistic ; it rushes headlong into en-
thusiastic beliefs founded upon the merest hearsay

or imagining ; it invents lies and excuses with incredible swiftness and an entire disregard for pro-
babilities, or for cause and effect ; it has no conception of responsibility, of duty, or any other
abstract virtue.   Withal, it is kindly and ferocious
by turn, cowardly in the face of stern power,
merry when the sun shines, lazy as the day is
long—childlike always.

The bold shamelessness of Russian official lying
has long since passed into a proverb, yet it remains
still so difficult a thing for the Western mind to
lay hold of, that able travellers are to this day
deceived on every side.   Within the past five
years books have been published by English and
other travellers, professing to tell " the truth about
Russia " which were literally padded from first to
last with Muscovite falsehoods.   Only last summer,
for example, Mr. Arnold White, who had been
journeying through the Empire to secure confidential information for Baron Hirsch, returned
and gravely reported for facts about Moscow a
pack of lies which had been told him by the
officials of the Holy Synod, the falsity of which
was demonstrated on the first moment of inquiry.
He was told, to take only one incident, that the
cruelties perpetrated in driving the Jews from
Moscow in March of 1891 were due to the mistaken and excessive zeal of "a late Chief of
Police," and he repeated this for truth in his
report.   As a matter of fact there was no " late "
Chief of Police at all.   Yourkoffsky, the Cossack

adventurer, who did these cruel deeds, had been Chief of Police in Moscow for six years, and was Chief of Police still. Only a child or a Russian officer would venture upon such a lie as this.

This infantile quality has its fullest exemplification in the confidence with which the Russian regards the commercial future of his country, once all the people who know how to conduct commerce have been chased from it. Over and over again, in the official literature of the Persecution, one finds it set forth with the utmost naïveté that Jews and other foreigners were necessary in Russia to open up avenues of trade and establish industries, but now that they have done this they can safely be driven out. The Russian admits frankly that he was not intellectually equal to the task of establishing such industrial commerce as Russia enjoys, but he never dreams of doubting his ability to carry it on now that it has been established. Much less does it occur to him to question his moral right to kick out and despise all those who established it.

Thus we return to the expulsion of the Jews. Undoubtedly they owe it to their nationality that they are the first to feel the effects of the Pan-Slavic upheaval—but they are being put out because they are not Russians, not because they are Jews. The expulsion of the other non-Russians will follow—nay, is already in progress.

It was natural to begin with the Jews. In every imperfectly civilised country—and unfortunately in at least one country which regards itself as very completely civilised—the materials for an anti-Jewish movement always lie close at hand. In Russia this unhappy people had from the first lived under extraordinary conditions. A whole thick volume of laws existed, all designed to keep it a race apart. Every moujik knew that the Jew was a pariah, a creature who in official eyes had fewer rights than himself, or even than the despised gipsy. When an ignorant man low down in the social scale finds somebody lower still, mere contact breeds a lust for persecution. Somewhat higher up on the ladder, the small Russian merchant, artisan, and trader had the additional grievance of disastrous competition with the Jew, who could actually add up figures in his head without an abacus, who never drank, rarely took holidays, understood how to buy, and could not be dismayed by hard work. Still higher up, the Russian professional and larger commercial circles had this feeling in a form intensified by the greater magnitude of the competition.

In one sense, the religious antagonism was a less potent factor in Russia than in Germany or Hungary. The Russian of the last reign was but a lackadaisical theologian, and took only less interest in the creeds of those about him than he did in his own dogmas. But with the sombre and sinister revival of ecclesiastical energy which followed the rise to power of Pobiedonostseff, the Orthodox Church was able to add the spirit of religious intolerance to the commercial, social and racial elements which, under the new reign, threatened Jewish security and peace.

Hence, when a wretched personal intrigue, to be detailed later on, put into certain base minds the idea of a *Judenhetze* in Russia, it was an easy matter to secure anti-Jewish riots. And later, when the Pan-Slavic vision had expanded into a demand for the expulsion of foreigners in general, what more natural than that the crusade should start with the Jews?

The Russians are the excuse-makers of the world. The police had scarcely begun their work of expelling Jews who were too poor to buy temporary immunity before all Russia blossomed with reasons for the expulsion. The Jews were all usurers, money-lenders, vampires who sucked the choicest Russian blood, promoters of dishonesty in business, &c. These charges began in the imagination, but it was not long before the Russians had persuaded themselves of their truth. Every bankrupt Russian merchant, who has misconducted his business with drunken stupidity and indolence for years, will tell you now that he has been ruined by Jewish chicanery; every bad Russian workman, who never properly learned his trade, and has lost every job he ever had through drink, ascribes his lack of work to Jewish competition; every moujik, who is too lazy properly to cultivate his field, and whose labour is mortgaged ahead for two or three years to the local

B

publican, while his children have neither clothes nor food, feels convinced that his misfortunes are all in some way due to the Jew.

More than that, the Russian Jew labours under the disadvantage of the fact that the large majority· of English, German and other foreign merchants and manufacturers in Russia take the side of the Russians against him. This is not difficult of explanation. All commerce in Russia—all financial activity of whatever kind—is in the nature of a game, in which all the people who are not Russians—Jews, Germans, English, Armenians, Greeks, and Tartars—play for the possessions of the Russian, he himself not being smart enough to take a place among the gamesters. In this game the competitors do not like one another, but race prejudice enables the others to more or less unite in a common dislike for the Jew.

What the actual facts are concerning the Jew in Russia, I hope to be able to state with some degree of conclusiveness later on. It is enough here to say that, whatever his faults, they are not those with which the present popular clamour in Russia charges him.

# CHAPTER II

## THE PARIAH COMMUNITY

PROPERLY to follow what has happened and is happening in Russia, not to speak of the still more impressive events to come, one must first of all realise that all over the empire the administrative power is above the law. It is by the failure to comprehend this that men even of Mr. Goldwin Smith's intellectual rank are led to write and print misleading and mischievous nonsense about Russo-Jewish matters.

In Anglo-Saxon countries, when we speak of a law-abiding community, we mean that the people therein obey the laws and give the officials appointed to administer the law a minimum of trouble. There is no equivalent phrase in Russian, and there is no need for one. That the people obey is taken for granted. It is the officials who do not observe the laws, but who instead use the vast and conflicting jumble of ukases, decrees, and Ministerial instructions as a general basis for doing whatever they want to do. There is no study or science of jurisprudence in our sense of the word. If a Governor-General sees that the drift of Imperial or Ministerial inclination is in a certain direction, his underlings and all the small officials who serve the courts and police offices of the province make a search and find a thousand and one smart ways of interpreting what is called the law to suit His Excellency's purpose, which, of course, is to keep abreast of the St. Petersburg current. If this current is suddenly arrested, if it backs, shifts, flows off at a tangent, the law as promptly assumes a wholly different complexion.

Moreover, if warrant for any given line of action which seems desirable to the local officials is not to be found at all in the law, the fact does not deter them for a minute. They go ahead without it, confident that there will be no one to bring them to book, and that, even if there were, they can rely upon Ministerial recognition of the fact that their excessive zeal was well-intentioned.

I am not writing at random in this or exaggerating anything. If it were necessary, I could fill a chapter of this book with quotations of perfectly authenticated cases in my notes of administrative actions which had no earthly excuse in law. What law, for example, authorised M. Alexeieff, Mayor of Moscow, during the summer of 1891 to order that no more sick Jews should be admitted to the hospitals of Moscow? This is only one of scores of such incidents, some of which it will be useful to cite further on. And as for grotesquely-strained constructions of the law, now stretched one way to form a pitfall, now wrenched the other way to clutch and fleece the victim, they form a leading feature of the whole story of the persecution.

For this reason, less importance attaches to the formidable list of anti-Jewish laws which exist in Russia than might be supposed. Three years ago a compilation of them was published at Kieff which covers 290 octavo pages of close type, and of these laws nineteen-twentieths have never been translated out of the original Russian. Since that book was printed there have been enough additional ukases, notes, and rescripts on the subject half to fill another such volume. It would be an incredibly dull official who in all this huge repository of contradictory laws and interpretations could not find new ways of commending himself to M. Pobiedonostseff.

Four years ago a commission was appointed to codify the existing laws and suggest new ones governing the residential privileges of Jews within the empire, and their rights of holding property and engaging in business. This commission, in the spring of 1891, made a report, which all Russian Jews know of by hearsay and refer to as "the sixty-five projects." This report was drawn up by M. de Ploeve, the chief assistant in the Ministry of the Interior, and the chosen penman of the persecution. It is said that the majority of the commission made a different kind of report, recommending more tolerant measures, and that the Czar refused to receive this and took M. de Ploeve's stringent suggestions instead. It is also

alleged that none of the Ministers save M.
Dournovo, who is M. de Ploeve's nominal superior,
originally favoured the adoption of this minority
report.

However that may be, the "sixty-five projects"
were hanging like a nightmare over Israel last
summer and autumn, while I was in Russia. It
was understood that nothing more was needed to
make them laws save a formal act of ratification
by the Council of the Empire, and the announcement of this was looked for from week to week.
Copies of these "projects," surreptitiously obtained,
began to circulate through the Empire, from one
official to another. A devoted man, at great risk
to himself, was able to procure for me one of these
written copies, and smuggle it out of the country
to me where I waited for it on the Hungarian
border. When the task of getting it translated,
and of comparing it section by section with existing laws as far as they are obtainable in any
language but Russian, had been completed, I found
that the mysterious "projects" were really little
more than a restatement of previous regulations.
What is new in them considerably limits Jewish
privileges, and elaborates the machinery for harrying them from country to town once they have
been driven inside the Pale. They also provide
punishments for even unwitting offenders not previously authorised by the law. But to my knowledge things have been done all over Russia for
which not even these new projects afford a warrant,

although, like all Imperially-approved " projects," they have been practically in force ever since the first high officials were able to find out about them.

These " projects " remain to this day unratified. This fact may be due to the Ministerial dissensions of which so much has been heard during the past winter — dissensions which, together with the general disorganisation incident to the famine, and the collapse of the Imperial Exchequer, seem to have paralysed governmental action in many other directions. But even if affairs in Russia had pursued their normal course, it is quite likely that the " projects " would still have remained in a pigeon-hole.

It had been taken for granted that the extreme severities of the past autumn and winter were based upon these mysterious " projects," of which so much was heard and so little known. I find now that this, with the exceptions noted above, is not the case. All this only enforces what was said at the outset—there is no need for laws in order to enable the placemen of the autocracy to harass, persecute, despoil, and expel the unhappy Russian Jew. The leash has been slipped. The whole official pack, from Governors-General down to the poorest Cossack, are in full cry at his heels.

To rehearse a few elementary facts : What is known in Russia as the Pale consists of fifteen Governments, or *Gubernia*. This territory, where Jews are allowed to live and into which they are being chased from all other parts of Russia, was all stolen by the Russians from other people. What is called Little Russia—the *gubernia* of Tchernigov, Poltava, and Ekaterinoslav — was conquered from Poland in 1670. The Crimea, or government of Taurida, was taken from the Turks in the following century. White Russia— that is, the governments of Vitebsk and Mohilef —came in from Poland on the first partition in 1772. The later partitions brought in at varying times the Polish governments of Kovno, Wilna, Grodno, Minsk, Kieff, Podolia, and Volhynia, while the further dilapidation of Turkey yielded Kherson and Bessarabia. These fifteen governments are the Pale. They stretch from within a few miles of the Baltic Sea, southward to the Euxine, and eastward to the land of the Don Cossacks.

This territory was supposed in 1879 to contain about 25,500,000 inhabitants, of whom 3,000,000 were Jews. I say "supposed," because Russian statistics are wildly inaccurate, and are confessedly made up from tax lists, village registers, estimates of neighbours, and everything except actual counting. No better means exist now upon which to base a speculation as to the entire number of Jews in Russia. The number is placed all the way from 4,000,000 to 10,000,000. Probably the estimate of Paul Dimidoff, whose pamphlet* is of great value on the whole Russo-Jewish question,

---

* "Juden-Elend im Lande der Romanows," geschildert von Paul Dimidow. Berlin. 1890.

giving them a total of 6,000,000, is most nearly correct. The Jewish rate of increase is almost as abnormally large as that of the French Canadians in Quebec. Hence, we may say, roughly, that thirteen years ago there were 5,000,000 Jews in Russia, of whom 3,000,000 lived in the Pale, something more than 1,000,000 in Poland, and something less than 1,000,000 in Russia proper.

These Jews in the Pale constituted nearly or quite 12 per cent. of the entire population of the Pale. Of the urban population they constituted a vastly greater proportion. In the towns and townships of Mohilef, for example, they were 94 per cent. of all the people ; in those of Volhynia, 71 per cent. ; Minsk, 69 per cent. ; Kovno, 68 per cent., and so on down to 15 per cent. in the towns of Ekaterinoslav.* Thus it will be seen that they were already congested in the towns. In fact, their enforced residence in these fifteen districts made the Pale distinctively a place of towns. In the Pale and in Poland the number of inhabitants in towns was 223 to every 1000 of rural population, whereas in the rest of Russia, excepting St. Petersburg and Moscow, the proportion of town to country was only 59 to 1000, and even in the governments containing the two great cities mentioned it only rose to 221 to the 1000.

Yet even with this tremendous preponderance

* "The Jewish Question in Russia." By Prince Demidöff San-Donato. Translated from the Russian by J. Mitchell. London. 1884.

of Jews in the towns of the Pale, it is estimated
that there were from 400,000 to 500,000 Jews
living outside the towns.  The laws, and even
more, the spirit of their administration, rendered
theirs a most precarious life.  They had legally no
right to own land, and they rented only under all
sorts of restrictions and liability to plunder.  But
the overwhelming pressure of competition for
existence in the crowded towns created a necessity
for their spreading into the country which literally
bore down opposition.  They paid blackmail to
the police and the higher authorities, and continued to live, or, rather, to exist.

Both in town and country existence for these
Jews was a problem which never came to an end.
Of all the gross misconceptions to which ill-informed
writers have lent their minds, there is none at once
so cruel and grotesque as that which Mr. Goldwin
Smith reflects when he paints the Jews of the Pale
as prosperous usurers.  I have never seen anywhere else in Europe, not even in the poorer part
of Ireland, which I know well, a more terrible
poverty than is the rule of their lives.  It does not
need the evidence of an eye-witness to show the
absurdity of the other view—the figures do that.
Let one only try to conceive each ninety-four Jews
in the towns of Mohilef, for example, waxing rich
and fat by lending money to the six Christians who
remain.  Since Dr. Johnson's islanders earned a
precarious livelihood by taking in one another's
washing there has been no other such comical

economic paradox. In truth, not a third of the Jews, even outside the Pale, have had money enough to buy railway tickets to the frontier. Inside the Pale the most grinding poverty has always reigned.

Another feature of the Pale claims attention before the question of laws is touched. If we include Poland, it will be seen that its entire western edge is upon the frontier of Germany, Austro-Hungary, or Roumania. This border line is nearly fifteen hundred miles in length. By law a strip thirty-three miles in width (fifty versts) along this whole frontier was marked as land upon which Jews might not live. Thus, a territory about the size of the State of New York was sought to be closed to them. But in the lax days of Alexander II this further attempt to bottle up the Jews in the towns of the Pale also failed. As they had pushed their way into the rural districts, so they slid past the policeman, greasing the palm outstretched behind his back as they went, into the interdicted frontier zone.

Here, as in the country part of the Pale, they lived under constant liability to police raids and official exactions ; if not in terror of their lives, at least at the daily mercy of every one in authority, and subjected to ceaseless blackmail.

We have, then, 3,000,000 of Jews living in the Pale, of whom five-sixths were huddled together in 114 towns, in four of which they were over 80 per cent. of the population ; in fourteen from 70 to 80

per cent. ; in sixty-eight from 50 to 70, and in
twenty-eight from 20 to 40—none of them wealthy
towns or centres of rich industries—and one-sixth
lived outside the towns, dependent daily upon the
whim of rapacious officials.   In any case existence
would have been difficult for a people thus forcibly
restrained.   It was made almost impossible by a
great volume of hostile laws.

In addition to the ordinary taxes borne by all
Russian subjects alike (and these the heaviest to
be found anywhere in Europe), a whole series of
special taxes were invented and enforced against
the Jews.   There was a tax on every animal
slaughtered according to the Jewish or *Kosher*
rite, and another upon every pound of Kosher
meat afterward sold from it; these imposts made
meat cost a third more to the Jews than to other
people.   A percentage tax was levied by the
Government upon all rents of houses, shops, &c.,
received by Jews, and on the profits of all
factories, breweries, vinegar manufactories, and
other industrial establishments carried on by Jews.
A heavy legacy duty was exacted upon all capital
bequeathed by Jews.   Printing presses owned by
Jews paid annually for a licence.   The Jewish
head of a family had to pay a special tax for the
privilege of wearing a skull cap during family
prayers, and the very candles, which every Jewish
housewife must light Friday evenings, yielded a
revenue by taxation to the Russian Government
of £28,000 per annum.

All these taxes are still levied, and all the other impositions to be mentioned are still in force. I speak of them in the past tense only to show what the Pale was like before the May laws added despair and choice between flight and death to the original burdens.

If a Jew became converted to Christianity he received a money payment of from £2 to £4 ; if he was married, and his wife declined to follow him to baptism, her refusal *per se* divorced her, and she might not marry again, but her husband could take a new wife on the morrow, and, moreover, could baptise, against the deserted wife's will, all her male children under the age of seven. Precisely the same privileges were extended to the Jewish wife who should become a convert.

There could be no synagogue in a town containing less than eighty Jewish houses, or house of prayer in one with less than thirty Jewish houses ; and the robbery of plate and other effects from these was not sacrilege. Jews who held public worship or prayer in any other place than the synagogue or legal house of prayer were liable to imprisonment.

Jewish youths of the age of twenty-one were stripped of practically all the safeguards and legal reservations which enable Russians to escape military service. No Jew could be a member of the Recruiting Committee which makes up the conscription lists. The ordinary rules exempting young men from service who were the sole supports of families only occasionally applied in the case of Jews. Moreover, worst of all, if in a certain district the number of Jewish recruits presenting themselves fell below the proportion which had been expected, enough Jews could be taken from the exempt class to make good the deficiency.

Let us pause at this to note a peculiarly characteristic Russian trick. These conscription lists were (and are) compiled upon the basis of the village or district registers. The way in which these are kept in itself suggests a whole chapter on Russian administration. It is enough here to point out that at its birth every male child is put on the registers by the doctor, but if he dies his name can only be taken off by the certificate of the village priest or pope. This affords one of the means of livelihood which the pope watches most closely and employs most profitably. Unless the dead urchin's name is removed from the register, the family is liable to produce him, or an equivalent, as a recruit when the twenty-one years have elapsed. But in the case of Jews the pope cannot certify to the death of a child. The parent must apply in person for a death certificate to the Governor of the province and bring witnesses. This means a long journey and great expense, which not one in a score can afford. The result is that many names are carried on in the registers to the military age of Jewish boys who died in infancy. It was for this that the law quoted above was

THE PARIAH COMMUNITY 31

made, by which this bogus deficiency may be made good by seizing other Jewish youths throughout the district.

Thus it comes about that, while the Jews constitute only 3.95 per cent. of the population of European Russia, the army conscriptions for a series of twelve years (1875–86) show the average proportion of Jewish soldiers to be 5.97 per cent.

Yet there is no lie of which Russian writers and apologists are more fond than that the Jews continually evade their military duties. The truth is that, by a device of counting dead men, they are called upon for much more than their proper share of the annual recruiting force, and the very operation of this trick is made a reproach to them. As for asking for military enthusiasm among the Jews, let it not be forgotten that no Jew can become an officer in the Russian army, or even an officer's servant, and that the Military Regulations are studded thick with insulting and injurious references to and restrictions upon him and his religion.

The restrictions upon trade, upon intercourse with other markets, upon the holding of property, upon practically every relation of life, under which the Jews of the Pale suffered twenty years ago were literally without number. The legal limitations alone fill a volume; they were everywhere mixed up with a sliding scale of illegal exactions which the local authorities imposed for their personal benefit.

In substance the Jew could do nothing at all

without paying blackmail.   The humblest Jewish artisan—for example, a tailor—could be raided by the police if when he made a coat for you he brought it to you with the buttons sewed on. There was a law which said that Jewish artisans should sell only the product of their own handiwork.   "Very well," the police would ask, "do you pretend that you made these buttons yourself?" To such a question there were only two answers : one was to yield in despair and surrender the trade-guild passport which it had taken years to gain the other was to give the policeman three roubles.

Thus underhand dealing became a law of existence.   So far as the power of a despotic empire could do it moral degradation was thrust upon this people.   Money became the one thing which could make life tolerable—money for the police, money for the informer, money for the local magistrates, money for every harpy and blackguard with the will and power to molest. Whenever men engage in an unhealthy and unnatural competition those with the worst and most dangerous qualities rise to the top, trampling the weaker and softer ones under foot.   We have seen something like that in Wall Street, where there are no laws abridging virtuous happiness or making dishonesty the condition of life.   In the terrible Jewish Pale the wonder is that any religion, any charity, any rudimentary notion whatever of honesty survived.   The truth is that the great bulk of the Jews of the Pale, like the hideously poor everywhere, remained a simple and devout people, clinging doggedly to their despised faith, helping one another where they could, and keeping up virtues of temperance, family affection, and chastity which their Russian taskmasters scarcely knew by name.

But in those days there were methods of escaping from the Pale.

The Jews of Western Europe, even in the darkest days of blind mediæval persecution, had their brethren dwelling in the palaces and castles of the rulers of the land, clad in rich raiment and commanding respect for their long beards from even the ribald men-at-arms—I mean the physicians. In Russia in our own century the Jewish doctor made the pioneer experiments with that ticklish affair, the toleration of a Slav. After him came the Jewish scholar, then the Jewish merchant prince. All this will be traced in detail further on. It is enough here to say that at last, by the edicts of March 16, 1859, Nov. 27, 1861, and June 28, 1865, the Czar Alexander II threw all Russia open to Jews who could fulfil certain conditions.

Besides the Jewish physicians and surgeons, graduates of universities, and merchants of the first guild, who still retain the right of residence outside the Pale, skilled artisans were now allowed to move into Russia proper, and settle where they pleased. They did this under restrictions and conditions of espionage and arbitrary attack which in any free land would seem incredible, but to

C

them this enlargement of their horizon was so
wonderful that they still refer to the time as the
" golden age " for Jews.

In no place, for example, were they allowed
equal civic or religious rights with Russians ; nowhere were they permitted to forget what indeed
the law of 1876 explicitly reminded them of—that
" Jews are aliens, whose social rights are regulated
by special ordinances." *  But, subject to the old
laws, which now for fifteen years were but languidly
enforced by the local officials, nearly or quite a
million Jews came to live in St. Petersburg,
Moscow, Kieff, Nijni-Novgorod, Smolensk, and
the other larger towns outside the Pale.  Here
they settled themselves in something like security,
educated their children, extended their business
operations, and multiplied after their kind.

For these fifteen or twenty years life was perhaps in some small degree easier in the Pale, as
well.  The Jewish population, which previously
had been increasing with dread rapidity, became
about stationary under the reduction by this outlet
of eastward emigration.  The ruling poverty was
scarcely lessened, because the best workmen and
the most active spirits were those which had
strayed off into Russia proper.  But there was a
little more bread to eat for those who were left
behind, and, under the influence of a kindlier
atmosphere wafted from St. Petersburg, the burden

* " Law upon Status," vol. ix. note 7, § 835.  1876.

of blackmailing officials pressed less heavily upon them.

It was a season of stagnation inside the Pale— sorrowful enough for any of us to contemplate, but representing in retrospect now an almost ideal peace to the inhabitants. It was a time of hopeful energy, of high educational and professional distinction, and of growing aspirations and achievement to the Jews in Russia outside the Pale. The story of how they reached this promising position, and of the effect it had upon their character as a race, and upon the conditions about them, will be told in its place, and I trust will be thought worth the telling.

The story of how, suddenly and without warning or reason, this work of a score of years of toleration and intelligence was at a stroke undone ; of how hundreds of thousands of people were and are still being torn from their homes, swindled and robbed of their possessions, and driven like criminals into that present pen of horrors, the Pale, or beyond the borders of their native land, it will be difficult to tell with either completeness or adequate force.

# CHAPTER III

## THE BARBARIAN AND HIS STORY

THE traveller, making his slow way in summer over the vast, sprawling, sparsely settled continent called Russia, is struck by nothing else so much as the weird likeness presented everywhere to the more backward agricultural districts of the United States. The fine dry air, the splendid sunsets, the majestic movement of the rolling clouds, are all American ; so, too, are the unspeakable country roads, the grey, old, unpainted wooden houses and sheds, the well-curbs with long reaches, and the huge piles of cordwood bordering every road. The very locomotives have bulging smokestacks, after a fashion now almost forgotten in America, and fill the rural atmosphere with the pleasant scent of burned hard wood. The railway stations and the buildings about them are all of wood, decorated with stereotyped patterns of carpenters' ornamental scroll work, and painted with that single priming coat of ochre which one associates always with the temporary structures of a picnic ground. The forests are of birch and ash. Water melons are everywhere for sale, and the fields are white with buckwheat. The panorama from the car window is literally crowded with suggestions of the New World.

Russia is indeed a new world—so new as to tread upon the heels of the hindermost thing in old worlds. Watching and pondering its varying manifestations, I could never rid myself of the thought that it was a kind of America in which the early civilised settlers had been overwhelmed and absorbed by the aborigines. Everywhere one got the sense of departed glories, of vanished arts and forgotten knowledge. To the genuine aims and works of a real race had succeeded the squalid views and surface purposes of a mongrel and half-caste people, through whose feeble and fickle hands everything was slipping back into barbarism.

There was a different Russia once—a Russia which moved quite abreast of Christian Europe, which in art and architecture, in skilled industries and in general learning, was not inferior to the England or France of its time. The Northman Viking dynasty which Rurik founded at Novgorod and which his children enthroned at Holy Kieff was as western in spirit as that of Charlemagne. The three daughters of Yaroslav wedded the Kings of France, of Norway, and of Hungary, and his grandson took for wife Gyda, the daughter of the English Harold. In that far-off time architects, painters, workers in mosaic, and teachers and scribes were brought in great companies from Greece to the Courts of the Russian Princes, and art and letters flourished there as they did not flourish in Saxon England or Carlovingian Germany. The Greek mosaics still decorate the walls of the *Sophieski Sobor*, or cathedral of St. Sophia at Kieff, a building founded by Yaroslav in 1017. The tomb of that Prince, in a neighbouring chapel, shows much more art and skilled workmanship than the so-called tomb of Athelstan in Malmesbury Abbey, or any other western carved remains of that period.

It is even on record, established by the pictures in the manuscript Chronicle of Nestor (A.D. 1285) and other contemporary works, that in those days the dress of the Russians, nobles, merchants, and peasants alike, was practically that of Western Europe.

The change began when, early in the thirteenth century, the Tartar hordes of Ghenghis Khan burst across the Ural Mountains and overran Russia to the Dnieper, killing 50,000 people in Kieff alone, and devastating the land. Thereafter the House of Rurik for more than three centuries waged a desperate and continuous warfare against these succeeding waves of barbaric invasion. The history of every individual town in Old Russia through this 300 years' nightmare is made up of conflagrations and massacres. The dynasty of Rurik may be said to have died thus fighting, for when Ivan the Terrible finally crushed the Tartars, it was only to clear the ground for domestic anarchy, in the darkness of which his line perished.

The Russian who emerged from this anarchy wore his shirt outside his trousers. This badge of reversion to Asiatic standards, to which he has steadfastly clung ever since, is strictly symbolical. The old Russia of the saints and martyrs, of the Yaroslavs and Vladimirs, was definitely gone. We cannot tell how deep was the soil in which those early fruits of civilising art and literature sprouted. Perhaps it would have exhausted itself in any case. As it is, the Tartar wars burned it into utter and hopeless sterility.

The close of these wars and of the obscure and wasting confusion which followed, brought to view, as I have said, a new Russian—clad like an Oriental, and sunk in more than Oriental ignorance and degradation. Ethnologically he did not know who he was—and to this day he has not discovered. He seems in truth to have been an amalgam of all the lowly elements which had survived those awful centuries—a mixture of Lett, Finn, Lapp, Cossack, vagrant Slav of a thousand different tribes, all coloured and tainted by the savage licence of ten generations of Tartar conquerors. He spoke varying jargons of a debased Slavonic language. Of the highly elaborated Byzantine system of Christianity—which, after the final separation from Rome in 1054 evolved a far more complicated dogmatic theology than the Latin church knew—he had retained almost nothing, but had become merely a worshipper

of sacred pictures, which is all that he is to
this day.

Three generations of strong Romanoffs—
Michael, the founder, his son Alexis, and his
son Peter—devoted something over a hundred
years to the attempt to civilise this new Russian,
and bring him into the fold of European nations.
The first two of these Czars laboured chiefly to
establish the foundations of the throne to which
their family had been called, to systematise representative and legal institutions throughout the
land, and to restore some sort of spiritual life to
the nominal Christianity which had survived.
The third, that amazing Peter the Great, had
vaster dreams. He built St. Petersburg as a
window through which his people might study
Europe. He compelled married Russians to
abandon the acquired Oriental idea of secluding
their wives, and enforced their unveiled attendance
upon the "Assemblées" which he instituted. He
made his subjects shave their beards. He dressed
his army in the wigs, three-cornered hats, and
broad-skirted coats of Western warfare. He
created a navy, and visited half the Courts of
Europe to learn new tricks of civilisation. From
first to last, the paramount idea in his strange,
wild, tumbling brain was to drag Russia forcibly
out of the arms of Asia, and make her European.
While he lived, the work seemed to be well done.
When he died it collapsed like the proverbial
house of cards.

The Romanoffs practically ended with the great Peter. There had been four of them, all good men, and three much above the average of men. There followed now thirty-eight years of pitiful waste and retrogression, during which two vicious young male idiots and three loathsome elderly drabs in succession astounded Europe by hitherto undreamed-of spectacles of buffoonery, crime, ferocity, and animal lust enthroned. At the end, what problematical drops of Romanoff blood remained in existence were to be found in the veins of a peculiarly vile and disgusting young Duke of Holstein-Gottorp, whose mother was supposed to have been the great Peter's illegitimate daughter. This German Duke was made Czar as Peter III, and a few months later was murdered by his wife, a German Princess of the house of Anhalt-Zerbst, who now herself ascended the throne as Catherine II.

During all this time—indeed, from a period long before the accession of the Romanoffs—almost every Sovereign, good or bad, strong or foolish, had added something to the already huge expanse of Russian territory. From the fall of the Byzantine empire to the destruction of the Teutonic knights, through all the weary centuries of mediæval warfare, pillage, and smashing of dynasties, Russia has steadily annexed territory right and left, north and south. How Catherine the Great still further augmented this vast domain by the spoliation of Poland, or how she strove

with her notable powers of mind and will to carry
forward Peter's task of Europeanising Russia, need
not be dwelt upon here.

No drop of Romanoff blood flowed in the veins
of her descendants, the five Czars who have filled
the throne since her death in 1796. The pretence
was scarcely made at the time that her son, Paul,
was actually the child of his nominal father; no
historian treats it now as even a probability.
Mirabeau and other observers of the Court in the
next generation have left amusing accounts of the
precautions taken to prevent the madman Paul
from being the father of a new imperial line. His
wife, a Wurtemberg princess, seems to have made
no secret of them, and the paternity of the handsome Nicholas, at least, was always popularly
connected with an Alsatian grenadier of humble
origin but lofty destinies. However that may be,
the Czars since Catherine have been wholly
German. They have behaved like Germans,
creating a prodigious bureaucracy in imitation of
Teutonic models, dressing and drilling their
soldiers in German fashion, forming all the details
of their Court after German notions of what a
Court should be. Alike under mad Paul and the
sentimental Alexander I, under grim, stalwart
Nicholas and the romantic Alexander II, the
work went on of striving to Europeanise Russia.
Though each pursued this ideal in his own peculiar
way, their ruling desire was the same—to confirm
and solidify Russia's place among civilised nations.

It requires a mental effort to realise that we now confront a Russia which, after 200 years of reluctant shambling and shuffling along under the whip on the road to civilisation, stops short and declares that it wants to go back—that its true affinities are with Asia, not Europe.

Moreover, those who hold the whip are now themselves of the same opinion. The moujik and the small Russian merchants and artisans have never wanted to be civilised. It is a new thing, though, for them to find that their masters in St. Petersburg feel that way too. Under such conditions the backward movement has already attained a tremendous momentum.

A strange figure in the human gallery is this moujik, who, stubbornly and placidly resisting for two centuries all the efforts of a powerful autocracy to make him something different, remains to-day just the man he was when the Tartar invasions ended and the Romanoffs began to create the modern Russia. He still wears his shirt outside his trousers, in silent protest against the pretence that he is a European.

If he were really as far away from us as he thinks he is and desires to be, one might find much in his curious character to like and to dwell almost tenderly upon.

The childlike qualities so markedly developed in most Slavonic peoples find their fullest expression in him. He is, moreover, an exceedingly docile and kindly-natured child. He bears with

uncomplaining patience, in all his weary pilgrimage from the cradle to the grave, an accumulation
of burdens such as no other people in the world
are acquainted with.   He dislikes work with all
his heart, yet tramps through life on the treadmill
of toil ordained for him without protest or bitterness.   When he gets drunk, which is whenever
beneficent chance affords, he leans for hours
against a fence or wall, smiling gently at the
passers-by.   If he makes any demonstration, it is
to throw his arms about some other moujik's neck
and kiss him.   The drunker he is, the more affectionately fraternal he becomes.

Lifelong communion with the vast flat-stretching
plains of his country, with its enormous tracts of
uninhabited land, of marsh and low-lying forests,
has made him a silent man.   Nothing is more
surprising to the observer in Russia than the
spectacle of two or three hundred moujiks going
to or from their work, or even out upon a holiday,
from whom no sound whatever proceeds.   Great
throngs of thousands will assemble at Moscow or
St. Petersburg to watch a procession of ikons or
a military review, and preserve absolute noise-
lessness for hours.   Paradoxical as it may seem,
they are a talkative, even garrulous, people by
instinct.   But their conversation is limited to the
dialogue.   Two moujiks alone will talk each other
to death.   Three moujiks together are reserved.
A half-dozen will say next to nothing at all.

Doubtless this queer trait reflects the universal,

omnipresent burden of suspicion under which their lives are passed. They are never sure that they are not outside the law, because the law means only the personal disposition of the individual policeman or small official toward them. In the cities, for example, the moujiks who traverse the principal streets all walk in the middle of the road. Noting this in St. Petersburg, I commented upon it to an English friend long resident there. He told me that at the Christmas time last year, when the great shop windows of the Gostinny Dvor were filled with their richest holiday display, he saw a moujik, or labouring man, attracted by a show of gaily-dressed dolls, come up on to the sidewalk and approach the window to look. A policeman roughly bade him be off, and the moujik, taking off his cap in apology, crept humbly back again to the middle of the road. No doubt that man will go through life without once questioning the existence of a law forbidding him to look in shop windows, if, indeed, he ever arrives at the point of distinguishing between law and the whim of a policeman.

Although the traveller in Russia gets a great idea of the variety and appetising scope of the Russian cuisine, the moujik lives very badly. The present terrible famine has only made him a little worse off than he was before—the margin between him and starvation was already so pitifully slender. His staples of food are the *kasha*, a sort of thick gruel, mainly of buckwheat, baked in a bowl, and eaten with grease ; the *schtchi* or soup of a white cabbage peculiar to Russia, eaten both fresh and sour, and rye bread.  He knows little or nothing of the taste of meat, save occasionally when he is lucky enough to get a little piece for his soup. He consumes great quantities of weak tea, but rarely tastes sugar in it, for the reason that the tariff and bounty swindles combined make sugar cost five times as much as it does in England. He drinks *vodka*, a raw and deadly spirit, by the pailful when it is given him, and habitually spends a large share of his pitiful earnings in buying it. One of the most melancholy and hopeless features of the existing famine has been the universal certainty that the moujik, if he was given relief in any portable form, would at once march off to pawn it for drink.

He has, as a rule, a stiff, coarse, mud-coloured beard, and wears his thick hair cut short and shaved at the neck, but very long in front; in imitation of the portraits on the ikons, he parts it in the middle, which imparts to even the greatest ruffian an air of sweet gentleness deceptive in the extreme.  The older men have exceptionally heavy and shaggy eyebrows.

The moujik wears a pink shirt—a peculiar tint of pale red which never varies—and wears it all exposed, like a tunic, belted at the waist.  His big bagged trousers are tucked at the knee into boot-legs.  These boots become to the eye an even more familiar symbol of Russia than the red shirt.

The first thing one notices after the Russian border has been crossed is that every one wears high boots—the customs officers, the train officials, the railway porters, the cabmen, the soldiers, the policemen—on every side nothing but high boots. Even the country women wear them when they do not go barefooted.

The rural moujik, who represents five-sixths of the population of the empire, lives in a little unpainted wooden hovel, rarely built with a second story, and thatched with straws. These shanties are clustered together in hamlets, in groups of fifteen or twenty. Many miles will intervene, as a rule, between this rustic village and the next— miles of wild, flat land, probably unbroken by even a road, and without fence or wall or other sign of habitation, much less a house.

His communal system of land division and his dependence upon the decisions of the Mir, or village Parliament, need not be entered upon here. The careful explanation of all this which Dr. Mackenzie Wallace made fifteen years ago has been widely studied, and still remains the best statement of the matter in existence. The trouble is that the moujik, whom Mr. Wallace even then suspected of not turning his emancipation to the best possible advantage, has since gone steadily backward. As I have pointed out broadly that the Russia of the fourteenth century was more civilised than the Russia of the seventeenth, so it is unhappily true that the moujik of to-day is a much less thrifty and prosperous creature than the moujik of 1875.

To some extent this is his own fault. His passion for drink and his childlike inability to see the value of consecutive application have led him into the vicious trick of mortgaging his labour whole years ahead. The Government encourages him to drink, because the *vodka* tax is one of the principal sources of official revenue. But equally harmful to him. are the protective tariff laws, which make everything he has to buy twice or thrice as dear as it is anywhere else, and beyond that almost the whole burden of direct taxation falls upon his overloaded shoulders. This poverty-stricken wretch, who when times are bad or harvests fail is daily brought face to face with starvation, has to pay an annual passport tax of five roubles—about $3— to begin with, and his land, house, and other taxes make up an aggregate at which the poor man in any other country would stare in open-eyed amazement.

His great poverty at home and the nomadic instinct in his blood make the moujik a notable wanderer. Very often he is in a way an artisan as well, and picks up a little work in various towns as he passes. Wages, however, are so low in Russia—the latest report on the subject assumes that while an English cotton spinner, working 10 hours a day, earns 70 roubles a month, the Russian cotton spinner, working 12 hours a day, earns 19¼ roubles a month*—that the most marked success in securing employment hardly raises a strolling moujik above the level of pauperism. Many trades are like that of the carpenter, chiefly in the hands of travelling bands who go from place to place, put up houses for those who want them, and then roam elsewhere. These carpenters, working bareheaded in the open air, perform marvels of skill with the adze, which is often their only tool. If trades unions were not sternly forbidden by law, these capable craftsmen would be a prosperous people. Even as it is, they seemed the most contented men in Russia. While at work they sleep herded together in rough little shanties put up for temporary use by themselves, and share everything, wages included, in common. In the long twilights of the North the traveller sees their cooking fires coming out one by one on the vast, desolate landscape like the first evening stars in the sky.

Less skilled labourers also go about in companies seeking employment as roadmakers, harvesters, or farm hands, living meantime in much the same way. These itinerant bands, when they have been long enough together, sing in concert at their work. It is said that the stay-at-home moujik now rarely does this. The soul of music

* Report from the British Embassy at St. Petersburg on "The Condition of Labour in Russia." Summarised in the *Times* of January 21, 1892.

has been scared and frozen from him. He used to have a musical instrument of his own, as national as the cymbal in Hungary, the pan-pipe in Roumania, and the guitar in Spain; nowadays he knows nothing but the German concertina.

These groups of wanderers, moving at will over the immense tracts of sparsely-populated country, include also the pilgrims, of whom through the year a half million are on foot in Russia, and the tramps, if, indeed, there can be drawn a satisfactory line of demarcation between the two. And now—not for the first time in Russian history, indeed, but threatening results novel to our generation—there is added the sinister spectacle of the remnants of whole communities, with their children and their cattle, roaming gaunt and wild-eyed across the never-ending plains, driven under the lash of famine and the plague.

I have lingered thus, at length, over the moujik because he is the foundation upon which all things truly Russian are built. His character and condition furnish the key to the entire Russian situation. The relatively small class of Russian petty traders, master artisans, and other townspeople not of the educated orders is made up of the moujik with his shirt worn inside his trousers. There is very little other discernible difference.

This class is a small one, because it is racially artificial. The Slavonic—or at least the Russo-Slavonic—character does not lend itself to the development of what in England is called the

RUSSIAN PEASANT TYPES
(*Government of Smolensk*)

middle class. There is the moujik, and then nothing indigenous between until you come to his master. What does intervene is chiefly not Russian at all.

The history of modern Russia is full of confessions that the Russian by himself is "no good." The three strong monarchs of this period, Peter the Great, Catherine II, and Nicholas, all laboured hard at the task of colonising the Empire with people from other lands, by whose example in industry, thrift, and intelligence the native Russian might profit. In turn Dutch, German, Swedes, and Swiss were brought in and established in villages or on the soil as models. The experiment in one sense succeeded ; these strangers prospered and flourished beyond expectation, branching out into new fields, creating commerce and industries which had not previously existed, and thereby enriching the State as well as themselves. But in only the smallest degree can they be said to have served the original purpose of their Imperial promoters. A certain infinitesimal proportion of the native element was caught up by the current of activity they set in motion, and spurred into imitation. But the overwhelming bulk of the native population declined to learn or imitate or be in any wise affected. Thus to this day you may see German agricultural colonies settled as far back as the great Catherine's time, with neat and comfortable buildings and closely-cultivated fields, the proprietors of which are all men with money in the bank or out at interest; while next to them are Russian farm hamlets made up of filthy hovels, with fields tilled in the most slovenly and half-hearted manner by moujiks, who in their wildest dreams could not imagine themselves being free from debt.

This points the fact at which, perhaps too slowly, we have arrived, namely, that the commercial and industrial activity and prosperity of Russia are almost wholly in the hands of people who are not Russian. It is not alone that the business of St. Petersburg, Moscow, Kieff, and Odessa is principally conducted by people whose fathers or grandfathers crossed the frontier. The great annual fairs, of which that at Nijni-Novgorod is the best known, and the innumerable minor fairs at which, in true Oriental fashion, supplies and wares are still concentrated and distributed, are alike dominated by everybody rather than the full-blooded Russian.

The same thing is true outside of trade. If a Russian landed proprietor stands out among his fellows as a successful farmer, if he secures good returns from his estates and gets his rents paid regularly, in nineteen cases out of twenty he has a German steward. It need hardly be added that this steward, in the very act of deserving well of his employer, will have made himself bitterly disliked by the moujik.

Here is struck the keynote of all that we are considering. The Russians as a whole lack the qualities which, from the standpoint of Western civilisation, command success. They see the alien wax prosperous and commercially powerful in their own country, where they grow constantly poorer. They are said by those who know them well to be the most amiable people in the world ; their amiability would have to be superhuman to stand such a test as this.

Among the strangers within the gates who monopolise the commercial activity of Russia and struggle together for its rewards, the Jew is naturally foremost in attracting attention. He is first of all marked off from the others by an arbitrary cleavage of race, religion, and blood prejudice. Beyond that, as we have seen and shall still more in detail observe, the law has fenced him round with restrictions peculiar to himself, rendering him in all men's eyes a suspect creature, like a ticket-of-leave man or a registered harlot. Still further, the limitations placed upon him have forced him to work in a field where whatever he does must be unpopular, and where his success in securing even existence must seem a sort of crime to the rest.

The ground having thus been cleared, and some idea, meagre and imperfect as it is, having been given of the external conditions of the question, it will be possible hereafter to keep more closely to the subject of the Jew in Russia and his tragic story.

# CHAPTER IV

*BEGINNINGS OF THE RUSSO-JEWISH QUESTION*

THE Jew represents at once humanity's oldest and least familiar fact. The records which he embodies visibly before us in his curled hair, in his eager eyes and bended nose, in his gestures, his utterance, the peculiarities of his family and religious life, belong to the very childhood of the race. We feel or simulate a tremendous interest when the palace tomb of another Rameses is dug out from under the drift of desert sands, or a new triumphal tablet of some forgotten marauder king is unearthed from the dust heaps of Nineveh. Our library shelves are filled with the literature of these efforts to grasp the likeness of these dead peoples, to fathom the secret of who they were and where they went to. Our scientists measure skulls and compare jaw-bones and wage with one another an endless war of words to solve for us the identity of the Hittites, the origin of the Assyrians, the disappearance of the Egyptians.

All the while we have with us a people older than any of these vanished races, to whose real history we pay very little attention indeed. The Old Testament, we know, and braggart Josephus may still be the reluctant resource of boys in Puritan households of a Sunday afternoon. But the connected story of this ancient folk has not to this day, save in Graetz's massive German work, been intelligently told. Yet how superbly strange and impressive a romance it is !

The Jews are the sole survivors of antiquity. With the calm, meditative gaze of a tent-dwelling people, they watched the dawn of human history. They knew and gave a name to that mysterious first race which went off into the darkness as the shadows lifted—that unknown elder son of the night for traces of whom we now blindly grope— the "Canaan" of Scripture, the Turanian of modern hypothesis. The Jews saw Chaldea, Assyria, Babylon, Media, Egypt, Phœnicia, Greece, Carthage rise, flourish, and fall. They saw Rome tower up in the West; expend the greatest effort of its vast power in smashing and levelling Jerusalem, and then go down itself. They saw one by one the Byzantine, the Gothic, and the Frankish Empires soar skyward, darken the heavens with the wings of dominion, and tumble to earth again. They saw Spain withered up by the flames she herself had lighted in the *auto da fe* of the Inquisition.

Persecuted by all, cursed, feared, quarantined, fettered by all, the Jews have survived all. One need not look alone in Asia Minor for peoples whose practical extinction they have witnessed. Three centuries ago the Grand Duke of Lithuania

was a powerful monarch in Central Europe,
strong enough to make himself King of Poland.
As late as 1566 the Lithuanian nobles in Diet
assembled decreed that Jews should wear a
yellow head-covering to distinguish them from
Christians. Last winter a friendless emigrant
girl was discovered here in the streets of London
speaking a language none could understand,
though the linguists of several learned institutions were applied to. Finally an amateur phi-
lologist wrote a letter to the papers describing
the sounds of the girl's speech, and this led to
the discovery that she spoke Lithuanian. The
gentleman who wrote solving the mystery began
by explaining to his readers where Lithuania was!

Only one small phase of this race's wonderful
history comes properly within the scope of our
inquiry. It is a common popular error to assume
that what is called "the dispersion" was
incidental to, and consequent upon, the fall of
Jerusalem. Four centuries before that triumph
of Titus there were large and influential colonies
of Jews in all the important cities of the East.
Alexander the Great was deeply interested in
them as a people, and gave them many privileges
not extended to other conquered races within
his vast empire. His successors, especially the
Ptolemies in Egypt, inherited and even emphasised
this attitude, until there were said to be a million
Jews in the city of Alexandria alone. Exaggerated
as this estimate obviously is, it serves to indicate

how generally the Hebrew race must have been distributed throughout the immense territory which the Greeks held by conquest long before the Christian era.

History and legend throw a great deal of light upon the character and achievements of some of these earlier colonies. We are peculiarly rich in records of the *rôle* the Jews of Alexandria played in civilising that part of the world, and, later, in influencing that strange, evanescent outburst of Arabian and Saracenic culture* from which to this day we draw so much unsuspected inspiration. We know, too, how strong and popular a force the Jewish residents of Rome exerted even in the days of Augustus.

It is only in Russia that we get next to no trace of their original settlements and earlier history. Perhaps this is not to be wondered at, for the story of the Russians themselves is wrapped in myth and fable up to the tenth century. It is apparent, however, that there were Jews inhabiting the basins of the Volga, Don, and Dnieper fully 500 years before Christ. At the time of the coming of the half-legendary Viking Rurik, in 864, the Jews were an important element in the population along these rivers, and in the east and south of what is now known as Russia, and had been for ages before Russians as such were heard of.

* "History of the Intellectual Development of Europe." By John W. Draper, M.D., LL.D. Vol. i. ch. xiii. New York. 1876.

In the Crimea there are, at Chufut Kaleh and Mangup, cemeteries of the Karaïm Jews, with tombs far antedating the Christian era. The monuments here, and the ancient parchments preserved at Chufut by the Rabbi Fircowicz, and in the Fircowicz collection in the Imperial Public Library at St. Petersburg, tell a story unique in the history of Judaism. The Hebrews settled here actually converted the barbaric pagan hordes of the Khazars to their religion in the eighth century, and the larger part of the Karaïm Jews in South Russia to-day speak the Tartar language among themselves. They are, however, very few in number—perhaps not more than three or four thousand. Madame Novikoff did not allow this to deter her from denying that the Russians treated their Jews badly, and then, when confronted with facts, explaining that she referred to the Karaïm Jews and not the schismatic Talmud Jews, as if these latter were an unimportant minority, instead of outnumbering the others 1000 to 1.

This brings us to the grand theological question with which Jewish history is so dishearteningly entangled, and which, however briefly, we must touch upon. I have spoken of the conversion of the heathen Khazars, whose realm extended from the Caucasus to the Don and Volga, and whose kings thereafter professed the Jewish faith, as unique in the records of Israel. It need not have been, were it not for the fact that the Jewish religion was in its essence a national creed. The policy of its priests and exponents was entirely one of exclusiveness. With this solitary exception of the Khazars, proselytism to the Jewish faith has been unknown.

It is, of course, useless to speculate upon what might have happened had the spirit of Judaism contemplated a propaganda among Gentiles. The Jewish Jehovah reigns now in men's consciousness wherever the idea of one God exists—among Mohammedans not less than all varieties of Christians—dethroning Bel, Jupiter and Woden alike. The Jews, however, have had little or nothing to do with this world-wide extension of their monotheistic idea. They kept their Jehovah for themselves, and never dreamed of preaching Him to outsiders. Rome, with its addition of the doctrine of the Trinity, and Islam, with its addition of the Prophet, divided the great propaganda between them.

This fact bears a curious relation to our immediate theme, because it is recorded that when Vladimir, seventh in descent from Rurik, and the first authentic figure in Russian dynastic history, decided to forsake the heathen gods of his Norse fathers, he gave serious consideration to the idea of embracing Judaism. From this it would seem that the Jews settled in Kieff and the Ukraine, far away from the centres of population of their race, and influenced by their success with the Khazars, had developed a missionary spirit. Whatever

their attitude may have been, Vladimir finally
chose Christianity instead, and is now enrolled
among its saints.

It has always been noticed that the conditions
which produce the most luxuriant growth of saints
provide the largest measure of unhappiness for
the Jews. Christianity had not reached its fifth
generation in Russia before it had a calendar with
scores of native saints and had chased all the Jews
out of Kieff. This first persecution dates back
to 1110, under a monarch whose wife was the
English Princess Gyda. There was nothing
unusual about it. Indeed, it furnishes proof that
Russia had, during those four generations, taken
great strides toward civilisation as Western
Christendom understood it. Bear in mind that
this was the pious century in which the authorities
of Toulouse accepted a large sum of money from
the Jews in commutation of the privilege of
Christian citizens to strike them in the face on the
streets during Eastertide.*

Thereafter for centuries we get no glimpse
whatever of the Hebrew in Russia. We may be
sure, though, that during the long nightmare of
the Tartar invasions it was looked to that he got
his full share of the woes and anguish which the
unhappy land suffered. How terrible this share
must have been we can guess from the fact that
the mediæval Russian Jew, unlike his fellows in
every other country, has left no written sign. We

* Vaissette's " History of Languedoc."

know absolutely nothing of his story during those darkened ages.

Meanwhile the Jew of Poland emerges into the light of history. At the beginning of the sixteenth century there were computed to be 200,000 Hebrews in the various provinces of Poland and Lithuania. Some had been settled there for centuries, coming through the German and Austrian States from Italy, Spain and France; others had been driven or had escaped thither from Russia. They enjoyed exceptional privileges, as Jewish rights went in those days—had entire religious freedom and tolerably broad civil liberty. The spectacle was a unique one in Europe, where Spain's savage crusade with stake and rack seemed much the more natural and proper thing. Jews in other lands thought of Poland as a veritable Land of Goshen. So many German Jews crossed the frontier and settled there, to escape the persecutions and levies of their own petty Princelets and robber Barons,* that their language, in the corrupted Hebraised German known as Jiddish, became the speech of the race.

This happy toleration was too good to last. Under it the Jews had largely lost their exclusiveness, and lived side by side with the Christians in entire amity, and were artisans, merchants, and farmers like the rest. The reproach of usury, cast upon them and earned by them in other countries where persecution drove them from more

* Stobbe. "Die Juden in Deutschland." 1866.

honourable pursuits, was not deserved or heard in
Poland.* But, as the power of the Polish throne
diminished, and the authority of the nobles and
clerics increased, matters began to wear a different
face. The Jews, after many generations of friendly
equality and frank community with their neighbours, found themselves legislated once more back
into the vicious old circle of being forced to do
certain things and then hated and abused because
they did them.

Then came the upheaval of the Russo-Tartar-
Cossack wars and invasions (1648-67) ending
with the treaty of Andrussoff, whereby the second
Romanoff Czar, Alexis, obtained Smolensk and
the Ukraine. This was the country in which
Jews, as I have said, had lived for two thousand
years. The Czar at once drove them all out.
Thereafter all was misery.

There succeeds now a period of nearly 200
years, filled with acute disquiet or active
oppression for the Jews. The refugees from the
Ukraine who had settled in Little Russia were
expelled in 1727. No Jews from without were
allowed to enter Russia upon any pretext. The
few physicians and other professional men of the
excluded race who did manage to remain in Russia
were in continual jeopardy of insult and expulsion.
Over and over again Russian statesmen who
were anxious to develop the resources and trade

* Professor S. Bershadsky. "The Lithuanian Jews." St.
Petersburg : 1883.

possibilities of their backward and barbarous land, hinted at the advisability of bringing in some Jews. The Imperial will was resolutely opposed.

In 1743, for example, the Senate recommended that Jewish traders should be allowed to enter Riga and Little Russia on temporary visits "for the promotion of the welfare of the Empire and the development of commerce." The Empress Elizabeth wrote with her own hand on the report : " I seek no gain at the hands of enemies of Christianity."* When the broad-minded Catherine II ascended the throne these efforts were renewed, but she too resisted them, and says in her Memoirs, "their admission into Russia might have occasioned much injury to our small tradesmen." † She was too deeply bitten with the Voltairean philosophy of her time to have, or even assume, any religious fervour in the matter, but though in 1786 she issued a high-sounding edict "respecting the protection of the rights of Jews of Russia," the persecution on economic and social grounds continued unabated.

By this time it will be seen the laws did, however, recognise the existence of Jews in Russia. The explanation is that the first partition of Poland and the annexation of the great Turkish territory lying between the Dnieper and the Dniester had brought into the empire such a vast Hebraic

* Observation No. 8840. Continuation of Vol. xi. of Code of Laws.
† The Zaria Journal, Vol. vi. " Catherine as an Authoress."

population that any thought of expulsion was hopeless. Holy Russia could keep herself uncontaminated no longer. The thief was compelled to submit to the pious discomfort of keeping the unholy part of his plunder along with the rest.

The rape of Poland and the looting of Turkey had brought two millions of Jews under the sceptre of the Czar. The fact could not be blinked. They were there—inside the Holy Empire, whose boast for centuries had been that no circumcised dog could find rest for his foot on its sanctified territory. To an autocracy based so wholly on an orthodox religion as is that of the Czars, this seemed a most trying and perplexing problem.

The solution they hit upon was to set aside one part of the empire as a sort of lazar house, which should serve to keep the rest of it from pollution. Hence we get the Pale.

Almost every decade since 1786, the date of Catherine's ukase, has witnessed some alteration made in the dimensions and boundaries of this Pale. Now it has been expanded, now sharply contracted ; this city and that has been exempted from the laws governing the territory about it ; deeds have been made lawful in one of its provinces which were penal offences in the next ; lifelong residents have been " decanted," as the old Burgundian phrase went, from one district to another—all in the most wanton and whimsical fashion, according to the freak of a despot or the interest of a Minister. To trace these changes would be to unnecessarily burden ourselves with details. It is enough to keep in mind that the creation of the Pale was Russia's solution of the Jewish problem in 1786, and is still the only one it can think of.

Side by side with this naïve notion that Holy Russia could be kept an inviolate Christian land in the eyes of Heaven by juggling the map, there grew up the more worldly conception of turning the Jew to account as a kind of milch cow. Traces of its dawn may be discerned in Catherine's later years, when Jews were allowed to enrol themselves as merchants in certain towns and enjoy the privileges given other people on condition that they paid double taxes. The local consistorial organisation which they had received from the Polish kings was, alone among all their institutions, retained, avowedly because it made the collection of these unjust taxes easy.

Later this view of the possible profits to be derived from the Jew came to be expressed with utmost frankness. In 1819 Jewish brandy distillers were allowed to go into the interior and settle "until," as the ukase said, "Russian master distillers shall have perfected themselves in the art of distilling." They availed themselves of this permission in great numbers, and at the end of seven years were all summarily driven out again, a new ukase explaining that "the number of Christian distillers was now sufficient." The Imperial

E

ukase of July 29, 1827, speaks of the laws about the Jews as " Government measures adopted for deriving State advantages from this race."

The past century's history of the Jews in Russia is made up of conflicts between these two impulses in the childlike Slavonic brain—the one to drive the heretic Jew into the Pale as into a kennel with kicks and stripes, the other guardedly to entice him out and manage to extract some service or profit from him. Now one, now the other, of these notions has from time to time obtained ascendency, as whim dictated or need compelled. On occasion the two appear together, yoked side by side, yet pulling in opposite directions. It is to this that the Russian laws about the Jews owe their wild and chaotic contradictions, and their inextricable jumble of confusion as to what may and may not be done.

The Panslavists of Russia nowadays sum up all their arguments against the Jew in the word "exploitation." It has come to be a part of the Russian language. A conversation in Russia about the Jews would be impossible without it. Those who use the word so glibly seek to convey the idea that the Jew is being driven out because he has "exploited" everybody—the noble, the landed proprietor, the merchant, the moujik. This allegation has been made so steadily that I daresay a great majority of Russians now actually believe it themselves. Certainly the opinion of the outside world has been largely influenced by it.

The sober truth is that it is the Jew who has been " exploited." I have shown how frankly the Russian Government used to confess its purpose of turning the Jew to account—sternly curtailing or abolishing all the natural rights which would minister to his own happiness or welfare, but using him wherever he seemed likely to be of service to his Russian neighbours or to the Government.

It was in this strictly utilitarian spirit that the keeping of taverns and rural grogshops throughout Poland and the Pale was put into the hands of the Jews. The fact that some of them still remain in this business is one of the chief reproaches levelled at the whole race by the Russian anti-Semites. But no one explains that they were put into this business, first by the great aristocratic proprietors and then by the Government, for the admitted reason that they alone among the population could be trusted to themselves to keep sober the while they sold drink to others. Both the Imperial revenues and the incomes of landed proprietors had for their chief item the tax and profits on the drink traffic. Both the Finance Ministers and the big landlords have always been anxious to increase rather than diminish this traffic. The special Imperial Commission of 1812, appointed to consider the advisability of forbidding Jews to retail *vodka* in the villages, reported that the Jew was most useful in that capacity, and that if he was sent away the business would fall into the hands of the native moujik, to the destruction of business and moujik alike.

In the same way, one hears continually of the Jewish usurer. To believe the average Russian's talk, all the money-lending in that whole great empire of debtors is done by the Jews. As I have said in a previous chapter, this is wild nonsense. The rich Jewish usurers in Russia can be counted on one's fingers. But the significant thing is that these big money-lenders and, to use an American provincialism, "note shavers," have always been hand in glove with the Russian authorities. They are still powers in the land. Nobody has heard a word about their being expelled or even troubled. The reason is that they are systematically " exploited " by the Russian officials.

A curious story told me partly in Kieff, partly in Odessa, illustrates this. One of the oldest and most distinguished native families in the Ukraine is that of Kotchubey, the princely head of which is the best remembered of Mazeppa's victims. The Princes of the house of Kotchubey are now much better known in Paris than they are in their ancestral Poltava. The last of them to live on his estates in old Russian fashion was Prince Victor Kotchubey. An elderly English gentleman who has lived since youth in Little Russia told me that some thirty years ago he was in the office of an English firm which was introducing agricultural machinery in the South. One day there entered a tall, fine old gentleman in a silk hat and dressed in the height of the London fashion. He spoke English perfectly, without even an accent, which greatly delighted the young British clerks. They were still more charmed to learn that he was Prince Kotchubey, the chief proprietor of the district. He ordered one of the machines to be taken to his estate for trial, and expressed courteously his pleasure at learning that these smiling young English clerks would attend this trial on the morrow.

They went, anticipating the most sumptuous hospitality. The trial began without the Prince. Soon thereafter appeared on the scene an old man dressed in Russian moujik fashion—huge boots, a tunic-like shirt open at the throat, a fur cap, and with a whip in his hand, who scowled about him and brusquely questioned the clerks in Russian. With difficulty they recognised him for the Prince; they begged him to speak English, and, when he refused, to allow them at least to reply in English. He roughly told them that if they could not speak Russian they had no business in Russia, and roundly abused them and their machine, which, deeply crestfallen, they took back with them. Later, when a friend asked the Prince if this account of his treatment of the English youths was true, he replied : " Yes, it was my fantasy."

The heirs of this old savage were, after the fashion of their land, stupidly prodigal and waste-

ful youngsters.   They got into difficulties.   A
Jew named Michaelowitz, living at Vannitsa, and
said to have begun life in great poverty, lent
them some money.   Other loans succeeded, with
renewals, interest accumulations, &c., until ruin
stared the Kotchubeys in the face.   Then some of
their advisers took the matter up, and discovered
that Michaelowitz had been guilty of gross frauds.
Suit was begun against him, and also a criminal
action, brought by the judge of the district.   He
was in prison some days before he got out on bail.
He hastened off to St. Petersburg, where Ignatieff
was then Minister of the Interior.   The next
thing was that the judge who was prosecuting
Michaelowitz found that the case had been taken
out of his hands and turned over to a judge in
Odessa, who was Ignatieff's friend.   Michaelowitz
was now promptly acquitted, having been his
own solitary witness.   Shortly thereafter Ignatieff
turned up as the owner of one of the Kotchubey
estates, valued at 300,000 roubles, and which
Michaelowitz is said to have grabbed upon a
loan of 125,000 roubles.   To-day Michaelowitz
is thought to be worth 3,000,000 roubles.

This kind of Jew stands in no fear of molesta-
tion.   He has friends, confederates, partners at
Court.   The Jewish brothel-keeper, the Jewish
receiver of stolen goods, the rich Jew of any questionable variety, has not been so much as menaced
by the expulsions ; he has friends among the police.
These excrescences upon the Hebrew community

are cited by every Russian who defends the May laws in justification of them. It is characteristic of the whole tragic farce that this handful of men, whose delinquencies are quoted as warranting the persecution of a nation, are themselves not persecuted at all.

During the Napoleonic wars, and peculiarly at the period of the invasion, the laws against the Jews were very largely relaxed, and Czar Alexander I made a personal appeal to them for help against the French. It was given, and in return the Imperial promise was passed that they should be given equal rights with other Russian subjects. But by 1822 this pledge had been so completely forgotten that the same Czar abolished most of the consistorial organisation, with its independent communal jurisdiction, which they had enjoyed since the days of the Polish kings.

In 1825 Nicholas ascended the throne. Within a year he had earned from the Jews that sinister title of "The Second Haman," by which Israel still recalls him. The events of his reign, intimately connected as they are with what the world to-day indignantly witnesses under his grandson, will be studied in the ensuing chapter.

# CHAPTER V

THE Jews of Russia called Nicholas " The Second Haman." They could think of nothing more opprobrious. The Book of Esther was, and still is, by far the most familiar of their sacred writings. The story of the victory of Mordecai appeals powerfully to their indomitably hopeful fancy. Scrolls containing it, and ornamented by marginal pictures of gibbets and hangmen, are everywhere to be found among them. Every Jewish boy in Muscovy is proud of being able to recite the names of Haman's ten sons without taking breath. The gallows upon which they were all hanged looms ever darkly triumphant in the Russo-Jewish imagination.

Undoubtedly the thirty years' reign of Nicholas, from 1825 to 1855, was filled with special hardships for the Jews. At the time they thought nothing could be more terrible than their position. But looking back upon it now, it does not seem so bad. In those days they at least could comprehend the intentions and aims of the despotism which oppressed them.

The Czar Nicholas, a man of immense personal

force, tireless energy, and original ideas, which from their very narrowness ran deep and strong, had an intelligent theory about the Jews. He wrestled for thirty years with the task of carrying out this theory, but, though a great number of Jews got hurt during the process, he accomplished very little else.

Nicholas succeeded to an inheritance wasted by war and weak misgovernment, and generally run to seed. He threw himself with his whole strength and pride of character into the work of regenerating the empire. His notions of what regeneration meant were, of course, very curious; they might easily have seemed backward and reactionary to one of the Pharaohs. But he was at least sincere and devoted and consistent in his labours. He permitted nothing to be done of which his intelligence did not approve simply because it had been the habit to do it. The most awful brutalities of his reign had a reason of some sort behind them.

This powerful and resolute Czar had, as has been said, a theory about the Jews. He recognised their exceptional mental qualities and their economic value to the State as no other European Sovereign save Napoleon had ever done. He believed that they could be made of the utmost use to Russia if—and this "if" was the key to his whole attitude—they could be cured of their religion. The first half of his reign was devoted to harsh bullying, to persecutions in novel forms; the latter half brought milder devices and more specious tricks—but cudgelling and coaxing had alike for their end the breaking down of Judaism as a creed and race caste.

Nicholas had an essentially military mind. He began his propaganda against Israel through martial channels. In April of 1827 he issued a ukase rendering Jews liable to military conscription like other subjects. Unlike other subjects, the Jewish recruits had to serve twenty-five years without ever being eligible to promotion. But, though no instructions were committed to paper, it became speedily understood in the army that the Czar desired heavy pressure to be put upon the Hebrew soldiers to win them over to baptism. This pressure became universal, and naturally took the shape of cruel torment to the obdurate.

But this process was too slow. Accordingly Nicholas invented a scheme of military colonies or schools, to be planted in the remote South, to be devoted to the combined conversion and martial training of Hebrew youths. This was an adaptation of the plan of settling regiments of the line about in the farm lands among the Crown serfs, which General Arakcheieff had proposed and carried out under the preceding reign. These colonies were an absorbing topic of agitation in Russia during the last days of Alexander I, and gave cause to numerous riots which were suppressed with bloodshed. The Jews now think of Arakcheieff as having also been the agent of Nicholas, in the establishment of the Jewish colonies. The facts are, however, I believe, that

Nicholas did not like him or employ him, and that he died in retirement some few years after that Czar's accession. It was only the idea that was indirectly derived from Arakcheieff.

Under this pretty plan, press gangs were now deputed to prowl about the Pale and forcibly abduct Jewish boys of from five to ten years of age. These were carried off to the southern settlement camps, and, after a violent baptism, were trained to the use of arms and brought up as soldiers. Jewish boys are, however, extremely precocious in the matter of theological learning. Their religious education begins so early that at eight their convictions are quite as well grounded as those of their elders. Some of these lads used to resist baptism. Then it was the commandant's thoughtful custom to put them in solitary confinement and feed them on salt herrings, without water to drink, until they consented to accept the baptismal rite.

I myself talked with a venerable man in Moscow last July, who was one of these " colonists," as they are called, in his youth, and who was brought by the herring test to the baptismal font. He was very proud of his forty-five years' service in the army, and carried himself with the dignity of a veteran of the Grenadier Guard. But neither this nor his juvenile apostasy prevented him from devoting his whole time to the succour and assistance of the poor Jews, then as now being hunted out of their homes in Holy Moscow.

Some of these Jewish urchins, thus forcibly converted, rose to rank in the Russian army. More than one of the generals of Nicholas are said to have come from this class. Those were days when generals were not necessarily educated men.

This trick of baptising boys and giving them new names, and the steady pressure so roughly exerted upon the Jewish conscripts, render it difficult to trace either the extent to which the army of Nicholas was filled with Hebrews, or the measure of admixture of Jewish with Russian blood throughout the Empire. It is known that Nicholas paid great attention to this press-gang method of gaining young Jewish recruits. They were most valuable, because the great landed proprietors, who were supposed to offer each year for enlistment a certain proportion of their serfs who had just reached the age of twenty-one, habitually bribed the recruiting committees to accept worthless and decrepit moujiks of forty-five and fifty years. As the term of service was twenty-five years the ranks were being continually depleted by the failure of these worn-out serfs to keep up with the rest.

But it was not alone through the machinery of the army that the proselyting screws were put upon Israel. In every walk of life rewards were busily dangled before the eyes of Jews if they would forsake Judaism. The local officials, eagerly interpreting and putting into execution the desires

of their master, did abominable things. Sometimes they also did comical things. An elderly
rabbi told me that even so late as the days of the
Crimean war he remembered policemen stationed
at the corners of the streets leading to the Jewish.
quarter in his native town, their business being to
catch Jews as they passed and cut off with scissors
their long earlocks, or *pies*, and the skirts of their
caftans, or long-tailed coats.

Nicholas, too, made numerous serious efforts
to plant Jews upon the soil as agriculturalists.
The story of these attempts is one of the most
melancholy in the whole unhappy records of the
race—at once melancholy and grimly grotesque.
We all remember the scene in "Great Expectations" of the little boy who, scared out of his
wits by the apparition of the mad old spinster in
her wild bridal array, hears her awful voice bidding
him get down on the floor and play. In the same
fashion the wretched Jew, physically feeble,
poverty-stricken, underfed, cooped up in the
crowded ghetto of his town, densely ignorant of
even the names of plants and farm implements,
was suddenly commanded by an imperial voice of
thunder to be an agriculturist.

Great colonies of Jews, sometimes numbering
hundreds of families, were now gathered up pro-
miscuously, transported across to the desolate
prairie lands of Novorossüsk and dumped down
upon the unbroken soil to thrive by agriculture.
In any case the experiment could have promised

scant success. As it was managed, it became simply murderous. A staff of officials, almost as numerous as the colonists themselves, was appointed to control the thing. Each family was supposed to be granted 175 roubles, but of this the officials gave the family only 30. The rest purported to have been expended in buying land, farm machinery, &c., and building houses. But seven-eighths of it was really stolen, and such colonists as did not die on the road found only groups of shanties not fit for pigs, and implements which broke in their hands. Here, under the control of brutal officials who knouted the incapable, but could not instruct or advise the industrious, these unhappy town Jews died of epidemics or starvation. The chief digging they did was the digging of graves.

The report of M. Stempel, who was superintendent of the Ekaterinoslav settlements, made in 1847, and which was not specially sympathetic to the Jews, presents an almost incredible tale of suffering.* It is quoted from the official documents in Prince Demidoff's book, and pictures the colonists as arriving at the beginning of winter, to find a cluster of wretched huts, damp, half open, and too low for a man to stand upright in, prepared for them to inhabit. These cabins had, let it be borne in mind, cost the Government enormous sums of money. The Jews begged to

* Archives of Kherson—Bessarabian Board of Administration. Report of Feb. 15, 1849. No. 116.

be allowed to reconstruct these shanties ; permission was refused by the officials. Stempel, the superintendent, then suggested that the Jews should be allowed to find shelter in neighbouring villages until spring. This also was refused, and they were peremptorily ordered to occupy the houses assigned to them. Those who had already sought refuge in the villages round about were driven back by Cossacks under circumstances of the greatest barbarism. Epidemics of scurvy and small-pox broke out shortly after.

It is only by the study of records likè these, and of the laws forbidding Jews to own, lease, or till land save in such "colonies," that we can understand why the Russian Jew seems to have no vocation for agriculture. It would be a highly miraculous thing if he had.

All this helps us, too, to comprehend the remarkable solidarity, at once so pathetic and so prejudicial, into which the Russian Jews have been driven. Once you cross the Russian frontier, you can tell the Jews at railway stations or on the street almost as easily as in America you can distinguish the negroes. This is more a matter of dress—of hair and beard and cap and caftan—than of physiognomy. But even more still is it a matter of demeanour. They seem never for an instant to lose the consciousness that they are a race apart. It is in their walk, in their sidelong glance, in the carriage of their sloping shoulders, in the curious gesture with the uplifted palm.

Nicholas undoubtedly secured in one way or another the baptism of many thousands of Hebrews. But he solidified the others into a dense, hard-baked, and endlessly resistant mass, the like of which no other country, perhaps, has ever found taxing its digestive powers. It is interesting to note that by that very ukase of 1827, extending conscription to the Jews, the Iron Czar unwittingly contributed to this undesirable end.

In a previous chapter it was mentioned that the Empress Catherine II allowed the Jews who came under her rule by the spoliation of Poland to retain, alone among all their ancient Polish privileges, their institution of the consistory, simply because it provided a simple and satisfactory machinery for the collection of taxes. Nicholas in the same way turned this remnant of Jewish self-government to account by making the *kahals*, or consistories, responsible for the furnishing of quotas of Jewish recruits. This placed a tremendous weapon in the hands of the Elders and orthodox leaders in every Jewish community. The old people of the strict Talmudic sect had it in their power to deliver over to the bondage of the army, at their own discretion and at any time, any young Jew who offended them, or whose opinions they regarded as dangerous because heterodox. No more effectual means could have been devised for stamping out every vestige of independent thought or impulse. The theocratic heads of each little Jewish community became absolute in their authority. One

might almost say that they had the power over
life and death in their hands. Naturally they
used it to enforce observance of the minutiæ of
the law, to widen the gulf between them and the
Christians round about, and to augment the
melancholy isolation of their race.

The abolition of these consistories in 1844, by
which the Hebrew population was made subject
to the ordinary civil jurisdiction, might have done
some good if it had been a complete measure.
But the duties of collecting taxes and of making
up recruiting lists were still left to special Jewish
bodies. Thus the real root of the evil was not
touched.

Of course, there are those who will not regard
it as an evil at all. I am not insensible to the
picturesque and inspiring side of the picture—the
spectacle of this little persecuted people clinging
doggedly to the smallest detail of their despised
faith, and risking everything they have in the
world for the sake of perpetuating in its least important particular the ceremonial of their ancient
worship. But in sober fact this view of the case
is most apparent to those who know least of the
Russian Jew. This theologico-racial isolation of
his, much as it may appeal to the generous imagination, has done him only harm. It has not made
him broad or tolerant; it has helped neither his
mind nor his body. Its effect, on the contrary,
has been to develop unlovely and unlikeable qualities in him. It has made him selfish, fanatical,

F

narrow-minded, ignorant of what civilisation likes
and respects—in a word, unsympathetic. It is,
more than anything else, responsible to-day for
the fact that no nation on earth desires him as an
immigrant ; that in every city to which he comes
he finds committees of his co-religionists formed
for the purpose of sending him somewhere else.

Even his virtues are of the unsympathetic sort.
He is a temperate man, generally a teetotaler ; he
is a creature of tireless industry, undergoing the
most arduous tasks for the smallest rewards ; he is,
perhaps with the exception of the Irish Catholic
peasant, the only uniformly chaste man in Europe ;
he is a faithful husband and a marvellously good
father, taking the harshest forms of self-denial as a
matter of course in the effort to provide education
and a start in life for his children ; he is innately a
peaceful man, and, in whatever country he may be,
a docile and law-abiding citizen.

Let us take this rather unique catalogue of
virtues and use it to illustrate a contrast with the
London dock labourer, with whom all England
and the world at large sympathised in his great
strike three years ago. This person, if he drinks
at all, is about the drunkenest man on the
habitable globe ; his indolence is a thing which
no employer can describe in language fit for publication ; his haunts and the unspeakable streets
about them swarm with drunken and vicious
women, young and old ; he almost rivals the
miner of the north country as an habitual wife-

beater; his neglect of his children is at once the scandal and the gravest problem of East London; fisticuffs, street brawls, and the breaking up of political meetings are his unfailing delight.

Yet we all took the deepest interest in seeing the dock labourer succeed in his strike for what we felt in our bones would probably turn out to be only extra beer-money, and no new country would object to him as an immigrant. *Per contra*, the miseries of the Russian Jew had to mount up in the scale until they suggested the horrors of the Spanish Inquisition before the world really took much interest, and, as I have said, nobody wants him as a settler.

Of course one might explain this by quoting the sage old remark that, after all, there is a good deal of human nature in the average man. But there is something more in it than that. The Russian Jew has suffered from the internal effects of this huge legal compression we have been tracing. He has been driven into the most contracted conceptions of things—into the least expansive and least informed variation of an exclusive creed, and into a fierce struggle for existence outside the bounds of natural and legitimate industry. The notions of tolerance for others or indulgence to himself are equally unknown to him. He alone among the scions of his race in Europe has produced next to nothing in art, music, or letters. When we have named the two brothers Rubenstein, the sculptor Antokolsky, and the young poet Frug, the list is well-nigh exhausted. If it were not for these, and for a certain journalistic activity among the more modern Jewish graduates of the universities, one might call the Russian Jew a barren and sterile thing in the gallery of nationalities.

He would, indeed, be a hopeless problem upon our hands were it not for the strange, almost startling, recuperative power in his race. The grandsons of these bearded and caftaned refugees, now flying in dumb and ignorant despair out into the unknown Christian world, will be recognisable cousins of Heine and Mendelssohn, of Spinoza and Eduard Lasker.

But to return to the chronicle. Nicholas is figured to our mind always as the very type of Sovereign who would not learn anything. In the matter of the Jews the latter years of his reign show a considerable change of attitude. After 1845 we do not meet many of those arbitrary and wanton ukases, curtailing Jewish privileges or driving the Hebrew population from certain towns, which are up to that date so cruelly abundant. These expulsions from towns were generally based upon the petition of the Christian merchants. Among the edicts ordering them are many curiosities. The Christian guilds of Knyshin, for example, in 1845 procured the expulsion of Jews from their town ; in 1858 we find them admitting that this had done injury to the place and begging that the order be revoked. Even queerer is the record of how, in 1829, the Karaïm Jews of Trok, in the Government of Wilna, obtained a decree expelling the other Jews from the town.

We see that the basis alike of antagonism and concession was economic. It was, in fact, a sort of barbaric variety of the protection idea. Every man who thought he could make more money if he were relieved of Jewish competition was an advocate of expulsions and a policy of repression. Where the Government here and there enlarged Jewish privileges it was admittedly because it had come to be seen that the country would profit by it.

As railways began to be built in Russia, and commerce and manufactures took on a new meaning and importance, the value of the Jew became more apparent. It is this fact which makes the closing part of the reign of Nicholas seem tolerant by comparison. A good many of the earlier restrictions were lifted. Jewish contractors were allowed to make bids for the carrying of Government stores and even the building of roads and railways. The farming of brandy manufacture came to be almost wholly in their hands, and now even the inspectorships over this business were filled with Hebrews, for the reason that they were superior in both honesty and bookkeeping skill to native Russians.

Nicholas, also, in his later years, exhibited a great liking for educated and intellectual Jews. Hebrew doctors, dentists, and lawyers were in

demand.  To this Czar is due the exception made
in Russian laws in favour of Jews who have
graduated at the higher schools of the empire,
by which they are allowed liberty of residence
throughout the realm.  The facilities which he
finally offered to the Jews in the matter of education were not, however, very generally improved
during his reign.  They remembered his earlier
devices of abducting and forcibly baptising their
boys, and suspected some new scheme of conversion or perversion in this opening of the schools.

With the death of Nicholas and the advent of
Alexander II a new era dawned.  Dr. Mackenzie
Wallace has drawn a spirited and comprehensive
picture of the literal stampede all Russia made to
reform everything.  History records no more
interesting phenomenon than this frenzy with
which the whole Slavonic mass set to work ripping
up old institutions, knocking over old idols, and
beginning life afresh  We have to do, however,
with only one minor aspect of this universal but
delusive awakening.

Almost the first thing the young Czar did was to
revive a commission to inquire into the condition of
the Jews, which Nicholas had decreed in 1840 and
then allowed to lapse.  This commission sent out
a list of inquiries to all the Provincial Governors.
These gentlemen returned voluminous reports, all,
without exception, favourable to the Jews.  Of
course it must be remembered, in this as in everything else, that Russian officials report to the

Czar what they suppose the Czar wants to hear. The air was surcharged with Radical electricity. Everybody knew that the heir apparent had been in opposition and was still a Liberal. Rumours of the emancipation of the serfs already sounded in men's ears. Nothing seemed more natural than that he should be a friend of the Jews, since he was so unlike his father. Hence these reports sent in by the Provincial Governors are not to be taken as quite trustworthy testimony. Yet they are of value as showing how much interested officials could find to praise in the Russian Jew, once they felt the Imperial tastes ran that way. Indeed, for the ensuing fifteen years the official literature of Russia was to abound in testimonials to the industrial, commercial, and educational value of the Jew, emanating from the most authoritative sources.

Upon the strength of these reports were issued the ukases of 1859, 1861, and 1865, already referred to, by which Jews of the first mercantile guild and Jewish artisans were allowed to reside all over the Empire.

It is just as well to remember that even these beneficent concessions, which seem by contrast with what had gone before to mark such a vast forward step in Russo-Jewish history, were confessedly dictated by utilitarian considerations. The shackles were stricken only from the two categories of Jews whose freedom would bring profit to Russia. I venture to call attention to this at the risk of seeming ungracious to the memory of the " Liberator Czar," because otherwise one gets a false perspective in the picture. There has never been any time when the Jews in Russia were treated like other people. Even in this period which we have now reached—this "golden age," as they call it now in bitter retrospect of regret—the milch-cow theory ruled their fortunes. They were treated better than before only because more enlightened views as to their usefulness prevailed. Those Hebrews who seemed unlikely to be of public use were kept, as before, cooped up in the Pale or running the gauntlet of police persecution.

The official records of this period are filled with recommendations from local officials pointing out places in the interior where skilled labour was needed and where Jewish artisans and artificers would be of service. Many of these are accompanied by the specious argument that if the Jews are allowed thus to settle in the interior, a few in each town, they will the more easily become converted and amalgamated with the Christian population. Ministerial decrees over and over again explain themselves on these practical, not to say sordid, grounds. In 1867, for example, Jews were for the first time allowed to rent flour mills and factories on rural estates, because "no one but Jews can be found there to manage these mills and factories, such management requiring special technical knowledge and experience." Nowhere is it ever suggested that the burdens resting on the Hebrews are lightened because it is the civilised and human thing to do.

Still, the quarter century following Alexander II's accession in 1885 fairly deserves its appellation of the "golden age" when what preceded it is recalled. It seems almost beatific by comparison with what has followed it.

# CHAPTER VI

## "THE GOLDEN AGE"

WHAT is called the "golden age" of the Jews in Russia may be roughly said to have lasted for twenty years—from 1857 to 1877. It began with the efforts of a high-spirited, broad-minded, and eager young Czar to profit by the terrible lesson Russia had learned in the Crimean war, and to so widen and reform the national structure that no such catastrophe could ever again overwhelm monarch, army, and people alike. It ended in the dismal confession of a dispirited and pessimistic old Czar, who found himself against his will embarked in another only less disastrous war, forced gloomily to recognise that his efforts had been in vain, and that it was beyond the power of any human force to civilise and satisfactorily govern Russia.

It is the universal testimony of fair men in Russia that, all circumstances considered, the Jews bore very well the measure of prosperity now meted out to them. I have talked with numbers of Russian gentlemen who are frankly anti-Semitic, but who admit that fifteen years ago they were satisfied with the progress the Jew had made

ALEXANDER II
(*The Liberator Czar*)

under the existing liberal conditions, and regarded him as a good and valuable citizen. So late, indeed, as 1880 the Christian merchants of Moscow signed what we would call a round-robin setting forth the excellent qualities of their Jewish associates on the Bourse or in the mart, and of the Jewish artisans settled in the city, and protesting against the introduction in Russia of the odious *Judenhetze* then rampant in parts of Germany. The first man to sign this was M. Alexeieff, now the bitterly anti-Semitic Mayor of Moscow!

During these twenty years of relative enfranchisement the Jews came a long way out of their shell. The cruel line of race and creed demarcation which we have seen so deeply drawn in previous reigns became less prominent in men's thoughts—in places faded away altogether.

In nothing was this beneficent effect more plainly exhibited than in the matter of education. I have pointed out that, although Nicholas nominally freed the public schools to Hebrew children, the old suspicion of his motives prevented any general advantage being taken of this step. But this not unnatural hesitation vanished at once under the new reign. The Jews have in every land and in every age been distinguished for the prominence they give to the education of the young. In Russia they had the added incentive of securing the special privileges for their sons which still attach to the Jew "of the higher education." Every father who now could, by doubling his own labour and self-denial, send his son to school, did so. In the cases of bright and promising Jewish boys whose parents were too poor, it was a common thing for the neighbours of the village or quarter to raise a purse among themselves to send them to school.

As the native Russian has less of this innate regard for learning than any other white man alive, it follows that the proportion of Jewish scholars in the schools far exceeded that borne by the Jewish to the general population. It was almost equally a matter of course that these Hebrew students should carry off the great bulk of the prizes. They started with a swifter and more facile brain ; they had the advantage of a home training in another language, or perhaps two other tongues,* besides Russian, and they were sustained and spurred on by the peculiar significance of that goal toward which all struggled—the freedom of "the higher education." So it was not unusual to see in a school where only one-sixth were Jews every one of the prizes taken by this minority.

Many of these Jewish graduates of the *gymnasia* and universities entered the professions as physi-

---

* The importance of this it is impossible to exaggerate. The poorest and lowliest Russian, Polish, Bohemian or Hungarian Jew, through his Jiddish, knows enough of German to transact business in it. This gives him an enormous advantage, with strangers, over his neighbours who speak only the outlandish language of the country. But of course it also makes him all the more hated by those neighbours.

cians, lawyers, and engineers. Others embarked
in commerce, happy in their exemption as belonging to the "higher education," until they could
win the other title to emancipation as "Merchants
of the First Guild"

The constitution of this privileged commercial
class is a curious one. A Jewish merchant inside
the Pale who has annually paid taxes amounting
to 1000 roubles (something over $600) for five
consecutive years may then go and establish himself provisionally in a city of the interior. Here
for a further term of ten years he must pay this
same amount of taxes. Then his term of probation
is over, and he may thereafter live wherever in
Russia he pleases, and even buy land, subject to
certain testamentary restrictions.

Neither of these two classes, the *intelligensia*
nor the Merchants of the First Guild, ever, however, became numerically important. Save in the
three professions I have mentioned, the Jewish
alumnus had very little chance of a livelihood in
Russia outside of trade. He could not be a professor, he generally did not want to be a rabbi,
and the civil service was practically closed to him.
The result is that after a few years he either
drifted into business or emigrated. As for the
other class, it seems unlikely that there ever were
at any one time more than 2000 or 2500 Jewish
Merchants of the First Guild. The number in
Moscow, for example, was estimated by well-
informed people for me last summer at 120.

There are only two or three other cities in Russia
where there could be more.

And these two classes, moreover, concern us
the less in that they have scarcely been touched
by the persecutions. No doubt their time is
coming, but as yet they retain the privileges of
1865.

Of the "something less than 1,000,000" Hebrews
supposed to have been living in Russia outside
the Pale at the close of Alexander's II's reign, the
overwhelming bulk were neither alumni and
Merchants of the First Guild nor usurers; they
were artisans and the families of artisans.

In the preceding chapter I have instanced som
of the requests which came from all parts of Russia
proper, after the Crimean war, for the colonisation
of skilled labourers, and have shown that the
shackles were stricken from the Jewish artificer
inside the Pale primarily to meet this demand.
Official records of the period make it clear that
Alexander II himself desired to see the Hebrew
population so completely distributed and scattered
over the Empire that it would lend itself to amal-
gamation. His lieutenants never rose to this
height of statesmanship. They, indeed, threw
open the gates of the Ghetto and let 60,000 or
70,000 Jewish craftsmen out; but they followed
these to the remotest parts of Russia, with the
whole lumbering mass of machinery which had
made their previous existence a burden.

Wherever they settled these artisans could not

buy property or take up a permanent residence.
Everywhere they were " sojourners," members of
a class known in Russian law as the *Inorodzy*, the
other members of which are " the Kirghiz Tartars,
the Samoyedes, the Kalmuks, the tribes on the
Caspian, the nomads of the Stavropol Government,
and the inhabitants of the Komando Islands."
This Jewish artisan, settling, let us say, in Tula,
had each year to get his certificate of good
character from the police of that place, and his
residential passport from the Jewish community of
his original place of domicile, renewed. If from
whim or by accident the renewal of either was
delayed for a day beyond the stated time, the
fact transformed him and his family on the instant
into pariahs, wholly outside the law and helplessly
liable to whatever measure of persecution and
spoliation the police might choose to inflict.

Beyond all this he was entirely subject to the
will of the artisan guild in this new town. Before
he could take up his abode there at all, he had to
pass a practical examination in the working of his
particular trade. This was always a fruitful source
of injustice and iniquity. The examiners would
habitually find out what branch of shoemaking or
watchmaking he knew best, and then set him to
show his proficiency on another branch. This
trick had its uses in more ways than one. It
enabled the Christian craftsmen of each little town
to regulate the number and skill in workmanship
of their Jewish competitors; it allowed them to

pass in as artisans other Jews who really had no trade at all but would pay for an artisan's certificate, and it afforded a broad and fertile field for the cultivation of blackmail, which the Christian guild and the police tilled industriously on shares.

Although we are studying a "golden age," there were still other restrictions which might as well be set down here. The law of 1865 permitted the Jewish artisan emigrating from the Pale to take with him his wife, children, and infant brothers and sisters. These, as his family, shared such precarious right of domicile as he was able, by the means enumerated above, to secure. But if he died, back these others all had to go into the Pale again. Similarly, if he fell ill or was disabled and hence was no longer able to work at his trade, he must return to the village in the Pale whence he came, and where he had been unable to earn a decent living even when in health.

It will be seen that the gilding does not bear overmuch examination. On the other hand, it ought to be explained that while these harsh restrictions and many others remained on the statute books, they were by no means sternly or strictly enforced. The police used them just enough to extract a comfortable livelihood.

But there was still another class of Jews who, under the liberating edicts of 1857–65, left the Pale to spread through the towns of Russia proper. The merchant of the First Guild might "take with himself" as many Jewish clerks as he "needed." I have put within quotation marks two portions of the sentence, because upon their phraseology has turned, as will be seen later, the ruthless expulsion of thousands of people. But in the days of Alexander II a loose and amiable construction was placed upon this concession, with results not wholly fortunate.

Considerable numbers of Hebrew clerks, book-keepers, accountants, and superior salesmen were brought into the interior, under the obvious meaning of this permissive clause. But there were also large numbers of less useful Jews who were neither artisans nor clerks, and who had no legal right to leave the Pale at all, but who followed on after the others. The recent opening of Oklahoma furnishes a rude sort of parallel for this overflowing of Israel from the Pale. Lots of people joined the throng who had no business to be in it—that is, who were without money, a craft, or a legal status—and greatly added to the complications and difficulties of the others.

These outsiders, if I may use the term, may have lacked trades and passports, but they had enough tenacity and assurance to make good the deficiency. They became small traders, hawkers, hucksters, messengers, money-changers, petty speculators, and the like; running a desperate race always, and being incessantly chivied by the police, like fakirs at a country fair, yet somehow scraping a living together. Soon their audacity

G

and the appetite of the police joined forces and
devised a scheme from which mutual profit could
be extracted. It is universally alleged on the
anti-Semitic side, and as stoutly denied on the
other, that these outsiders got themselves fraudulently registered as clerks of the Merchants of the
First Guild, and that in payment for this privilege
they rendered themselves useful to their pseudo
employers—the connection helping them to make
money with which to buy police immunity. The
closest inquiry led to the conclusion that such a
class did exist, but in nothing like the numbers
popularly given in Russia.

It is almost entirely from this grade of unauthor-
ized Jews, so to speak, that the usurers, brothel
keepers, and general rich scoundrels about whom
the Russians talk so glibly, have arisen. They
owed every step of their progress, as now they owe
their freedom from persecution, wholly to the
venality of the Russian police and officials.

The commercial and industrial value to Russia
of this change in the treatment of the Jews was
immediately recognised. The Jewish traders and
artisans who now spread themselves over the
empire at once multiplied by tens or scores the
traffic of the districts in which they settled, and altered the whole scale of prices in entire departments of manufacture. Elderly men remember
still the wonderful effect produced in small places
like Podolsk or Riazan by the advent of the Jewish
watchmaker and silversmith, who would actually

repair timepieces to make them go instead of to
secure their early collapse and another job—and
whose charges bore an intelligible relation to the
labour he had expended.

The great and almost universal cheapening of
prices which followed this pacific dispersion of
Israel, and which to this day is angrily remembered
by the native Russian tradesman, is of service as
pointing an essential difference between the two
races.

The Russian tradesman dislikes exertion, and
has almost a Turkish contempt for hurry or eagerness in traffic. He has no notion whatever of the
theory of quick returns. His idea of commerce is
to mark a fifty or sixty per cent. profit on his goods,
and then sit down and drink tea and play draughts
till God sends him a customer.

The Jew, on the other hand, comprehends to its
utmost the value of turning his money as rapidly
as possible, and he has a real delight in activity.*
He will sell each week at a profit of 10 or 5 per
cent. a stock of goods as big as that which cum-
bers the Russian's store for six months. If 5 per
cent. is not forthcoming, he will take less, down to
the lowest margin which will effect a sale and return something. Prince Demidoff says that he
will even sell without a profit at all, if the demand

---

* The great Pan-Slavist, Aksakoff, says in his " Investigation of
Trade at the Ukraine Fairs " (St. Petersburg, 1858), " while a rouble
will be turned over twice by a Russian trader, in the hands of a
Jew it will be turned over five times."

for that special line hangs fire, in order to hasten off and embark the capital in a more promising venture.

This conception of business did not endear the Jewish merchant to his Russian competitor. Still less did the amazing energy with which he threw himself into his work. The restless, nervous, tireless industry of the Russian Hebrew in pursuit of the object he has in view is in truth one of the chief objections to him. He sets a pace which the others find impossible.

In Kieff a very intelligent Russian took the trouble to explain to me why he objected to the Jews. There were a number of commonplace and familiar reasons, which did not stick in my memory. One, however, interested me. Formerly, he said, the peasants used to drive into town on market days and sell their produce in the open square. Then it was possible for honest citizens to sleep comfortably in their beds till 8 or after, and then stroll down at their leisure to the market, after their first breakfast. But now the Jews go out on the country roads for miles, at 4 or 5 in the morning, intercept these peasants and buy the produce as it lies in the carts. This my Russian friend regarded as monstrous.

As I have said, the development of trade, the opening up of new avenues of commerce, the founding of new industries, and the cheapening of articles of common use which followed this partial emancipation of the Jews, was of inestimable service to Russia. It is impossible, however, to estimate it for what it was really worth, for the reason that it is, from every economic point of view, inextricably mixed up with the Emancipation of the Serfs.

The main bulk of the Hebrew host let out of the Pale by Alexander II found all Russia turned topsy-turvy by the sudden setting free of these millions of serfs. The opinion of the most thoughtful and best-informed men I know in Russia is that, without the services of these Jews as middlemen, as cheap producers, and as hard workers, the emancipation experiment would from the start have been a failure.

However that may be, it is the wildest and most fanciful nonsense to say that such measure of failure as is apparent now is due in any way to the Jews. Something like universal bankruptcy exists in Russia at the present day, undoubtedly. There is said to be not one Land Bank in the empire which, if it closed its affairs, would prove solvent. The Nobles' Bank is so sadly the other way that not even the lottery loan, which M. Vishnegradsky has authorised, against Russian law, and used his Ministerial power to compel other banks to take up, can possibly put it on its feet. But the Jews are not the creditors. The multiplying swarm of Grand Dukes, each with his two millions of roubles of capital ; the rapacious gang of officials and politicians, of whom Ignatieff is a type ; the vast thousand-armed devilfish of an

Orthodox Church, sucking in everything portable
from every quarter, and piling up in its maw literally tons of gold and silver ; the incapable native
producers and traders, with their ceaseless clamour
for higher tariffs ; the wildly-debauched colonies of
spendthrift aristocrats in Paris and on the Riviera
—these are the people to whom Russia owes her
bankruptcy—not the Jew.

Fortunately this assertion need not rest on my
own authority.    Very striking proof of its truth is
at hand.    Since the present famine became a
reality in the minds of the governing officials in
St. Petersburg, there has been an interesting
relaxation in the vigilance of the Press Censorship.
Presumably this means nothing more than that a
general demoralisation has spread through the
departments, as a result of the crisis.    However
that may be, it is certain that from last autumn to
the present time the newspapers of Russia have
printed much bolder remarks upon public affairs
than ever before, and have apparently not been in
any way molested.    The three articles published
in the St. Petersburg *Viedomosti* on the 11th, 15th
and 25th of October, 1891, to the substance of
which I desire to call attention, would six months
earlier have brought the *gendarmerie* down upon
the office within an hour of publication, and would
probably have landed the editor in prison.

These articles were given the title of " Lie and
Truth."    They dealt with the familiar Russian
assertion that the Jew "exploits" the moujik, and

is alike a social and commercial curse to Russia—
and dealt with it, not by abstract arguments but
by the production of solid and unanswerable
statistical evidence.

Too much importance cannot be attached to
this proof that the presence of Jews, so far from
injuring the moujik, benefits him.  His prosperity
is much greater in the districts containing a large
Jewish population than it is in parts where no
Hebrew is allowed to live.  Demonstration of this
is furnished by the figures of the new Government
Peasant Land Bank, whose operations extend
over the 15 provinces of the Pale, and 26 other
provinces of the interior.  The Pale, as we have
seen, is crowded with Jews; the Interior contains
practically no Jews at all.  The report of the
Land Bank for the five years 1885–9, make this
remarkable showing as to the condition of the
Orthodox peasantry (the only persons permitted
to buy land) in the two contrasted districts :

Land bought by peasants in the Pale     .  67.2 per cent.
Land bought by peasants in the Interior .  32.8  „   „

Value of this land in the Pale  .    .   . 87.7 per cent.
Value of this land in the Interior   .   . 12.3  „   „

Of the total moujik population in these 41
provinces, the Pale contains considerably more
than half, it is true, but the prosperity of this
section as compared with the other is not to be
accounted for in that way.  If we follow the
figures further, this is brought out very clearly:

Peasant population of Pale (15 provinces)   58.3 per cent.
Peasant population of Interior (26 provinces)   41.7 „   „

Area of peasant purchases in Pale   .   470,299 desiatines.
By population ratio should be   .   .   407,463   „
                           Excess   .   62,836   „

Value of land bought in the Pale   .   23,496,795 roubles.
By population ratio should be   .   .   15,618,369   „
                           Excess   .   7,878,426   „

There can be no answer to figures like these.
They show us that in the dread Pale, where the
unhappy Jews are huddled together in the most
terrible poverty and driven to the most desperate
devices to keep body and soul together, the
Russian peasants have two million sterling more
money to invest in land on their own account, than
have the moujiks in the interior where no Jew is
to be found. If this indicates " exploitation " anywhere, then obviously the Jew and not the moujik
is its victim.

The Government report for the same years,
1885-9, on the amount of unpaid taxes due from
the peasantry, is quite as remarkable. The Land
Bank statistics covered only 26 of the interior
provinces ; these official tax-arrears returns embrace all Russia, but this only serves to exhibit
the condition of the Orthodox peasantry of the
Pale in a still more favourable light :

Unpaid taxes in Pale (15 provinces) .   36,041,590 roubles.
Unpaid taxes in Interior (35 provinces, 237,984,768   „

Debt *per capita* inside Pale   .   .   .   26 kopecks.
Debt *per capita* outside Pale   .   .   .   83   „

Students of sociology attach great importance to statistics based upon the death rate. In a country like Russia, and among a people like the moujiks, the question of health and of life itself is most intimately connected with that of material prosperity. Tried by this test, then, we secure much the same results. The *Viedomosti* quotes only the returns for the three years 1884–6. They show that the death rate in the 35 interior provinces where there are no Jews was 35.6 per thousand, whereas inside the Pale it was only 29.8.

Fully as interesting, from another point of view, are the statistics relating to crime. Enough has been said about the Pale to indicate that there, if anywhere under the sun, the Jew might feel justified in setting all laws, human and divine, at defiance. Yet the records of these three sample provinces of the Pale show that even where the Jew is poorest, most ignorant, most oppressed, he still behaves himself better than his Russian neighbours :

*Town population Province of Vilna.*

| | | | |
|---|---|---|---|
| Jews | . 66.3 per cent. | . Jewish criminals | . 52.1. |
| All others | 33.8 „ „ | . Other „ | . 47.9. |

*Town population Province of Vitebsk.*

| | | | |
|---|---|---|---|
| Jews | . 60.2 per cent. | . Jewish criminals | . 49. |
| All others | 39.8 „ „ | . Other „ | . 51. |

*Town population Province of Kovno.*

| | | | |
|---|---|---|---|
| Jews | 80.4 per cent. | . Jewish criminals | . 50.1. |
| All others | 19.6 „ „ | . Other , | . 49.9. |

To get the full significance of these figures, it must be kept in mind that a thousand actions which the Russian himself is entitled to perform are crimes when done by a Russian Jew. Even praying in an unauthorised synagogue puts a man in the criminal classes—certainly would enrol him in one of the tables of Jewish offenders quoted above. There are no Jewish judges, no Jewish juries, no Jewish policemen. To say the least, we may be sure that the statistics do not err on the side of leniency to the Jew.

The sober truth is, that nobody in Russia has dreamed of paying any debt to a Jewish trader or artisan these eighteen months. The sums due throughout the Empire to individual Hebrews who have been driven out of their homes, no kopeck of which they can ever hope to see, would in the aggregate mount up to many millions. Thus at every step last summer I encountered or heard of some respectable head of a family, who could have gone away in relative comfort if his outstanding credits had been available or negotiable, but who in reality needed charity to assist him and his household to the frontier. Yet it is they who are denounced as "exploiters" of the Russians!

But it is important not to forget that we are studying a "golden age."

Up to the reign of Alexander II, the rich Jew was practically unknown in Russia. The Hebrew

doctors and dentists in St. Petersburg were prosperous, and here and there throughout the empire
some merchant more daring or more useful to the
police than the others had managed to lift himself
out of the slough of penury which engulfed his
race. These were very few in number, however,
and are now hardly remembered.

But in the new order of things after the Crimea
there was room and scope for the millionaire Israel-
ite. Apparently the fortunes of those who now
climbed the ladder of finance and attracted the attention of all Russia were at the time much exaggerated. The load of blackmail which they had
to carry was too heavy and too continuous in its
pressure to make the amassing of really great
wealth possible. But, undoubtedly, Warschoffsky,
Horwitz, and the elder Poliakoff became rich and
powerful capitalists. I mention these names because they belong to a little family group, the character and fortunes of which played an important
part in the tragic sequel. Intermarriages among
their children bound these three strong and self-
made men together. It was the era of railway building, and they, by superior shrewdness and energy,
secured the most important contracts all over the
empire. To this day, when an accident happens
on a Russian railroad from bad rails, defective
roadbed, or rotten bridge, the Russian always
ascribes it to the Jewish contractors.

It does not concern our inquiry to dwell upon
the careers of these great business and building

magnates. Probably they were no better and no worse than the active, aggressive, strong-handed men who in every new and undeveloped country come to the front, carry through big constructive projects, and reap the rewards. The building of our own Pacific road produced just this type of men and much the same kind of questionable methods. The difference was that in the United States the Crédit Mobilier exposure and Congressional interference made every detail of the scandal public property. In Russia many Ministers and officials and even princes of the blood waxed wealthy side by side with the railway contractors, but there was never a protest raised by anybody.

Smaller Jewish contractors grew up under the shadow of these great men, and thrived by intimate relations with the officials. The collusion was notorious. I have already spoken of Ignatieff, and the manner in which he shared with the Vannitsa Jew, Michaelowitz, the plunder of the Kotchubey estates. He was hand in glove with all these Hebrew contractors, who, by Ministerial favour and even higher influences, gradually got control of the public works. What was true of him was true of practically every other Russian politician and office-holder of importance. We have seen how, in the days of Catherine, Paul, and Nicholas, the poor Jews were treated by the Government as a kind of milch cow. The same idea was still in force, only it was the officials who had learned now to create and then exploit rich

Jews for their own personal benefit, at the expense of the country at large.

These things came to a climax in the Russo-Turkish war of 1877–8. Here again a dozen volumes could be written upon what must be condensed into a few paragraphs. Briefly, that war was a veritable debauch of corruption. Its very inception was a cold-blooded swindle. Ignatieff, as Minister to Constantinople, sedulously sent home lying reports about Turkey's weakness, the disorganisation of her army and finances, and her utter inability to defend herself at any point. He as untiringly used every means in his power to stir up the Balkans to a point where Russian interference should seem to have become a matter of national honour and Imperial dignity. So enthusiastically was he backed by the whole official hierarchy—each member keenly scenting plunder in the air—that the Czar was at last reluctantly forced across the Rubicon. War was declared.

In Russia everything is done by contract—war included. What happened now simply staggers the imagination. Ten thousand civilian officials wrestled with ten other thousand army dignitaries for their share of the spoils. Minister struggled against General, Mayor hurled himself in fierce rivalry with Colonel. As a result, the army was so heartlessly and completely robbed by every one that it barely missed being starved out of existence ; indeed, Russia would have been whipped to her knees if thievery and bribe-taking had not been almost as prevalent among the Turkish Pashas as well.

In this wild rush for booty the luckless Jew was literally overwhelmed by superior Muscovite numbers. Like little Jakey, in the whimsical story of the synagogue being stampeded by a cry at the door of "job lots!" he was killed in the deadly crush.

The contracting machinery in Russia had been invented by the Jews and was in their hands. The three Hebrew capitalists I have mentioned, with numbers of their less powerful co-religionists, secured most of the contracts for supplies, horses, munitions, &c., at the outset. But the official appetite had all at once grown so savage and ravenous that they could not for a moment hold their own against it. They would themselves have been eaten had they not thrown everything else to the monster. Every Russian will tell you that the late Grand Duke Nicholas, brother to the Czar and Commander-in-Chief, stole enough for his own purse to have fed an army corps during the campaign, though he is said to have died last year heavily in debt. Thousands of officers only less splendid in rank took only a smaller share. The present Czar, then heir-apparent, was so indignant at this shameless wholesale robbery that he complained formally to his father, and an inquiry was ordered. The culprits were too lofty in rank to be exposed. The inquiry came to nothing.

Doubtless the Jewish contractors had embarked upon the business with confidence that at least a proportion of the spoils would be theirs. They made a cruel mistake. Not only were profits denied them—they did not get back even the principal of their investment. They were robbed openly and without mercy. Warschoffsky was broken mentally as well as financially by this spoliation, and hanged himself. The older Poliakoff, going to his funeral, fell dead with heart disease in the house of mourning.

In this sinister fashion ended the "golden age!"

# CHAPTER VII

## IGNATIÉFF AND THE MAY LAWS

THE last thing which foreigners who study the contemporary history of a country get to understand is the part played in the making of that history by powerful journalists. No Englishman, for example, comprehends in the least the influence upon the American civil war exerted by editor-politicians like Horace Greeley and Thurlow Weed. In the same way, it is very difficult for any one outside of England to realise how largely the events of the past decade in these islands have been affected, mischievously for the most part, by Mr. William .T. Stead.

A Russian newspaper man, of whom very few people in Russia itself, and practically none at all outside, have heard, enters our story at this point, and from the moment of his début becomes an important factor in its tragic development. I allude to Mr. Suvorin, the owner and editor of the *Novoe Vremya*.

A most characteristic anecdote is told of the manner in which he first became interested in the Jewish question. M. Suvorin was a journalist and popular writer of *feuilletons* for the most liberal papers in that era of comparative Liberalism in Russia, that is to say, from 1865 to 1875. Then a distressing domestic tragedy broke down his working power, and forced him for a time into retirement. He had so far emerged from this, when the Russo-Turkish war came in 1877, as to have under his control an obscure and unremunerative paper. Excited by the rumours of great fortunes being made at the seat of war, he went down to Bucharest in company with an inventor, even poorer than himself, but who had some novel sort of copper kettle to sell. Suvorin conceived the plan of enriching himself by getting this kettle adopted for use in the camps of the Russian Army, and to effect this he sought an interview with Samuel Poliakoff, the great Jewish contractor, then in Bucharest. But Poliakoff, harassed and worried by incessant conflict with the bigger Russian robbers, perhaps already foreseeing the ruin which was to overtake him and his colleagues, was in no mood to trifle with this unknown and threadbare adventurer. He brusquely sent Suvorin about his business.

Suvorin returned to St. Petersburg with his kettles, and began attacking Poliakoff in his paper. His rage, however, was too great to appease itself upon any one man, even though that man were the millionaire Poliakoff. It spread itself out to embrace the Jews of Russia. At another time the police would have made short work with unauthorised journalism of this sort. But it chanced just

H

then to play into the hands of the most influential man in Russia—General Nicholas Paulovitch Ignatieff.

The Jews in Russia always mention this man's name under their breath and with a shudder of hatred. More often he is not mentioned by name at all, but designated with a word which means "The Infamous." I have been told by others that the Jews exaggerate Ignatieff's power for harm to them, and that he has by no means so fully earned their hatred as they imagine. Upon this, of course, I cannot pretend to pass. I know only that they universally ascribe to his malice, greed, and inhuman wickedness and cruelty the sum of their miseries, and that they trace the whole painful record of their persecutions and woes since 1877 by references to the details of his career.

I have shown in the preceding chapter the motives Ignatieff had for crippling and destroying the group of great Jewish contractors. Apparently cognate motives now led him to throw the protecting mantle of his power over Suvorin, and to give his support to the anti-Jewish crusade of the *Novoe Vremya*. From that moment the *Novoe Vremya* became an important paper. After the suppression of the *Golos*, in 1882, it took the position it has since held as the most influential journal in St. Petersburg, or in Russia. And Suvorin has grown now to be a rich man.

The rise of the *Judenhetze* in Prussia at this

particular time (1879) was of tremendous assistance to Ignatieff and Suvorin. It is the habit to assume that this agitation in North Germany was the beginning of the whole thing, and that the fever of persecution only spread over the border into Russia after it had become epidemic from Berlin to Pomerania. So admirable an authority as Dr. Wilhelm Müller takes this view.* But the facts are the other way. The *Novoe Vremya* had been attacking the Jews for months before the first outbreak of feeling in Germany, and Ignatieff, now become Governor of Nijni Novgorod, was openly against the Jews.

The German riots did, however, point the means to a practical demonstration of anti-Semitism in Russia. Up to this time, such unhappiness as the Jew in Russia had suffered had come from maladministration, from bad laws, rapacious and brutal officials, and the jealousy of Christian guilds of traders or artisans. He had got along well enough with the Russian people themselves. I do not pretend that he was beloved, but he had not been exposed to popular insult and violence. Indeed, as has been explained heretofore, he quite generally represented, in the minds of the Russian masses, cheap prices for goods and an industrious distribution of the necessaries of life. Therefore, no one had thought of beating him or burning down his house.

* The annual publication "Politische Geschichte der Gegenwart." By Wilhelm Müller, Professor in Tübingen.

But now, all at once, anti-Jewish riots began in Russia. It was interesting to note that they were all in Southern Russia, a section far remote from German influence. In each case they were in towns containing a large population of Greek stevedores and labourers, and these Greeks had a practical monopoly of the violence. This was in itself significant. But then it was discovered that a band of young men from St. Petersburg—young students, clerks, and ne'er-do-wells generally—was travelling about the country, and invariably appeared in a town a day or so before the outbreak of the riot. These *agents provocateur* did their work too clumsily. They grew inflated by their success, and appeared on the streets blowing whistles, marching in step, and otherwise calling attention to their organisation.

The scandal became so obvious that the Christian merchants of Moscow signed a protest against it. I have already mentioned the fact that M. Alexeieff, the present Jew-baiting Mayor of Moscow, headed the list of signatures. This protest, being intrusted to Dr. Bunge, a fair and honourable man, then Minister of Finance, was shown to the Czar in person, along with convincing proofs as to the bogus character of these riots. It is believed to have been due to direct Imperial interference that they thereupon came suddenly to a stop.

The Czar Alexander II, now in the sixties, saw his reign closing in disaster, confusion, and

·dishonour. The hideous carnival of corruption which had paralysed his armies during the recent war, and so well-nigh brought them to defeat, disheartened him. Individually, here and there, as in the case of these fraudulent riots, he could intervene on the side of decency. But his utmost efforts could effect no more than might a cup of water dashed against a burning house. Small wonder, then, that he ceased to try.

Misgovernment, wholesale robbery, over-taxation, the failure of the emancipated moujiks to prosper under the double burden of their own ignorant indolence and the stupid greed of the landed classes—in a word, the blight of barbarism, had created widespread conspiracies of revolt. Society was honeycombed with murder clubs and anarchist associations. The Government of the "Liberator" Czar hardened into a despotism of the most malevolent type. In the years of 1879-80 not less than 60,000 Russian subjects were exiled to Siberia "by administrative order" without any trial whatever.*

It may be well believed that the Czar himself grew utterly despondent. He had tried to do such great things—with this squalid and evil result! Most of all—worst of all—he came to doubt the value of having striven to educate his people. The disaffection all came from the educated classes. To this day Russia offers the grotesque paradox of a country spending great

* Dr. Wilhelm Müller.

sums upon universities and higher schools, a large
proportion of the graduates from which are sent
in chains to Siberia shortly after their education
has been completed.   But in those fateful years
practically every educated Russian was a suspect.

Naturally a state of affairs in which education
is a ground for suspicion must have seriously
affected the Jews.   They were pre-eminently an
educated class in Russia, for reasons which have
been heretofore discussed.   It is said that the
Czar came to believe that the Nihilist movement
drew its chief inspiration and instruments from the
Jews.   Obviously this belief would have been
fostered by all the officials of the Ignatieff stamp
who surrounded him, and it was openly promulgated in the *Novoe Vremya.*

There seems to have been extremely slight
ground for this belief.   Mloditzki, who attempted
the life of Gen. Melikoff, was a baptized Jew, that is,
a Hebrew who had formally accepted Christianity.
One of the heroines of the conspiracy which finally
accomplished its purpose was Jessy Helfmann,[*]
the daughter of Jewish parents, but herself a professed freethinker.   Aaron Zundelevic, the brave
founder of the "secret press" in St. Petersburg,
who learned the compositor's trade and taught it
to four companions for this sole purpose, was the
son of a little Jewish shopkeeper in Wilna.[†]   This
almost exhausts the list.

[*] "Underground Russia." By Stepniak. Page 112. London: 1883.
[†] Ibid., page 202.

In fact, the Jew does not lend himself to the notion of conspiracy. In every country he has been the patient, long-suffering, even servile non-resistant, never the rebel. All over Russia I was struck by the absence of political feeling in the talk of representative Hebrews. I never met one in whose presence I could feel, " Here is a man who would give money to the Nihilists." Of course this proves nothing. In Russia more than anywhere else the desperate man keeps anxious guard over his speech, his face, his demeanour. But the three Nihilists of Jewish blood whom I have mentioned were revolutionists because they were Russians; no hint is given anywhere that they took up arms to avenge the sufferings of their Hebrew brethren. No suggestion is ever heard of even the possibility of conspiracy or revolt among the Jews on account of Jewish wrongs. Their fault is to be over-docile and too submissively loyal.

All the same, Nihilism gave the Jews a bad name. When the terrible blow of March 13, 1881, was struck, an insidious whisper about a Jewish murder plot crept all over Russia in the wake of the dreadful first news. Within six weeks the Jewish quarter of Elizabethgrad was sacked and burned, and the reign of terror inaugurated which was to destroy thousands of homes, reduce 100,000 Jews to poverty, and stain the history of the century with incredible records of rapine and savagery.

The temptation to linger upon the tragedy of
the Czar's assassination, concerning which such
strange and sinister stories are afloat in Russia, is
very great.  And though it is only in its effects
that it belongs within the proper scope of our
inquiry, a brief glance at some of the surrounding
circumstances will be of use.

It is well known, of course, that General Gourko,
General Drenteln, and other police and palace
officials knew all about the plot to blow up the
Winter Palace for months before the explosion
came.  That was clearly demonstrated in the investigation.  It was proved that detailed information
as to the conspiracy and its purposes and methods
had been put into their hands in November of 1879.
The explosion, which killed and maimed so many
of the Finnish guard and the servants, and which
only missed destroying the whole Imperial family
by the accident of dinner being kept waiting for a
tardy guest, came in February of 1880.

The discovery that the very men who were
ruling Russia with Oriental ferocity, in the name
of "law and order," were capable of this mysterious negligence, or criminal connivance—one
hardly knows to this day what to call it—
impelled the Czar to energetic action.  He
abolished the office of Governor General of St.
Petersburg, which Gourko had held, and installed
Gen. Loris Melikoff as a kind of military dictator.
Drenteln, the Chief of Police; Count Tolstoï, the
Minister of Education, and other representatives

of the venal and stupid despotism which had grown up since the war, were thrown out of office, and men of a different type, or at least governed by a different spirit, took their places.

There was a year of Melikoff's Government. To the foreign student, who looks back now over the reforms actually put into operation, to say nothing of those proposed and believed to have been contemplated, the period seems one of unique good feeling, and of unparalleled efforts to abate the evils of which Russians justly complained. Those who lived through this time in Russia do not think so highly of it. They say that no doubt the intentions in high quarters were excellent. But the 30,000 officials charged with interpreting these intentions throughout the Empire simply ignored them and went on in the same old brutal and arbitrary rut. General Ignatieff was Governor at Nijni Novgorod. There were, thirty other Governors like him in as many other *gubernia*. They did practically as they pleased, and what pleased them most was to neutralise everything which the hated Armenian, Loris Melikoff, essayed to do.

There came rumours at last that the Czar, under Melikoff's inspiration, was about to grant a Constitution. What purports to be a copy of this proposed instrument has since been published. Whether it is authentic or not, there is no doubt that a circumstantial statement as to the Czar's intention to issue some such decree had spread throughout the higher official circles.   It was even declared that the new Constitution had been signed and was to be promulgated on March 14, 1881.

On March 13 the Czar was blown to pieces by dynamite bombs.

The most that is charged in conversation in Russia is that the officials responsible for the safety of the Czar knew all about the fatal conspiracy, just as a year before they had been cognizant of the Winter Palace plot ; that they could have prevented the tragedy by continuing the simplest of precautions, and that, from the point of view of the mutinous and disaffected aristocrats and bureaucrats, they chose a strangely opportune day for the relaxation of these precautions.   This much can be said fairly enough, because there was a public, or semi-public, trial of some of these delinquent police officials. They were found guilty of negligence which had contributed to the death of the Czar, and were sentenced to *three years' residence in the pleasant northern town of Archangel !*

But back of what is said lies a world of terrible hints and suggestions.   It is not for me to attempt to reduce them to language.   They may, indeed, have no tangible basis in fact.   But they have taken hold of men's minds in Russia, and they more than vaguely outline in the public consciousness a picture of perfidious murder more awful even than that of the Czar's mad grandfather, Paul.

Be that as it may, the enemies of Melikoff and of the murdered Czar's liberalising experiments came at once into power. It is true that Melikoff lingered along in his anomalous post of dictator for a brief period, and that the new Czar seemed for a little to be attracted by the notion of attempting still further reforms. But any expectations built upon this apparent hesitation were short-lived enough. Ignatieff had hastened to St. Petersburg at the news of the assassination, and was promptly made Minister of Domains. Two months thereafter he and his group had achieved a complete conquest. Melikoff had been driven out in disgrace and exile, and Ignatieff was in his place.

Many other names might be cited of men whom the old Czar distrusted or despised, and whom he had striven to deprive of influence in the State, who now mounted swiftly into prominence and power once more. Gen. Gourko, for example, whose dismissal we noted above, was made Governor General of Poland. Drenteln, who had shared with Gourko the odium of the Winter Palace explosion scandal, was given the fat berth of Governor General at Kieff. But the chief of the former suspects who now assumed control, and the one who gave character to the whole painful episode, was Ignatieff, the new Minister of the Interior.

Count Ignatieff was at this time in his fiftieth year. He had led a life of adventure and brilliant achievement in the far East, and in his younger

days, before he created a new order of reputation
in diplomacy and politics, had enjoyed in Russia a
celebrity not unlike that of the late Col. Burnaby
in England. He was of noble birth, a millionaire,
a scholarly gentleman of great linguistic attainments and delightful manners, and the husband of
one of the ablest and most fascinating ladies in all
Russia. He was a statesman of widespread, cosmopolitan acquaintances and connections. He
had seen and studied most of the nations of the
earth. Even his enemies admitted his high
abilities. His industry and energy were beyond
those of any other Russian in public life.

It might well be thought that such a man, stepping into the foremost post in the empire at the
beginning of a new reign, would have before him a
long, distinguished, and lofty career. As a matter
of fact, he was brusquely, almost contemptuously,
put out of office after a short thirteen months.

Ignatieff—long since christened " The Father
of Lies "—has industriously circulated the story
that he retired because the Czar failed to approve
his project of reviving the ancient *Zemsty Sobory*,
a kind of constituent assembly, or States General,
which Peter the Great destroyed. This pleasant
tale has come to be generally credited, and has
even, in certain weak-minded quarters, cast a sort
of halo of liberalism around Ignatieff's foxlike
head. The truth is that Ignatieff would have as
readily cut off his hand as committed himself to
any abstract governmental scheme, of whatever

nature, which ran the slightest risk of encountering the Imperial disfavour.

It was not the *Zemsty Sobory* project which caused Ignatieff's downfall. He was disgraced because unanswerable proof was brought to the Czar that he was using the persecution of the Jews to extort blackmail, and that he had taken advantage of his position to exempt his own estates from the disastrous effects of the May Laws, while those of the Imperial family suffered.

The Jews themselves were never under any illusions as to the motives of their tormentors. The first great anti-Semite riot at Elizabethgrad, in April 1881, only preceded by a day or two Ignatieff's accession to office, and very shortly after came the terrible fires and looting at Kieff, where 2000 Jews had the roofs burned over their heads. It was clear enough that a definite purpose underlay these outbreaks and inspired the attacks in the *Novoe Vremya*. There could be but one explanation of Ignatieff's attitude.

If there had been any doubt, his circular rescript to the Provincial Governors in September 1881, must have cleared it away, In this he disclosed his whole line of campaign. "While energetically protecting the Jews from violence," he said, "the Government recognised the need of equally vigorous measures for removing the existing abnormal relations between the Jews and the native population and for protecting the people from that injurious activity of the Jews which was the real cause of the agitation." In these, and in other not less menacing phrases with which Ignatieff prefaced his directions for the formation of local commissions to inquire into the subject, the Hebrews discerned the foundations for a colossal superstructure of blackmail.

While the "inquiry" went on, the riots increased in frequency and violence. The minor officials had caught their cue, and circulated the most shameless lies about the Nihilists being entirely composed of Jews, and about fresh Israelitish plots for the murder of the new Czar. They even winked at the distribution and placarding of a bogus ukase which purported to give imperial sanction to the spoliation of the Jews. Synagogues were burned and Jewish quarters sacked in dozens of southern towns ; Sarah Bernhardt was publicly mobbed as a Jewess in Odessa ; the Christmas-tide horror in Warsaw, where 900 houses and shops were broken into and pillaged and 10,000 people driven into the wintry streets, ran its cruel course without interference from the garrison of 20,000 troops, whose commandant, like Drenteln at Kieff, "would not trouble his soldiers for a pack of dogs of Jews."

All this had been done, bear in mind, without the issuance of any new adverse law or regulation. The legal status of the Jew remained precisely what it had been under Alexander II. The difference lay in the spirit which now, from Ignatieff down to the humblest *tchinovik*, animated the bureaucracy. Tens of thousands of Jews had fled across the frontier before the culminating tragedies of Warsaw and Balta. The flight then became an exodus.

Meanwhile rumour was busy with an expulsion edict which Ignatieff had ready for promulgation. An abstract of this edict was surreptitiously confided to the leading Jews of St. Petersburg, accompanied by the intimation that Ignatieff was still open to reasonable arguments upon the subject. Details of what followed have been given to me by men of weight and position, who took part in the conferences held. The Minister's "openness" of mind took tangible form in this proposition : For the sum of 1,000,000 roubles he would guarantee to except St. Petersburg from the provisions of the coming ukase. The principal Jews of St. Petersburg gave anxious consideration to this offer. They finally decided to decline it, upon grounds which were given to me in this order : First, the immense difficulty of raising such a sum of money : second, the danger of being found out : third, the impossibility of believing that Ignatieff would keep his word.

It is said that some few made private terms on their individual account with Ignatieff. The community as a whole refused to pay the bribe he demanded.

His answer was the " May laws." These temporary orders, as they were officially called, were confined in their operation to the Pale.

They comprised only three clauses, one compelling all Jews within the fifteen provinces henceforth to live in towns; one suspending all their mortgages and leases on landed estates, and also their powers of attorney for managing estates; and one forbidding them to carry on business on Sundays and the principal Christian holidays. These famous edicts bear the date of May 15, 1882.

The first emotion is one of surprise that these laws, which so profoundly stirred all Christendom, should contain only such limited and relatively inoffensive provisions. They involved hardships, no doubt, and measurably complicated the problem of existence which, as we have seen, had always pressed so cruelly for settlement within the crowded and poverty-stricken Pale. But, compared with the evil reputation they bear in the world's memory, they do not seem so dreadful after all.

The point is that these laws, which were all that Ignatieff dared venture ask the Czar's signature for, and which he issued as "temporary orders," because he feared their rejection if submitted to the Council of the Empire, bore only the smallest relation to the ferocious outburst of persecution associated with their name. They merely cast the shadow of imperial authority over the Ministerial *Judenhetze.*

The savage orgy of official violence which ensued was independent of all laws. No pretence was made of confining it to the Pale.  The creation of Melikoff's dictatorship, and, later, the reign of martial force following the assassination, had disorganised completely such traces of system and responsibility as had previously restrained the local officials.  Every man in uniform had become a law to himself.  The mere rumour of the " May laws " served to precipitate a headlong rush upon the unhappy Jews.  We need not dwell upon the results ; sufficient are the horrors of our own immediate day.  It is enough to note that the excesses sent a wave of indignation surging all over the civilised world, which found vent in ringing protests and the prompt organisation of committees of succour and relief.  The amazing statement is made now that between April of 1881 and June of 1882 not less than 225,000 Jewish families—comprising over a million souls and representing a loss to the Empire of £22,000,000—fled from Russia! *

The May laws had been issued but a month when there came a sudden and strangely unexpected deliverance.  Ignatieff retired from office on June 12.

As I have said, he has industriously built up the fiction that his downfall was due to his desire to re-establish a mediæval variety of Parliamentary institutions in Russia.  The lie is characteristic.  He was turned out because convincing

* "The History of the Year"—October 1881 to October 1882. London : Cassell, Petter, Galpin & Co.

I

proof of his attempt to extort a million roubles
from the Hebrew community of St. Petersburg
was laid before the Czar. With this exposure of
the shocking venality and beast-like battening on
human misery which underlay the persecution, it
came to an abrupt end.

An additional reason for Ignatieff's tumble was
given me by a Russian official, whom I met in
Bucharest, and who had been in 1882 in a
position to know very well what was going on.
According to this narrative, Ignatieff took the
precaution, after the May laws had been drafted,
but before the Czar had seen them, to send his
venerable and infirm mother down to Kieff, near
which all his great Southern estates lie, and have
her on his behalf privily renew all the contracts
with his Jewish farm-managers and tenants for
another twelve years. It was only after his
mother had telegraphed to him the fact of the
contracts having been renewed, that he secured
the Imperial signature to the May Laws and
promulgated them. This was very clever—
almost as clever perhaps, as that earlier performance of his at Constantinople, when as Russian
Ambassador he combined with the Grand Vizier
to officially deny the current and correct report
that the interest on a certain Turkish loan was to
be defaulted, to sell this and other Turkish
securities "short" on a market thus fraudulently
inflated, and, when the crash came, to each pocket
profits said to have mounted into the millions—

but one important circumstance had been overlooked. The Czar's uncle, the late Grand Duke
Nicholas, also owned large estates near Kieff.
When the May laws were promulgated, Nicholas,
who had been taken by surprise, hurried to fore-
stall their action by seeking to renew the contracts
with *his* Jewish managers and tenants. They
told him that he was too late, and expressed their
regret that he had not acted sooner, say when
Count Ignatieff renewed all his contracts on his
neighbouring properties. The Grand Duke,
astounded at this, made inquiries, and carried the
proofs of Ignatieff's perfidy straight to his nephew,
the Czar.

It is stories like these which explain why the
Jew's only name for the Russian is "*Afoinka
ganev,*" that is to say, "the thief." I give it as it
was narrated with circumstantial detail to me, by a
Russian who did not dislike Ignatieff, and who
related the anecdote with evident pride in the ex-
Minister's shrewdness. How much, if true, it had
to do with Ignatieff's downfall I cannot pretend
to say. But it is interesting, if only from the
proof it affords that Jewish managers and tenants
were valued by owners of big agricultural estates
above their Slavonic neighbours. To this day, it
is the fact that the subordinates who superintend
and carry on the bulk of Ignatieff's widely
extended property interests and affairs are
Hebrews.

Ignatieff's successor, Count Dmitri Tolstoï, had

belonged to the reactionary party as Minister of Education, and could in no sense be regarded as a reformer. But, following Ignatieff, he was veritably Hyperion to a satyr. He recalled his predecessor's September circular, and, although the May laws were not revoked, all official demonstrations against the Jews were summarily stopped.

People said that at last the new Czar had asserted himself, and congratulated one another upon the beneficent promise which this involved to Russia and to civilisation. We pass now to a study of the manner of man this new Czar is, and of the unhappy means by which that promise of his early reign has been turned into Dead Sea fruit of curses and of crimes against humanity.

# CHAPTER VIII

## THE CZAR AND HIS COUNSELLORS

WHEN the witty Abbé Galiani declared that Virtue was more dangerous than Vice, because its excesses were not open to the restraints of conscience, he might well have beheld, in prophetic vision, the present Czar of Russia.

Alexander III has now been more than eleven years on the throne; he held an independent command in a great war fifteen years ago; he has been a brother-in-law to the Prince of Wales for over a quarter of a century; yet to this day he is the least-known personage in Europe. It is not alone that foreigners have little information about him. His own subjects know even less. When they have told you that he is an extremely good and honourable man, personally; that he loves his wife very much, and finds his greatest enjoyment in being with her and the children, and that he is very strong and works hard, you discover that their impressions are exhausted.

There is something at once grotesque and pathetic in this Russian ignorance about the Czar. No anecdotes are told of him. No allusions are made to him in ordinary conversation. A hush falls upon any gathering, all over Russia, at the mere casual mention of his name. I have more than once seen this strange and sudden constraint manifest itself in a Russian family circle, where English was being spoken, and it was entirely certain that the servants could not understand a word of our talk, when I asked about the Czar. Their silence said plainly that this was a subject to be left alone. I know of no other country in the world where this weird awe at the very sound of a human being's name can be duplicated. On a miniature scale, emotions of this sort may have been created in bygone times in some lonely part of England, where a merciless and mysterious highwayman held every road under a nightmare of terror, and no one knew or dared guess who his confederates might be.

The Czar's plans are never published. The flag is kept flying on each of his palaces whether he is living there or not. The people of St. Petersburg rarely know whether he is in residence there or somewhere else. That is a question which no Russian asks of another. I was in the capital during the visit of the French fleet. The English newspaper correspondents had absolutely no means of learning from day to day what was going to happen. The officials gave them plenty of information, of course, but it was all false. The Czar never appeared at the times and places they indicated, but invariably did appear when the correspondents were chasing

wild geese in other directions. It is said that
the officials were themselves as much in the dark
as the rest. Once, while I was walking with
one of these journalists across the open square
in front of the Winter Palace, and we were in
doubt whether to visit the Hermitage Gallery or
take the boat for Cronstadt, I suggested that we
ask a uniformed officer who had strolled out of
the Palace if the Czar was to inspect the fleet
that day or some other. My companion laughed
aloud at the idea. "We should probably both
be arrested—you certainly would be shadowed all
over Russia," he said, in explanation.

The veil of mystery which envelops the Czar's
intentions almost wholly masks his individuality.
In addition to his great personal goodness, it is
understood that he is a taciturn man, and it is
apparent that he is growing very fat. Every
Russian, moreover, is familiar with the fact that he
wears a large full beard, a fact which is not
without significance, by the way, for since Peter
the Great established the cult of shaving this is
the first male ruler of Russia who has shaved no
part of his face. But there popular knowledge of
Alexander III abruptly ends.

It was my fortune to get to know several
people—nether Russians nor Jews—who see a
good deal of the intimate side of imperial life,
and who talked with a certain degree of freedom
about its more important features. It was not
much that they could tell, after all was said and

done, but it at least threw some light upon the baffling enigma with which the outside world has laboured since 1881. I offer it for nothing more than the candid talk of men who know the Czar, and are personally well affected towards him.

Alexander III is a man of rather limited mental endowments and acquirements, who does not easily see more than one thing at a time, and who gets to see that slowly. In other words, he is a born "potterer." He has no idea of system and no executive talent. He would not be selected to manage the affairs of a village if he were an ordinary citizen. It is the very irony of fate that he has been made responsible for the management of half a million villages.

He has an abiding sense of the sacredness of this responsibility, and he toils assiduously over the task as it is given him to comprehend it. Save for brief periods of holiday-making with his family, he works till two or three o'clock in the morning examining papers, reading suggestions, and signing papers. No man in the empire is busier than he.

The misery of it is that all this irksome labour is of no use whatever. So far as the real Government of Russia is concerned, he might as well be employed in wheeling bricks from one end of a yard to the other and then back again. Even when one tries to realise what " Russian Government " is like—with its vast bureaucracy essaying the stupendous task of maintaining an absolute personal supervision over every individual human unit in a mass of a hundred millions, and that through the least capable and most uniformly corrupt agents to be found in the world—the mind cannot grasp the utter hopelessness of it all. The ablest man ever born of woman could do next to nothing with it—at least, until he had cleared the ground by slaying some scores of thousands of officials.

Alexander III simply struggles on at one little corner of the towering pyramid of routine business which his Ministers pile up before him. Compared with him Sisyphus was a gentleman of leisure.

This slow-minded, mercilessly-burdened man knows very little either of the events close about him or of the broader currents of contemporaneous history outside. He had the customary elaborate education from which most Princes mysteriously manage to extract so little benefit, and he seems to have got less of it than usual. He was a man grown before his elder brother's death pushed him forward as heir to the throne. A belated effort was then made to engraft upon his weak and spindling tree of knowledge some of the special fruits of learning which a future Emperor should possess. He was docile and good. Some of his teachers established a powerful personal influence over him, the effects of which were afterwards to be of such terrible moment, but they accomplished little else.

The old Czar, Alexander II, viewed his heir

with melancholy aversion and distrust. He was
kept down as much as possible, and made to feel
his father's unsympathetic attitude in many ways.
Once or twice he was subjected to disciplinary
measures, which have been described to me as not
readily distinguishable from imprisonment. This
is only another way of saying that, like most other
heirs apparent, he became the focus of attraction
for all the elements of disaffection in civil service
and army alike. It does not appear that he ever
assumed the leadership of these elements or had
anything to do with their intrigues. The only
instance of interference attributed to him is that
already mentioned, when he appealed to the Czar
to investigate the gross financial scandals thrust
upon his notice at the seat of war. But the old
Czar none the less regarded him as fully identified
with the reactionary forces of the Empire, and was
troubled with gloomy forebodings as to the character of his reign.

This natural dulness of mind and the enormous
burden of routine work ceaselessly pressing upon
it, go some way toward accounting for the one
feature about the Czar which most puzzles outsiders
—namely, that he doesn't seem to have any notion
whatever of what is going on in his own country.

He reads two papers—the *Novoe Vremya*,
which Suvorin learned how to make pleasing to
his tastes and feelings, even before he became
Emperor, and the *Grashdanin*, which is edited
by a bright man of position for whom the Czar

has a great liking, Prince Mastchersky.  To these personal relations is ascribed the peculiar licence allowed to the *Grashdanin*; one continually finds in it a freedom of expression which no other editor, not even Suvorin, would dare venture upon. While I was in St. Petersburg, for example, the *Grashdanin* quite frankly deprecated the craziness with which Russia was dancing about in its welcome to the French fleet.   Similar utterances in another paper would have involved prompt conflict with the censor.

But the *Grashdanin* is no whit freer than the *Novoe Vremya* in the handling of what is called news.   The newspapers of Paris, curious as they seem when judged by English or American news standards, are mines of information compared with the journals of St. Petersburg.  They contain only the baldest and barest skeleton summary of the world's events, laying great stress upon births and deaths within the blue-blooded pale of royalty, and for the rest chiefly chronicling accidents, fires, and like non-contentious happenings.   Such political writing as is permitted them is almost wholly confined to foreign politics, and is usually in controversial comment upon utterances quoted from the Berlin, Vienna, or London press.   But these utterances must have been originally harmless, or they would have been blacked out by the foreign press censor before the Russian editors got them.

It is understood that the Empress receives and

reads the *Times*. The question is often raised
whether she does not bring to her husband's attention the facts about Russian misgovernment which
its St. Petersburg correspondent has for years so
bravely published. It is said that on occasion she
had done this, and that, moreover, upon the
suggestion of her brother, the Crown Prince of
Denmark, and the Prince and Princess of Wales,
she has tried to put before him something of the
amazed disgust with which Russian doings seem
to have inspired Christendom. Many varying
stories are told of these efforts to improve the
annual Imperial holiday at Fredensborg, in Copenhagen Court circles. It is said, for example, that
some one of the English royal party which was
there last autumn to meet him nailed a copy of
*Darkest Russia* on an inner door of his apartments,
half-jokingly, half in earnest. In another quarter
it is averred that the Czarina ventured last
September to show him a letter she had received
from her sister, the Princess of Wales, on the
subject of the Jewish persecutions, and that the
Czar, losing his temper, brought his hand down
vigorously upon the table and commanded that
the topic be not mentioned again in his presence.

But the poor little frightened and saddened
lady, over whom hangs day and night the haunting horror of a violent death for those she loves,
can have but small heart for this mission. The
one consolation of her unhappy life is the tender
affection in which the weary and puzzled big man,

her husband, holds her.   Why should she vex and grieve this affection by repeating to him the malicious things which outsiders are saying about his work ?

That they are malicious, I am assured that the Czar firmly believes.   How should he learn otherwise ?   When these German or English accusations of cruelty, of injustice, of crime are brought under his notice, let us assume that he makes inquiries.   To whom does he address these inquiries ?   Obviously to the officials.   And quite as obviously these officials swear with solemnity and fine unanimity that the allegations are all monstrous falsehoods.   A sharper, bolder, more energetic ruler might contrive to force his way behind this barricade of official assurances which surrounds the throne, and get once in a while at something like the truth.   Alexander III does not even try to do this—and doubtless would fail if he did try.

Indeed, under the skilful manipulation of one of these officials, these attacks upon Russian honour and civilisation have had quite a different effect upon him from that contemplated.   So far from awakening him to the truth, they have rendered him sullenly and obstinately enraged at their authors, and at the foreign communities which credit them.

The trait of family affection, which is developed in the Czar to almost a morbid state, colours his attitude toward Russia.   He thinks of the

whole Russian people as his children; to his mind
they are all under one roof—his roof. Above
everything else, he will strive to protect the family
reputation.    If scandals arise, his chief desire is to
hush them up, to prevent their being noised
abroad.    He will make an effort to see justice
done, and to punish the offenders, but his foremost solicitude is that it may all be done quietly.
Hence one from time to time witnesses in Russia
the phenomenon of an apparently influential
official being suddenly, without warning or trial,
pulled down out of sight and secretly sequestered.
He may never reappear again, and all that people
will guess about the affair will be that in some
way his misdeeds became known to "the little
father."

This quality, upon which those who are informed
about the Czar lay great stress, quite naturally
prevents his taking kindly to foreign criticism.    In
truth, it makes him furious, and for that reason,
again, he avoids reading or learning about it.

This picture of the Czar, based upon the talk
of people who know him and like him, might easily
be expanded in the direction of personal gossip,
but that is not desirable here.    In some respects
these private hints run counter to generally accepted notions.    For example, public belief holds
firmly to the idea that the Czar is a very devout
man, and that since the Borki accident he has
been a religious monomaniac.    I am assured that
he takes his personal religion very easily indeed,

and has never expressed any concern in the ministrations of the palace chaplains save that they
should make their sermons shorter. In the same
way, he is popularly thought of as an ardent pan-
Slavist, whereas my information is that he and
the dominant Court circles, as distinguished from
official circles, are against pan-Slavism.

These are notes of contradiction which tend, I
frankly confess, to disturb the balance of the
theory I brought away from Russia with me. They
render certain current phenomena less easy of
comprehension than they would have otherwise
seemed. But they could not be suppressed with
candour, and, after all, giving them their greatest
weight, they but serve to show afresh what an
inexplicable chaos of confusion and clashing cross-
purposes the whole Russian question presents.

One further personal point, and we may leave
the individuality of the Czar and take up once
more the thread of events. Alexander III is
called by sundry enthusiasts the Peacemaker of
Europe. The informants to whom I have referred
agree that, though he is by nature a kindly man,
he is not at all swayed by humanitarian views, and
has no more abstract hatred of war than has any
other trained soldier. His objection to war is,
however, very strong, and it is based entirely
upon his dread of the physical discomfort to which
a man of his increasing bulk would be subjected
in the saddle. This sounds almost comical, but
it is given to me for sober fact.

We have seen how this slow, commonplace, conscientious man wavered and trembled in hesitation when, in March of 1881, the murder of his father suddenly threw upon him the overwhelming weight of Czarship. Much has been told me of the brief period in which the new Czar, startled and shaken by the frightful tragedy, yet even more moved by dazed contemplation of the herculean task devolved upon him, dreamed of attempting to follow in his parent's footsteps, and keep the poor little plant of Liberalism alive. There is neither time nor space here in which to dwell upon this phase of the story.

It is enough to note once more that nothing came of this momentary first impulse. The reactionaries, Ignatieff at their head, swarmed back into place and power. It is true that after thirteen months, as has been related, Ignatieff's effort to blackmail the Jews of St. Petersburg was revealed to the Czar, and he was summarily thrown from office. His successor, Count Tolstoï, reversed the policy of the Government against the Jews. But in other respects there was little or no change. Officialism grew stronger year by year; cliques of Ministers and Governors gathered more and more fully into their hands the vast powers of the autocracy. Even when the Czar most actively bestirred himself he could not control the ten-thousandth part of the things they did in his name.

So far as the Imperial family exerts any influence

upon the head of their house, it is probably on the
wrong side.   Of the Czar's uncles, brothers to the
late Alexander II, two have recently died—
Constantine, who was a learned and liberal-minded
man, and suspect on that account, and Nicholas,
who was neither learned nor liberal, but had too
evil an official and financial record to enjoy his
nephew's respect or confidence.   The remaining
uncle, the Grand Duke Michael, is a scholarly and
sensible Prince, who used to be able to do a certain amount of good in his post as President of
the Council of the Empire, but who is now sixty
years old and has grown tired of the thankless
task of resisting that awful dead weight of the
bureaucracy. The first-named of these three, Constantine, left a son bearing his own name, now
an alert-faced, bright-eyed officer of thirty-four,
who is considered to be intellectually the best of
the Romanoffs. This Constantine Constantinovitch
has written one or two books, and a poem at
which the Czar is said to have lifted his eyebrows.
He bears one of those vague and intangible repu-
tations for Liberalism which grow so easily from a
despotic soil, and is worth remembering, not for
what he has done, but for what numerous Russians
imagine he may do, if the affairs of their country
drift still further downward to absolute chaos.

One of the Czar's four brothers stands out with
prominence as a strong and powerful figure in imperial counsels.   Of the other three Alexis is too
easy-going and pleasure-loving to worry his hand-

K

some head about politics, Serge is a foolish man with nothing to say for himself, and Paul is too young to carry weight, even if he gave promise of capacity. But the Grand Duke Vladimir is a potential and genuine personality.

In many respects, Vladimir, who is only two years younger than the Czar, is the truest descendant of Nicholas that Russia has seen. He has more of the stalwart and somewhat sinister comeliness of his grandfather than any of the others. He inherits, too, a large share of that remarkable despot's great energy and personal force. Whatever he sets about doing gets done. He has a bitter kind of wit, which sometimes achieves the painfully rare feat of making the Czar laugh. His robust vigour and clear way of seeing and going straight to the point also commend him to his brother's confidence. How strong he is may be seen from the fact that his wife, a Mecklenburg Princess, and in resolution and marked individuality a fit mate for Vladimir, has been able to defy for eighteen years the tremendous pressure brought by Court and Church to bear upon all non-Orthodox wives of Grand Dukes to accept the Greek faith. If Vladimir chose to play a part for himself in Russia, he might work untold results. Although there are two lives between him and the succession, people have an uneasy feeling that somehow, some time, he will be Czar. But thus far his chosen *rôle* has been that of his brother's right-hand man. He is openly a reactionary—a frank

H.I.H. THE GRAND DUKE VLADIMIR

believer in autocracy, sustained if needful by gibbet
and grape-shot.  When, a little while ago, it was
rumoured that he was to succeed General Gourko
at Warsaw, the fact that Gourko is the most mercilessly savage governor any living Pole can remember, did not prevent a thrill of dismay running
through Poland at the prospect of the change.
To conclude, Vladimir is the man of whom Ministers and high officials stand in most dread.

There are very few of these bureaucrats dimly
discernible in the thick shadows of Russian despotism whom we need trouble ourselves to distinguish, even by name.  When Count Dmitri
Tolstoï died, a less able and less scrupulous man,
Dournovo, became Minister of the Interior.  Some
time before this, a minor official named Vishnegradsky had the fortune to write a report on Russian
finance which attracted the Czar's attention—and
won from him the curious declaration that it was
the first document of the sort he had ever been
able to understand.  The lucky author was made
Minister of Finance.  There will be more to say
of him in the sequel.  The Czar from the outset
has insisted upon personally directing at least the
foreign policy of his Empire, and, accordingly,
M. de Giers, a supple and observant courtier,
remains in only nominal control at the post of
Foreign Minister.  The Czar's former military
tutor, Vannoffsky, is Minister of War, and, with
the Grand Duke Vladimir and Dournovo, is at
the head of what is called the war party.

But more important than any of these, more important than the Czar himself, is the thin-faced, slender, spectacled man who since 1880 has been Procurator of the Holy Synod — M. Pobiedon-ostseff.

This remarkable personage fascinates the imagination. He is as unintelligible to the modern Western mind as Torquemada. Indeed, one must go back to mediæval times for every parallel which he and his work suggest. The whole situation created by him is like nothing else in history so much as that which Spain presented under Ferdinand and Isabella, where the influence of a man we cannot now at all comprehend persuaded a gentle, wise, and kindly Sovereign to stain her reign with the most hideous and stupid of crimes against humanity, and to gratuitously work the destruction of her country.

Pobiedonostseff is a learned lawyer who was one of the present Czar's tutors in his youth. His tastes led him, however, when the opportunities for preferment arose, to choose the ecclesiastical side of the autocracy in which to serve. That he is a sincerely and fanatically pious man, as the Greek Church understands piety, seems beyond doubt. During the great fast of the year he retires to the Sergieff Monastery and mortifies the flesh as vigorously as any anchorite, remaining for days on his knees, fasting and beating his forehead against the stone floor. This does not prevent his telling the most amazing and barefaced lies, as it

"THE GRAND INQUISITOR"
(*M. Pobiedonostseff, Procurator of the Holy Synod*)

did not prevent his coolly persuading the Czar to steal Maurice Hirsch's million roubles. His religious fervour contemplates without blinking the prospect of ten millions of Jews, Lutherans, Catholics, and dissenters generally being despoiled, evicted, harried by Cossacks and driven like criminals from their homes.

This theory of serving God with falsehood, with theft, with shameless treachery, with torture, massacre, and wholesale persecution, has in other times possessed the brains of great and good men of our own Western races. But these men have all been dead three or four hundred years. Russia and M. Pobiedonostseff have only just reached the point where Europe stood when Columbus discovered America.

Everything is nowadays ascribed to the ascendency which Pobiedonostseff exerts over the mind of the Czar. In one sense that is true. The Procurator of the Holy Synod had long-standing claims upon the affection and respect of the new Czar when the present reign began. He became a trusted adviser; then, little by little, the power behind the throne. He grew to guide the Czar in the selection of new Ministers and officials and in the distribution of honours and of rebukes until the whole official world of St. Petersburg dreaded him, and fawned upon him as Paris did in its time before the " Gray Cardinal." To-day the enormous power which he wields is exerted much more through these eager official sycophants, who owe their places to him and scramble over one another in their haste to carry out his most faintly hinted desire, than through direct personal contact with the Czar.

It is indeed likely that he himself has been swept along much more rapidly, and to greater lengths than he had dreamed of, by the head-long zeal of these underlings. He set in motion the Governmental machinery for the repression of dissent, originally, because he was an active-minded man who took his duties seriously, and who saw that anything like spiritual revivals outside the Greek Church must be stopped if Orthodoxy was to survive. Once begun, this spirit of repression quickly ripened into a rage for persecution. From the exiling of M. Pashkoff in 1882, for the crime of holding Bible meetings among the fashionable people of St. Petersburg, to the expulsion of six millions of Jewish people, begun in 1890, is a tremendous step. But the one is the natural sequence of the other. The prosecution of the Pashkoffski was the match which set fire to the prairie.

From the hunting of this almost ridiculously small and unimportant quarry, the whole massed pack of Russian officials have excited themselves into a gigantic *wild-jagd* of heretics and unbe-lievers all over the Empire. Franzos tells of a Polish prince, Czartoryski, who went gunning among the Jews of his district of Podolia, "because there was so little game left in the neighbourhood.* There is a good deal of this same barbarous lust for blood-letting sport in what we are witnessing now. A shot is being taken at everything that rises—Mennonites, Stundists, the Molokani, the Finns, the Catholic Poles, the Germans, the Jews alike. Only the Moham- medan subjects of the Czar's eastern empire are not molested, save here and there in isolated instances, and that not until recently. But for all other non-Orthodox game there is no close season.

Of this vast and terrible persecution the outside world knows but little. We can never hope to learn the thousandth part of the truth.

But it is possible to get approximately at the facts, so far as its Jewish victims are concerned. For many reasons they attract more attention and excite a greater interest throughout the world than do their companions in misery. Moreover, the previous existence of entire volumes of laws adverse to them has rendered it the easier for the police to harry, plunder, and expel them *en masse*. But in his study of the repellant details of the year of terror now drawing to a close, and in following the still more shocking events which the near future threatens, the reader must re- member that the Jews are only one among many unhappy sects and classes whom Pobiedon-

---

* " The Jews of Barnow." Stories by Karl Emil Franzos. Edin- burgh and London : 1882. One of the most striking and effective works of our generation.

ostseff is mercilessly driving to despair, ruin, and exile.

It has seemed important to dwell at length upon the peculiar conditions existing in Russia, and upon a historical examination of the dull incompetency, ignoble greed, semi-civilised vanity, and stark-mad fanaticism which, confusedly struggling together for evil, have produced this savage spectacle at which humanity now revolts. We have hereafter to consider nothing but the persecution itself.

# CHAPTER IX

## THE HOLY SYNOD AT WORK

THE ascending progress of the Procurator of the Holy Synod, M. Pobiedonostseff, in influence and authority, is marked at each successive stage by fresh impositions upon the Jews.

I have noted that when Count Dmitri Tolstoï succeeded Ignatieff, "the Infamous," in the midsummer of 1882, the persecution which had been begun under the May laws came to a halt. It is true that the laws themselves were not revoked, but it was everywhere understood that, like such a countless number of other ukases and edicts, they had lapsed into what President Cleveland called "innocuous desuetude." So late as November 1884, when a question arising under them was referred to the Governor General of Wilna, he declared that the May laws had been suspended.

Within two years—that is to say, by 1886—the power of Pobiedonostseff had grown so great, and the might of the ecclesiastical arm had so overshadowed the lay forces of the bureaucracy, that a blow could be struck at the Jews more cruelly shattering in its effects than any of those aimed by the May laws. It has been pointed out that the Russian Hebrews had now, for more than twenty years, displayed a feverish, almost fierce, anxiety to educate their children. They had everywhere seized upon this as a great object of their lives, as the one thing above all others which promised better days for the Israel that was to come. And it has been explained how, under this potent stimulus, the Jewish children all over Russia attained a remarkably disproportionate percentage of proficiency in the schools, academies, and universities of the Empire.

With the true malignity of genius which makes a grand inquisitor, Pobiedonostseff struck at the heretic Jews through these children for whom they were sacrificing so much. For several years before experimental measures in this direction had been ventured upon. First, the number of Israelitish students to be admitted to the Military Academy for Medicine was limited to 5 per cent. of the entire number. (This, it may be said in passing, turned out to have been a preliminary step toward the complete exclusion by law of Jewish physicians from the army, which is now an accomplished fact.) Next, similar restrictions were placed upon the proportion of Jewish students in the Mining Institute and the Engineering Institute for Public Roads. Shortly after, the number of Jewish boys allowed to study in the Institute of Civil Engineers was cut down to 3 per cent., and the doors of the Veterinary Institute at Kharkoff, the only school of its kind in Russia, were shut in their faces altogether.

It may be imagined with what dismay Jewish parents saw one professional avenue of escape from the ghetto after another being thus closed to their children. But this was mere play—the cold-blooded toying of a cat with a mouse—by comparison with what was to follow.

On December 5, 1886, and on June 26, 1887, the Czar signed two edicts which together gave the Minister of Public Education the power to restrict the number of Jewish pupils in every school, primary, advanced, technical, and the rest, throughout the Empire. This Minister, Delianoff, who had only recently been elevated to the post by the influence of Pobiedonostseff, and was then, as he has been ever since, acting wholly under the guidance of the Procurator of the Holy Synod, took prompt advantage of this Imperial warrant. He issued an order defining the maximum number of Jewish youths hereafter to be admitted to any and all the schools of Russia, from the most elementary grade up to the universities. Inside the Pale they were never to constitute more than 10 per cent. of the whole number of pupils; everywhere outside the Pale, with two exceptions, they were to be restricted to 5 per cent. The exceptions were St. Petersburg and Moscow, where 3 per cent. was to be the rule. This order remains to this day the law, and M. Delianoff, who issued it, figures now in the "Almanach de Gotha" as a Count.

The full significance of this barbaric measure
can only be realised when it is remembered that
in eighty-two towns of the Pale the Jews were
more than half the inhabitants, and in four
towns constituted over 80 per cent. of the population—and that, too, in 1884, before the latest
crusade had chased literally hundreds of thousands
of other Jews into these towns.    It means, for example, that in towns like Mohilef, where, roughly
speaking, there are 3000 Christians and 47,000
Jews, only one Jewish boy can attend school for
every nine Christian boys who have been entered
as pupils.    There would be in this town of a
school age, say, 600 Christians and 8000 Jewish
youths.    Even if we assume that every one of the
former class went to school, (which, of course, is
in Russia a wholly fantastic hypothesis,) we would
have only sixty-six Hebrew lads entitled to éven
the rudiments of a public education—and the
terrible corollary of 7934 others forbidden to go
to school at all.

I have chosen for illustration the extreme case,
so far as the proportion of Jews in a town is concerned.    But when we consider that only a very
tiny section of the "Christian" population of
Russia ever dream of sending their children to
school, whereas the poorest Jews make that the
chief purpose of their lives, the illustration ceases
to be exaggerated.    To render the Jews dependent for educational facilities upon the schoolgoing
propensities of the least ambitious and most sloth-

fully ignorant population in Europe was practically to debar them from education altogether.

This whole matter of education in Russia presents an aspect of the Russo-Jewish question which the Americans, English, and Germans, above all other peoples, will find instructive and impressive. Indifferent to learning as the great bulk of the Russian peasantry and lower classes are, they show more fondness for the schools than do their rulers. We have in Russia the absolutely unique spectacle of a Government exerting its powers to prevent its own Orthodox people obtaining an education. Since 1887 almost every year has brought its administrative order directing further restrictions upon the admission of pupils. Only a few months ago I was told in St. Petersburg of a new regulation, under way, which would make it practically impossible for the child of any poor man in Russia to get into school at all.

Doubtless these reactionary measures had their origin in the conviction that education was responsible for Nihilism. But, once started, this backward march in school matters became quickly merged in the general barbaric retrograde movement. The gloomy and wooden-headed despotism which is tearing down theatres in St. Petersburg, which suppresses news, songs, and literature alike, which treats as criminals and outcasts all who decline to worship relics and sacred pictures, which has restored the knout, and which to-day refuses to allow private charity to intervene between its stupid helplessness and the terrors of a great famine—it is not strange that this despotism dislikes schools.

It only adds to the grotesque and savage imbecility of the thing to learn that this order limiting the percentage of Jewish pupils in schools was accompanied by another sharply reducing the number of Christian children who might thereafter be received, the effect being, of course, to still further cut down the Jewish percentage.

Credulity fairly staggers under the additional fact that when the Jews, after their first shock of amazement, meekly begged permission to establish more schools for their young at their own expense, they were met with a refusal.

There were at this time (1887) some 1200 Jewish schools, with a total attendance of 28,226 pupils. Of these schools 77 were more or less supported by the State ; the rest were small private classes, quite often for technical instruction, with an average attendance of about 20 children. These schools have now almost wholly disappeared, in the convulsions and disorder of the past two years. From their environment, and the hopeless conditions surrounding the race which supported and filled them, it may be imagined that they never reached a high plane of excellence; indeed, they were in many cases merely a Russo-Jewish adaptation of the old Irish hedge school.

Such as they were, however, the Jews were prepared to multiply their number and assume the entire expense of the education of their young. No poverty - stricken and oppressed people could have proposed a heavier self-sacrifice. Rich Hebrews in other lands backed up this offer by tenders of assistance — Baron Hirsch, for example, proffering a donation of $10,000,000 to found technical schools and institutes for the Russo-Jewish youth. In some few instances these offers were accepted. Philanthropic Jews were allowed to build a technical school at Vinitza and a mining institute at Gorlovka, both avowedly for the education of Jewish boys. But when they were opened, the Government coolly stepped in and compelled them to admit nine Christian youths in one case, nineteen in the other, for every Jewish pupil. Much more numerous were the instances in which the officials took the money offered by the Jews for the establishment of Jewish schools, and frankly put it in their own pockets.

These were mere local variations. The Minister of Public Instruction, so far as the central authority went, refused the petition of the Jews to be allowed to build schools of their own. With fine Oriental irony he invited their attention to the fact that the new order limiting Jewish scholars to a small percentage of the whole number was really in the interest and for the protection of the Jews, inasmuch as it now for the first time officially guaranteed their right to any share whatever in public school education.

Even Torquemada enjoyed his little joke, they say.

To preserve a historical balance, it is important to note that this first great anti-Jewish blow struck by Pobiedonostseff was coincident with the opening of the Lutheran persecution in the Baltic provinces. In the autumn of 1886, just about the time that the Council of Ministers was drafting the edicts mentioned above, the Czar's brother, the Grand Duke Vladimir, visited Riga, and with his characteristic brutality of frankness publicly warned the German populations of Courland and Livonia that it had been decided completely to Russianise them, peaceably if possible, but with any extremity of roughness if force became necessary. And in the spring of the following year the Ministerial order on Jewish education, or rather non-education, synchronised with the arbitrary edicts which forbade the German Lutheran pastors in the Baltic provinces longer to teach or control the schools they had built, and which changed the language in those schools from German to Russian, prohibited the use of German on the railways, and decreed the re-modelling of the University of Dorpat over into a Russian institution.

As we go further we shall see the savage crusade against the Jews linked at every step with cruelties or treacherous wrongs perpetrated upon other non-Orthodox people living under the shadow of Czardom—now the proscription of the

Stundists, now the priest-hunts in Catholic Poland, now the exiling of the Molokani, now the shameless and excuseless betrayal of Finland—all parts of one great barbaric scheme.

The Ministerial order of early 1887, closing the schools to all but an infinitesimal fraction of Jewish youths, was a sufficient hint to all the officials, big and little, throughout Russia, who desired either to win favour in the highest circles or make a little money for themselves by harrying the Jews. That the persecution did not at once become general seems to have been due to the restraining influence of Count Dmitri Tolstoï, who, as Minister of the Interior, to the last managed to keep his head above the advancing tide of Pobiedonostseff's authority. In May of 1889 Tolstoï died, and thereafter nobody has so much as tried to stand up against the Procurator of the Holy Synod.

But even before Tolstoï's death, in fact from the date of the education order, the lynx-eyed underlings scattered over the Empire had seen well enough how things were drifting. While they to some extent pretended to please their immediate master, the Minister of the Interior, the spirit of all their actions was dedicated to the rising power, Pobiedonostseff. Evidently the best way to please him was to squeeze the heretic. Thus it happens that, while the years from 1883 to 1890 are ordinarily thought of as an interval interposed between two outbursts of militant anti-

L

Semitism, the truth is that the lull really covered only two or three years, and that the persecution whose horrors have finally aroused civilisation began in 1887.

The change which came over the attitude of the provincial authorities when they grasped the fact that Pobiedonostseff was the rising man, and that he was hostile to the Jews, showed itself at first by a revived activity in enforcing the long dormant and disused May laws. As I have said, these laws were limited in their jurisdiction to the Pale. Accordingly, everybody in uniform began busily hustling such Jews as still remained in the country parts of the fifteen prescribed govern-ments off their land and into the towns, and either arresting or blackmailing any Israelites who dared to appear in the market-places of the Pale on Sunday.

This Sunday prohibition, which last autumn brought about the terrible riot at Starodoub, with the usual accompaniment of Jewish lives lost and Jewish shops and houses plundered and burned, is one of the most characteristic features of the anti-Jewish laws. The Hebrews, of course, religiously abstain from labour on Saturday. It was considered by Ignatieff an extremely smart trick to forbid them to do business on Sunday as well.

In its essence, this meant that the Jews could only have five earning days against other people's seven. Although there are laws on the books prohibiting Christian labour or business on Sunday, they are a complete dead letter. Every traveller in Russia knows that Sunday in the markets and business streets differs in no respect from any other day, save that there are no Jews about. Having remained idle on Saturday for their own Sabbath, they are compelled to observe Sunday for the Christian Sabbath—the while the Christian himself works or barters from morning till night, and the market places are filled as well with Tartars, Gipsies, and Persians, whom no one molests.

This renewed driving of the rural Jews into the towns, already overcrowded, and this arbitrary curtailment of their chances of earning a livelihood soon produced most melancholy results. In every civilised country the Hebrew has a lower death rate and makes a better showing in vital statistics generally than the rest of the community. This fact, whether it be due to unique dietary laws, to exceptional supervision over marriages, or whatever other cause, remains a fact. In Russia alone this has not been the case. Insufficient food, wretched shelter, overwork, and the ceaseless strain and terror of a hunted animal have made him from the beginning a degenerate creature physically.

Yet even in Russia, up to the enforcement of the May Laws, it was supposed that Jews never suffered from phthisis. Throughout the reigns of Nicholas and Alexander II the army examiners found no traces of this disease among the Jewish recruits. Very soon, however, after the Holy Synod began the completion of Ignatieff's work, and the swarming ghetto in each dirty, ill-built, undrained, half-starving town of the Pale saw with horror new crowds of homeless and destitute Jews being hounded in, to deepen the prevailing misery and share the fight for bread from day to day, there was a different story to tell. The rejections for phthisis, from nothing at all, rose to 6.5 per cent. among Jewish recruits, against 0.5 per cent. among all other Russians. Other maladies kept almost equal pace in ravaging these crowded quarters of hunger and helpless squalor. On the score of general physical unfitness, the rejections among Jewish youths of the conscription age mounted to 61.7 per cent. against 27.2 among the other recruits examined.

In the very latest drawing of recruits, that of January 1892, only 6 per cent. of the Jewish youths who presented themselves for the *tirage* passed the medical examiners, while of the Russians 65 per cent. were accepted.

These figures furnish a ghastly comment upon the Russian plea that their Jews are all rich usurers.

It may be imagined that in this outburst of official hostility not very strict attention was paid to keeping within the laws which it was pretended to enforce. As has been explained, every *tchinovnik* is his own law. Villages consisting almost wholly

of Jews were ransacked to find those of the race
whose residence did not date back prior to May
1882, and these were all incontinently packed off
to the towns. In this search many were found
who had been born on the spot in the sixties or
earlier, but who had no papers to prove it ; off
they went with the others. Again, there were
cases of artisans, resident in one of these villages
all their lives, who went for a week or a month to
some other place for work ; on their return they
were treated as new-comers, their former residence
being ignored. This happened to soldiers returning from service to their native village. An
instance is recorded of a man living all his life
in the village of Palitzki who was absent five
days to get married, and on coming back to his
home was driven out as a stranger having no
domicile.

I could fill a chapter with incidents of this kind,
many of them related to me by the victims themselves in Hamburg, Berlin, Königsberg, or here
in London. But there is too much else of even a
more painful sort to tell.

These were not the only tricks to which resort
was had. The whole gamut of barefaced knavery
was swept. To take one among a throng of examples, the immediate suburbs of large towns had
heretofore, for municipal and other purposes, been
treated as parts of the towns themselves. Now
these were decreed to be villages, and all the Jews
accordingly driven out of them into the densely

packed pest-holes of the towns. Impudence even went so far as to deny that Reshilovko, a place which had long been styled in all official documents as a town, was a town at all, and in its new and arbitrarily-acquired character as a village all the Jews had to leave it within forty-eight hours.

What has thus far been related happened, be it remembered, in the Pale, and between the years 1886 and 1890. Up to this latter date no attempt was made openly to revoke the permission of Alexander II, in 1865, under which hundreds of thousands of Jewish artisans, clerks, and others had moved eastward out of the Pale, and made homes for themselves all over Russia proper.

The difficulties under which these people laboured, even in the palmy days of the golden age, have been described in a preceding chapter. Naturally enough, such a fierce persecution could not break forth in the Pale without some of its effects being felt by the luckier Jews outside. These effects took many whimsical forms, according to the fancy of the Governor, the needs of the police, or the feelings of the population in each separate Government. In some *gubernia* the Jews experienced nothing more than a perceptible accession of rigour in examining their passports and guild warrants; in others, they began to be treated almost as if the protecting laws of 1865 had been annulled.

These laws, it will be remembered, permitted
Jewish artisans to settle wherever they liked in
Russia upon the condition of proving to the
satisfaction of the local trade guild their proficiency
in their handicraft.  But, as I have said before,
law in Russia is strictly a matter of construction.
The same official will interpret the same law in
three different and contradictory ways in as many
hours if it seems important to do so.  Accordingly
the more active and unscrupulous Governors,
Judges, and Chiefs of Police, sniffing the eager air
of persecution blowing straight over the steppes
from St. Petersburg, now all at once discovered
that this word "artisan" ought to be looked
into.  The law said "artisans"—ah yes, but who
were artisans?

The mere hint was enough.  The Governor of
Smolensk led off by deciding that butchers, bakers,
vinegar manufacturers, and even glaziers, were
not properly artisans.  Many of these crafts had
been living for years in Smolensk without the
slightest hint of doubt as to their legal status;
now they were all incontinently sent packing.
The Senate was appealed to in the matter of the
vinegar-makers and decided that they undoubtedly
were artisans.  This made no difference; the
declaration of the local artificers' guilds to the
contrary continued to be a better authority.

Very strange results were obtained by this outbreak of provincial definitions of the word artisan.

In one Government for example, musicians and cooks would be decided to be good artisans, while pavers and coachmen would be excluded. Perhaps in the adjoining Government the rule would be exactly reversed. Moreover, a handworker might be assured of his regularity one week and be visited by the police the next, because in the meantime the status of his trade had altered in the minds of the local authorities.

On a large number of the private railways of Russia the bulk of the engine-drivers were Jews. They had in fact almost as closely a monopoly in this employment as Scotchmen are said to enjoy as steamship engineers. They had obtained this because they were found to be soberer, more active and intelligent, and more to be depended upon, than the moujik. A secret circular• was now sent out, informing the railway companies that engine-drivers were not artisans and that their Jewish employées must go. And of course go they did.

In Moscow twenty-four Jewish compositors were expelled upon the decision that printing was not a trade, but an art!

So matters went on into the year 1890, the position of the Jews becoming more and more intolerable as the spirit of the Holy Synod more fully permeated the ramified branches of the bureaucracy. It was reported about that the Czar regarded the escape alive of himself and

family from the terrible railway accident at Borki
as the direct and miraculous intervention of
Providence. The facts were that the imperial
train was being driven at the rate of ninety versts
an hour over a road calculated to withstand at the
utmost a speed of thirty-five versts; that the
engineer humbly warned the Czar of the danger,
and was gruffly ordered to go still faster if possible ;
and that the miracle would have been the avoid-
ance of calamity. But facts don't get about in
Russia, or pass unrecognised if they do. What
was apparent was that a great devotional mood
had seized upon the Czar and the Court circles.
The contagion spread like wildfire : in a twinkling
officials, soldiers, policemen, traders, moujiks,
flocked to the churches, cabmen blocked the
streets in front of shrines to make their obeisances
from the driver's box, and the country roads were
populated once more with concourses of tramping
pilgrims.

It was in the height of this sentimental religious
fervour that reports leaked out about the Government's intention to revoke the guarantees of 1865,
and put the May laws in force all over the Empire.
Copies of the proposed edicts were obtained,
smuggled out over the frontier, and published to
the world. The Holy Synod stopped counting
its beads long enough to issue a categorical denial
that any such measure had ever been discussed,
and Russian Ambassadors at foreign Courts were

instructed to give solemn assurances that the report was pure invention.

When they had lied long enough, the edicts which they swore had never existed even in thought were promulgated. It was a triumph of mediæval barbarism. Everywhere throughout Russia it was understood that, to celebrate God's protection of the Czar at Borki, there was to be a burnt-offering of Jews.

H.I.H. THE GRAND DUKE SERGE

# CHAPTER X

## THE APPOINTMENT OF SERGE

THE whole year of 1890 was clouded, as has been said, by reports of new and savage laws about to be decreed against the Jews. In July the *Times* published in London, from its accomplished St. Petersburg correspondent, Mr. George Dobson, what turned out to be a tolerably accurate forecast of these projected laws. The statement was solemnly denied by Russian officials, as were all other rumours of prospective persecution, but through the indiscretion or venality of local administrators it became known that these denials were lies made out of whole cloth. It was discovered that a series of questions had been addressed to the provincial Governors by the Minister of the Interior, each asking an expression of opinion upon some proposed new penalty or increased restriction, and that an overwhelming majority of these Governors had hastened to express admiring approval of these barbarous propositions. No other answers, of course, could have been expected. To prevent ambiguity in the replies, the intended acts of oppression had been carefully specified. All the Governors had

to do was to copy these and say " Yes " to them.
Then they were laid before the Czar as the
recommendations of his official deputies throughout the Empire.

I have said that their assent was a matter of
course. In the first place, every new oppressive
law increases the chances for gain to the Governor
and all his creatures; inquiry as to his approval
in such a case is like asking an official in another
country whether he would like an increase of
salary. More important still, an interrogatory of
this kind is a plain indication of what the central
authority wants—and to discover this and satisfy
it is the controlling passion of every Russian
official's abreast.

One of the Governors did, however, salve his
conscience—perhaps also his pocket—by revealing
the text of these Ministerial inquiries to the Jews.
It may be said in passing that there are to this
day scores of officials in Russia who are openly
fervent Jew-baiters, yet who secretly provide
information of this kind to the Hebrew community for pay.

Other Governors, being informed by these
inquiries of the intentions of the Ministry, began
at once to act as if the suggestions which they
had approved were already laws. In October the
second anniversary of the Czar's escape from
death at Borki was celebrated, and stories were
circulated to the effect that the Czar had received
personal revelations as to the intervention of God

to save his life. The ignorant, drunken, and greedy village priests, who had now obtained a welcome addition to their incomes by having been given control over the primary schools, eagerly circulated these tales, and built up the wildest and most fantastic concoctions of miraculous visions with which to further darken the poor wits of the superstitious peasantry.

The Czar himself seems to have been affected by the outburst of fanatical orthodox excitement which this Borki anniversary precipitated. I have been told by a trustworthy man, who himself saw the document referred to, this story in illustration. An influential Russian dignitary, with brains enough to see what stupid mischief Russia was doing herself, contrived to have put into the Czar's own hands a memorial tersely setting forth the actual facts of the Jewish question, recounting the miseries inflicted upon helpless and unoffending people, and showing how inevitably this criminal folly must react upon the Empire. Alexander III read the paper carefully and wrote on the margin that he had been much impressed and touched by it. "But," the imperial hand added, "we must never forget that it was the Jews who crucified our Lord and spilled his priceless blood!"

In this same October, a score of Governors in different provinces, apparently by some malignant concert, began driving out all the Jews who had charge of, or were employed in, flour mills. In more intelligent times they had been drafted into this business—in fact given a practical monopoly of it—for the sole reason that they were the only people who knew enough to conduct it. Now, in spite of the fact that without them the flour mills would have to be closed, they were all expelled on the plea that they were not artisans. 'It is to incredible idiocies of this sort that the famines in Russia are largely due. In 1887, Mr. Dering, Secretary of the British Embassy at St. Petersburg, reported that there had been "permanent famine" since 1866 in 148 out of the 625 administrative districts of Russia, and that in 71 of these alone there were 300,000 chronic paupers. It was in these districts that many of the flour mills were now closed, on account of the Crucifixion!

The public notoriety of the St. Petersburg expulsions dates from this same fateful October of 1890. They had really been going on for a year or two, but so quietly as to have escaped general notice. To this day it is practically impossible to get information about the clearance of the Jews from the capital on the Neva. I have obtained some figures to be printed in their proper place in the narrative ; but they had to be compiled from the most recondite sources, and have not only never been published, but will convey novel information to the St. Petersburg Jews themselves. The truth is that the Jews of St. Petersburg have never had any organisation or cohesive bond of union. They scarcely know one another ; they have never acted together. The extent to which this is true of Moscow and other large Russian cities would amaze those who talk so glibly about the close solidarity and trades-union combinations of the Jewish communities.   But it is peculiarly the case in St. Petersburg.

The then Chief of Police, General Groesser, a curious, not to say comical, despot, about whose whimsical and purely savage vagaries a volume might be written, had been quietly chasing the Jews out for a long time.   Now, under the impulse of this new craze for persecution, he began to issue public orders concerning the marked men of the race.   For example, on October 30 he promulgated directions that, in each case where a Hebrew was sent away for lack of residential rights, his whole family must be packed off with him.

The Minister of War, Vannoffsky, was not going to lag behind Dournovo, Groesser, and the rest in putting into action the Czar's pious feelings. Military orders were issued directing that all Jews should be driven from the Caucasus, to prevent their perverting the religious faith of the army !

At about the same time a decree from the Minister of Instruction extended to converted or baptised Jews the provisions of the previous law limiting the proportion of Jewish students to be allowed in universities.   This affected a large class of the brightest young scholars in the university towns, who, for the sake of pursuing their studies, had made the sacrifice of formally accepting Christianity as it is understood in Russia.   Now most of them found their sacrifice to have been in vain—and were sharply chased back into the ghettos.

In the succeeding month, a ukase was issued ordering that in the future no Jew should be baptised unless his entire family became converts at the same time. This, it was explained, was to circumvent the device adopted in their despair by numerous Hebrew families threatened with ruin and enforced exile—viz., of sacrificing one male member of the household to the Christian font as a kind of scapegoat, and then enrolling his relatives as his servants, so that all might remain.

Concurrently it was decreed that Jews should no longer be received into the Catholic, Lutheran, or other dissenting folds, but must be baptised, if at all, into the Orthodox Church. This monopoly having been given to the Orthodox priesthood, they promptly established a probationary term of six months for would-be converts from Judaism. Up to that time anybody could be baptised immediately upon application, and many stories were afloat like that of the great banker, Horwitz, who is said to have once been warned away from the Hotel Dussaux in Moscow, and to have gone out and returned within the hour with a certificate of baptism. This swiftness of procedure was made possible by the rivalry between the Lutheran and the Orthodox pastors for baptismal fees. The moment the latter were given a monopoly they sat down and blackmailed the Jew at their leisure.

This question of the "conversion" of Jews is a most difficult one about which to secure facts in Russia. I have shown in previous chapters how strenuously Nicholas strove, alike by forcible abduction and torture and by bribes, to break down Judaism as a religion. Everybody will give you a different estimate as to results. Russians of education and position have gravely assured me that the baptised Jews greatly outnumbered those who remained in their creed, which of course is absurd nonsense. But the Russians discover and suspect Jews now everywhere, as Richard III saw ghosts in his tent on Bosworth Field. Their mania for this is like that which prompted good people in the time of Eugene Sue's "Wandering Jew" to believe that every third man was a Jesuit in disguise.

Jewish authorities, on the other hand, say that the "conversions" have been on an average only 1300 per year—or something like .002 per cent. of adults.

However this may be, the formal desertions from Judaism have been almost wholly confined to the educated classes and to residents in cities like St. Petersburg and Moscow. In this latter place, of which I saw much more than of any other Russian city, the proportion of "converts" has always been exceptionally large. The story is told there of the Lutheran Church, of which all the officials, beadles, ushers, and the like were named Blumenthal, Rosenberg, Morgenstern, and

M

so on, and into which, one Sunday when special services had drawn a large attendance, a Russian wag strolled with his hat on. The "baptised" dignitaries, scandalised, hurried toward him with indignant gestures. " Oh, I beg pardon," he said, looking blandly from one Semitic face to another; " I thought I was in a synagogue."

Very often, in the two great cities mentioned, one will find Hebrew families in which the parents hold by the old faith, but have had their children baptised as communicants in the English church. Where the sons are destined for commerce, this Anglican connection is especially valued. In such cases, it is hardly necessary to add that the claims of religion rest lightly on both parents and children. I encountered in the south of Russia an elderly Jewish merchant, who had lived in Alabama in slavery days, and had subsequently served in the Confederate army. In the quaintest imaginable jargon of Jiddish, German, and half-forgotten English " as she is spoke " in the cotton belt, he told me that he was himself too old to change his creed now, but that his sons were being brought up as Christians. This kindly old man was almost frantic with delight when he learned that I was a Freemason. It was many years since he had met one before, because the order is most sternly forbidden and outlawed in Russia. He wore on his watch-chain, however, the jewel of the State Lodge of Alabama, and confided to me that the Russians were far too ignorant and stupid to ever guess that it was a masonic emblem. After this subject had come to be mentioned between us, it was absolutely impossible to get him to talk of anything else. I was eager to obtain from him information upon events in his own neighbourhood, of the present day. To my every question he would reply, " Oh, mister, the suffers is most pitiful,"—and straightway hark back to Masonry on the Mississippi " befo' the wah." He told me that, however lackadaisical some of the other brethren might be, he used to be always on hand before his lodge was opened. I recall, with a certain effect of pathos, how he assured me, with tears in his eyes, that the dream of his life was to sell out and end his days in some country where he could attend lodge meetings every afternoon. In his long solitude he had so brooded upon masonic recollections that they had come to colour all his views of nationality, religion, business, even existence itself. I shall never forget how his countenance fell when I confessed to him that in England one's lodge only met once a month, and that even then I generally forgot to attend.

The outbreak of administrative persecution, to which allusion has been made, with its gloomy background of constantly increasing rumours of fresh oppressive laws to come, stirred what remained of liberalism in Russia to protest.

The *Novosti*, now the only paper of importance which had not joined in the anti-Semitic hue and cry, on November 6, 1890, reprinted from Katkoff's *Russian Messenger* of 1858 a curious and forgotten document, the resurrection of which came like a slap in the face to Alexander III. In that third year of the reign of his father, "the Liberator Czar," a paper called *Illustration* made some casual remark which was considered insulting to the Jews. Thereupon 147 of the best-known Russian authors, poets, journalists, professors, scientists, &c., signed a protest against offensive allusions of this kind. In this list, which the *Novosti* now reprinted, were the names of Turgenieff, Bestujeff, Kostomaroff, Kriloff, Pogodin, Katkoff, Aksakoff, and dozens of others of the first rank in the world of letters and of thought. There was grim satire in this republication of these names, which the censors saw and appreciated enough promptly to serve the *Novosti* with a first warning.

But there was something more than irony in the act. It became known that the reprinting of the 1858 protest was in the nature of an experiment preliminary to the publication of a protest of 1890, with Count Lyof Tolstoï leading the list of signatures. This new memorial was understood to be much milder in tone than the other, and to have been signed by practically all the literary and scientific lights of the empire. I say "understood," because it was never printed. The chief of the censor's office, M. Feoktistoff, sent a circular around among the Russian editors forbidding them, under the severest penalties, to publish what he termed this "impudent and senseless" petition.

It was characteristic of Russia that this same Feoktistoff had himself signed the infinitely more vigorous protest of 1858.

This still-born petition was the last discernible sign of Russian Liberalism, so called. In the carnival of brute force which ensued—this terrible contest between autocracy and assassination which the world still watches in round-eyed amazement— the man with a petition had no place.

What is now going on in Russia is so awful that we forget how shocking the events of the winter of 1890 seemed at the time. Nihilists were being tried by scores, and sentences of life-long imprisonment or exile meted out right and left. One murder plot after another was revealed, or invented—each followed by a cloud of arrests or sequestrations. Officers high in the army and in aristocratic circles shot themselves to escape a worse fate. Universities were closed, and hundreds of students dragged off to jail.

In Poland the brute Gourko instituted a reign of terror novel even in that unhappy land. In mid-winter 14,000 Polish engineers, conductors, fire-men, and mail clerks on the railways were summarily thrown out of employment, and the decree was posted up that henceforth none but Russians should be allowed to work on Polish railways. Simultaneously, 11,000 German and Austrian subjects, clerks, salesmen, agents, and the like employed by private firms throughout Poland were expelled from the kingdom without warning and without excuse. Poles who dared to comment upon these outrageous measures were knouted to death, or marched publicly in chains off to Siberia. The huge and ever-increasing Army of Occupation—already furnishing in Poland one soldier for every twelve men, women, and children of the civic population—assumed fresh licence to plunder, maltreat, and outrage the people in imitation of their General. Poles cannot trust themselves to talk of the horrors which since Christmas of 1890 have been their portion. There are no words for these monstrous deeds. I have myself been told by eye-witnesses, by relatives of the victims, stories of the treatment of gently-nurtured Polish girls, and of dutiful and irreproachable Polish wives and mothers, which I could no more listen to with dry eyes than they could relate to me unmoved.

So the New Year came—ushering in the year of our Lord 1891—destined to be the most tragic in modern Russian history.

While rumour was still busy with those mysterious anti-Semitic laws which were to come, a scattering fire of minor decrees of persecution was maintained. During the opening months, another Minister, Manassein, Minister of Justice, joined the group who had already prostituted their departments to the savage resolution of Pobiedonostseff, and issued an order that no more Jewish barristers should be admitted, and that those already practising should be expelled. The Jewish paper, the *Voskhod*, was suppressed. General Gourko commanded, apparently out of pure wantonness of brutality, that hereafter all Jewish recruits in Poland when sent to be examined by the inspection committees should be marched in *étape*, that is, chained together like criminals and in the company of jail-birds. There is rarely lacking a comic side to these things in Russia; in early February there was a public agitation inside the St. Petersburg Society for the Prevention of Cruelty to Animals in favour of having the Society interfere with "the cruel manner in which the Jews slaughter cattle."

It was vaguely understood at this time that one Minister, Vishnegradsky, was standing out against the final declaration of a Jewish crusade. This bright manipulator of finance, as we have seen, did not owe his advancement to Pobiedonostseff. He was the Czar's own selection. The rise of M. Vishnegradsky is curiously characteristic of his country and his race. He was the son of a poor village priest, and came up to St. Petersburg to seek his fortune with scarcely the traditional green three-rouble note in his pocket. He was fortunate enough to attract the attention of the Hebrew banker, Baron Gunzburg, and in this way engrafted himself upon the great railway and contracting projects of that sanguine period.

He had not only a smart eye for figures, but a ready tongue and a forehead of brass. Even after he had become an official, and was a wealthy man to boot, he used to be retained by Messrs. Warschoffsky, Horwitz, and other great promoters to attend meetings of railway companies and commercial organisations generally, and make speeches in favour of their interests. An occasion was mentioned to me upon which his fee for his services was 15,000 roubles.

A friend of mine in St. Petersburg, an elderly man who has known M. Vishnegradsky closely for many years, assured me that, with the possible exception of Dr. Miquel, he regarded the Russian Minister of Finance as the cleverest administrator in Europe. But in his position he does not rely upon official ability alone. "Vishnegradsky," said my friend, "is very sly. He saw that Pobiedonostseff created a great impression upon the Czar by every now and again quoting a Bible text in his conversation. Now when Vishnegradsky talks with the Czar he quotes two texts where the Procurator would only introduce one. Thus he is very strong with the Czar."

The Finance Minister need not have been so tremendously clever to discern the monetary and commercial ruin which an extreme anti-Semitic policy would involve. It can well be understood how, for the credit of his own department, he should have resisted to the last the increasing pressure of the forces of fanaticism, intolerance,

PRINCE DOLGOROUKOFF

and savage lust for plunder which the Grand
Inquisitor was marshalling.  For one thing, he
was just bringing to a successful close a great
State loan, to be negotiated by the chief Hebrew
houses of Europe, a loan which should crown his
administration with honour.  How necessary was
it, therefore, to keep quiet about the Jews!

On April 7, 1891, M. Vishnegradsky was able
to announce to his Imperial master, and two days
later to the public, that he had concluded arrangements with the Rothschilds, Bleichröder, and
another Jewish banking-house for a loan of
600,000,000f.

One might well believe that the Czar and his
Jew-baiting Ministers had been holding their
hands till this announcement could be made.
Almost on the morrow the blow fell.

Some weeks before, it had been announced
that the Prince Dolgoroukoff, who had been
Governor-General of the Province of Moscow for
many years, and who was spending the winter in
Paris, had retired from his office, and that his
successor would be the Czar's third brother, the
Grand Duke Serge.

At the time the excitement over Nihilist plots
and the open turbulence of the students was so
great that it was said and believed that the Czar
intended to leave St. Petersburg altogether, and
restore Moscow to its ancient dignity as the imperial capital.  The appointment of Serge was
explained on the theory that he was going to

prepare the historic seat of the Muscovy Czars against the coming of his august brother.

The true story of the appointment is quite a different affair. It has never been told in print, and it is so vitally connected at every step with the most painful aspects of the Jewish persecution that I feel no apology need be offered for briefly recounting it here.

The old Governor-General, Prince Dolgoroukoff, was a very characteristic and likeable type of the best that the ancient Russian aristocracy affords. A descendant of Rurik, the head of a family with a thousand times more noble Russian blood than flows in the Imperial veins, and which more than once has been in rivalry with the Romanoffs for the throne itself, the Prince perpetuated in his person the distinctive qualities and traits of a good boyar. Full of the sense of dignity in his descent and his office, he yet gave courteous audience daily to all, rich and poor alike, who had the slightest claim upon his time. Although by nature luxurious, perhaps indolent, he resolutely forced himself to supervision of every detail of his official duties. He was specially watchful in keeping his subordinates in place, and in sharply preventing their usurpation of the smallest iota of his powers and responsibilities. In short, he was such a Governor-General as very few Russian provinces ever had.

He was queer in other ways  For one thing he was honest. Moreover, he liked to see justice

done.  He was quite capable of publicly punishing and humiliating an under-official whom he
caught injuring or robbing a poor man.

He had been just to the Jews, nothing more.
The oppression which the law clearly dictated had
been meted out to them in Moscow as elsewhere.
Only Dolgoroukoff would not allow his underlings
to blackmail and persecute them outside the law.

Such a great noble, not very pious, not at all
servile, who was actually on amiable terms with
educated and able Jews, was naturally an eyesore
to Pobiedonostseff and the Jew-baiting clique.
So long as he held supreme office in Moscow—
the most important dignity below royalty itself—
no crusade upon Israel could be successfully embarked upon.  The Holy Synod marked the old
Governor-General down in its black books.

The civil Governor of Moscow, Prince Golitzyn, was a man much more after the Inquisitor's
heart—a dull and malignant man, who could not
possibly have been given office in any other
country under the sun, and in Russia only obtained
it through powerful aristocratic connections.  This
Golitzyn had long striven, in a muddle-headed
way, to distinguish himself by effusive brutality of
zeal in carrying out what he imagined to be the
Czar's desires.  To his chagrin, no recognition
had come, and Dolgoroukoff kept so vigilant a
watch and curb upon him that he despaired ever
being allowed to win it.

Prince Golitzyn's estate at Illinskoïe marches

with that of the Grand Duke Serge, and the two men are intimate associates. It is supposed that through this arose the suggestion of Serge's taking Dolgoroukoff's place. However suggested, there was soon a powerful cabal formed to bring this result about. Various sinister figures in shady politics were brought into the intrigue—Ignatief and Suvorin among them—and it was not difficult to enlist Pobiedonostseff in it. Perhaps he invented the Hebraic pretext, which was finally agreed upon as a basis for action. At all events, M. Alexeieff, the Mayor of Moscow, wrote a letter to Pobiedonostseff declaring that there were 120,000 Jews in Moscow (there never were over 30,000), that they were ruining religion, sapping loyalty, and destroying trade, and that they had evidently bribed Dolgoroukoff to acquiesce in all their scoundrelly schemes.

Pobiedonostseff showed this letter to the Czar, and so played upon his suspicion of dishonest officials, his aversion to the Jews, and his desire to give his brother some show of usefulness in the State, that the appointment of Serge was secured. This desire is intelligible enough, since the problem of what to do with the ever-multiplying swarm of Grand Dukes lies very heavily upon the Czar's mind. There are at the present writing not less than twenty-four of these princes of the blood. Each upon his birth has set aside a certain sum, partly family property, partly from the public funds, which will have grown by compound interest to the capital amount of 2,000,000 roubles by the time he attains his majority. Alexander III has a provident mind, and early in his reign occupied himself with devising means of combating this Grand-ducal scourge. By a family statute of July 1886, he ordained that hereafter the title of Grand Duke should not descend beyond the grandson of a reigning Czar, and at the same time he greatly increased the difficulties in the way of Grand Dukes marrying. Morganatic marriages are sternly forbidden, and the Imperial consent to other alliances is given in a grudging fashion. But it still is not likely that Serge would have been given such an important post, had not the intrigue against his predecessor been so astutely mixed up with the Jewish question.

This base device of blackening Prince Dolgoroukoff's character is still employed, despite the fact that the octogenarian Governor-General died in Paris very shortly after his enforced resignation. To this day every Russian official has at his tongue's end the malicious lie that Dolgoroukoff was in the pay of the Jews, and continually borrowed large sums from Lazarus Poliakoff, which he was never asked to repay, to discharge the interest on his enormous debts.

The falsehood is as foolish as it is mean. Prince Dolgoroukoff lived and died a very wealthy man. One estate alone of the several he possessed yielded an annual income of 46,000 roubles. At the time of his death he had a current deposit

of 70,000 roubles in a single Moscow bank.  These
are facts within my own knowledge.

The Grand Duke Serge—a scrawny, hollow-
eyed, narrow-browed man of thirty-five, everywhere throughout European Courts known to be
the least intelligent and respectable Romanoff
since the time of Paul, and in Russia familiarly
called by a name which involves offences hardly
to be hinted at in type—was in March gazetted as
the new Governor-General of Moscow.

There is the greatest difficulty in speaking
fittingly of this person.  A writer in the Pompeian
decadence might have shrunk from saying all
there is to be said about Serge.  There are men
in the mines in Siberia, or were a few years ago,
who were exiled by the old Czar for having been
associated with this son of his in conduct of the
most debased and abominable sort.  There is no
mystery about this in Russia.  Everybody knows
who is meant when "the classic" is mentioned.
No one ever professes doubt as to the man's
character and habits.  English-speaking peoples
have become more familiar with his name than
with that of any other Romanoff prince, for the
reason that, in 1884, he married a Hessian
princess, the daughter of the late Princess Alice.
This childless lady remains a wife only in name.
Nothing could be more tragically pitiful than the
way in which, a couple of years ago, she was
prevailed upon to join the Greek church, on the
assurance of Serge's chaplain and of Count

Stenbock-Fermer, his Intendant, that her nominal husband would alter his demeanour toward her once she was in the Orthodox fold.   It is known that Abbot John of Cronstadt, the most important religious figure in Russia, had the courage to ask her if her "conversion" was not obtained under these abhorrent circumstances, and was fiercely warned by the Czar to mind his own business.   It is needless to say that the pledges thus given were not kept.   Serge continues the unspeakable thing he was, and is hissed by the populace on the rare occasions when he appears in public in Moscow.

It was to "purify" the city for the entry of this obscene simpleton that the Cossacks and police made that famous midnight descent upon the poor Jewish quarter in Moscow which ushered in the new persecution.   How this first raid, recalling nothing else so much as an attack by savages upon a frontier settlement in American colonial days, was followed by the inhuman sacking and clearing of an entire suburban district; how there came the edicts, sentencing practically the whole Jewish population of Moscow to exile and beggary; how thick and fast thereafter succeeded the ukases which have turned every part of Russia into a hell of torment to an entire race—this is what remains to be told.

# CHAPTER XI

To even begin to comprehend Russia, one must have seen Moscow. Viewed solely as a spectacle, I should think there is nothing else in the world more remarkable. Considered as the key to the strange, baffling enigma of the retrogressive Tartar Empire in Europe, it furnishes the most fascinating and enthralling of studies. Frankly, Moscow ought to have a book by itself. To compress mention of it into a few paragraphs confronts me as a necessity, which is also a grief.

This weird, Arabian Night's dream of a metropolis conveys to eye and mind alike the impression of being lost on the map—of having strayed a thousand miles or so westward out of its reckoning. The spectator from the cupola of Ivan's tower beholds a vast barbaric encampment sprawling over a space which a London might occupy— a veritable Asiatic city of white and pale red walls, low, green roofs, Oriental gardens, and still more Oriental domes and minarets. These domes rise on every side—to the number, they say, of nearly 2000—some green or blue, some glowing with burnished gold, like poppy-heads and ox-eyed

daisies above a field of mixed clover. At in-
tervals tall slender towers lift themselves up like
palms, to flower at the top in a lacework of engirdling balcony. Around this a man is for ever
walking, day and night, to watch for fires—just as
they were doing in Bokhara a thousand years ago.

In the centre of all, high-banked upon the river-
side, looms the historic Kremlin, with its Tartar
name, its white-and-gold mosques dating from
remote pre-Tartar times, and its huge red palace,
built by that modern Tartar, Nicholas, less than
fifty years back, yet looking more savage than all
the rest.

Gazing upon this spectacle, one forgets that he
is only a thirty hours' ride from German soil. He
seems immeasurably nearer to Samarcand than to
any civilised portion of the globe.

And this is what Moscow feels. Its interests
and its affections turn ever eastward.

St. Petersburg by comparison is a pitiful thing
—a dreary, commonplace, pretentious imitation of
alien standards, with wide, empty streets, huge,
desolate-looking palaces, and a sparse population
which seems no more at home than does an
Ogallalla chief in a silk hat. St. Petersburg
represents what the Czars have desired that
Russia should pretend to be. Moscow represents
what Russia really is.

Moscow has little that is characteristic to show
of the times since Ivan the Terrible. It is true
that the Romanoffs came from the neighbourhood

N

—their mediæval boyar residence in the Varvarka is still a sight for tourists—but two of their three generations, what with establishing a dynasty, waging foreign wars, and fighting the Nikon schism, had no time for building, and Peter the Great built a capital for himself on the Neva instead. Moscow, too, bore scarcely any part in the European masquerade begun by Peter, which was sunk into an orgy by his widow, niece, daughter, and idiot grandson, and lifted into a tragedy by the Ascanien wife of this fool. Moscow through all this century of neglect and desertion held its peace with true Eastern patience. When the time of sacrifice came, it burned itself on the altar without reluctance, without hesitation. All that is truly fine in barbarism shines in the history of Moscow.

As one would expect, it is in Moscow that the lamp of Pan-Slavism has been kept alight. It has been the home of successive generations of national spokesmen and leaders who ceased not to protest against the Court effort to Germanise Russia. It was here that Aksakoff uttered the famous watchwords of the reactionary party, " It is time to go home!" Here, too, only a few years ago, the Mayor, M. Alexeieff, made the celebrated speech about planting the double-cross of the Greek orthodoxy upon the Mosque of St. Sophia in Constantinople.

The people of Moscow live almost without newspapers, or, better, without European news.

Scarcely a breath of the outside Western world touches them. The untravelled among them have only the vaguest and most childlike notions about Berlin, Vienna, or London; and these notions, when they are not indifferent, are profoundly contemptuous. Their devotion to their barbaric Church, its ritual, its fast-days, and its miracle-working ikons, puts to shame the perfunctory observances of St. Petersburg. They think of the Protestants and Catholics of Europe as mere unimportant sects. They feel themselves to be, as they are, the citizens of Russia's true autocratic and ecclesiastical capital. They never doubt that in good time the Czar and the Holy Synod, sick of the vanities and poor Western imitations of St. Petersburg, will return to their real home, Holy Moscow.

Moscow has much the same feeling toward the Jews that the Emirs of Bokhara might have—that is, one of contemptuous tolerance in good-humoured times, of grim ferocity when the ugly mood is on. The mere suggestion that the Czar and the Holy Synod actively disliked them would be enough to provoke a persecution. These Moscovians, however, would have no thought of a fear of consequences such as might deter the Bokharan despot. They are proudly incredulous of Europe's power to make them afraid. Once, indeed, the French, under the mighty Napoleon, did reach the Holy City and stable their horses in St. Basil's; but the result of this invasion is such an awful landmark in history that the Moscow imagination never conceives the possibility of its repetition.

Hence, when it becomes known in Moscow that Western Europe, and particularly that meddlesome part of it presided over by the Lord Mayor of London, is protesting against something which Moscow is doing, the news impels Moscow promptly to do that something with increased fervour and energy.

As Moscow is the heart, the core, of the real Russia, so her treatment of the Jews during this terrible year 1891 most truly typifies the persecution throughout the empire. As was said at the outset, it would require many big volumes adequately to present the history of this persecution. It is not within my power or the proper scope of this work to tell the tithe of what happened in Moscow alone. But I have chosen to dwell at greatest lengths upon the events in Moscow, because it is here that one gets the clearest view of the foul hypocrisy, the meanness, the stupidity, and the savagery which have all over Russia marked this latest crusade.

In other places, too, it has been possible for an apologist to plead in extenuation that the brutality and violence were the work of the small local authorities, and that it was unjust to hold the Imperial Government responsible for the acts of obscure and remote agents. But in Moscow, as I have shown, the conspiracy began upon the very steps of the throne. A brother of the Czar

was made the stalking-horse of the plot to defame
and dispossess an honest and tolerant Governor-
General and to establish the Jew baiters in power.
The Holy Synod openly proclaimed the necessity
of "purifying" Moscow from the presence of Jews
before the Imperial Grand Duke Serge entered
upon his office.

Whatever may be said of the persecution elsewhere, there is no difficulty in fixing direct
responsibility for the unspeakable events of
Moscow upon Pobiedonostseff, Dournovo, and
Alexander III.

The general theory among the Moscow Jews
is that in March 1891 they numbered about
30,000.  It is very difficult to get at the facts.
As has been said, the Mayor of Moscow, in a
letter to Pobiedonostseff, unblushingly placed their
number at 120,000.  The man upon whose information and candour I relied most of all in Moscow
gave me the following estimate, which is somewhat lower than that popularly made, but may be
accepted as approximately correct :

### City of Moscow.

| Legal Divisions. | Families. | Souls. |
|---|---|---|
| A. Artisans and poorer classes ; two-thirds of whom were expelled from March–June 1891 . . . . . . | 3,500 | 17,500 |
| B. "Circular" people ; expulsions now going on . . . . . . | 800 | 4,000 |
| *C. Merchants of the First Guild . . | 120 | 700 |
| *D. Professional and higher education . | 200 | 800 |
| Total . | 4,620 | 23,000 |

* Not touched as yet.

*Province of Moscow.*

| Legal Divisions. | Families. | Souls. |
|---|---|---|
| E.  Suburb of Marina Rostscha ; extremely poor people . . . . . | 400 | 2,400 |
| F.  Rest of province ; all classes . . | 500 | 2,600 |
| Grand total . . . | 5,520. | 28,000 |

The distinction between the city proper and the province is important, because within the former the Cossack Chief of Police, Yourkoffsky, was supreme, whereas in the suburbs and elsewhere throughout the district Prince Golitzyn is responsible for what has been done. It is with reference to the latter in particular that documents exist which will come as a surprise, I venture to think, to the civilised world.

During the month of March, General Kostanda, a Greek born in Odessa, and then commandant of the troops in the Province of Moscow, was summoned to St. Petersburg to receive the edict appointing the Grand Duke Serge Governor-General, and get his own authorisation to act as *locum tenens* until the Prince should take up his new post. General Kostanda, a decent wooden man, returned to Moscow wearing a long face. To a police officer who met him at the station he gloomily confided the fact· that he had orders to settle the Jewish question in Moscow before Easter.

Within sight of the walls of the Kremlin—hemmed in away from the river, between that sprawling palace enclosure and the famous Found-

ling Hospital—lies one of the most deplorable
slums which any of the world's great cities contains.   It is the Zariadie quarter, and was the
home of most of Moscow's poorer Jews.   Here in
huge *podvories*, or houses serving at once as tene-
ments for the swarm of resident occupiers, and as
furnished apartment dwellings for Jews coming
into Moscow on temporary business, lived many
thousands of the Hebrew colony—at least half of
the city's Israelitish population.   These *podvories*
all have distinctive names.   The largest of them,
the Glebovskaya Podvoryeh, has a melancholy
fame in the local history of the Moscow Jews.
To this vast rickety old hive every strange
Hebrew entering Holy Moscow used to be escorted
from the city gate by mounted Cossacks ; here he
was compelled to live during the three days of his
allotted stay.   It seems incredible, but there can
be no real doubt that two years ago between 2500
and 3000 Jews of all ages were domiciled in this
one building.   It is the property of the Moscow
Eye Hospital, and the lessee, himself a Jew, enjoyed from it an annual income of 25,000 roubles.
Now he has thrown up his lease in despair, and
the great edifice is entirely tenantless.

A few days after General Kostanda's return,
this whole Zariadie quarter was surrounded at
midnight by the police, the mounted Cossacks who
serve under police control, and even the city fire-
men.   Strong forces were posted on the Moskva-
retsk and Ustinsky bridges, to prevent escape to

the right bank of the river, and all the streets and passages leading to the Ilyinka were closely guarded. Then, under Yourkoffsky's personal supervision, the whole quarter was ransacked, apartments forced open, doors smashed, every bedroom without exception searched, and every living soul, men, women and children, routed out for examination as to their passports. The indignities which the women, young and old alike, underwent at the hands of the Cossacks may not be described.

As a result, over 700 men, women and children were dragged at dead of night through the streets to the *outchastoks* or police stations. They were not even given time to dress themselves, and they were kept in this noisome and overcrowded confinement for thirty-six hours, almost all without food, and some without water as well. Of these unhappy people, thus driven from their beds, and haled off to prison in the wintry darkness, some were afterward marched away by *étape*, that is, chained together with criminals and forced along the roads by Cossacks. A few were bribed out of confinement; the rest were summarily shipped to the Pale. To-day they are scattered—who knows where?—over the whole face of the earth. They were chiefly artisans and petty traders. There was no charge of criminality or of leading an evil life against any of them. They were arrested and banished whether their passports were in order or not, and with them, alike to the *outchastoks* and into exile went their children and womenkind.

THE COSSACK, GEN. YOURKOFFSKY
(*Late Chief of Police of Moscow*)

With the exception of a partial account in the *Moskovsk Viedomosti* of April 9, 1891, nothing was ever printed about this astonishing event save a note in the St. Petersburg papers of April 12, which was transmitted to the continental press as well, stating briefly that " 150 Jews had been arrested in Moscow." This is worth noting, because it is the only reference to the Moscow barbarities which has ever been permitted to appear in the Russian press from that day to this. It also has a value as a characteristic example of Russian veracity. The number of frightened wretches thus descended upon and dragged from their homes was in reality about five times as great as was stated.

Startling as the number is, it would have been much larger but for a fortuitous accident. One of the police officers, who knew in advance of this barbarous project, happened to be a baptised Jew. He risked Siberia to save the friendless people of his blood. His first recourse was to send a warning note to the Rabbi, but the latter was attending a wedding somewhere and could not be found. Then the police agent sent a man in a cab to notify Jewish shopkeepers whom he could trust not to betray him. In this way a large number were warned, and did not go home that night.

It may be imagined that the tidings of this outrage filled the Jewish community of Moscow with consternation. Perhaps that is too strong a word. Israel is an inveterate optimist—and more so in Moscow than elsewhere in Russia. I could not learn during my visit in July and August that this first stroke at the poor defenceless wretches in the Glebovskaya Podvoryeh brought any definite consciousness of approaching mischief to the better protected classes of Moscow Jews. As the progressive blows were struck, they found each grade in the Hebraic social formation quite taken by surprise—quite unprepared by the misfortunes of a poorer class for its own calamity. To this day there are numbers of Jewish merchants of the First Guild in the large Russian cities who will not believe it possible that the Russian Government—though it has broken its faith with everybody else—can ever turn against them.

Moreover, the Jewish community in Moscow was almost completely lacking in organisation. We habitually think of the Israelitish element in every town as being so closely welded together in bonds of common interest, sympathy, and ambition that it overbears and breaks down the scattering competition of outsiders. This notion is more or less at fault in every civilised country. It is not true even of Moscow.

On the Bourse there, for example, I found Jewish merchants of the First Guild who had lived in Moscow for a dozen years or more, yet who barely knew each other by sight, and in two cases, I remember, not even by name. The explanation is that, under Dolgoroukoff's lenient rule, their race and religious barriers had fallen away, and they had formed associations with Christians instead. They came, too, from different parts of the empire or of Europe; their children in many cases were baptised, and they avoided intimate Jewish connections on their account. The Jewish community in Moscow spent 125,000 roubles annually in charity, but the sum was contributed by a very small number of individuals. During the terrible spring and summer of 1891 only 27,000 roubles could be raised among them for relief of the sufferers, railway tickets, &c. This must not be put down to niggardliness. On May 10 the *Novoe Vremya* declared there were 65,000,000 roubles' worth of bills on Moscow Jews in banks or in private hands which no one would accept or pay.

All the same, this midnight descent on the Jewish quarter sent a thrill through the whole body. It could not be believed that the thing was done with authority, and protests and appeals were filed, as if there was still a reign of reason and justice.

The merchants of the First Guild were not long suffered, however, to remain under this delusion. I have already explained how, under the law that each merchant might "take with himself" into the interior as many Jewish clerks as he needed, it became a not uncommon thing for artisans and small traders to settle in towns, nominally as clerks of some big Jewish merchants, but really doing business for themselves. I do not think there was much of this in Moscow. Indeed, the old Governor-General, Prince Dolgoroukoff, interpreted the word "need" so literally that he never granted permission to a Jewish merchant to employ a new Jewish clerk without referring the question whether it was "needful" to M. Naidianoff, President of the Bourse Committee, who ever since 1885 had invariably answered no. This, by the way, furnishes an interesting comment upon the stories of Dolgoroukoff's subserviency to the Jews.

But now of a sudden the Moscow officials discovered a new construction of the phrase "may take with himself." They began an investigating tour of the offices and counting-rooms of the Jewish merchants of the First Guild. Every clerk who could not prove that his employer had personally conducted him from his home in the Pale to his present place of labour, was given abrupt orders to get out. Many of the men thus put under sentence of banishment or ruin—for what could clerks do in the Pale?—had lived in Moscow more than half their lives, and were well-known and popular citizens. One old clerk in the Moscow - Riazan Bank, thus expelled with his family, had held his place and his residence in Moscow for thirty-two years!

For some weeks the police kept up a system of midnight descents upon the various podvories, not only in the Zariadie quarter, but elsewhere, as in Solianka, Staraia, and Ploschtchad streets. This running fire of irregular persecution, however, touching only the poorest classes as it did, was merely an overture to the real performance.

The first two days of the Passover, in April of 1891, will never be forgotten while the Jews remember Russia.

It is said to be to the felicitous invention of M. Alexeieff, Mayor of Moscow, that these days owe their sinister renown.   I saw that burly, swart, round-headed, heavy-jowled barbarian driving in his *troika* with Admiral Gervais, and he did not look as if he had ever invented anything.   He is a man of forty-five, and inherited great wealth and a large mercantile business from his father. The Jews lay stress upon the fact that his mother was a Greek—of a race which they hold in peculiar terror and aversion.   He is an ambitious demagogue, who ostentatiously divides the Mayor's salary of 7000 roubles among the clerks in the office, and himself spends from 100,000 to 120,000 roubles in entertainments and municipal ceremonies annually.   The year 1891 is said to have cost him 160,000, owing to his bringing all the officers of the French fleet from Cronstadt to Moscow, entertaining them at the principal hotel four days, and sending them back as they came, by special train, all at his own expense.

The fact that the old Governor-General had steadfastly resented this spread-eagleism, and done all he could to prevent the Mayor from posing as

the master of Moscow, furnished Alexeieff's chief
reason for joining the conspiracy against Prince
Dolgoroukoff. The same motive changed him
from an effusive, not to say loud-mouthed, de-
fender of the Jews in Alexander II.'s reign into
the most vehement and relentless Jew baiter to
be found anywhere in the dominions of Alexander III.

He burned to distinguish himself at the very
outset of the Grand Duke Serge's régime by a
more ingenious device of torture for Jews than
had yet occurred to any other anti-Semite. The
Levantine half of him prompted this peculiarly
Oriental piece of brutal cunning.

An imperial edict had finally been secured a
few days before, which swept away all the rights
of residence in Moscow given by the law of 1865
to Jewish artisans and handicraftsmen. This
decree was in the hands of the Moscow authorities some time before the Passover. It was
Alexeieff's idea to withhold it for a little and have
some sport.

On the first day of the Passover, after the Jews
had assembled in their synagogue, whispered
word was passed round of a ukase just promulgated which would hereafter make it difficult for
more Hebrews to come and settle in Moscow.
Later comers brought the text of this decree. It
was but a line or so, ordaining, in substance, that
"all Jewish artisans, small traders, publicans
&c., are forbidden to enter Moscow and the

Province of Moscow." It was dated March 28 (O.S.).

It is true that this came as a surprise, but the Jews gathered together in celebration of the paschal sacrifice did not, perhaps, regard it as an unmixed evil. Under the circumstances, with a hostile spirit plainly gaining force at St. Petersburg, and with the memory of the previous week's midnight arrests in their minds, it was natural that they should feel that there were already quite enough Jews in Moscow.

The next day, the second of the Passover, came what seemed at first to be another edict. It also bore date of March 28 (O.S.), and it said simply: " The Minister of the Interior, in connection with His Imperial Highness the Governor-General of Moscow, will straightway consider and adopt measures to secure the removal of the 'above-named Jews' from Moscow and the Province of Moscow."

" Above-named Jews " ? The puzzled community gazed at the words in bewilderment. Then a terrible light shone upon the paper. The two decrees were really parts of one edict. Yes! They bore the same date! The phrase " above-named," in the second, could only refer to the category enumerated in the first. They had been separated, and doled out on different days, in a refinement of savage cruelty. The laws of 1865 were annulled!

A shriek of dismay went up, drowning the

chant of the festival. Women swarmed screaming through the narrow streets to the synagogue. In thousands of homes parents looked at each other over the heads of their children with blanched faces—and, even as they gazed, heard the hoofs of the Cossacks' horses on the stones outside.

# CHAPTER XII

*MARINA ROSTSCHA AND THE "CIRCULARS"*

A DOZEN years ago a birch forest came up almost to the very gates of Moscow along the city's northern line. It was called Marina Rostscha, and this name was given to the residential suburb which, shortly after the war, began to extend itself beyond the municipal border. The first to discover this northern outlet were well-to-do citizens—everywhere in Russia as in the United States on the look-out for rural spots in which to build summer cottages—and their comfortable wooden villas now line the main road for some miles beyond the city limit. The forest has dwindled here into scattered groves of small trees, through the verdure of which may be discerned still other and more secluded rustic summer houses.

In a remote part of this straggling wood some Russian speculators of the humbler sort eight years ago built a village of little houses—they might even better be called hovels—and rented them to Jews who were too poor to pay police blackmail for the privilege of living in Moscow itself. At the Passover time of 1891 it is said

O

that 400 Hebrew families were huddled in this
squalid hamlet. They were perhaps the most
hopelessly poverty-stricken creatures in the whole
province, but they at least had homes of their
own—that peculiarly racial ambition which everywhere, under the most adverse and trying conditions, the Jewish people toil to gratify.

Like the very poor in every community, these
households hidden away in the forest were rich in
children. The families here were to be computed, I was informed, at the high average of six
members each.

I made a pilgrimage to this now historic place
on a rainy day in August of 1891. Three Greek
cemeteries lie upon this northern border of the
town—the largest of them just within the city
bounds, the others outside. After you have
passed these burial-grounds Marina Rostscha
begins, but there is a long drive through a com-
paratively open district before our part of the
woods is reached.

No more depressing spectacle can well be conceived. The white-stemmed birches, which lend
an indescribably sad aspect to all North Russian
scenery, drooped their delicate boughs like weeping willows and shuddered in the rain. The pale
green masses of distant foliage lost their outlines
in the gloomy grey mist exhaled by the drenched
earth. Little disused lanes, all deep mud and
puddles, here and there branched from the chief
thoroughfare to pierce the bosky thicket, and

where these cut a way through the trees the eye caught vistas of rude roadside shanties, which had once been homes, and now were but a forlorn and ugly part of the picture of desolation.

Somewhere in this rain-soaked and deserted wilderness I was told there were a dozen or more families of Jews still living in their cabins. I could not find them. We drove in and out for what seemed to be several miles without seeing a soul. In one of the lanes, finally, we came upon two Jews, an old, long-bearded man in cap and caftan, and a young fellow who looked to be in an advanced stage of consumption, dragging through the deep mire a truck laden with household goods. Some time before a big and rather foolish-looking vagrant dog had attached himself to us, and was following along after my droschky. The two Jews left their cart as we approached and withdrew to a safe distance until we had passed. My *isvostchik* laughed till the tears ran down his face as he explained to me, by panto-mime and the few German words he knew, how the Jews were always in mortal terror of dogs. Volumes could not have better told the tale of a hunted race.

The story of the clearing of Marina Rostscha is perhaps the most cruel and repellent episode in the whole record of that spring's barbarities.

As I have said, the Jews living here were of the lowliest class—artisans, petty traders, and street hawkers, porters, and day labourers. They

had congregated here, it is true, to avoid the
police, but this involves no suggestion of wrong-
doing on their part.   Their object in getting as
far away as possible from the police, was not
that they were criminals, but that they could not
raise the money to pay them for permission to
live unmolested in the town.   There is no record
of an arrest ever having been made among the
Jews of Marina Rostscha for a criminal offence.
The heads of families—all the men, in fact—
went daily to Moscow to work, returning in the
evening to their homes.   Some of their children
came in to the technical or handcraft school
maintained by the Jewish community of Moscow.
Most of them, however, studied their primers and
elementary books at home.

Of a sudden, without warning, on an inclement
wintry night, a troop of police and Cossacks
surrounded this out-of-the-way country suburb,
and, forming an engirdling cordon, proceeded to
carry out Prince Golitzyn's written order to expel
the entire community !

This order was executed with what even
Russians regarded as incredible brutality.   The
lights had been extinguished in almost every
house, and the unsuspecting people were asleep.
They were awakened by the crash of their doors
being broken open, and the boisterous entrance
of Cossacks, with torches and drawn swords.
The terrified inmates were routed out, and
driven with blows and curses into the night,

without being given time even to dress. They snatched such garments as they could and ran. The tales that are told are too harrowing to dwell upon. At least 300 families were thus dragged from their beds, and chased out into the wintry darkness on this first night's raid. Barefooted, half-naked, frightened out of their senses, these outcasts wandered helplessly through the black woods, moaning in their misery, or raising shouts in the effort to keep together.

Some of them, at last, were able to build fires in the forest, and gather around these the old and infirm, and the women with nursing babes at their breasts, or little children, who had made their way thus far with bare feet over the snow and frozen ground. The soldiers pursued them hither and stamped out these fires!

Others did not stop in their flight until they had reached the cemeteries, lying just outside the town. Here they found refuge, and, crouching for shelter among the tombstones, waited for morning. Here, when the mocking daylight came, it gilded pictures of anguish and horror which one may not attempt to describe. Take only this one little sketch from the panorama of suffering : it is the figure of a woman—by name Epstein—who, fleeing from her invaded home through the night, became separated from her husband and son, and made her way alone to the Miuski Orthodox cemetery. She is found by the morning light, lying insensible on the frosted grass among the graves.  Beside her is a dead child, to which she had given birth during the dreadful night.

No allusion to this amazing event has ever appeared in any Russian paper.  There was no editor who dared so much as to mention it. Although many deaths resulted, directly and indirectly, from the terrible shock and exposure of that night, there were no inquests, no investigations, no official reports.

News of the outrage did spread through Russia, by letters and by word of mouth, and some of the details found their way into the foreign press. Even the Russians were shocked, or at least annoyed, by the gratuitous savagery of the thing. In July M. Pobiedonostseff, speaking to Mr. Arnold White on the subject, said everybody deplored the violence shown by the "late" Chief of Police in the Marina Rostscha evictions.  This characteristic lie implied that the Chief of Police had either died or been removed.  Neither was the case.  The Cossack Yourkoffsky, who came to Moscow from the Kouban, whip in hand, an illiterate, uncivilised, menial police bully, and who worked his way up to mastery by dint of sheer brute cheek, was Chief of Police then, and continued to be until the beginning of this present year 1892, when he was superseded for complicity in a scheme of plunder, by forgery and embezzlement, which was on too magnificent a scale for even Russia to pass unnoticed.  That

his loss of office and disgrace had nothing to do
with the Jewish question, is evident from the fact
that his successor, Vlassoffsky, is an even more
celebrated Jew baiter, and won his promotion by
excelling all previous records of harsh brutality,
in the clearance at Riga. It was he who con-
fiscated 12,000 roubles belonging to a Jewish
charitable society (although it had a ministerial
permit), on the ground that its relief books
contained no Christian names. This same
Vlassoffsky it was who, wearied of the trouble
of arresting the Jews of Riga in their houses,
authorised their seizure on the streets, and gave
five roubles reward to a *gorodovoi*, who, on
bringing a prisoner in, said he knew he was a Jew
by his nose.

The raid through the forest was continued next
day, and for the following week, to find the
scattered and isolated houses which had been
neglected on the first descent. The refugees
were given three days in which to sell all their
goods and get out of the province. From this
condition to absolute spoliation was but a step.
At these "sales," out in the woods, chairs were
sold for a penny apiece; beds went for sixpence.
No one obtained money enough to buy a railway
ticket to the Pale. The reign of terror lasted
until all but some dozen or fifteen families of the
whole 400 had been driven from their homes.
Then an English lady, resident in Moscow, was
able by intercession with her bosom friend, the wife

of one of the Moscow officials, to secure a respite for the miserable remnant. These are the people whom I looked for and was unable to find last year. I am told that they, too, have gone now.

I have dwelt at length upon the barbarities of Marina Rostscha, because there they were exhibited on a circumscribed stage, and can be grasped in something like their entirety. It is hopeless to give an equally complete notion of what happened in the big city of Moscow simultaneously. All that can be said is that there were many hundreds of similar domiciliary descents, alike by day and by night, and that hundreds of families were as ruthlessly turned out on the streets as any of the sufferers in the forest suburb. The stories of individual affliction could be given here by scores. One distracted Jewish girl, an eighteen-year-old seamstress, named Malka Usilevna Chasgorine, who had come to Moscow from the village of Gradiansk, in Mohilef, being chased from her lodgings and refused food or refuge because she was a Jewess, threw herself into the river. She was rescued by a moujik, and kindly Christians made up a purse to enable her to leave town. There were two perfectly authenticated cases of young Jewish girls of respectable families and unblemished character, who adopted the desperate device of registering themselves as prostitutes, in order to be allowed to remain with their aged parents in the city where they were born!

Many instances could be cited where whole families for weeks feared to sleep at night in their own homes, but walked about in the suburbs until morning, or, worse still, took refuge in the bagnios and "bath-houses" which are the resort to Moscow's vilest elements—and were, in consequence, safe from police interference.

For this new crusade spared no one. Though the head of the family possessed the qualifications necessary for residence, it was now held that this did not extend to his children who were grown up. The police were the sole judges as to whether they were grown up or not.

As to that, the police were the sole judges of everything. They sent out many people who had a perfect legal right to remain. Mr. Friedland, a civil engineer, and Miss Seldowicz, a certificated physician, were both protected, nominally, by their professional degrees. That mattered nothing at all. The former, indeed, appealed to Yourkoffsky, and was ordered to leave within ten hours on penalty of being sent by *étape*.

In dozens of other towns in Central Russia—Kaluga, Tula, Ribinsk, Podolsk, and the like—clearances marked by the same brutality and the same savage disregard for law or decency went on in this Easter week. All over the empire the Jewish communities trembled at the startling news each day brought them, and looked to a tragic morrow for themselves.

In St. Petersburg General Groesser filled all the

railway stations with police, to detect and arrest travellers suspected of being fugitive Jews from Moscow and the interior. At the same time he issued an order under which most of the Jews living in the capital were to leave by May 3.

Suddenly it was announced that the expulsions had ceased. The first statement to this effect was officially suggested to the correspondent in St. Petersburg on May 5. The next day some of the inspired journals contained hints that the whole anti-Jewish policy would probably be abandoned.

Nobody seems to have guessed for the moment what this apparent abrupt *volte face* meant. In some quarters it was even supposed that Russia had seen the folly and inhumanity of its course, and repented.

In a couple of days, however, strong light was thrown upon this puzzling enigma by the announcement that Baron Alphonse de Roth-schild, the head of the Paris house, had decided to withdraw from that Russian loan of 600,000,000f. which was supposed to have been settled the previous month.* It turns out now that he notified the Russian Ministry of Finance of this decision on May 2. The ensuing declarations, that the Jewish expulsions had ceased, and were not to begin again, had no grain of truth what-ever. They represented merely the Russian officials' desire to throw dust in the keen eyes of

* See p. 185.

the Rothschilds, and lure them and the other great Jewish houses into going on with the loan. Even after the reported failure of the loan, and the consequent tumble of Russian securities on the Bourses, the St. Petersburg papers, and the Russian Embassies in various Continental capitals, kept alive the false report that the Rothschilds had not really declined, and that the loan was only delayed, not lost.

When this pretence could no longer be maintained, disguise was abandoned swiftly enough. On May 11 the *Novoe Vremya* launched a bitter and half-crazy attack against the Rothschilds, insinuating that their adoption of the Jewish pretext was a mere blind to cover their insolvency, and demanding immediate vengeance upon all the Jews in Russia. The *Grashdanin* and other anti-Semitic papers joined the hue and cry at full yelp. The Moscow *Gazette*, in this fierce delirium of passion, invented the remarkable theory that the Jews were polygamists, and urged that the police should forthwith take over custody of the Hebrew marriage rolls kept by the rabbis in the synagogues.

The persecution, despite official hints and statements, had never stopped at all. It may well be that the Finance Minister, Vishnegradsky, tried to stop it, at least until the loan was realised. There is no doubt whatever of his intense disgust at seeing the Rothschilds and Bleichroders driven away from his bait just at the critical moment by

the hair-brained fanatics and knaves in control.
He was, and is, by no means alone in this disgust.
I talked with many Russian merchants and men
of affairs on this subject. They rarely expressed
concern about the sufferings of the Jews. They
were unanimous in deploring the stupidity which
had precipitated their sufferings before the loan
had been actually secured.

On May 17, the Grand Duke Serge made his
formal entry into Moscow. At his side was his
wife, the pale and sad-faced Hessian Princess.
who is a granddaughter of the English Queen, and
who had only recently been dragooned into pretending conversion to the Greek Orthodox Church.
Nothing could be at once more pathetic and more
revolting than the true story of that "conversion."
The marriage, so called, took place in 1884.
Very soon thereafter those circles in Germany
and England which first catch gossip as it filters
down from royalty itself, began to be stirred by
strange rumours of a terrible nature concerning
the bride's unhappiness. It was not long before
the Princess left her unspeakable husband, revealing to her relatives as her justification a story of
his infamy which cannot be suggested in print.
These relatives, or some of them, persuaded her
to reconsider her action. Pressure was exerted
from the highest quarters in St. Petersburg, and
in more than one other great capital, and the
Princess Elizabeth finally with reluctance returned.
It is universally alleged and believed in Russia

that two of Serge's favourites, his chaplain and his intendant, Count Stenbock-Fermer, worked upon the credulity of this virgin wife by assuring her that her husband's neglect was due solely to her religious heresy, and that everything would be changed if she accepted the Orthodox faith. When she at last consented, there were special references made in sermons and Church papers to the certainty that the saints would now bless her with children.

The Jews of Moscow saw this couple—the half-witted and obscene Prince and the Princess who had protested to John of Cronstadt and to her relatives against the mockery of her "conversion" —ride in state through the Holy City to the Iverskaya Chasovnia, and prostrate themselves under the Ikon of the Iberian Mother of God before entering the Kremlin. Conceive the bitterness of the reflection in the minds of these Jews—that it was avowedly to purify Moscow for this pair that they and their children were being torn from their homes and sent to wander as outcasts over the face of the earth!

A fortnight later the Czar himself came to Moscow with his wife and family, on their way to the Crimea. A Jewish veteran named Israel Deyel, a corporal in the reserves, had written a most pathetic petition* that at least the Hebrew soldiers who had served their time might be allowed to remain in the city of their birth. It is

* See Appendix A.

known that the Czar actually saw this petition.
It is known also that Deyel was sent to prison,
and that the expulsions now proceeded more
fiercely than ever.

Up to the 23rd of July 1891, when the funds of
the Moscow committee had become exhausted,
nearly 27,000 roubles had been expended and
2365 railway tickets purchased. As children
travel free, this latter figure by no means measures
even the assisted part of the exodus. If we put
the children for whose elders tickets were bought
at the low number of 635, it would give us 3000
people who needed assistance to get out of the
town. The committee estimated that about one
in four of the Jews quitting Moscow had to apply
for help. This would raise the number of
refugees, from March up to the latter part of July
1891, to 12,000. Doubtless that estimate closely
approximates the truth.

I have described with some minuteness the
classes which made up these first 12,000 exiles.
There was a sprinkling of well-to-do people
among them, but the vast majority were artisans,
managers of small workshops, and others to whom
this sudden enforced expulsion meant ruin.

To be compelled thus without preparation all at
once to sell everything and get out—and that in a
hostile town where no Christian would pay the
debts he owed a Jew or buy his goods for more
than the merest pittance—did literally involve
ruin. A case came under my personal observa-

tion—that of a Hebrew joiner, some of whose excellent work I saw in the house of a friend—a hard-working, temperate man, who had been living by his trade in Moscow for twenty years. He had a large family and practically no savings. The few roubles he had put by went through May and June to keep the police quiet. In July, when he could pay no more backsheesh, he was brusquely given ten days in which to leave. His household effects were worth perhaps $100. He was able to sell them for $4. I speak of my own knowledge, because I saw the man quit Moscow with his family and saw my friend help buy the tickets through one of his clerks. He did not dare go to the station himself.

But up to the time of my visit to Moscow the more prosperous of the artisan class were still clinging to the hope that if they could only raise money enough for the police they might manage to remain. The Passover edict, it will be remembered, had only instructed the authorities of Moscow to "consider and adopt measures for their removal." That left a broad margin for bribery.

While I was in Moscow came the regulations of July 28, 1891. They bore this date, but they were not then officially promulgated. A week later their provisions were only a matter of hearsay, and copies were vaguely known to be in the hands of certain Jews.

The first three clauses dealt with the Jewish

artisan class, whose rights had been suspended in April. This new edict put an end to their hopes of buying further delay. They were now divided into three categories—(1) those living in Moscow only three years, unmarried or childless, and employing only one workman; (2) those of six years' residence, with four children and four workmen; (3) those having "a very long residence," a "large family," and more than four workmen. For these classes expulsion was decreed on this sliding scale: Within (1) from three to six months; (2) from six to nine months; (3) from nine months to one year.

Of course, this provision of a minimum and maximum time was solely for the benefit of the police. It may be imagined how they peddled out the extra time, by months, then weeks, then days!

This was bad enough, but its rigours had been largely discounted. Two-thirds of the people at whom it was aimed had already fled. There was, however, in the tail of these "regulations" of July 28 a sharp and unexpected sting. It was in these words:

"All those who have been living in Moscow by virtue of possession of Circular No. 30 of the Minister of Interior (Markoff) of 1880 are divided into two categories:

"A. All clerks, personal attendants, and those of small occupations must go within six months.

"B. All engaged in trade, especially in large

factories owned by Russians, must go within one year."

I was on the Bourse at noon one day when the first whisper that the "circulars" had been suspended was sent the rounds of the floor. A strange, motley, picturesque crowd is that which gathers on the Moscow Exchange—with sleek, well-clad city merchants and bankers rubbing shoulders against uncouth capitalists from the Volga, the Crimea, or far-off Archangel; with Tartar traders from remote Siberia and the Chinese border; with olive-skinned, doll-faced Persians; with bright-eyed, hawk-visaged Bokhara Jews; with Armenians, Cossacks, Finns, Poles, Greeks, Turks, English, and Germans; above all, with thin, silent, observant, masterful Russian Jews—a weird, cosmopolitan medley of races, of costumes, and of jargons, in which Russian is heard, perhaps, least of all.

I shall never forget how the whispered rumour about the "circulars" ran through this throng. One could trace its progress as it went; men ceased talking quotations and crops, and their faces lost the flush of commercial eagerness; little groups formed apart to discuss it in undertones. A hush fell over the hall. We were in Russia, and no man dared speak aloud about this thing he had heard.

The "circular" class, whose doom was thus announced, was composed of a much higher social grade of Hebrews than had previously been

P

touched.  The phrases " clerks, personal attendants," and " those engaged in trade " hardly
convey an idea of the half of those who in
Moscow held the circular of 1880.  Only a few
days before, a professional man of distinction
and means had said to me that he could not be
molested because he was protected by a Ministerial circular !

He was in London, a homeless wanderer,
before many months.  He had with him here, as
a companion in exile, an intelligent and energetic
young man whose firm in Moscow did an annual
business of £50,000, but who had not been in
trade the requisite number of years to secure the
privileges of a merchant of the First Guild, and
who was accordingly living under the " circular."
The decree of expulsion found him newly married,
with a handsome house which he had just fitted
up with something like £2000 worth of furniture.
He unhesitatingly resolved to leave the country
at once, and not haggle with the police about
the few extra months he might buy from them.
He applied to the railway officials—who are, of
course, also Government officials—for a car to
transport his furniture to the frontier.  They were
very sorry, but all their cars were in use, and it
might be months before they could let him have
one.  He learned on inquiry that this was their
stereotyped reply to all such applications from
Jews.  Then he tried to sell his furniture, and
encountered another combination against his race

of much the same stamp. No one would bid more than a few hundred roubles ; my recollection is that the sum finally offered was £60. Then the young merchant came to a heroic resolve. The last night he was to spend in Moscow—he had sent his wife ahead—he locked himself up in his house with saw and chisel, and by morning he had utterly disfigured and destroyed every stick of his fine furniture. If he could neither keep it nor sell it, at least he provided that no one else should enjoy it.

The " circular " class was supposed to comprise 800 families—a total of 4000 souls. There were a few poor people among them ; the bulk were in comfortable circumstances, and some—for the most part manufacturers, brokers, and agents— were what is called wealthy in Russia.

As an indication of this I had a letter from Moscow in October saying that, now the " circular " people were leaving, the scenes at the Smolenski station were of quite a different character from those I witnessed in the summer. Then one was chiefly impressed with the poverty of the poor fugitives being packed into third-class cars. Now, my correspondent said, most of those leaving went in second-class carriages.

Putting aside for a moment the cruelty and wrong done to these people, try to imagine the grave self-injury inflicted by a country which thus blindly chases out a whole great class of mer- chants, manufacturers, and skilled workmen, who are everywhere a stimulating and important factor in the commercial life of that country. The "circular" class alone are said to have employed in Moscow and vicinity 25,000 Russian workmen.

There was, indeed, in this edict expelling the "circular" people an obscure phrase excepting from its operation certain "very large factories"— but this in practice covered only four establishments, whose influential Russian owners had Jewish managers whom they desired not to lose. One clause provides that, if Jews of Section B can give the police good reasons, their stay may be extended another year. A gentleman whom I met in Moscow asked a police official if it would be a "good reason" that immediate expulsion would almost entirely ruin him and his family. I made a minute at the time of the reply :

"No," said the official quite good-naturedly, "you must show that *Russians* will be directly injured by your going. Injury to yourself is no reason at all. The Government doesn't care whether you have a shirt to your back or not."

# CHAPTER XIII

## THE FLIGHT FROM MOSCOW

OF necessity one must study an exodus on the road. I was not fortunate enough anywhere to see the *étape*—that melancholy survival of mediæval brutality of which Mr. Kennan makes so much. But on every side I heard stories of them, and was shown proofs that men and women against whom absolutely nothing but their nationality was alleged had been marched through the streets in chains and in the company of thieves and other criminal refuse.

It was not through lack of looking for one that I failed to see the *étape*. On fully a score of occasions, in various Russian towns, I watched the whole scene at the railway station at the hour when the cheap train was to start westward with its freight of homeless exiles. In Moscow I went almost every afternoon to witness at the Smolenski station the departure of the seven o'clock train for Brest-Litovsk, by which at that time practically all the refugees were making their way to the Pale. What I saw daily at this station remains still most vivid among my recollections of Russia. As a little boy I used to associate our

Civil War entirely with the old wooden depôt of my native town, where I saw troops gathered from time to time to go away, and watched the sobbing or even more cruel dry-eyed anguish of the wives, mothers, and daughters left behind. Those childish impressions—half forgotten for many years—all came back bright and sharply defined at sight of the Jewish fugitives in the Smolenski station.

Most of them were on hand an hour or more before the time for the train to start. The long, broad platform was dotted with piles of their luggage heaped against the walls. The character of this *impedimenta* showed obviously enough that its owners were going for good—spoke eloquently of a people torn up by the roots. There were pet pieces of furniture wrapped in sheets, and crockery encased in bedding and tied with ropes. One saw carpets, picture-frames, candlesticks, big leather-bound books, even bird-cages, all made into parcels as portable as possible, with a few to be taken free as personal baggage. Everywhere there were teapots fastened outside the hand-luggage, so as to be easy of access during the wearisome journey of two nights and a day across to the Pale.

The management of this baggage lay heavily upon the minds of the fugitives. They flitted incessantly about, dragging it from one point to another, as opinions fluctuated among them concerning the probable attitude of the railway officials toward it. At each platform along the train stood a peasant in uniform whom we would call a brakeman, and his principal task was to see that none of this unauthorised baggage got into the car, where now dozens of people were crowding themselves together on the narrow wooden benches. I watched for a long time the manœuvres of two or three groups of elderly men —thin, flat-chested, long-bearded men in caps and caftans—who stood guard over little heaps of household goods. Every now and again, when the brakeman's attention seemed to be diverted, one of them would dart across the train and try to hand something through the open window to a friend inside. Occasionally he succeeded; more often the guard ran over and forcibly intervened. In this latter case the Jew would go back and keep sharp look-out for a chance to repeat the attempt. Once I saw the brakeman, in his anger, dash a big, rope-bound chest, which they had nearly dragged into the car, to the platform with such violence that it was broken and its contents scattered for yards about. The men who had it in charge meekly got down and gathered them up and fastened the box together again. Then they dragged it to another part of the train, and eventually smuggled it through a window.

The whole pathos of the Jews' position in Russia —their long-suffering abasement, their fawning absence of dignity, their tireless patience,

their curious persistence of daring in little things
—was in this picture.

It could not be said that the train hands or any
other officials connected with the railway behaved
with special roughness to these Jews. Indeed,
with the solitary exception I have noted, wherein
one could not deeply blame the man, they seemed
to be rather amiably disposed than otherwise.
This was of interest, as confirming what, over
and over again, intelligent and candid Jewish
merchants and professional men had told me—
viz., that the Russian peasants do not themselves
dislike the Jew, and that both the persecution,
and the brutal spirit in which it is carried out,
proceed entirely from above, filtering down
through from the Czar and the Holy Synod, to the
lowliest policeman or *tchinovnik* who yearns for
promotion and the favour of his superiors.

The trainmen did, however, behave with con-
spicuous curtness to the three or four long-haired
village priests or popes of the Orthodox Church,
who were also travelling third-class, and who
bothered them with questions or by not having
the proper tickets for their luggage. One of
these, a quizzical-faced, drunken, and dishevelled
fellow, with a patched and muddy gown, and a
woman's straw hat perched jauntily on his head,
was at last thrown summarily out of a car and
went away smiling blandly.

The daily average of Jewish fugitives, during
my observations in July and August, seemed to

be about fifteen families. In only one instance did I see any going other than by the third-class or presenting an appearance of prosperity.

All the women, however, were dressed well. It was only too evident that they were wearing their best clothes. At Hamburg I encountered much proof of the existence of a class of female exiles who are in rags and tatters. They did not come from Moscow. These women at the Smolenski station—like most of the Jewesses I saw everywhere throughout Russia—were much less characteristic in type than the men. These latter—pallid, keen-eyed, nervous, bearded, Orientals in face, form, and gesture—could not be mistaken anywhere. But their wives and daughters for the most part looked like the comfortable and ugly Slavo-Saxon peasantry roundabout Leipsic. There were a few exceptions. I saw one little girl, poorly clad save for a thick black satin pelisse much too large for her, staggering along under a big bundle of bedding, who had a face that might have come from a frieze in the Palace of Saigon.

Only here and there did one see a young man among these exiles. The Jewish youth seems to be in the army or already safe beyond the frontier.

As a rule, there was little enough of tears or lamentation. During the four months then drawing to a close, over 10,000 people had come to that Smolenski station with all that was left of their belongings, had said good-bye to the only people in the world they knew, and had gone forth to strange lands or to the horrors of the Pale. It is small wonder that most of those I saw looked as if they had forgotten how to weep.

One hideous woman of fifty I recall, by the aid of a rough sketch among my notes, who cried a great deal. She was leaving behind her an even uglier son—a repellent-faced young man who was the object of her fondest grief. He was immensely bored by this, and was continually wandering off to talk with a group of menfolk, and being summoned back for fresh maternal kisses. The parting of two young sisters, who clung, sobbing, to each other through the window till the train moved, makes another picture in my memory. The one who was left fainted on the platform as the carriages began gliding by. Most marked feature of all were the prolonged fervent caresses bestowed by those who were remaining upon the little children in the cars. The babes were held up to the windows, and kissed and kissed again by the elders outside, with a depth of emotion which seemed to belong to the chamber of death rather than to a railway station.

To and fro, meanwhile, among these scenes of misery high Russian officials in uniform and well-to-do Russians of private station sauntered unconcernedly, lighting cigarettes and chatting as they strolled, without so much as a sign that they

were aware of the presence of these Jews about
them.   They positively never looked at them.   I
was given many quiet and friendly intimations in
Russia that it was considered extremely bad form
even to observe incidents and occurrences which
the authorities were responsible for.   If "well-
intentioned" Russians see the *étape* coming down
the street they look the other way.   Despotism
must regard this as its ultimate triumph.

On the evening of Thursday, August 6, I
visited the Smolenski station for the last time.
The scenes that evening attending the departure of
the train seemed to reach a climax of harrowing
interest.   There were more small children than
usual, perhaps.   The tragedy of it all—the ignominy, the injustice which had darkened these
wretched lives before, the cruel doubt and uncertainty of their future—oppressed my spirits.   I
could not resist the impulse to take off my hat as
the long "emigrant" train slowly moved out of
the station.   It was such a solemn salute as one
pays, in Roman Catholic countries, to the passing
of a hearse.

At that very moment the glass in the roof
overhead rattled with the concussion of cannon
reports.   Again and again, I know not how many
times, the noise of big guns firing not far away
shook the air.   The explanation was at hand outside.   Some mile further west were the grounds
of the French Exhibition in Moscow.   That
evening the Jew-baiting Mayor, Alexeieff, was

giving a banquet there to the visiting officers of the French fleet, who had journeyed from Cronstadt as his guests.

The hapless Jews in that train, as they took their farewell look upon the domes and minarets of the Holy City wherein most of them had been born, may have wondered what the cannon were firing for. The most acridly sarcastic mind among them could have hit upon no more bitter irony than is furnished by the fact that the salutes were being fired in honour of the partnership newly formed between this monstrous and unclean despotism and the French Republic!

From the Smolenski station it is but a short walk up the broad Dolgoroukoffskaya to the chief forwarding prison of Moscow. The high white walls, with their round, castellated towers at the corners, rise abruptly from the side-walk. The prison itself is a red brick building, well inside these walls, with few windows and those heavily barred. It is to this prison that all the Jews arrested on the night of the descent upon the Glebovskaya Podvoryeh were dragged; it is from this that they, and many who came later, have been sent away by *étape*—that is, marched down the public thoroughfare in chains, or under heavy Cossack guard, to the railway station.

Mr. Arnold White, accepting here as elsewhere the assurances that polite Russian officials have made to him over the dinner-table, has taken it upon himself to deny that any Jews were thus sent unless they were criminals. American officials in Russia have been quoted to me as authorities for this same statement.

A devoted man, to whom the Jews of Russia and of the world owe a greater debt than they can ever repay, and whose name it will be possible to mention when, a few months hence, he has left Russia for good, last autumn collected for me in various towns a list of eighty-eight persons who were marched out of Moscow by *étape*, and against whom no charge of criminal conduct—unless it be criminal for a Jew to shrink from beggary and expatriation—was brought. They were taken publicly through the streets, most of them in chains and all in the enforced company of common jail-birds, at eleven o'clock on Monday mornings. This list was published in the New York *Times* of December 7, 1891,* and subsequently in *Darkest Russia.* No detail of it has been controverted.

The gruesome-looking manacles which figure as a badge upon the cover of this book, and which are now in my possession, were worn out of Moscow on June 1, 1892, by Jossel Revsin, a Jewish artisan who was marched publicly away in a chain gang of criminals and vagabonds, solely because of his race and religion. In the same *étape* was another handcuffed Jew, Israel Rassner, and two Jewesses, Rivka Krein and Feiga Beresinova. The women were not in irons, but they were a part of the *étape.* All four were thus

* See Appendix B.

conveyed into the Pale, whence they eventually
emerged and made their way to England and
America. Although he did not learn their names,
these were the unhappy wretches whom Mr.
Romanis, the hard-working and candid corre-
spondent, saw being driven through the streets of
Moscow on June 1, and described in the *Daily
News* of June 6.

Space will permit only the most cursory glance
at the terrible story of Moscow during the year
which has elapsed since the Passover decrees.
No other city in modern times has offered such
a wantonly abhorrent chronicle of evil deeds and
cruel instincts to an offended Christendom.

The Grand Duke Serge will not, it is said,
complete his second year of office as Governor-
General. His brutal manners, his total neglect of
his duties, and the now general knowledge of his
personal character, have been too much for even
Moscow. He finds himself scowled at on the
streets, and hissed on the race-course. In consequence, he spends almost all his time out on his
estate of Illinskaya, surrounded by the group of
favourites whose names are mentioned under one's
breath. He pays no attention whatever to the
tasks imposed by routine upon a Governor-General.
Of these, by far the most important is the hearing
of appeals and complaints, and the reception of
petitions. Prince Dolgoroukoff used to see every
one. Serge sees no one. Of all the hundreds of
petitions sent to him, the first has yet to be

acknowledged or answered. To make matters worse, he does not even leave his chief intendant, Istomin, to attend to the Moscow business, but has him half the time at Illinskaya.

This Istomin is another sinister figure in the group which governs Moscow under the favour of the Holy Synod. He is a man of university degree, who, after several failures in life, went to St. Petersburg and was lucky enough to get on the blind side of Pobiedonostseff, who made him editor of his official paper at a salary of 8000 roubles. Working his way carefully, he obtained a pious reputation as a relentless anti-Semite and a capable man of affairs, and was picked out as bear leader and general manager to Serge, when that simpleton was selected for Moscow. The Jews of the " Holy City " regard Istomin as their real grand inquisitor.

Of the scores of domestic tragedies over which this man has been proud to preside, perhaps this is the most characteristic. It happened on October 23, 1891. A woman, the wife of a small merchant belonging to that division of the " circular " class ordered to leave by October 26, was so close to her time of confinement that removal threatened her life. Her husband, with a physician, haunted the approaches to the Governor-General's office for two days, before they could find any one in. At last they managed to secure an interview with Istomin. The physician explained to him that they asked for a fortnight's respite for the woman simply because if she started now upon a railway journey it was practically inevitable that a catastrophe would occur on the road.

Istomin replied that there could be no respite and that the woman must go at once. He added : " There is no reason why you should not take a separate compartment for her on the train and let a midwife travel with her."

And that was what was done !

Another narrative, dealing with people much better known and illustrating in a broader way the whole heartless business of crushing and ruining a family, has for its central figure Mrs. Mandelstamm, a venerable lady of refinement and culture, the mother of the well-known Dr. Mandelstamm of Kazan. Upon the death of her husband, in 1874, she went to Moscow to live. Her elder children were already domiciled there, and the younger ones were now given the advantage of the best educational facilities afforded by the Holy City. In the commercial disasters following the war Mrs. Mandelstamm's property became involved, and her oldest daughter, Mrs. W——, now a middle-aged woman with four children, was compelled to work as a saleswoman in a *Magasin* to help support the family. This did not prevent their household continuing to enjoy the respect of the entire community, and the fact that Dr. Mandelstamm of Kazan is a baptised Jew, and a man of high professional and popular position, was looked upon as guaranteeing them immunity from the persecution.  Suddenly, under the "circular" decree, the aged widow received warning to leave Moscow within four weeks.  Her son went to the palace, and personally saw Istomin, with whom he was acquainted.  Istomin promised readily to submit the case to the Governor-General, volunteering the assurance that His Highness was not such a barbarian as to refuse this good old lady the privilege of living and dying among her children in Moscow.  A few days later Dr. Mandelstamm called again upon Istomin, and that official without a word returned to him the petition he had submitted.  On it was written, in Serge's own hand, the incredible order that instead of the four weeks granted her by the police, the venerable woman must leave Moscow within twenty-four hours!

During this brief space of ti...c, the decrepit old widow made all her arrangements for leaving her home for ever, and started on her journey.  But first she witnessed the hurried marriage of her third daughter, Rosetta, to a young fellow-student at the University, named Weinburg.  This marriage was to have been deferred for a year or two—until both bride and groom had taken their degrees.  It had now to be precipitated in this summary fashion, in order to prevent the expulsion of Rosetta as well.

This visitation of barbaric wrath upon an unoffending family was not even now exhausted. The eldest daughter, Mrs. W——, was ordered to

Q

leave Moscow by April 26, 1892, a decree which she by a few weeks forestalled. After years of self-denying labour to support and educate her children—labour which has broken down her health and induced a pulmonary affection which can give her only a few more years of life—she is driven from her native land, a homeless and helpless outcast, with three daughters, the eldest of whom was studying the piano at the Conservatory, the youngest of whom is a child of ten. Her only son came of age this year, and has been drafted into the Russian army—to be expelled and follow the others into exile when he has served his term with the colours.

This truly mediæval catalogue of vicious barbarities is only one, and by no means the most cruel, of the bitter many which have been burned into the memories of the Moscow Jews. After July of this year 1892, there will remain scarcely a shadow of that Hebrew community which eighteen months ago numbered nearly 30,000 souls. The rabbis, the beadles, the members of the choir, the elders, have all been driven out. Even the sexton of the Jewish burying-ground has been sent away. No Jewish butchers remain. From the beginning, special care was taken to trace and expel all Jewesses who were employed in Hebrew households as cooks, a decision having been obtained that they were not artisans, and some one else having decided, or being said to have decided, that they were not domestic servants.

The expulsions of January 26, 1892, upon which date expired the time limit of the poorer class of "circular Jews," and of those artisans who had "six years' residence and four children, or employed four workmen," may be said to have reached a climax in horror which no one had dreamed possible. To the brutality of man was added now the awful savagery of the elements. The week was the coldest which even that arctic region remembered for years. On the day itself, the thermometer actually marked 34 degrees below zero, Fahrenheit. The gas could not burn in the street-lamps in such a temperature; great bon-fires were kept blazing in the squares and at corners, at public expense, to prevent citizens compelled to be out of doors from freezing as they walked; the schools were closed, and garrison drills suspended. On the 22nd, orders were issued that the forwarding of criminal convicts from the central prison should be stopped for the time being, owing to the terrible cold.

It was at such a time as this that nearly 2000 Jews were forced to take a last look at what had been their homes, and start off on their pilgrimage of exile. The weather was too bad for convicts to travel in; it was all right for people whose offence was having been born in Israel. Not until two days after the date of the expulsion— that is to say, until practically all the victims had departed—was the clemency which had from the first been extended to thieves and murderers stretched out to cover Hebrews as well. A police order was issued on January 28, deferring "the further expulsion of Jews from Moscow until February 1, in view of the extreme frosts." Mme. Novikoff might characteristically reproduce this decree as an example of the humane spirit inspiring the Russian Government. When it was pointed out to the officials that the expulsions had already taken place, they shrugged their shoulders and laughed.

One shudders at that laugh. That four little children were frozen to death in the streets, on their way to the railway station, is a mere incident of the hideous story. An educated young Jewish woman who was in Moscow that day, and has since joined her brother in London, grows faint and hysterical and blinded with tears when, even at this distance and lapse of time, she essays to tell the narrative of what she saw. I do not wonder at it. There were scores of wretched children, clad only in linen smocks or tattered summer clothing, whose hands and feet were frozen. The crowded platform, from early morning till midnight, offered at every step such scenes of heart-breaking misery of mind and wild physical anguish as belong to the battle-field alone.

With this final picture haunting the memory, let us leave inhuman Holy Moscow.

# CHAPTER XIV

### ST. PETERSBURG, ODESSA, AND KIEFF

ST. PETERSBURG is less characteristically Russian than any other city within the empire. It is a kind of fakir in architecture—a cosmopolitan charlatan borrowing styles and tricks of expression from numerous civilised sources, yet revealing its innate barbarism through them all. I have not seen it in the winter, when it is said to present a brilliant and attractive individuality entirely its own. Its summer aspect is one of profound melancholy, with vast sprawling empty streets, with huge gloomy deserted edifices, with waterways confined between silent quays, and bearing on their cold surface no signs of trade activity or social animation.

The far-famed St. Isaac's Cathedral suggests in turn St. Paul's in London and the Capitol at Washington; the Kazan Cathedral is a poor imitation of St. Peter's at Rome; the great building devoted to the General Staff is copied from Versailles; the palaces are plagiarisms from Venice, Amsterdam, and Berlin; even the shop-windows follow at a respectful distance after Parisian models.

In this city, built to order over a swamp by a Czar's caprice, and ever since its creation the centre and focus of the efforts of an alien imperial line to Germanise Russia, what may be called municipal feeling scarcely exists. It is dominated by the congregated bureaucracy of the empire even more wholly than Washington is ruled by Congress. Its population comes and goes, without rooting itself or forming enduring associations —like that of the capital on the Potomac. The signs, on its principal and fashionable business streets exhibit German names, French names, Dutch, Swedish, Finnish, and English names, with only here and there a Russian appellation.

The residents of St. Petersburg know and care so little about such civic facts and conditions as lie outside their own special ambitions or points of social contact, that it has been extremely difficult to collect statistics concerning the Jews of the capital. None of the people whom I met and talked with there had any definite notions on the subject. Most of them were under the impression that, with a few favoured exceptions, the whole Hebrew community had been cleared out years ago. This idea was borne out by my failure, during nearly a fortnight in St. Petersburg —on the streets, in the bazaars, at the garden theatres in the suburbs—to see more than one or two distinctively Jewish faces.

I learned afterwards that there were still a good many Israelites in St. Petersburg, but that they went about as little as possible, and particularly avoided places of public resort. One evening at the Arcadia Gardens I called my companion's attention to a young man walking with a girl who seemed to be his sister, and asked if they did not look like Jews. " The girl may be," was the reply. "If she is a registered prostitute nobody will object to her as a Jewess. But the man would only dare come here in case he had been baptised : otherwise he would certainly be insulted and compelled to go !"

The best clue to the figures of the persecution in St. Petersburg is furnished by the mortuary statistics of the city. In 1882 there were 480 Jewish deaths recorded ; in 1890 the number had fallen to 200. Assuming the death-rate to be 25 in the thousand, this would give us a Hebrew population of 19,200 in 1882 and of only 8000 in 1890. That is to say, in nine years 11,200 people had fled or been expelled from the city of the imperial residence.

The figures for the following year, or a portion of it, are more exact. I discover that the St. Petersburg Jewish Committee from June 13 to October 22, 1891, assisted 202 artisan families of 569 souls to leave the city. This does not include any of the refugees who were able to pay their own expenses. It also leaves out all the young men, no matter how indigent. The committee did not dare help them to get away for fear of incurring the charge of facilitating their escape from the conscription. From two independent sources the estimate is made that the whole number of expulsions from May to November was close upon 2000. They have been going on at this rate ever since.

All this has been done without the warrant of any edict or decree of expulsion. The Chief of Police, General Grœsser, who frankly declared that he was above the law, acted entirely on his own initiative. If any one tried to appeal to a higher authority, he was simply put out within twenty-four hours. The most common pretext for these expulsions—where any was vouchsafed at all—was that the victims did not work at their trades on Saturdays. But, as has been explained heretofore, no explanation or authority is necessary. General Grœsser, so long as he did not incur the wrath of the Czar or offend the Czar's master, the dread Pobiedonostseff, freely did anything under the sun in St. Petersburg that he pleased.

When the savage expulsion decree fell upon Moscow and the towns in the Province of Moscow at Passover time in April 1891, Grœsser filled the eastern and southern railway stations of St. Petersburg with police and Cossacks to intercept any of the persecuted race who might try to escape in that direction from their doom of returning to the Pale. Scores of travellers were arrested on arrival upon the vaguest and most shadowy suspicion of being Jews, and in not a few instances were detained in custody for days, though their passports showed the suspicion to be groundless. It is said that some of these people, out of sheer official perversity, were afterwards marched off by *étape*.

In Russia no man can exist without a passport. When the police take this passport away he is no longer alive in any civic sense. Every privilege appertaining to his human estate is suspended. He can appeal to no one. If it is the whim of some choleric barbarian in epaulets to send him to Siberia, off he must go, with no more chance of escape or redress than a captured fish flapping in the sportsman's basket. Even if he be a stranger, with the passport of a foreign Government, he is equally powerless. Only last November Mr. Joseph Pennell had his passport taken from him at Berdichef, and was refused permission to either telegraph or write to the British Consulate at Kieff or the American Legation at St. Petersburg. It eventually pleased the provincial authorities to transport him to the western frontier. If they had decided to send him eastward instead, he would simply have disappeared into Siberia without a sign.

The expulsions in ·St. Petersburg, which since 1882 had never wholly ceased, began again with renewed virulence in May 1891. The most notable victim was the young poet Frug, who came from the south to the capital in 1883. Although he had been refused admission to the university, his literary attainments won prompt recognition, and his writings, alike in verse and prose, were sought after by the most important Russian journals, including some that were avowedly anti-Semitic. Despite this fact, he would not have been allowed to live in St. Petersburg or anywhere else in Russia outside the.Pale, had not the device been adopted of enrolling him as a footman in the household of Mr. Warschoffsky, a Jewish lawyer having the right to employ one co-religionist as a servant. Only in November last even this humiliating privilege was arbitrarily withdrawn, and Frug was ordered to leave the city within twenty-four hours, on penalty of being sent by *étape*. There was no pretence that his writings were objectionable, or that he had committed any offence. It was only that he was a Jew.

Can a country be regarded as civilised, or as fit to hold friendly relations with civilised peoples, of which such a story as that can be truthfully told ?

It would serve no purpose to quote the details of the St. Petersburg expulsions. Mr. I. Rabbinovitch was sent in chains to Dünaburg for no offence save that of being a Jew. Moses Mordonchai Feinberg, a gold and silver smith, whose right of residence dated from 1871, and Eidel Solomon Gissing, whose permit extended back to 1868, were both reduced almost to beggary by summary and wholly unjustifiable orders to leave. So the list might be extended indefinitely.

When, in the summer of 1891, the *Times*
printed the statement that a synagogue in St.
Petersburg had been closed by the Government,
the Russian press at once denied its truth, and
the denial was accepted. The facts are that two
synagogues, not one, were shut up : they were in
the province of St. Petersburg, not the city of,
that name. One was at Narva, a manufacturing
town, where Jews work in the cloth and flax
mills and the chemical works. The other was at
Kolpino, where they are employed in the great
naval factory, founded by Peter the Great, where
engines are now made and armour-plate is rolled.
These Jews are said to be without exception
veterans whose service of twenty-five years under
Nicholas and Alexander II entitled them to live
anywhere in Russia. It was not thought expe-
dient to abrogate this privilege. The Government instead closed their synagogues. It is a
penal offence to publicly read Jewish prayers
save in a licensed synagogue. Thus these old
soldiers, against whom no thought of offence or
disloyalty was charged, were estopped from wor-
shipping God in the manner of their fathers.

These wanton things were not done in some
remote and inaccessible corner of the empire, by
officials beyond the control of the Central Government. They happened within the Province of'
St. Petersburg, under the direct authority of its
Governor, the Czar's friend, Count Toll.

The childlike foolishness of it all is, I am aware,

well-nigh incredible.  The outside world can comprehend neither its gratuitous malignity nor its
spasmodic want of system.  Why suppress the
synagogues of Narva and Kolpino, and leave
others unmolested ?  Why pack one man off in
chains, without a word of warning, and let another
remain months after his time has expired ?  Why
expel the poet within twenty-four hours, and take
no steps whatever against the brothel-keeper ?
Why toil to fill volume after volume with a conflicting jumble of statutes, and then act without
any warrant of law at all ?  There is no answer.
One might as well ask why the same horse which
shies at a piece of paper on the road will charge a
field battery without a qualm.

One of the least explicable of the late General
Grœsser's acts was his issuing an order forbidding
Jews to apprentice their children to artisans, in
order that they may learn a trade.  What on
earth the reason may be for this astonishing
regulation, its results have been painful in the
extreme.  Not even the veterans of Nicholas
have been exempted from this whimsical order.
One old soldier, Minin by name, some years ago
apprenticed his son to an umbrella-maker.  The
boy served his time, obtained his certificate as a
skilled workman, and began work for his master
as a journeyman for the period stipulated in his
indentures, living in his house meanwhile.  Under
this new edict the police declared this contract of
his illegal (though it bore Grœsser's signature) and

ordered the young man to quit work. Minin petitioned Grœsser and was rebuffed ; then he appealed to the Senate, whereupon Grœsser gave both him and his son twenty-four hours in which to leave St. Petersburg.

Another favourite device for harrying the unhappy people, now highly valued in large Russian towns, is ascribed to General Grœsser's ingenuity. By police orders, every Jewish merchant must hang out a sign, giving not the Hebrew names of himself and his father, but those names as it pleases the Russian wit to contemptuously parody them. Thus a man whose name is Samuel son of Abraham, must on his sign describe himself as Schmoulke son of Abramke— names which fill the Russian Jew with loathing. This serves numerous purposes : Jewish shops can be systematically boycotted ; in case of a riot the Christian mob can see exactly where to work its violence ; and the owners are compelled by their own advertisements to make themselves ridiculous in the eyes of the community.

Jewish merchants of the First Guild, residing elsewhere in Russia, cannot visit the capital now without liability to insult and expulsion. Though they have as much legal right in St. Petersburg as the Czar himself, the police pay domiciliary visits to their hotels and order them to get out of the city immediately.

It is reported that on a recent occasion, when Russia was casting about for a new loan, a great foreign banking-house was requested to send a confidential agent to St. Petersburg to consult with the Minister of Finance. The agent who was sent was a Hebrew, a financier of high standing and social position. Although it was known that he came on Government business, the police went to his hotel and so affronted and browbeat him that he turned about and went home again, and negotiations for the loan ceased then and there.

Incidents of this sort illustrate afresh the fallacy of the popular notion that the Russians are an astute people. They are smart in a small savage way, like a Sioux Indian on a Soudanese sheik. It is a cunning which falls so wide of our own standards of cleverness that we instinctively exaggerate it. An episode in Mr. Pennell's Berdichef experiences last November affords an excellent example of what I mean. An official representative of the Governor-General, sent down from Kieff to discover what this suspicious stranger was doing, went with him to a local photographer's to have developed all the film-negatives Mr. Pennell's kodak had made. There were street scenes, market groups, itinerant pedlers, pictures of tumble-down old rookeries, and the like. The official looked gravely through them, one by one, over the lamp in the dark room, doubtless deeply puzzled that any sane man should so waste time and chemicals. When the inspection was finished, only one negative had been laid aside for confiscation.  By merest chance this one had in it the upper part 'of a telegraph pole.  The *aide-de-camp* detected in this a subtle attempt to obtain information about Russia's military telegraph system, and had it destroyed on the spot.

It is not surprising that the official policy of suppression and exasperation which I have outlined above should have well-nigh destroyed business in St. Petersburg.  Competent men of affairs, who are concerned in the Russian trade, assure me that the existing commercial collapse is even more due to the demoralisation created by the Jewish expulsions than to the bad harvest.  In the first week of October 1891 alone, ten big Orthodox Christian business houses in Moscow failed, their aggregate liabilities being nearly £1,000,000. To this inaugural crash succeeded a winter of unparalleled financial stringency, punctuated by bankruptcy, and the spring of the present year, so far from promising improvement, brought the fall of the great Günzburg banking-house, attended by a whole train of minor failures.  Just as the Czar had the Jewish flour mills closed on account of the crucifixion, so he is understood to have personally interposed to prevent official aid being extended to save the Günzburgs from disaster.  It would be strange indeed if commercial confidence throve in such an atmosphere.

An even worse state of affairs exists at Odessa, where the stagnation which I saw last summer was during the autumn turned into a destructive

panic by the ukases blocking all cereal exporta-
tion.  Of that great congregation of prosperous
merchants who have built up the Black Sea
trade and developed far above all other portions
of the empire the grain belts of the Dnieper and
the Dniester, hardly any can hope to emerge
unscathed, and the majority are confronted by
absolute ruin.

On the surface of things this is ascribable, of
course, to the terrible failure of the crops and to
the ukases mentioned above.  In reality one of
the chief factors in Odessa's present tribulation
is the enforced idleness or absence of the small
Jewish middlemen, who formerly went through
the grain country buying the crops as they stood
and advancing the money for the harvesting
expenses.  Last year, from fear of confiscation
or expulsion before they could sell again, and
also from their inability to get credit at the banks,
they made no purchases.  As a result, in whole
rich districts the crops were never cut at all, but
rotted where they stood.

The Jewish exodus from Odessa has lacked
the sensational features we have seen displayed
at Moscow and St. Petersburg—for the reason
that the Hebrew community there was much
stronger and richer than in any other Russian
city, and could purchase civil treatment from
the police and provincial authorities—but in point
of numbers it must nearly if not quite equal that
from both the others put together.  It could hardly

be otherwise, when in the year 1890 the city contained 106,000 of them.

A large proportion of the Israelites in Odessa at the beginning of 1891 were foreigners, who had come from Austria, Roumania, Germany, Turkey, and elsewhere. Among them were some of the leading citizens of the town—lawyers, physicians with rich, fashionable practice, dentists, merchants, ship-owners, and manufacturers. They have all had to go.

Although Odessa is within the Pale, that fact has made very little difference with the unhappy Jews of Russian birth domiciled there. Odessa is a new city. Its amazing growth and splendid commercial position during the past twenty years have been largely the work of the Hebrews from other parts of Russia who moved thither in the sixties and seventies, under Alexander II's relatively enlightened rule. There Judaism held up its head as it never dared do in Moscow or St. Petersburg. There it maintained handsome synagogues, had its open share in municipal management, and stood on an admitted footing with other sections of the community. No Jew in Odessa hesitated to avow his race or talk about it. There were next to no converts to Christianity there.

Even in August of 1891, when I visited Odessa, the situation had gravely altered. The banks were avoiding transactions with Jewish merchants as much as possible, and in a country where

R

everything is arranged upon a credit system that in itself was ruinous. The forced realisations of those who had had to fly, and the general refusal of debtors to pay what they owed to those who remained, were completing the spoliation of the Hebrew community.

I saw them by scores, sitting about in the parks, gardens, and public places of Odessa, or wandering aimlessly along the beautiful parade which, perched high in the air, overlooks the blue Euxine. Their inability to look as if they were accustomed to leisure was pathetic. "Compulsory idleness" was written on every lineament of their thin, eager, olive-hued faces. You could read it in the sidelong glances they bent upon strangers passing by and in the restless manner in which they sat on the benches, as if ready to spring up and run on the instant.

Six months before they had been active, capable, self-reliant citizens, busily carrying on their share in the commerce of a bustling and prosperous port, maintaining comfortable homes, educating their children, and bearing themselves with a decent pride. They had been powerful enough, when the Governor-General issued an order authorising the police to punish Jews who failed to touch their caps to all officials, to compel the revocation of the order by simply refusing to enter any place of public resort so long as it was in force. Now the blight of barbarism had passed over them and turned them into the distraught, frightened, and wretched beings I saw.

"Holy" Kieff to-day probably exceeds Odessa in population, although it plays so insignificant a part in the thoughts of the outside world. In appearance it is as uniquely striking as "Holy" Moscow, but in character they are widely separated. Kieff and the district to which it gives its name really belonged to Old Poland. There is a large Catholic element in the city. Many ancient families of the Polish nobility hold big estates in the country roundabout—or did until within the last few years. For generations cruel Russian laws have existed for the purpose of breaking up these estates and preventing the children of the Polish owners from inheriting them, but until recently the officials were bribed to let them remain a dead letter. With the rise to power of Pobiedonostseff this parleying with the heretics came to an end. A little later Count Alexis Ignatieff, a younger brother of "The Infamous," was sent to Kieff as Governor-General.

This junior Ignatieff is a fat, rough, burly soldier of fifty. He is worth remembering, because many people in Russian official circles regard him as the coming man. Eight years ago he was Chief of Staff of the Cossack Guard. When the *circonscription militaire* of Irkutsk was formed in 1884, he was put at the head of it. His Siberian record is one of the most terrible

which even that home of horrors presents. He
had men flogged to death and female prisoners
tortured until even Russian journals protested.
Then he was promoted to the rich and powerful
berth of Kieff.

With the coming of this hard barbarian a new
impulse was given to the spoliation of the Polish
proprietors, the coercion of the university students
(an exceptionally restive lot in Kieff), and the
persecution of the Catholics, the Molokani, the
Stundists, and other "schismatics" of the South.

It may be imagined that he has not spared the
Jews.

No figures whatever are obtainable on the
subject of his expulsions. The province of Kieff,
as distinct from the city, is inside the Pale, and
last year was estimated to contain some 400,000
Hebrews. On the theory of ratio heretofore
adopted, this would mean that 60,000 people had
been chased from their homes in the villages into
the towns. There are no means of testing this
estimate. But to see the present state of Berdichef, the principal town in the province, is to feel
ready to credit any statement on this head, no
matter how wild.

This Berdichef was in 1890 supposed to contain some 60,000 inhabitants, two-thirds Jews.
It was then an overcrowded place, made up for
the most part of old and insanitary rookeries, in
which were huddled one of the poorest populations to be found anywhere in Europe. By

August, 1891, it was said that fully 20,000 additional Hebrews had been driven in from the surrounding country. The spectacle of their poverty and squalor was something too sickening for words. The whole place, with its filthy streets, its open sewers, its reeking half-cellars under the overhanging balconies, and its swarming throngs of unwashed, unkempt wretches packed into the narrow thoroughfares on the look-out for food, made a picture scarcely human. Mr. Pennell tells me that when he was there in November he was assured that, instead of the 60,000 Jews of August, there were then in Berdichef no less than 90,000.

It is understood that there is nothing else in the Pale quite so awful as the condition of Berdichef. Certainly the fugitives who find their way out of Russia from this point touch the lowest depth of destitution and enfeebled misery which the committees at Hamburg and elsewhere have to encounter. But there are over a hundred towns in that hell called the Pale where the same causes operate which have made Berdichef such an unspeakable charnel-house, and in each one the Russian police have done their brutal best to reproduce the conditions of Berdichef.

The "Holy" City of Kieff has always occupied a position in Russian law apart from the province of that name. The separation dates back into the mists of the Middle Ages. Kief is invested with unique importance in the Russian Orthodox mind. Here it was that the pagan descendants of Rurik first accepted Christianity; here St. Vladimir, seventh in descent from Rurik, built the first Christian church in 989; and here he lies buried in the Dessiatinnaya church, which occupies the site of his ancient edifice. When Poland and the Czar Alexis in 1657 divided the Ukraine between them the city of Kieff was excepted from the provision which gave the right bank of the Dnieper to the Poles. Thus the "Jerusalem of Russia," as it is called, came under the dominion of the Czars 136 years before the province lying outside its walls. This was not gathered in by the Muscovite octopus till the second partition—that of 1793.

Among the distinctions in law still maintained between the city and the province is this, that the latter is in the Pale and the former is not. For generations no Jews were permitted to live in the Holy City. The statute is still on the books forbidding any but merchants of the First Guild to reside in the town, and limiting them to the Libedsky and Plossky quarters. Side by side with this are other laws referring to other classes of Jews who live in the town. Prince Demidoff San Donato, in his admirable work, deals at length with the grotesque paradox involved in these contradictory enactments. Of course, what they meant, though he did not like to say so, was that the local officials had the Jews of Kieff at their mercy, and could blackmail them at will.

This is what is still going on in the "Holy" City. Judging by a study of the laws, I had expected to find no Jews at all in Kieff. To my surprise, they were vastly more in evidence there than in Moscow. The outburst of anti-Semitic fanaticism which had smitten Moscow, St. Petersburg, and Odessa hip and thigh, which had made the fair at Nijni Novgorod a blank failure, and established a reign of terror in every manufacturing and trade centre of the empire, was being used in "Holy" Kieff with strictly commercial prudence. They were not so silly in this sacred city as to slay the goose of the golden eggs, or even chase it away prematurely. A sagacious system of squeezing, with just enough brutality to make the pressure acute, commended itself instead to their judgment.

A favourite trick there, at the time of my visit, was to serve well-to-do Hebrew merchants with notice that their cooks or their coachmen, not being artisans, must leave the city. If the merchant cared to go to the necessary expense, he could convince the police authorities that his special servants were undoubtedly artisans. If he concluded, on the other hand, to let them go, he presently received a notification that his own position in the city seemed irregular. That meant business. Knowing perfectly well that they had laws enough, in assorted varieties, to make anything under the sun irregular, he walked up to the Captain's office and settled.

To this day we get from time to time news of a fresh raid upon unauthorised Jews in Kieff. In December, for example, there was the story that 150 public-houses kept by Jews had been closed in that city. Most probably it was a lie made out of whole cloth ; if it was not, then it showed the continued existence in Kieff of a great class of Jews who, by the law, should have been expelled long before, and who had at last come to the end of their power to pay blackmail.

It is an ingenious part of the scheme at Kieff to every now and again make some savage and sporadic onslaught upon a group of Jews, solely with a view to leading the St. Petersburg authorities to believe that the expulsions are being earnestly and thoroughly carried on. Quite of this character was the order of the Governor-General last summer summarily expelling all the singers, musicians, and actors of Jewish blood in the various theatres and cafés-chantants of the city. It happened that this involved the closing of every such place of entertainment in Kief. On the very night of the order "Robert le Diable" had to be abandoned at the Opera-house and the audience sent away, because the conductor of the orchestra was the only non-Hebrew connected with the performance. Naturally, an incident of this sort attracted universal attention. Tidings of it flew to St. Petersburg, and pleased Pobiedonostseff and the Czar. This served the purpose of diverting attention from those other

Jews who had not been sent out of Kieff, and who were paying through the nose for their immunity.

So this long chronicle of the persecution comes to an end. From the mass of notes still untouched concerning Nijni Novgorod, Kaluga, Simbirsk, Tula, Pavlovo, Vorsina, and numerous other places, examples of barbaric cruelty and heart-breaking misery could be cited to an almost indefinite extent. They would but repeat the story already told. Nor is it needful to refer to the savage anti-Jewish riots at Staradoub, Balta, and other points throughout the south during the past winter; they are still a part of the current news, and in truth relate more to the general famine-stricken and turbulent condition of the empire than to the special Semitic question.

In the interest of a complete narrative of the expulsions, it is necessary to now leave the land of oppression and to observe the phenomena of the exodus presented at and across the frontier.

# CHAPTER XV

## ISRAEL IN EXILE

THE indignant interest with which Christendom
has followed Russia's career of internal persecution
and inhumanity is, at its best, of a sentimental
character. However shocked the nations may
have been, none of them has allowed the feeling
to affect in any tangible way its friendly relations
with the Government of the Czar. But the
moment public gaze is shifted from the doings
inside the Empire to the great streams of fugitives
pouring across the border, humanitarian sympathy
takes on sternly practical limitations. We have
already witnessed the beginnings of what threatens
to be a policy of complete exclusion on the part
of the German Empire. Both England and
America display a growing nervousness over the
prospect of a sustained Semitic invasion, and are
not only applying such immigration regulations as
they possess with more and more severity, but
are quite in the mood to further strengthen their
defensive statutory machinery. There is no other
nation north of the equator, big or little, which does
not occupy practically this same hostile attitude.

It would be misleading, however, to ignore the

gradations in which this self-protective spirit is evoked and manifested. The United States, for example, have room enough for all new-comers who promise to be good citizens and helpful members of the community. Their interest is concentrated upon the inquiry whether the Russo-Jewish refugees come within this category. In a modified sense, this is true of England as well, although her reliance is placed upon the volunteer vigilance of the London Jewish Board of Guardians and Russo-Jewish Committee rather than upon the lax and meagre safeguards of British immigration laws.

But the two great Empires governed from Berlin and Vienna ask a very different question. They are already overcrowded and overburdened. There is not work enough now within their borders to keep in even relative comfort their own people. The utmost skill of their rulers is taxed to prevent vast war budgets from bankrupting the nation, and to repress the tendency of ill-paid or idle millions to revolt against their lot. To either of these great States the influx of any mass of poor people, seeking food and employment, would be a grave calamity—and this would be as true of Gentiles as of Jews.

The problem with which this whole Russo-Jewish question confronts the German and Austrian Empires is one which, in its ultimate working out, may profoundly affect the history of Europe. We have seen that Russia's action is twofold.

She drives all the foreign-born Jews out of her dominions. She roughly sweeps up all her native-born Jews and dumps them into the hundred or more towns of the Pale. That she should expel the aliens is, from her point of view, intelligible. But what earthly reason can there be for this strange policy of herding all her own Jews in the towns of these fifteen western provinces, where, in incredible squalor and helpless misery, they must eat each other or force their escape ? What conceivable commercial, social, or political end can be served by this course ? Is it merely the fantastic stupidity of barbarism ? Or is there deep method beneath the madness ?

Both in Austria and in Germany this massing of the unhappy Jews in the towns of the Pale is suspected to be a war measure of a unique and terrible character. When at last the great conflict comes, it is believed to be Russia's scheme to drive westward before her armies this whole Jewish population, making of it a moving *chevaux-de-frise* of flesh and blood, which the hosts of the Triple Alliance must cut through and dispose of before they can strike a blow at the advancing enemy.

Even if this hideous device proves impracticable, and the first shock of combat is on Russian soil, the conditions will not be much altered. The Jews, congregated in the towns along the whole frontier, will not less effectively serve as a barrier between the Russians and the invader.

It is enough, however, to have suggested this phase of the complicated subject. If there were no other reasons, it would sufficiently explain both the eagerness with which the authorities and the local Jewish communities of the German and Austrian border stations concert to pass all the refugees on as swiftly as possible to the west, and the sudden interest which the Prussian military authorities have taken in sharpening their watch upon the eastern frontier line.

The exodus has had six principal outlets. Of two of these—the departures by vessels from the Baltic ports, and from Odessa to the far south *via* Constantinople—little need be said. The former was never important. The latter has ceased to be so since Turkey was won over by Russia and France, and induced to close her frontier gates. There was a time when the solution of this great problem seemed to lie in the direction of Syria and Egypt, but the hopeless impracticability of dealing with the Turk, and the indisposition of the Jews themselves to go back into their worn-out Oriental cocoon, combined to dispel this idea. Of the four land routes, by far the most used is that which, traversing Northern Russia and Old Poland by Dünaburg and Wilna, enters East Prussia at Eydtkuhnen. The central section of the Pale and the district along the line from Moscow to Brest-Litowski sends its refugees through Warsaw to cross the frontier of the Vistula at Thorn.

The southern Pale and the whole section beyond
Kieff and Odessa is drained primarily by the
railway which crosses the Austrian frontier at
Podvolochesk, and to a lesser degree by the line
which enters Roumania at Ungheni.

With the partial exception of those travelling
by this last-mentioned route, the fugitives all
make their way toward Hamburg.

One of the unfortunate consequences of this
eagerness on the frontier, of which mention has
been made, to at all hazards keep the exodus
moving, is that very little inquiry is made there
as to the fitness of the people for emigration.
They are sent on to Berlin and Hamburg, where
the local committees must bear the responsibility
of detaining and sending back the worthless ones,
and of deciding what the others are good for and
where they are to go.

The scenes at the frontier stations are no less
touching and significant than those of the original
embarkation.  I have told how the exiles were
packed like sprats in the third-class cars, with
their wooden seats and fetid atmosphere.  By
the time they have reached the frontier—a journey
of from twenty to sixty hours it may be—weari-
ness, scant food and sleep, and the sense of friendless desolation have induced an air of half-
stupefied dejection.  They sit in silence, gazing
at nothing, with lack-lustre eyes which seem to
say again, "Sufferance is the badge of all our
tribe."

Mechanically, too, they obey the train officials who at the Russian terminus order them out of the cars. The men drag out the big hempen bags and boxes which they have had with them, and cluster about the baggage vans to watch for the appearance of their other chattels. The women and children huddle together on the platform, looking with furtive fright upon the strange new scene. At last all are passed through the station building and emerge at the other side upon another platform, where an empty train is drawn up. On these carriages are painted German words; the trainmen wear a novel uniform and have their trousers outside their boot-legs.

Then a curious thing happens. There are Russian soldiers, with a non-commissioned officer, stationed at every carriage door. Each male Jew must now show his passport bearing the police stamp of permission to leave the Empire, and explicitly stating the size and *personnel* of his family. He has had to spend money, and sometimes weeks of time, to secure this permission. If now there is any informality about it, or if the examining sergeant or gendarme chooses to sus-pect one, the Jew is roughly put to one side, perhaps to be detained at the local prison, perhaps to be sent back to the hole whence he was fleeing. At last all those who have a right to leave Russia have been got into the new train. It starts—and in five or ten minutes has passed the frontier.

On the German border this train goes unaccompanied by Russian officials. They used in earlier Bismarckian days to cross over upon German soil, and even swagger about the German Custom-house. A peremptory stop has been put to that, and along the whole extended Prussian frontier the Muscovites are now kept sharply in their place, and made to feel that they have neither friends nor well-wishers on the other side of the line. But on the Austrian and Roumanian frontiers they still assert, and are patiently conceded, the privilege of following the refugees into non-Russian territory, and standing by the while their baggage is opened and examined by the Customs officials.

A day and a night elapse before the slow train reaches Berlin : still another day and night are consumed in the journey to Hamburg. This will be the first German city they have seen, for they are not allowed to enter Berlin, but are conveyed around the outskirts of the capital by the Ringbahn to Ruhleben, and thence, after an hour's inspection and rest, sent westward.

The Jewish committee at Berlin, formed in June 1891 to receive and forward these exiles, has performed a humane and arduous task. Under its direction have been the various frontier committees—or *Sichtungskomitees* *—who are supposed to winnow the whole mass as it emerges from Russia, send back the undeserving, tabulate

* See Appendix C.

the remainder, and furnish Berlin and Hamburg with the necessary information. I say "supposed," because in practice this labour has been left to Hamburg. At the frontier and at Berlin the principal work has been in furnishing food and medicine, providing tickets for the penniless and arranging the transportation so that the resources of Hamburg may not be overtaxed at any one time. At Ruhleben some members of the committee are present whenever one of these Jewish refugee trains arrives. Every emigrant is given a cup of sweetened tea and a roll of *kosher* bread upon coming out of the carriage—the children getting milk instead of tea. On their departure—generally an hour or so later—each is given a bowl of pea-soup and more bread. A physician is also constantly in attendance. Much the same benevolence has previously been extended by the *Sichtungskomité* at Eydtkuhnen. These frontier committees also do succeed in detecting and stopping a large proportion of the Jews from Poland proper who try to smuggle themselves through as sufferers from the Pale beyond.

Pathetic stories were told me in Berlin of the terror and ignorance of the earlier refugees, who came shortly after the fierce Passover persecutions. The committee had arranged with the railroad authorities for the use of a disused tunnel in which to feed and examine the exiles during their halt at Ruhleben. The panic-stricken

S

wretches could with difficulty be brought to comprehend that at last they were among friends.
They were afraid to eat the food set before them
for fear it was not *kosher;* they fought against
giving up their tickets, to be exchanged for
others; especially were they terrified at being
compelled to enter the tunnel, which seemed to
them like another Russian prison. Some were
found who, at sight of this, suspected that they
had been brought to Siberia instead of Germany.
One woman, rather than go into the tunnel,
snatched up her two babes, and, screaming as she
ran, leaped upon the track before an advancing
train, and was rescued at great risk and by a
veritable hair's-breadth. The people who come
now are more tranquil, but still difficult to manage
often enough.

But Hamburg is the real place in which to
study the exodus. If I should seem to speak
with an excess of warmth upon this subject, let
me record in advance the feeling that I have
never in my life witnessed more genuine, unos-
tentatious, and intelligent philanthropy than I saw
at work here, and have never come into contact
with better, kindlier, more truly admirable men
than the Jews of the Hamburg committee.

Israel has always been an integral influential
element in this fine old *freie Stadt.* In Hamburg there has never been the vaguest dream of a
Judenhetze. When the anti-Semitic craze was at
its height in Berlin, Dr. Stœcker came to Ham-

burg to lecture. His audience pelted him off the platform, and he had to leave the town that same night. The Jews in the Republic of Hamburg number 20,000, or only 4 per cent. of the population. They constitute 10 per cent. of the membership of the Burgerschaft or Legislature, and furnish 20 per cent. of the graduates in the *Gymnasia* and other higher schools.

The old saying that "every country has the sort of Jews it deserves" passes a just eulogium upon Hamburg. In this proud, strong, broadminded, free city, where there has so long been one law and one code of courtesy for all races and creeds, the Hebrew community is a source of honour and of strength. It is more than ordinarily prosperous, devout without bigotry, and public-spirited in the highest degree.

The Hamburg committee embraces some scores of the foremost Hebrews in finance, commerce, and the professions. There are no honorary members, no drones. They all give personal attention to the work, and the division of this labour among the various sub-committees forms a piece of mechanism as exact and efficient as a Prussian regiment.

One of the most significant features of their work is the cordial assistance it has from the police and Stadt authorities. The two co-operate as if they were parts of a single body. Several of the buildings, including the men's bathhouse, used by the committee are the property of the city, and with the exception of one for which rent is paid, have been lent free of charge.

From the moment when the refugees land in one of the four Eastern stations of Hamburg, till the anchor is weighed on the vessel which is to bear them to a new continent, they are under the charge of the committee, and, if needful, are comfortably maintained at its expense.

After their reception at the station, the tickets given them at the frontier are examined, or new ones given them, and records made of all the names, and other particulars. They are then allotted to certain lodging-houses, with which contracts have been made. A complete bath is obligatory, and during this their clothes are disinfected. Such as need new garments—a very large majority—are supplied from the committee's warehouse. Besides the food at the lodging-houses, a generous midday meal is furnished at the Jewish soup kitchen. Small *Sichtungskomites* sit nightly, and pass upon every individual case of the thousands presented. Such help as is necessary is extended, and the applicant is sent to the point where his trade or previous work seems to give him the best chance of success. Generally from ten days to a fortnight elapse before he departs for his new home. Even on the voyage he is surrounded by the care of the Hamburg committee. There are stores of *kosher* meat and bread on the ship, and a Jewish kitchen, a *Schaumer*, and a doctor.

A volume would scarcely exhaust the curious sights which I came upon during my visits to Hamburg, and with which the hospitable town has been familiar since the spring of 1891.

The bath for the men—a public establishment on Bauerstrasse lent by the city—presented most whimsical spectacles. The men all received tickets for four baths—the first compulsory. One of the committee confessed with a rueful smile that the remaining three were not invariably used. It was evident enough that many of the poor devils had never been immersed in water before; none of them had the remotest idea of swimming. They hung back as long as they could, quaked their way in gingerly, and emerged from the tepid water gasping and shivering from fright. I was told that the women both needed and dreaded this ordeal even more than the men.

A whole floor of a big old building off the Alter Steinweg is devoted to the collection of clothing—cast-off or shop-worn—with which the rags from Russia are replaced. Here were great heaps of coats and trousers, still in their original shelf creases, contributed from remnants of stock by Jewish merchants, and other piles of garments collected from houses all over North Germany and Denmark. There were barrels full of hats, huge mounds of boots, some new, mostly old, and tables covered with underclothing, shirts, collars, and neckties. Many of these were elaborate and

expensive productions, which had simply gone
out of fashion, so when a Jewish mender of
umbrellas turns up at New York in a fancifully
embroidered dress shirt he need not necessarily
be suspected of bad faith. The committee-men
who were with me had great laughter over a
dress-coat which some kindly soul had contributed. I suggested that it might be useful
for a waiter. But it seems there are no Jewish
waiters.

A curtained screen across the big room shut
off the part devoted to clothing for women. Here
the pegs were laden with frocks of all sizes and
colours, with flaring decorations and wildly gay
patterns—relics of departed German fashions. I
was curious to know whether, if one of the
applicants fastened her heart upon some particular gown, she got it, or was put off with
something else. "Oh, yes," was the reply;
"we give her what she wants. Even Jewish
women, you know, must be humoured on the
dress question."

The mute record of many tears and saddened
homes lay on a table in the corner—a heap of
delicately made infants' clothes which had never
been worn. I saw two peasant women from
some unspeakable slum or other in the Pale look
at these wee garments of lace and ribbons, and
then look sadly at each other. They understood
the language of the little unused robes.

Most curious and droll were the metamorphoses effected in these clothing rooms. Grave, gaunt-eyed, bearded old men came out with jaunty white straw hats and the roundabout jackets of the dandies of 1884. A small boy, whose parents were the very lowliest I saw in face and demeanour and dress, got a costly sailor suit, much better than the German Emperor's children wear. One thick-nosed, bold-faced young man, who had been clothed afresh, came to us with a complaint that his hat did not correspond in quality with the rest of his outfit. It was rather a questionable hat, but his manner displeased my friends. "Do you want to pass, then, for a Baron in America?" one of them asked him.

The public dinner at 12.30 was spread in a room capable of seating about 130. In the three weeks preceding my first visit, in July, 5000 meals had been served here. There were a half-dozen members of the committee here each day, superintending the affair. When the thick pea-broth had been handed about, two of these committeemen stepped forward with bowls and tasted it. Then, as by a signal, the hungry people hastened to eat. They had been waiting for this proof that the soup was prepared in *kosher* fashion.

The virulent orthodoxy of these refugees, if I may so call it without offence, considerably complicates the task of looking after them in their

journey across Europe. They would rather not
eat at all than bite into any unsanctified morsel.
The very dishes in this soup kitchen which the
committee had started for their benefit, had to be
new. The *Schaumer*—a venerable, long-bearded
dignitary of the synagogue, something between
a beadle and a sexton, who presided in a black
skull-cap over the arrangements—had to give
them repeated assurances on this point. His
presence was a formal guarantee that everything
had been cooked according to the Jewish ritual.

The bread was all in small rolls, each of which
had pasted upon the crust a little paper *kosher*
label. In an adjoining room were barrels of
peas, of flour, and of sugar. I noted with curiosity
that these were all of the most expensive variety.
The prices in the books showed this, and it was
true of the other articles of food as well. Besides
the soup and bread, each person had one-third of
a pound of meat, with potatoes and greens.

There was no drink but water, of which they
drank tumblerfuls in quite the American way. I
commented upon this, saying that the costliness
of every other item forbade the theory that this
was for economy's sake, but, pointing out that
English paupers, or, for that matter, French and
German too, would get something besides water
to drink, even if their food was of the cheapest
and worst. " These people would not drink anything but water," was the reply. " We tried some

of the older and more feeble of them with beer at the outset, but it made them sick, and they begged off from having any more."

In this cookshop 14,128 meals were given during the month of July 1891, 23,579 in August, 13,682 in September, and 5676 in October. The falling off is ascribable in large measure to the rigorous religious fast-days of the early autumn, which rendered the Jews unwilling to travel or indulge in real meals. The greatest number of meals served on any one day was 1360 on August 4. The daily average for the entire period from the formation of the committee through to the beginning of winter was 530. Thus far in the year 1892 the average has been somewhat smaller, owing to the partial closing of the German frontier and the cholera outbreak.

I have not been able to secure exact figures from Hamburg concerning the exodus. In round numbers, about 75,000 refugees seem to have passed through that port since the 1st of June 1891. The committee reports having entirely provided for, alike in food, clothes, transportation, and some small start in life, 20,000 people. They have partially helped 30,000 more. Something like another 25,000 have come to Hamburg and gone away without asking for help or applying to the committee—and very possibly the number may be still larger.

In the matter of finance, the German Central

Committee has raised, including all sources of contribution, something over £100,000. There are objections to examining in detail the expenditure of this sum, and it moreover by no means covers the heavy individual outlay, to which almost the entire Hebrew community has been subjected. The Hamburg committee's books, for example, showed last autumn that they had received £27,000 from the General Committee, and had raised £11,000 more on their own account in Hamburg in addition. This fell, however, far short of representing what had been expended in that city alone upon the ceaseless stream of fugitives passing through. Several of the more important local committees have also been given permission to draw upon Baron Hirsch for current expenses, when their funds from other sources were exhausted for the time being. Hamburg, for instance, was last winter authorised to draw upon him, if needful, to the extent of £20,000.

The most valuable indication of the extent of the new exodus, and of its curious fluctuations, is afforded by the following figures, for which I am indebted to the courtesy of members of the Russo-Jewish committee at Berlin. They give by weeks the number of adult Hebrew emigrants received at Ruhleben and forwarded to Hamburg —the diminution during October being due to the fast-day observance already alluded to :

| Week ending— | | Week ending— | |
|---|---|---|---|
| July 10, 1891 | . 2,517 | January 2, 1892 . | 943 |
| July 17 . | . 2,796 | January 9 . . | 820 |
| July 24 . | . 3,452 | January 16 . . | 695 |
| August 1 . | . 2,675 | January 23 . . | 693 |
| August 8 . | . 2,700 | January 30 . . | 741 |
| August 15 . | . 1,812 | February 6 . . | 776 |
| August 22 . | . 2,700 | February 13 . | 894 |
| August 29 . | . 2,912 | February 20 . | 1,010 |
| September 5 | . 3,019 | February 27 . | 641 |
| September 12 | . 3,690 | March 5 . . | 560 |
| September 19 | . 3,355 | March 12 . . | 602 |
| September 26 | . 2,200 | March 19 . . | 798 |
| October 3 . | . 1,207 | March 26 . . | 652 |
| October 10 . | . 795 | April 2 . . | 264 |
| October 17 . | . 632 | April 9 . . | 66 |
| October 24 . | . 749 | To 23 . . . | 42 |
| October 31 . | . 686 | April 30 . . | 481 |
| November 7 | . 1,526 | May 7 . . . | 754 |
| November 14 | . 1,507 | May 14 . . | 1,154 |
| November 21 | . 1,437 | May 21 . . | 1,581 |
| November 28 | . 1,234 | To 31 . . . | 1,563 |
| December 5 | . 1,075 | | |
| December 12 | . 1,364 | Total, 47 weeks . | 63,861 |
| December 19 | . 1,023 . | | |
| December 26 | . 1,068 | | |

These figures take no account of children. Adding these, at the lowest estimate, would more than double the total given above. It is also quite within bounds to assume that, of the total number of Jews fleeing from Russia, not more than two-thirds pass through Berlin. Still further, no record is presented here of the considerable number of refugees who have been able to bear their own expenses, and have not troubled the committee. Some authorities estimate this class at one-fourth of the whole. It seems to me safer to call it one-fifth. Upon that basis we have then a total flight of approximately 205,000 souls in nine months. By the lowest estimate, the year ending in October of 1892 will have seen not less than 225,000 human beings driven from their homes, and the land of their birth.

It does not fall within the scheme of this work to trace the exodus beyond the converging point of Hamburg, whence it radiates again to every quarter of the globe. Years must elapse before judgment can be passed upon this new Israel out of bondage. The stupendous plan of Baron Hirsch, evolved by the wisdom of the chief men of the race, and endowed by his vast donation, is not yet fairly in operation, and can at best benefit but a fraction of this great host already dispossessed and expatriated. The minor colonies in the United States, founded partly from his bounty, partly by the philanthropic efforts of American Hebrews, have not thus far progressed beyond the experimental stage. The English-speaking communities all over the world—accustomed alike, whether in the huge human hives on the Thames and the Hudson, or the more open spaces of Australia, the Cape, California and Canada, to offer refuge to the oppressed and wretched of whatever race and tongue—hold the bulk of this prodigious foreign mass still undigested, unassimilated.

Those who are not prone to broadly hopeful views of humanity may without much trouble find warrant for both present discomfort and future apprehension in the character and dimensions of this latest invasion. Doubtless nothing that could be said here would ease the one or allay the other. But I trust that at least some service will have been done by the attempt to examine both the religious and the racial causes underlying this phenomenon of nineteenth-century history, and to become acquainted with the forces which, having been employed for generations to plunder, narrow, debase and demoralise the unhappy Russian Jew, expend themselves now in the final act of throwing him out, a penniless and helpless wastrel, for others to take care of.

The study has in the nature of things been one of sustained gloom—a picture in which the only lights fall from the torches of Cossacks on their midnight raids, or from the sinister candles burning in front of the modern Torquemada's *ikons*. The story of a whole people being insulted, degraded, and abused by system, denied the commonest of human rights by law, and at last stripped bare, torn from their homes and driven out of their country, could not well be made pleasant reading. Yet, now that it has been told, I find myself wondering whether the most pathetic and hopeless feature is not, after all, its disclosure of what the Russians themselves are like. The woe-begone outcast in cap and caftan, wandering forth dismayed into exile, will take heart again. His children's children may shape a nation's finance, or give law to a literature, or sway a Parliament. At the least, they will be abreast of their fellows ; they will be a living part of their generation ; they will be free men, fearing neither famine nor the knout.

The Russian marches the other way.

# APPENDICES

## A.

PETITION presented in Moscow, in May 1891, to the Czar by Israel Deyel, a corporal in the Veteran Reserve, and for the writing of which he was imprisoned.

*(Translated.)*

Most Serene, Mighty, and Exalted Sire and Emperor Alexander Alexandrovitch, Autocrat of all the Russias, Most gracious Father :

A most humble petition from reserved Jewish soldiers and under-officers living in Moscow :

May God hear, and may the Emperor have mercy !

We, most faithful subjects, reserved Jewish soldiers and under-officers, venture to lay at the feet of your Imperial Majesty our most humble petition not to extend to us the Law of 28th March of this year, touching the transportation of Jewish artisans from Moscow and the Government of Moscow, and not to subject us soldiers, both artisans and non-artisans, to removal from these places.

May it please your Imperial Majesty to have your most gracious attention drawn to the fact that the above-mentioned Law, subjecting thousands of poor Jews to utter ruin, must press with special harshness and injustice upon us soldiers, who have borne your Imperial Majesty's service, and who, at the first call of their country, must advance again to serve the Throne and Fatherland. Deign to note, moreover, that such a heavy and degrading restriction, depriving us of the right to

live where we best may throughout the Empire, does discredit
to the military calling and casts undeserved ignominy upon us,
many of whom, having had the honour to serve in the Sheor
regiments, have had the high privilege to wear the sign of the
Most Exalted Name of your Imperial Majesty, and the names
of personages of the Imperial family.  Many of us have had
the honour to receive, for zealous service, your Imperial
" Thank you ! "

The prohibition to us soldiers to live freely within the
borders of our Fatherland, for which we bound ourselves by
oath not to spare our lives, is deeply felt by all Jews and many
Christians to be a limitation gravely inconsistent with the
noble designation of soldier.    Military service opens to other
persons of all callings, and even to peasants, the possibility of
attaining reputation, rank and nobility.    To us Jews may it at
least give freedom to live at peace throughout the Empire, and
may it lift from us the ignominy of compulsory confinement
within the " Pale of Settlement "—where the driven-together
mass of Jewish inhabitants, separated from their more prosperous
and civilised co-religionists to whom the Law accords privileges
of free residence and rights of property, live in poverty,
ignorance and evil circumstance, the unavoidable results of
their calamitous condition.

A non-Jewish soldier, when going forth to fight and die for
his Fatherland, may find strength in the trust that the near
ones he leaves behind will be watched over by the community,
and receive the paternal care of the Government, and the
generous favour of the monarch.    But a Jewish soldier has to
face death for his Fatherland with the bitter consciousness
that she has separated him as an outcast from all her other
children, humiliated him, and by her laws has deprived him of
the means to decently exist himself, and to provide for the
family he leaves behind.

He can only pray to God that the authorities and the
Government may not ascribe the offences of individual Jewish
wrongdoers to a natural evil disposition in the whole nation ;
that they may not punish all other Jews indiscriminately
because of these few; and that the Judophobe newspapers

may not, with malicious design, poison the minds of the population against us, and move the authorities to bring us into disfavour with the Government.

This is our humble prayer: may our Fatherland render us justice, and your Imperial Majesty show his exalted grace, to the end that all reserved and retired Jewish soldiers and under-officers, whether they be artisans or not, may graciously be granted the right to live unreservedly throughout the Empire, and that those who have served in the ranks during their entire term may be accorded certain small other privileges, such as the right to trade, and to enter the service of private persons and of public institutions.

Thus may be fulfilled the saying: "A prayer to God and service to the Emperor is never in vain."

Reserved Under-Officer,<br>ISRAEL DEYEL.

MOSCOW, *May* 15, 1891.

---

## B.

THE St. Petersburg *Official Messenger* of so recent a date as August 22, 1892, published by authority a sweeping denial of all the statements hitherto made "regarding the alleged cruelties attending the expulsion of Jews from Russia. In particular, says the Reuter's despatch summarising this official utterance, the allegation that Jews were conveyed in chains from Moscow and St. Petersburg, and forced to travel on foot to their destination, and in some cases even transported to Siberia, is declared to be entirely without foundation. "In Russia," the official organ adds, "none but convicts are put in chains, and these even are not transported on foot." The journal concludes by emphatically declaring that no cruelties or acts of violence have been perpetrated against the Jews, and that all newspaper statements to the contrary are pure inventions.

In the face of this circumstantial, though strangely belated, denial, I reprint the list of 88 Jewish residents of Moscow who were marched publicly through the streets of that Holy City from the Central Forwarding Prison to the Smolenski, or

T

some other railway station, by what is known as the *étape*.
Every name has been verified by personal investigation, and is
vouched for by men of the highest respectability in Moscow.
The list only partially covers the Jewish representation in the
*étapes* of a few months in the spring and summer of 1891, and
of course indicates only an infinitesimal fraction of those thus

THE SMOLENSKI RAILWAY STATION, MOSCOW.

outraged throughout the Empire. The women, who are distinguished by italics, wore no chains ; the men all bore manacles
similar to those which are portrayed on the cover of this book.
Not one of them was a "convict," or charged with any crime
save that of race.

Opposite each name is the place to which that person was
sent. Those towns marked (*) are not in the Pale. That
means that one-fourth of these Jews were either twenty-five-
year veterans or were otherwise of the privileged classes permitted since 1865 to reside anywhere, and that, when removed

from Moscow during 1891, their domicile reverted to some other place where Jews are not allowed to reside, and from which they would also in time be chased. In three cases the same name occurs twice—where people ventured back to save some relic of their property or collect a debt, and were again expelled.

| Name | Sent to |
|---|---|
| 1. Israel Marfis | Wilna |
| 2. Itzko Aisik | Novgorod.* |
| 3. Movscha Perschin | Mstislavl. |
| 4. Schelma Berlin | Mohilef. |
| 5. Israel Schabak | Kronstadt.* |
| 6. Adam Schinavitch | Novgorondsk. |
| 7. Itzko Reiffmann | Grodno. |
| 8. Elia (Evsel) Grischmann | Podolsk,* |
| 9. El-Baer Liachtiger | Konsk. |
| 10. Moissei Bieloi | Toula.* |
| 11. Berka Bieloi | Toula.* |
| 12. Meyer Blechman | Egorievsk.* |
| 13. Chaia Benstein | Mohilef. |
| 14. Pessia Sverlova | Polotzk. |
| 15. Srul Berkovitch | Toula.* |
| 16. Iovel Grischmann | Podolsk.* |
| 17. Piness Leif Katzev | Mohilef. |
| 18. Bina Blovstein | Libau. |
| 19. Israil Yonte | Orscha. |
| 20. Peretz Leib Cohan | Goldingen. |
| 21. Mendel Epstein | Vitebsk. |
| 22. Rivka Krein | Telschi. |
| 23. Affraim Faimann | Pokrov.* |
| 24. Mendel Moros | Vitebsk. |
| 25. Wulf Bloch | Orschmiany. |
| 26. Leibh Eviossar | Vitebsk. |
| 27. Schlema Schneeweiss | Vitebsk. |
| 28. Sara Gutermann | Orscha. |
| 29. Biela Scherr | Wilna. |
| 30. David Kantor | Serponkhov.* |
| 31. Boruch Friedmann | Igumen. |
| 32. Jankel Volkovitcher | Mohilef. |
| 33. Raphael Raitzyn | Dünaburg. |
| 34. Morduch Chessin | Mstislavl. |
| 35. Selman Spetner | Borissov. |
| 36. Benjamin Moskin | Mstislavel. |
| 37. Selig Mirschovitch | Orscha. |
| 38. Leiba Poliakoff | Surans. |
| 39. Isidor Tager | Rieschitzy. |
| 40. Hirsch Rabkin | Vitebsk. |

| Name | Sent to |
|---|---|
| 41. Schmuel Aronovitch . . . . . . | Rossienny. |
| 42. Leiser Kravitsky . . . . . | Klin.* |
| 43. Jossel Kaplan . . . . . | Rossienny. |
| 44. Jossel Chenvkin . . . . . | Klimoffka.* |
| 45. Itzko Burdess . . . . . . | Wilna. |
| 46. Itzko Sterch . . . . . . | Tukum. |
| 47. Abraham Bernstein . . . . . | Troky. |
| 48. Srul Krivoschief . . . . . | Bobruisk. |
| 49. Faibisch Schur . . . . . . | Gorky. |
| 50. Berka Drisin . . . . . . | Dissna.* |
| 51. Bentzian Sliokin . . . . . | Kieff.* |
| 52. Bassia Riabkin . . . . . . | Mohilef. |
| 53. Faiva (her grandson of eight) . . . . | Mohilef. |
| 54. Jehiel Veitmann . . . . . | Bogoroditsk. |
| 55. Siska Bam . . . . . . | Polotzk. |
| 56. Itzko Rapaport . , . . . . | Egorievsk.* |
| 57. Ruvim Blankstein . . . . . | Vologda.* |
| 58. Schlioma Streltzin . . . . . | Mohilef. |
| 59. Jankel Itelson . . . . . . | Orscha. |
| 60. Salmon Goldberk . . . . . | Sienny. |
| 61. Jankel Fechtonbaum . . . . . | Kadin. |
| 62. Itzko Grünblatt . . . . . | Slutzk. |
| 63. Sachary Faveleff Starinsky . . . | Slutzk. |
| 64. Chaim Wolf Edelstein . . . . | Rossienny. |
| 65. Rivka Krein (twice) . . . . . | Telschi. |
| 66. Jankel Galkin . . . . . . | Podolsk.* |
| 67. Jossel Revsin . . . . . | Klimovitschky. |
| 68. Israel Rassner . . . . . . | Mohilef. |
| 69. Feiga Beresinova . . . . . | Mohilef. |
| 70. Wolf Shatzkess . . . . . . | Grodno. |
| 71. Elka Toffe . . . . . . | Dünaburg. |
| 72. Jossiff Schmuelovitch . . . . | Orel. |
| 73. Movscha Trotzky . . . . . | Wilna. |
| 74. Isaac Pschenitza . . . . . | Warsaw. |
| 75. Meyer Blechmann (twice) . . . . | Egorievsk.* |
| 76. Movscha Meyer Suria . . . . | Vilkomir. |
| 77. Evsel Grischmann (twice) . . . . | Podolsk.* |
| 78. Indel Movscha Roschkin . . . . | Slonim. |
| 79. Itzek Choloss . . . . . . | Rossienny. |
| 80. Mordka Geldenreitik . . . . | Orschmiany. |
| 81. Itzek Geiner Chanyss . . . . | Bratzlov. |
| 82. Itzko Zivkin . . . . . | Mstislavel. |
| 83. Elia Bernovitsch . . . . . | Toula.* |
| 84. Herman Zeilon . . . . . . | Warsaw. |
| 85. Abraham Blovstein . . . . . | Vologda.* |
| 86. Xenia Riva Drevlovska . . . . | Dorrogobousch. |
| 87. Irael Denell . . . . . . | Orschmiany. |
| 88. Elonor Zeilon . . . . , . . | Warsaw. |

## C.

THE visible head of the almost world-wide organisation for the reception, care, and distribution of the Russo-Jewish refugees, is the "*Deutsches Central-Komitee*" at Berlin, which, oddly enough, has its correspondence addressed to No. 40 Holy Ghost Street. This central body comprises some of the most eminent Hebrew citizens of the German capital, including Justizrath Meyer, Rechtsanwalt Breslauer, and Karl Emil Franzos.

The more detailed work throughout Germany is divided into three branches or departments—East Prussia, Upper Silesia, and the Seaboard.

The *Hauptgrenzkomité* of East Prussia has its headquarters at Königsberg, and consists of the chairman of the five provincial committees of Insterburg, Prostken, Memel, Eydtkuhnen and Tilsit, under the presidency of Rabbi Dr. Bamberger, of Königsberg. The most important of these minor bodies is the frontier or *Grenzkomité* of Königsberg, which comprises 100 men and women, and is split up into eleven sub-committees, covering "sifting," lodging, clothing, commissariat, transportation, forwarding, care for the rejected, medicine, legal points, changing of money, and advice to independent travellers. The five lesser frontier committees already mentioned represent some 80 workers, who, under general direction from Königsberg, receive the fugitives direct from Russian soil.

The *Oberschlesische Hilfscomitee* in Beuthen, a town 116 miles south-east of Breslau, and the centre of a network of railways leading from Southern Poland and Cracow, is presided over by Amtsgerichtsrath Levy, and has general supervision over the small frontier "sifting" committees at Myslowitz, Ratibor, Kattowitz, Lublinitz and Laurahütte. In association with these, but organised by the *Israelitischen Allianz* of Vienna, are the Austrian frontier *Sichtungs-Komitees* of Cracow, Podvolochesk, Oswiecim, Husiatyn and Czernowitz.

Infinitely the most important of the "*Komitees an den Hafenpläzen, etc.*," is the splendidly organised and effective

Hamburg Committee. There are minor bodies of the same sort at Bremèn, Stettin and Posen.

In addition to these committees engaged in actual daily contact with the great problem, there are 31 towns in Germany which have auxiliary committees formed to assist the Russian Jews.

The list would not be complete without mention of the powerful Jewish organisations in Vienna, Buda-Pesth, Paris, Antwerp, Brussels, Amsterdam, Copenhagen, Rome and Zurich, which co-operate cordially with the German central committee. London and New York, the former through its Anglo-Jewish Association, the Russo-Jewish Committee and the Committee of Deputies of the British Jews, the latter through its National Committee, the United Hebrew Association and the United Hebrew Charities, have the still more arduous and trying task of receiving this vast emigrant host after Europe has sent it forth, and finding a permanent place for it inside the pale of civilisation.

# INDEX

Her mind drifted to the image she had once had of him—Maximilian Hart, the powerful, ruthless, intimidating mover and shaker who always got what he wanted.

The master player. He'd moved her, shaken the whole foundation of her world, but what, in the end, did he want with her?

Right now, Chloe couldn't bring herself to care.

She loved being with him like this.

And she was going to revel in it as long as it lasted.

# Emma Darcy
## THE MASTER PLAYER

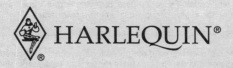

# HARLEQUIN®

TORONTO • NEW YORK • LONDON
AMSTERDAM • PARIS • SYDNEY • HAMBURG
STOCKHOLM • ATHENS • TOKYO • MILAN • MADRID
PRAGUE • WARSAW • BUDAPEST • AUCKLAND

Recycling programs
for this product may
not exist in your area.

ISBN-13: 978-0-373-23642-8

THE MASTER PLAYER

First North American Publication 2009.

Copyright © 2009 by Emma Darcy.

www.eHarlequin.com

**Printed in U.S.A.**

**All about the author...**
*Emma Darcy*

**EMMA DARCY** was born in Australia, and currently lives on a beautiful country property in New South Wales, she has moved from country to city to towns and back to country, sporadically indulging her love of tropical islands with numerous vacations.

Her ambition to be an actress was partly satisfied when she played in amateur theater productions, but ultimately fulfilled when she became a writer. Initially a teacher of French and English, she changed her career to computer programming before marriage and motherhood settled her into community life. Her creative urges were channeled into oil painting, pottery, and designing and overseeing the construction and decorating of two homes, all in the midst of keeping up with three lively sons and the very busy social life of her businessman husband.

A voracious reader, the step to writing her own books seemed a natural progression to Emma, and the challenge of creating wonderful stories was soon highly addictive. With her strong interest in people and relationships, Emma found the world of romance fiction a happy one.

Currently she has broadened her horizons and begun to write mainstream women's fiction. Other new directions include her most recent adventures of blissfully breezing around the Gulf of Mexico from Florida to Louisiana in a red convertible, and risking the perils of the tortuous road along the magnificent Amalfi Coast in Italy.

Her conviction that we must make all we can out of the life we are given keeps her striving to know more, be more and give more, and this is reflected in all her books.

I dedicate this book to all the readers who have traveled through my worlds and shared the smiles and the tears with me.

# CHAPTER ONE

HE watched her. The launch party for the new hit television show was packed with celebrities, many of the women more structurally beautiful than the one he watched, but to Maximilian Hart's mind, she outshone them all. There was a lovely simplicity about her that attracted both men and women, a natural quality that evoked the sense she would never play anyone false. The quintessential girl next door whom everyone liked and trusted, Max thought, plus the soft sensuality in her femininity that made every man want to go to bed with her.

There was nothing hard, nothing intimidating about the way she looked. Her blonde hair was in a soft short flyaway style that invariably seemed slightly ruffled, not sprayed into shape. There were dimples in her cheeks when she smiled. Her face had no sharp lines. Even her nose ended in a soft tilt. And her body was how a woman's should be—no bony shoulders, no sticklike arms, every part of her sweetly rounded and curved, not voluptuously so, not threatening to other women but very inviting to any man.

Though her eyes were the real key to her attraction, their luminous light blue colour somehow suggested that her soul was open for listening to and empathising with anything you wanted to tell her. Nothing guarded about those eyes. They drew you in, showing every emotion, transmitting an almost mesmerising vulnerability that stirred a man's protective instincts as well as the more basic ones.

The wide generous mouth was almost as expressive as the eyes, its soft mobility reflecting the same feelings from a grimace of sympathy to a scintillating smile of shared joy. She had the gift of projecting whatever you wanted from her and you believed she truly felt it, not an actress playing a part. It was a gift that could turn her into a huge star, and not just in the television show he'd bought and had rewritten to showcase what he'd seen in her.

Oddly enough, he wasn't sure she wanted to be one. Her domineering mother wanted it. Her ambitious script-writer husband wanted it. She did what *they* wanted, never raising any objection to it but there had been occasions when Max had glimpsed a lost look on her face—moments when she thought no-one was watching, when she wasn't required to be someone else's creation, when she was not *on show*.

She was on show tonight and the party people were flocking to her, wanting to share her spotlight, fascinated by her unique charisma whether they wanted to be or not. The crowd around her kept shifting, changing, forced to give way to others who wanted a piece of her if only for a little while. Although Max noted that those most closely connected to her life left her to shine alone.

It didn't surprise him. Neither her mother nor her husband enjoyed the role of background person, which they inevitably became if they attached themselves to her in public. He tore his gaze away from her to glance around, unsurprised when he spotted her mother schmoozing up to a group of television executives, increasing her network of contacts she could use. Max had disliked dealing with her. Unavoidable since she had appointed herself her daughter's agent. He kept any business meeting with her short and coldly rebuffed any attempt at a more personal connection with him.

Pushy, full of her own ego, Stephanie Rollins was the worst kind of stage-mother. Her vividly dyed carrot-red hair yelled *notice me, remember me,* even without its butch shortness, which accentuated her abrasive attitude of *I'm as good as any man and better than most*. Though there was nothing butch about her body, which she dressed with in-your-face sexiness; cleavage on show, tight skirts, extremely high heels to bring attention to her shapely legs.

Everything was used as a weapon in her fight to win her own way and there was nothing Max liked about her. Even the name she'd chosen for her daughter—Chloe—seemed deliberately artful, aimed at being remembered. Chloe Rollins. It rolled off the tongue, yet it always struck a false note with Max. It seemed too contrived for the person he saw in Chloe. Something simple would have suited her better.

Mary.

Mary Hart.

His mouth twitched with amusement at the fanciful addition of his own surname. Marriage had never appealed to him. He didn't want a wife. Sexual urges were satisfied with one woman or another and his butler and cook did everything else a wife could do. Besides, Chloe Rollins already had a husband and Max didn't believe in poaching other men's wives, not even for a casual affair. Having a messy private life had no more appeal than having a messy business life. Max stayed firmly in control of both.

He wondered what use her husband was making of this party and his gaze roved around the crowd, seeking the handsome charmer Chloe had married, Tony Lipton. *He* was well named. The guy was full of glib lip but Max didn't think much of his writing ability. None of the lines he came up with had any emotional punch. They invariably had to be edited, sharpened by other writers on the script-writing team for the show. Tony Lipton wouldn't be on the team at all but for his inclusion in the deal with Chloe.

Interesting…he was not currying attention. He was right off at the edge of the party crowd, half-turned away from it and having what looked like a very tense exchange with Chloe's personal assistant, Laura Farrell. Angry frustration on his face. Angry determination on hers. Tony grabbed her arm, fingers digging in with a viselike grip. She wrenched herself free of it and whirled away from him, her face set in seething resentment as she barged through the crowd, making a beeline for Chloe.

Max's instinct for trouble was instantly alerted. There were media people here. He did not subscribe to the view that any publicity—however bad—was good publicity. Any distraction from the success of the show was not welcome, particularly anything unpleasant centred on the star.

He moved, carving his own way through the crowd, but he was coming from the opposite side of the room—impossible to intercept Laura. She reached Chloe first, shoving past the cluster of people surrounding her, moving into a stance of close confrontation, her body language screaming fierce purpose, her hands curling around Chloe's shoulders as she leaned forward and whispered something venomous.

Definitely venomous.

The shock on Chloe's face—the totally stricken look—told Max this was big trouble. Fortunately he was only a few seconds behind Laura, close enough for his tall and powerfully built physique to shield that look from most of the nearby spectators.

'Get out of my way, Laura,' he commanded, the steely tone of his voice startling the woman into releasing Chloe and swinging around to face him.

He moved swiftly, cutting straight past her, curling an arm around Chloe's waist, scooping her close to his side, walking her away from the source of her distress, his head bent towards her, talking intently as though he had something important to impart, his free arm held out in a warding-off gesture that would deter anyone from interrupting the tête-à-tête.

'Don't make any fuss,' he dictated in a low

urgent voice. 'Just come with me and I'll take you to a safe place where we can deal with this problem in private.'

She didn't respond. She stared blankly ahead and walked like an automaton, carried forward by the force of his momentum. It was as if she had suddenly become a shell of a person with nothing going on inside. Max reasoned that whatever Laura had told her had to have been one hell of a shock to reduce her to this state.

His immediate aim was to protect her, protect his investment in her, and he did it as ruthlessly as he went after anything he targeted. He didn't care what her mother or her husband thought of his action. He steered her straight out of the Starlight Room—the premier function room in this five-star hotel—ignoring calls for his attention, quelling any pursuit of them with a forbidding look. No-one wanted to get on the wrong side of Australia's television baron. He had too much power to cross, and Max had no scruples about using it as it suited him.

He'd booked the penthouse suite for his convenience tonight. Wanting to enjoy his own private satisfaction in Chloe Rollins, he hadn't invited his current mistress to the party so there was no risk of any acrimonious scene if he took Chloe there. It provided a quick and effective escape for her.

He didn't bother asking for her consent. She wasn't hearing anything. Didn't seem to be aware of anything, either. There was no word or sign of protest from her as he led her into an elevator, rode up to the top floor, escorted her into his suite, locked the door behind them and saw her seated in a comfortable armchair.

She did not relax against the soft cushions. Max wasn't sure she even knew she was sitting down. He moved to the bar and poured a generous measure of brandy into one of the balloon glasses provided. He poured himself a Scotch, intent on appearing companionable rather than intimidating, when the brandy jolted her back to life.

She wasn't comfortable with him, never had been. He didn't set out to charm people and was probably too forceful a personality for her to easily like. But right now he was the man in charge and he wanted her to accept that situation, give him her trust, confide the problem and let him resolve it because clearly she was incapable of dealing with it herself and he needed his star actress to keep performing as only she could. Maximilian Hart did not take losses on any project he engineered.

'Drink this!'

A large balloon glass was shoved forcefully at

the hands lying listlessly in her lap. Her dulled mind registered that she had to take it or it would tip over and spill its contents. She wrapped both hands around it to hold it steady.

'Drink!'

The hard command rattled her into lifting the glass to her lips. She sipped and liquid fire seared her palate and burned a path down her throat. Heat scorched up her neck, flooded into her cheeks and zapped her brain out of its numbed state. Eyes filled with pained protest automatically targeted the man who had made this happen.

Maximilian Hart.

A shudder ran through her at the realisation that *he* was standing over her, the power that always emanated from him kicking into her heart and causing her stomach muscles to contract.

'That's better,' he said, satisfaction glinting in the dark eyes that shone with too much brilliant intelligence, invariably giving her the impression that nothing could be hidden from him. He'd seen it all, knew it all, and cared only for what advantage it could give him in the world he was master of.

It was a relief when he turned away from her, putting physical distance between them as he strolled over to the armchair facing hers on the other side of a sofa and a glass coffee table, which was placed to serve any occupants of the lounge suite. He sat down, folding his long, strong body into the chair, his elegant hands casually nursing a drink of his own.

He was a strikingly handsome man, though that was a totally inadequate description of him. The dark good looks—black hair, strongly chiselled face, deeply set brown eyes, tanned skin, perfectly sculptured mouth—added to his air of distinction, but it was the aura of indomitable power that gave him a charismatic impact, which made all the rest seem merely a fitting outer framework for the dynamic person who could take over anything and make it work.

Somehow it heightened his sexuality, almost to the point of mental and physical assault on everything that was female in Chloe. She wanted to recoil from it, yet could not switch off the magnetism he exerted, tugging out feelings she shouldn't have with this man. It was alarming to find herself alone with him.

Her gaze jerked around, taking in what was obviously an executive suite. With a king-size bed. Which instantly reminded her of the one Tony had insisted they buy for their bedroom.

Had he used it with Laura?

Is that where he'd so carelessly committed the worst betrayal of all?

'What did Laura Farrell tell you?'

The question pulled her gaze back to Maximilian Hart, forcing her to meet his riveting dark eyes—no escape from telling him the truth. She could feel the pressure of his will-power pounding on her mind and knew he wouldn't tolerate any evasion. Besides, it couldn't be covered up. Laura didn't want it covered up. And neither did she. No argument in the world could make her resume her marriage after this.

'She's been having an affair with my husband.' A double betrayal—a woman she'd trusted as a friend and the man who'd pretended to love her. 'She's pregnant...carrying his child.' The child Tony had denied her because this new television show was too big an opportunity to pass up. Her mouth wobbled at having to speak the final sickening words. 'He won't leave me for her because I'm...I'm his cash cow.'

She closed her eyes as bitter tears welled into them.

'He certainly won't want to leave you,' came the cynical comment. 'The critical question is... will you leave him?'

A huge anger erupted through her, cracking open a mountain of old wounds she had buried in getting on with the life her mother had pushed her into from infancy onwards, cutting off other options, leaving her no choice but to follow the path set down for her. Her marriage to Tony was part of that…the baby she'd been talked out of having. *No more, no more, no more,* screamed through her mind.

She dashed away the tears with the back of her hand and glared at the man who was querying her response to the situation. 'Yes,' she answered vehemently. 'I won't let you or Tony or my mother sweep this under the mat. I don't care if it hurts my image. I'll never take him back as my husband.'

'Fine!' he said with a casual gesture of dismissal. 'I just wanted to know how best to deal with the situation, given our abrupt departure from the Starlight Room.'

'I won't go back there, either,' she threw at him in full-blown rebellion. 'I don't want to see or talk to Tony or be anywhere near him. Nor do I want to listen to my mother.'

He regarded her thoughtfully for several moments, the powerful dark eyes probing, assessing, speculating, making her feel like a butterfly on a pin being minutely examined. She wrenched her gaze away from his and took a gulp of brandy, wanting its fire to burn away the humiliation of being nothing but a cash cow to the people who had brought her to this.

Maximilian Hart was no different, she savagely

told herself. He only cared about her because of the huge investment he'd made in the television show, redesigning it as a vehicle for what he perceived as her special talent. Whatever *that* was. Though she was grateful to him for getting her out of the Starlight Room. She couldn't remember him doing it but he'd obviously observed the impact of Laura's revelation and acted to minimise its effect on the launch party.

*The show must go on.*

But not tonight.

Not for her.

'Since you don't wish to be reached by your very tenacious mother, nor your husband, who will undoubtedly be plotting how to dump this on Laura Farrell and make himself out to be the innocent victim of a woman deranged with jealousy…' He paused a moment watching for her reaction to that scenario.

Chloe was rattled by it.

'Which, I assure you, would be a lie,' he went on sardonically. 'I observed them in very intimate conversation together just prior to her assault on you. She was furious with him. The connection between them was not fantasy.'

'The baby would prove it anyway,' she muttered bitterly.

'Not if Laura is persuaded to have an abortion.'

Chloe looked at him in horror.

He shook his head. 'Not by me.'

Tony. And her mother. She knew without him telling her they would both see that as a way out of an unsavoury scandal, a way of smoothing everything over so she would keep going as they directed. Her head started to throb at the thought of all the arguments they would subject her to.

'I've got to get away from them. Got to…' She was barely aware of saying the words out loud. Her mind was desperately seeking some way of escape, but everything she had was tied up with Tony and her mother…her money, her home, her whole life.

'I can protect you, Chloe.'

Startled by a claim she had not been expecting, she stared at him in anguished confusion. The look of arrogant confidence on his face reminded her of how powerful he was. The dark eyes bored into hers with a relentless strength that set all her nerves twittering. Of course, Maximilian Hart could protect her if he wanted to. But what would that mean?

'You need to move to a safe refuge where the security is so tight no-one can reach you unless you want them to,' he said matter-of-factly. 'It's no problem to me to arrange that.'

A peaceful haven, sheer heaven, she thought,

though practical issues instantly raised difficulties. 'I'd have to go home to get my clothes.'

'No. Professional movers can pack and deliver them to you.'

'I don't even have my credit card with me.'

'I'll put a lawyer to work sorting out your financial situation. In the meantime I'll set up a bank account for you that will cover your needs until you're in charge of your own money.'

She winced. 'My mother will fight to keep control.'

'I doubt she has more weapons than I have,' he drawled, ruthless intent gleaming in the brilliant dark eyes.

He was right.

Her mother was no match for him.

Freedom shimmered in front of her.

'Trust me, Chloe. There is nothing I can't do to set you on an independent path. *If* that is what you want.'

Seductive words, pulling her his way. *Yes* teetered on the tip of her tongue. Only the sudden sharp sense that she'd be walking out of one form of possession straight into another held it back.

'Why would you do this for me?' The words tumbled out on a wave of fear—fear that he meant to mould her into what *he* wanted, and the promise of independence was the lure to trap her into something worse than she had known.

'I don't want any disruption to the delivery of this show, which has been—and is—a project I've planned for a very long time. You're the key player in it, Chloe. I need you functioning as only you can. If that means freeing you of every distressing influence, ensuring you won't be got at by people who'll cause you grief, I'll do it. Throw a blanket of security around you that no-one can break without your permission. All I ask in return is that you keep working on the show for as long as your contract runs.'

Protecting his investment.

It made sense.

Maximilian Hart was always linked to success, never failure.

This wasn't a personal thing to him. It was business. He simply didn't want her private life adversely affecting what he had put in place.

Her fears suddenly seemed ludicrous. Strangely enough, she felt a surge of confidence that she could do as he asked—keep playing her part in the show—if she didn't have to deal with her mother or Tony or Laura while she did it.

'I'll make them go away,' he said softly, somehow tapping straight into her thoughts. 'Just say the word, Chloe.'

Her battered mind started swimming with a vision of a white knight fighting all her dragons instead of a dangerous Svengali of a man planning to use her for some devious purpose of his own. It was more than seductive. It propelled her into accepting his offer without any further fretting over it.

'It *is* what I want,' spilled from her lips.

'Yes,' he said as though he'd known it all along and had only been waiting for her to confirm it. He rose from his chair with the air of a man relishing the sniff of battle. 'You'll be absolutely safe waiting for me here. You probably need to eat something. Order whatever you like from room service. Make yourself comfortable and relax, knowing you don't have to face harassment from any source tonight.'

'Where are you going?'

'Back to the Starlight Room.' He smiled a smile of intense private satisfaction. 'By the time I've finished there, I doubt anyone will have the desire to harass you about your decision.'

Her decision.

An independent decision.

She felt weirdly awed by it as she watched the man who'd made it so easily possible walk away to begin putting it into effect. Maximilian Hart. Who had the power to do whatever he set out to do. And he was about to use his power to free her from the life she'd wanted to escape from for as long as she could remember.

# CHAPTER TWO

'WHAT'S going on, Max?'

The question was shot at him the moment he re-entered the Starlight Room—it was Lisa Cox, the editor for the entertainment section in one of the major newspapers, sniffing a story that might have more sensational value than a report on a launch party and waiting to pounce on the major source for it. She was a sharp-faced woman with big curly hair, inquisitive eyes and a dangerous tongue.

'You whip out of here with Chloe, who looked like death,' she swiftly put in. 'You come back alone...'

'Chloe is resting,' he blandly stated.

'What's wrong with her?'

'The energy drain of the party, continually responding to people without pausing to eat or drink. I think she needed a fast sugar-hit,' he said with a frown of concern.

'Does she have diabetes?'

'I'm about to speak to her mother about Chloe's condition, if you'll excuse me.'

He stepped aside, his gaze already scanning the crowd for a carrot-red head.

'Is this going to be a problem for the show?' Lisa threw at him.

He returned a freezing-off smile. 'No. Someone needs to take better care of her. That's all. And I'll make sure it's done.'

Closure on that issue. No gossip to pursue.

Stephanie Rollins had moved to the far corner of the room, obviously involved in a heated discussion with Tony Lipton and Laura Farrell. They were unaware of his return, probably the only three people in the room who were since the crowd literally parted to make way for him as he took the most direct path to where they stood.

Laura Farrell was tall, model-slim, straight brown hair falling to her shoulder blades, wearing an elegant black dress, in keeping with her personal style of always appearing in good classic clothes. She had amber eyes—cat's eyes. Max had seen envy in them when she was looking at Chloe. Contempt, as well. As though Chloe was stupid and didn't deserve her status as a star.

It was a completely different story when Chloe

was looking at her—sweetly helpful, indulgently helpful, happy to do whatever was asked of her. The two-faced bitch had shown her true colours tonight. Max was looking forward to banishing her from Chloe's orbit.

Tony Lipton, as well, even more so, the smarmy con man riding his gravy train without any real caring for the woman who'd been carrying him. With his streaky blond hair and green eyes he could almost be a clone for Robert Redford in his prime, but his only talent was for looking good and talking himself up. The fall is coming, Max silently promised him as Tony caught sight of his approach, was visibly alarmed by it and quickly warned the others.

The two women sprang aside, automatically making room for him to join the group. Laura's face held a mixture of fear and belligerence. She had to know she'd dug her own grave as Chloe's personal assistant but she was going to fight to come out on top with a hefty slice of Chloe's wealth through Tony's mistake in getting her pregnant. No doubt she'd get long-term support out of his divorce settlement. The pregnancy would not have been a mistake on her part.

There was tight-lipped anger on Stephanie's face. She'd obviously been counting the cost of the inevitable fallout and didn't like the score.

She'd like it even less when he slapped her with Chloe's total disaffection from her domination.

The tension amongst the group was palpable, waiting for him to present them with a platform from which to push their hotly contesting barrows. Max wasn't about to give it to them in full view of interested spectators.

'No doubt you're all concerned about Chloe,' he said, barely keeping an acid sarcasm out of his voice. 'I've taken her to a private suite. I suggest you all accompany me out of here so the situation can be discussed in private. I urge you not to speak to anyone as we go. You won't like the consequences if you do.'

'You can't do anything to me,' Laura jeered defiantly.

'Shut your bloody mouth!' Tony sliced at her.

'Take my arm, Stephanie,' Max commanded, holding it out for public linkage to Chloe's mother.

No hesitation there.

Max shot a steely look at the gravy-train specialist. 'Follow us, Tony, and bring your woman with you.'

The perfect golden tan on his face didn't look so perfect stained with a guilty red flush, but Max didn't pause to take pleasure in the effect. He retraced his path across the room with

Stephanie Rollins in tow, his head bent to her in a pose of confidential conversation, murmuring a string of platitudes about the need to look after Chloe more carefully.

It only took a matter of minutes to have the three of them away from the party and in an elevator being whisked up to what they undoubtedly expected to be a showdown with Chloe. On the executive floor he led them to a door where a butler was standing, ready to let them in and hand over the pass card to Max, who had arranged for this second suite to be available on his way down from the one Chloe was now occupying.

They trooped in.

He closed the door.

Stephanie was the first to react. 'Where's Chloe?' she snapped, eyes suspicious of having been maneuvred into a place that held no advantage to her.

'Where she wants to be…out of reach from any of you,' he replied, sweeping all three of them with a look of icy contempt before addressing Stephanie. 'Since you hired Laura Farrell as Chloe's personal assistant, I suggest you now fire her. She will not be welcome anywhere near Chloe again. Is that understood, Stephanie?'

She nodded, too smart to argue against what he was telling her point-blank was unfixable.

'I wouldn't work for her again anyway,' Laura mumbled.

Max ignored her, targeting Tony next. 'You're fired from the script-writing team.'

'You can't do that. I've got a contract,' he spluttered.

'I'll buy it out. My lawyer will be in touch with you to settle. Consider the contract terminated as of now. I don't want you anywhere in the vicinity of Chloe when she's working on the show.'

'But…'

'Go quietly, Tony,' he advised, threat underlining every word as he added, 'I could have you blacklisted from the whole television industry.'

'For God's sake! I just made a mistake in my private life. It has nothing to do with my profession,' he protested.

'It's not private when it affects my business. Go quietly, Tony,' he repeated.

He shook his head in shattered disbelief that his dalliance with Laura Farrell would bring such fast and comprehensive reprisal—banished from the golden star circle, in danger of being completely exiled from celebrity stamping grounds, and without Chloe at his side he had no leverage to change what was being dealt out to him.

Satisfied that Tony was now fully aware of consequences, Max turned his attention back to

Chloe's mother. His strong inclination was to get rid of her altogether, but family bonds were tricky. Without consulting further with Chloe, he had to check himself on that front.

'I don't believe you've acted in your daughter's best interests, Stephanie, which you should have done both as her mother and her agent.'

'This is none of my doing,' she cried, one hand flying out in a cutting dismissal of Laura and Tony.

'You chose Laura and you allowed Tony to attach himself to Chloe's career. Bad judgement on both counts,' Max bored in relentlessly. 'You will meet with me at eleven o'clock tomorrow morning in my city office for a discussion on whether or not you will continue to be her agent.'

'That's between me and Chloe,' she vehemently argued.

'No. She has given me the power to act on her behalf and I shall, Stephanie. Believe me, I shall. You might want to bring a lawyer with you. Mine will certainly be there.'

'Let me talk to her,' came the swift demand, a flicker of fear behind the calculation in her eyes. 'We've got too much history for you to interfere like this.'

'Chloe does not want to listen to you,' Max stated unequivocally, pushing the position through with calm ruthlessness. 'I suggest you accept that your domination of your daughter is over and your best course is to move into damage control rather than try fighting me. I am a very formidable opponent, Stephanie.'

He left that threat hanging for several moments, letting it sink in before announcing, 'I will now leave you to return to the Starlight Room. None of you will be allowed back into it tonight. The butler will evict you from this suite in thirty minutes. A prompt exit from the hotel would be your wisest move.'

He turned his back on them, let himself out of the suite, gave the butler his instructions, then, not anticipating any pursuit from the group he'd left to contemplate their future, he took an elevator down to the function room floor and rejoined the party in the Starlight Room.

Lisa Cox caught hold of him and inquired, 'Chloe not returning?'

'No. She's been on a publicity treadmill this past week and needs a rest from it,' he said in casual dismissal. 'Why not chat to some of the other cast members, Lisa? I'm sure they'd all be happy to give you their view of the show.'

He smiled to wipe out the concern he'd displayed earlier and moved off to do some mixing with the cast himself, making his presence felt at the party for the next forty minutes, which was long enough to publicly distance himself from Chloe's absence and long enough for the unholy trio to have made their departure from the hotel.

Then excusing himself on the grounds of celebration fatigue, he made a show of retiring for the night, returned to the executive floor, checked that the second suite he'd acquired was empty, then continued on to the one where he'd left Chloe. Only a little over an hour had passed since she'd made her decision. If she'd developed cold feet about it, he'd have to convince her there was no going back. Actions had already been taken.

She belonged with him now.

The thought jolted him, carrying with it as it did an immense satisfaction. It was too strong, smacking of a possessiveness that was alien to him where women were concerned. In maintaining his own freedom he'd always respected their freedom to make their own choices, as well. But he did own Chloe Rollins in a professional sense, for the duration of her contract with him, and she was now free in a personal sense, giving him the opportunity to pursue his interest in her. That was what was giving him this extra buzz of excitement.

She was the most fascinating woman he'd ever met and she was no longer tied to her husband. He could take her, keep her with him, explore the woman she was inside and out, for as long as he wanted to.

Chloe had not moved from the armchair where Max had left her. A review of her life had been churning through her mind—the whole horrible hollowness of being more important to her mother as an image on a television screen than a person with real needs that were ignored or dismissed.

She'd fallen in love with Tony because he'd seemed to focus entirely on her, the woman, making her feel truly loved, caring about what she wanted. All pretence. No sooner were they married than he'd started allying himself with her mother, adding to the pressure to maintain the image on the screen, sugar-coating it by telling her how special she was.

She'd fallen out of love with him very quickly, disillusioned by how he manipulated their life together to his liking, not hers, but he'd been easier to live with than her mother so she'd done whatever he'd required of her to make the relationship harmonious enough, even to this last deal with Maximilian Hart—Tony angling to be part of the script-writing team, arguing that he could share the show with her, be on hand to look after her interests, ensure she had everything she wanted.

Lies.

All lies.

He'd spent more time with Laura than with her, bedding Laura, getting Laura pregnant, while still pretending to be a loving husband. Not that she'd believed it anymore. He loved her career, the contacts, the celebrity whirl. She was the vehicle for the life he wanted, the life her mother wanted.

The marriage had felt empty long before this. Which was why she'd wanted a baby. A baby's love would have been real and she would have loved it so much. So very much. A child of her own to do everything right for.

Chloe had kept sipping the brandy, liking the fire in her belly. It made her feel alive, made her feel more determined to take charge of her life once this contract with Maximilian Hart had been fulfilled. It felt good to have him on her side, knowing he would help her get through this huge change in her life. It made perfect sense that he didn't want her so encumbered by problems that she couldn't shine in his show. She understood that a man like him would want this project to fulfil the potential he'd envisaged. While it was true she was a key player in making that happen, Maximilian Hart was the master player, orchestrating whatever was needed to achieve the desired success.

A man like him…

The phrase had slid through her mind. She tried to analyse what it meant and all she could come up with was a sense of absolute control of himself and everything he did. Maximilian Hart exuded power. Was that what gave him the sexual magnetism that invariably rattled her? It probably rattled every woman who was subjected to his presence.

Chloe was totally unaware of time passing. Hearing the door to the suite being opened jolted her into leaping out of the armchair and turning to face the man who'd done whatever he'd done to ensure she was free of harassment. That was much easier to accept when he was not here. The moment Maximilian Hart came into view, her heart started skittering with nervous apprehension.

'It's all right,' he instantly assured her. 'You won't have to see any of them again unless you wish to.' His gaze dropped to the empty balloon glass she was still nursing in her hands, then quickly swung around the tables in the room. 'You haven't eaten?'

'No. I…' She flushed, remembering his instructions to order something from room service. 'I just didn't think of it.'

He smiled reassuringly. 'You don't have to if you don't want to, Chloe. I'm feeling somewhat peckish myself, so I'm going to order us club sand-wiches, which you can eat or not as you please.'

She watched him move to the writing desk, pick up the telephone, speak to room service. He added French fries to the order, then asked her, 'Tea, coffee or hot chocolate?'

'Hot chocolate. And tomato sauce.'

He raised a quizzical eyebrow.

'I like tomato sauce with French fries,' she explained, not caring if it sounded childish. She suddenly felt peckish, too, and wanted to enjoy the food he'd ordered.

His smile was one of satisfaction this time. Chloe wished his smiles would make him less daunting but they didn't. They gave her the sense he was one move ahead of her and they were designed to make her feel better about falling in with him. He was probably ten moves ahead of her. She needed to get her wits together and find out what he'd done on her behalf.

Having completed the room service order, he wrote something on the notepad beside the tele-phone. 'I've booked another suite for myself and stopped all calls to this one so you're assured of an uninterrupted night. When you're ready for break-fast tomorrow morning, call me on this num-ber—' he tapped the notepad '—and I'll join you to plot out the next steps that have to be taken. Okay?'

She nodded, relieved to know he wasn't thinking of spending the night with her. Not that she had worried about that in any sexual sense. It was a well-known fact he was currently connected to the model Shannah Lian, a gorgeous redhead who oozed class. While Shannah had not attended the party with him tonight, probably because of some other commitment, Chloe didn't connect the model's absence to any interest Maximilian Hart might have in herself.

This was business for him. However, he might have thought she shouldn't be left alone, and the simple truth was she couldn't relax in his presence. Her gaze drifted to the bed. It would be good to climb into it, knowing she was alone. A shudder of revulsion ran through her at the thought of Tony having sex with her after he'd been with Laura. Never again!

'Tony will not be connected to the show anymore, Chloe. I've fired him from the scriptwriting team. Laura Farrell will be gone, as well. They're both out of your professional life.'

Clearing the set for the show to go on, Chloe thought, but their banishment did give her a vengeful satisfaction. 'Good!' she said, swinging her gaze back to the man who'd used his power to free her from them in the workplace. 'Thank you.'

He strolled towards her, gesturing towards the armchair she had vacated. 'Room service will take a while and we need to talk about your mother.'

She sat down, seething with rebellion against anything her mother might have suggested to him, ready to fight any continuance of the control that had blighted her life. He took his time, settling in his armchair, the dark eyes observing her edginess, making her feel even more tense.

'Do you want to keep her as your agent?' he asked.

'No.' The word exploded from a mountain of resentments. A rush of doubts followed it. She had no idea of the legalities of the situation. 'Do I have to?'

He shook his head. 'I took the liberty of arranging a meeting with her tomorrow for the purpose of ending the business relationship between you.'

He'd already taken the initiative! Chloe stared at him in awed silence.

He made an offhand gesture. 'You still have the choice.'

'I don't want her in charge of anything to do with me anymore,' Chloe said vehemently.

He nodded. 'My lawyer will sort it out for you.'

Just like that! She shook her head in amazement, scarcely able to believe that the shackles of a lifetime could be broken so easily. 'My mother will fight against it. What did she say when you arranged this meeting?'

He shrugged. 'She wanted to speak to you, which I would not allow.'

'I don't want to listen to her.'

'I did pass that on,' he said dryly, totally unruffled by whatever arguments had been thrown at him.

Of course he wasn't emotionally involved, Chloe reasoned. To him it was a clear-cut business issue of ending an agent/actor contract and settling the financial fallout.

'Do I have to be at the meeting tomorrow?' she asked anxiously.

'Do you want to be?' He didn't seem to be the least bit concerned about it, again leaving the choice up to her.

'No.' She could well imagine the harangue she would be subjected to—the long list of all her mother had done for her. Except it wasn't for her. It had never been for her.

'Are you frightened your mother will persuade you to keep her on as your agent?' he asked curiously.

'No. I just don't want to listen to her. If you can work it without me…'

'It will undoubtedly go more smoothly without

you. I'll have my lawyer join us for breakfast in the morning. You can give him your instructions and he'll act on them.'

'I think that would be best.'

Another decision made—by herself, for herself.

'Yes,' he agreed, rising from his chair. 'If you'll excuse me, Chloe, I'll call him now. Will eight o'clock suit?'

'Yes, but…' She looked down at her blue silk party dress. 'I have only these clothes.'

'A bathrobe will be fine for breakfast,' he assured her. 'I'll arrange for clothes to be brought to you from the hotel boutiques when they open. Don't worry about appearances. The big picture is more important.'

The big picture…one *she* was drawing, not her mother or Tony or even Maximilian Hart, who was giving her choices, not making decisions for her. She watched him move away, taking out his mobile phone to make the call to his lawyer. Somehow his power didn't feel quite so intimidating anymore. He was using it on her behalf—the white knight slaying her dragons.

She couldn't help liking him for it.

# CHAPTER THREE

STEPHANIE ROLLINS did not bring a lawyer to the meeting. She walked into Max's office wearing power clothes—purple dress, wide red belt, red high heels, red fingernails—with the overweening confidence of a woman who had always held sway over her daughter and didn't believe that was about to change. Not even the presence of his lawyer shook her, not visibly. She viewed them both with a haughty disdain, as though Max was merely following through on his word, putting on a show.

The assumption was implicit that whatever Chloe had said to him last night, she would have backtracked on it this morning. There would be too big a void in her life without her mother. She wouldn't be able to cope on her own, had no-one else to turn to now that Tony Lipton had committed the unforgivable, destroying his credibility.

Max greeted her with cold courtesy, introduced her to Angus Hilliard, who headed his legal department, saw her seated and returned to his own chair behind the executive desk. 'As it turns out, there is no need for any discussion, Stephanie,' he said, gesturing for Angus to hand her the document severing her services as Chloe's agent.

She took it, read it, raised derisive eyes. 'This isn't worth the paper it's written on. Chloe will come back to me once she's calmed down. If you hadn't interfered last night, given your support…'

'Which she will continue to have.'

'Oh, I'm sure you'll look after what you perceive as *her* interests for the duration of her contract with you. It serves *your* interests. But after that…'

'I can steer Chloe to a reputable agent who will not take the exorbitant percentage of her earnings that you do,' Max slid in, his dislike of this woman so intense he intended to completely sabotage her influence over Chloe.

Anger spurted into her eyes. 'Without me she would be nothing. Chloe knows that. I engineered every step of her career, had her trained to be capable of carrying off any role, chose what would be the best showcase for her, pushed her into becoming the star you are now exploiting.'

'Yours is not the face that lights up the screen,' Max stated cuttingly. 'You didn't train you daughter to do that. It's a natural gift, which you have exploited for your own gain. In actual fact, you are nothing without her.'

Max enjoyed ramming that home, seeing the furious frustration in her eyes.

'You think you've got the upper hand?' she threw at him defiantly, rising to her feet and tossing the legal notice of separation on the desk. 'When your contract with Chloe is up, I'll see that she never signs another one with you.'

He eyeballed her with all the ruthless power at his command. 'Don't count on it, Stephanie. I'd advise you to use what you've milked out of your daughter to get a life of your own.'

She stared back, blazing fury gradually giving way to speculative calculation. 'Why are you doing this? Why are you making it so personal?'

He shrugged and relaxed back in his chair, a sardonic smile playing on his lips. 'In this instance, the role of crusader for justice appeals to me.'

Her eyes narrowed. 'Or have you got the hots for Chloe? Seizing the moment?'

That shot was too close to the bone to ignore. He produced a mocking look. 'I am somewhat occupied with Shannah Lian, who, I doubt, would take kindly to that suggestion. Whatever my reputation with women, Stephanie, I'm not known for playing with two at the same time.'

'Whatever your interest is in Chloe, you'll

move on. You always do,' she retorted, her chin lifting belligerently. 'And once you lose your interest in her, she'll come back to me.'

*Never*, Max thought with such violent feeling it surprised him. He watched Stephanie Rollins sail out of his office on her triumphant exit line, silently vowing she would not triumph. The door was slammed shut behind her to punctuate her power and Max instantly started planning to negate it.

'Phew! I'd hate to be in that woman's clutches,' Angus commented.

Max swivelled his chair to face the end of the desk where his lawyer was seated. Angus Hilliard was in his forties; bald, bespectacled and in the habit of hiding his incisive brain behind a mild manner. 'The trick is not to give those long red fingernails anything to draw blood from. She's had her pound of flesh, Angus.'

'That's for sure.' Behind the rimless glasses the lawyer's grey eyes glittered with the urge to act. 'From what Chloe told us over breakfast about everything she'd earned as a minor, I could probably get her mother for fraudulent appropriation of…'

'No. We don't dig up the past,' Max said firmly. 'Better for Chloe to close the door on that victimisation rather than relive it in court. I'm not sure she'd be up for it. Focusing on what she can do with the future is a far more positive step. And to give her the chance to take it, we have to stop her mother from getting to her.'

'Needs a bodyguard,' Angus suggested. 'Want me to arrange it?'

'Yes. Make it someone she'll feel comfortable with, a fatherly type, an experienced guy in his fifties. Have him come to my Vaucluse residence this afternoon for an interview with me.'

'Will do.' His mouth curved into a bemused little smile. 'I've never seen you as a crusader for justice, Max, but I have to admit…there's something about Chloe Rollins. Makes you want to do things for her.'

Her bodyguard would feel it, too, which was why Max didn't want some attractive young hunk tuning himself in to her needs. He needed time to re-organise his affairs, time for Chloe to like having him in her life, and he wasn't about to allow an attachment to develop with anyone else. He had to keep her on hold until he was ready to move.

'A rather special something,' he agreed, rising from his chair, smiling as he added, 'And it's no big deal for me to rescue and protect her. A small but satisfying challenge.'

Angus laughed. 'That's the Max I know. Very satisfying, winning against the monster mother. You're going back to the hotel now?'

'Yes. You'll tie up all the ends with Tony Lipton's contract?'

'With knots that can't be untied.'

Max nodded. 'Thanks for your help, Angus.'

He left, assured he hadn't shown his hand to anyone where Chloe Rollins was concerned. Nor would he until the time was right. A secret pleasure…the spice of anticipation…Max knew he would enjoy both as he waited.

Chloe could not relax. Her mind kept whirling around the idea of an independent life. It had shamed her this morning, revealing to Max and his lawyer how impossible it had been for her to strike out on her own. At eighteen, when she'd wanted to break free of her mother's demands on her, the money that was supposed to have been put in a trust account over the years of her childhood and adolescence was simply not there.

Her mother had been in control of all her earnings and had used them as she'd seen fit; buying a home for them, spending it on whatever she'd decided was right for Chloe's career, and right for her own as an agent to be reckoned with. With no funds and no training for anything else, her dream of independence had crumbled. She'd resigned herself to working as her mother directed, though insisting her financial share of any contract go straight into a bank account that only she could draw on.

She didn't actually dislike the work. Having constructed dream worlds for herself ever since she was a child, it was easy to slip into whatever role a director wanted her to play, but sometimes she yearned for a real life—one where there was no pretence involved, no putting on a show, no expectation of her beyond being herself.

Without her mother and Tony constantly pushing her into whatever limelight could be arranged, she could make her own choices, as she had been doing since Maximilian Hart had stepped in and given her that freedom. The thought of his meeting with her mother this morning made her shudder. Being there would have been awful. She was glad he had given her the option of letting him handle it. But learning how to handle things herself from now on was a necessary step to complete independence.

The telephone rang.

It had to be him.

The hotel people had been instructed not to put any other caller through to this suite.

She hurried to the writing desk and snatched up the receiver, her heart pounding with apprehension over what had occurred with her mother. 'Yes?' spilled anxiously from her lips.

'All done here,' came the calm reply. 'Your mother has been legally notified that she is no longer your agent. I'm on my way back to the hotel. Did you find something you liked amongst the selection of clothes sent up from the boutiques?'

So many questions were flooding her mind, it was difficult to focus on his enquiry. 'Oh…oh, yes I did, thank you. The salespeople took the rest back. I've jotted down the prices of what I chose to keep so I can repay you when I have access to my bank account.'

'No problem,' he said dismissively. 'I take it you're now happily dressed and ready to appear in public.'

Panic hit. 'How public?' Were there reporters ready to pounce outside the hotel, firing questions about Laura and Tony?

'Only lunch at the hotel, Chloe,' he assured her. 'I've booked a table for us at the Galaxy Restaurant. You'll be quite safe there in my company.'

Safe and hopefully more relaxed with him in a public restaurant, Chloe thought in relief. Alone with him in this private suite made her feel tense and nervous, too aware of her vulnerability to his powerful magnetism. 'Okay,' she said quickly. 'How did the meeting go?'

'We'll talk about it over lunch. Should be with you in half an hour. 'Bye now.'

Half an hour…

She put the receiver down and walked into the luxurious ensuite bathroom to check her appearance. The decor of this hotel—The Southern Cross—was all done in white, silver and shades of blue, which Chloe found very attractive. Blue was her favourite colour and she'd been instantly drawn to the blue-and-white polka dot dress, which she was now wearing.

It was a lovely soft silk in a wraparound style, with a wide white leather belt fastened with studs, which were covered by a large leather button. She'd chosen white toe-peeper high heels to go with it, and a plain white clutch bag, which was also fastened with a button. To her it was a smart, classy outfit that would come in handy for many occasions and was well suited for lunch in the premier restaurant of this hotel.

She'd carried a mini hairbrush and a few make-up essentials in her evening bag last night, so had been able to look reasonably presentable at breakfast this morning. She refreshed her lipstick, gave her hair a few flicks with the brush and decided no-one would find anything to criticise about her appearance. Especially not her mother, who wouldn't be there.

That thought lightened Chloe's spirits as she wandered back to the living area of the executive suite. This was a new day for her, and for the first time she noticed it was a beautiful day outside. The hotel was situated along the walkway to the Sydney Opera House and the floor-to-ceiling windows overlooked Circular Quay, as well as giving a magnificent view of the great coathanger harbour bridge. The sky was a cloudless blue, the water was sparkling and Chloe idly watched the ferries gliding into the quay and out again.

Her pulse rate instantly quickened when she heard the door to the suite being opened. There seemed to be nothing she could do to counter or defend against the strong impact of Maximilian Hart. He strode into the living area and stopped dead at seeing her standing in front of the long windows. The wild thought came to her that she had made some kind of surprising impact on him. Which was probably absurd, but for a few moments of stillness, there seemed to be an electricity in the air, zapping between them, vibrating along every nerve in her body.

'Mary…'

The name fell so softly from his lips, Chloe wondered if she'd heard correctly. 'I beg your pardon?'

He shook his head, a bemused little smile curving his mouth. 'You reminded me of someone.'

A woman he'd cared about? Chloe would have

liked to ask about her, the momentary softness from him strongly piquing her curiosity, but almost instantly he shrugged it off and was the powerful man in charge again, walking purposefully towards her.

'Nice dress,' he said. 'It suits you.'

She flushed at the compliment though there was really nothing to it, only a bit of warm approval, and he didn't linger on it, moving straight to business as he handed her a sheet of paper.

'This needs your signature. It gives permission to the removalist company to enter your apartment at Randwick, pack up all your personal possessions and transport them to the guest house on my property at Vaucluse. I'll have it faxed to them once you've signed and they can get the job done this afternoon.'

It was all said in a matter-of-fact tone. Chloe took the sheet of paper, stared at it, tried to swallow the shock of the refuge he was offering. She wanted her things out of the apartment, needed a place to put them, but for it to be so closely connected to this man felt...dangerous. She hadn't thought ahead, didn't have an alternative plan to offer, yet....

'There must be apartments to let.' She raised anxious eyes to his. 'I don't feel comfortable about...'

'I can't guarantee your security anywhere else, Chloe.' The dark eyes mocked her fear of him. 'You won't be living with me. The guest house is quite separate to the main residence. The important issue is protection against any harassment, and not only from your mother or Tony. Once this scandal breaks, the media will go into a feeding frenzy, which means the paparazzi dogging your every move. You will be completely protected on my property. Consider it a pro tem arrangement, while you think about how best to handle your future.'

Yes, she did need time to make a proper plan—one she could and would stick to—and knowing all too well the tenacity of her mother, the point about protection against harassment was very appealing. Tony, too, might try to change her mind. Besides, how would she escape the inevitable outcome of all this with reporters chasing her and paparazzi shoving cameras in her face if she was trying to manage on her own? There was so much threatening her bid for freedom and Max was holding out safety from all of it.

She heaved a sigh to relieve the tightness in her chest. It didn't help. Another disturbing thought struck. 'There could be talk about us if I do this. I mean…with me leaving Tony…being with you…'

He looked sardonically amused by the intimation they could be lovers. 'I'll make it perfectly clear you're my guest, Chloe. I'm simply looking after the star of my show while she's dealing with a traumatic episode in her life.'

Heat surged into her cheeks again. It had been absurd of her to feel any danger in going with him. He wasn't about to use or abuse her. Besides, he was attached to another woman.

'Shannah Lian might not like it,' she blurted out.

He shrugged. 'I can take care of my own business, Chloe.'

Of course he could. Take care of hers, too. She felt foolish for even questioning the situation when he had already taken all aspects of it into account. 'Do you have a pen?' she asked, deciding her best course was to accept his offer.

He handed her one. She moved over to the coffee table, signed the permission note, then passed the pen and paper back to him with a smile of gratitude. 'It's very good of you to do all this for me.'

His smile smacked of deep, personal satisfaction. 'I'm a mover and shaker by nature. It pleases me to be of service to you.'

The white knight…except his eyes were dark and simmering with a pleasure that suddenly felt very sexual to Chloe. Her heart skipped a beat.

Shockingly, her vaginal muscles clenched. It took an act of will to ignore this totally unwelcome physical arousal and divert her mind to something else.

'After you'd gone this morning I looked through the newspaper,' she babbled. 'I thought there might be some mention of the…the scandal. When you went back to the Starlight Room, didn't anyone say anything?'

'I made sure the story didn't break last night. I didn't think you were up to handling a hounding by the media and you're too exposed to it here in the hotel.'

Caring for her…

That was even more seductive than his physical magnetism. It was terribly difficult to keep any defences up against how he affected her.

'The story won't remain hidden,' he went on. 'Someone will talk. I simply bought enough time to set up a secure environment where no-one can gain access to you without your permission.'

She shook her head over how much care he had taken. It was extraordinary. But then *he* was extraordinary. The master player in action on her behalf.

'Thank you,' she said huskily, finding it difficult to even speak in a normal voice. She swallowed hard to work some moisture down her throat and ruefully added, 'Despite what you tell people, it will cause gossip, you know, with me leaving Tony and staying at your place.'

He looked at her consideringly. 'Will that worry you?'

She thought about it for several moments before answering, 'No. It will probably lessen the humiliation of the scandal, do my pride good being linked to you.' An ironic little smile accompanied the plain truth. 'You're a bigger fish than Tony.'

He laughed, his brilliant dark eyes lighting up with twinkles of amusement. 'Let me know if you get the urge to fry me.'

'Not much chance of that,' she swiftly retorted, heat racing into her cheeks again. 'You've never been caught.'

'Nor likely to be. I think most people would call me a shark.' He cocked a challenging eyebrow at her. 'You could try casting a net around me.'

It struck her that was precisely what *he* was doing, casting a net of security around her with ruthless efficiency. 'I don't have your power.'

'Not mine, but you do have power, Chloe,' he said on a more serious note. 'A different kind. It tugs at people. Even me.'

The self-mocking glint in his eyes told her that

the white knight role was out of character for him. His true nature *was* that of a shark, always on the hunt, going after whatever attracted him, taking however many bites he wanted out of it, then cruising off, looking for other appealing prey to satisfy him. There wasn't a net that could hold this man. She'd always thought him intimidating, dangerous, powerful, and that impression was still very much in force.

However, it gave her a weird little thrill to know she tugged at something in him, too. Her mind shied away from the thought it was sexual. She was still married and he had Shannah Lian. It was probably more an arousal of sympathy that he didn't usually feel. Anyway, it made her feel less of an image he liked on the screen and more of a person he cared about.

'Well, whatever I have that tugs at you, I'm very grateful for it,' she said. 'You've provided me with an escape I couldn't have managed myself.'

'I hope it leads to a happier future.' He smiled, holding out his arm for her to take. 'Let's go and enjoy lunch.'

She grabbed her clutch bag from the coffee table and linked her arm to his, determined not to worry about his motives for helping her. 'What about the fax to the removalist company?' she reminded him, wanting her personal belongings out of the Randwick apartment and in her own possession as soon as possible.

'I'll hand it to the executive butler on this floor before we go down to the restaurant, instruct him to have it sent immediately.'

Chloe felt giddy with the thought that separation from her mother and Tony was being cemented in less than a day and she hadn't even had to face any fights over it. She hugged the arm of the man who had done this for her as they walked out of the hotel suite together, thinking how lucky she was to have a shark on her side, patrolling the waters around her, keeping bad things away.

Her whole body tingled at being in such close physical contact with him but it wasn't a tingle of fear or alarm, more one of excitement, pleasure in being attached to the power that had affected her freedom. She was acutely aware of the muscular strength of his arm, the whole male strength of him appealing to her female instincts, stirring a wish that he could always be at her side.

Which was totally unrealistic.

And weak, Chloe sternly told herself.

She had to learn to be strong on her own.

But right now, it felt amazingly good to be with Maximilian Hart.

# CHAPTER FOUR

HILL House—a simple name for what was almost a historical mansion at Vaucluse. It had been built by Arthur Hill, an Australian shipping magnate who'd made a fortune early in the last century, and it had been lived in by his descendants until the last member of his family had died three years ago. There'd been a lot of publicity about it when it was put up for auction—photographs in magazines, a potted history of the Hill family, proceeds of the sale to go to various charities. Maximilian Hart had outbid everyone else for it.

At the time, it was generally assumed he'd bought it as another investment, which he'd sell when the market would give him a huge profit. After all, why would a jet-setting bachelor want to live in a mansion? Penthouse apartments would be more his style. Yet so far he had kept it and lived in it.

Maybe it was the privacy that appealed to him,

Chloe thought, looking at the high brick wall enclosing the property as Max operated a remote control device that opened the huge iron gates facing them. They swung apart and he drove his black Audi coupe into the driveway to the house, pressing more buttons on the device to relock the gates.

While she had been quite relaxed over lunch in the hotel restaurant, sitting beside him in his car on the way to an indefinite stay on his property had made her feel nervous again. So much proximity with Maximilian Hart was a rather daunting prospect. His kind and generous consideration of her needs could not be faulted, yet her instincts kept sensing an undertow that was pulling her into dangerous waters with him, especially when they were alone together.

The man was sexual dynamite. He stirred feelings and thoughts that were terribly inappropriate. As the gates clicked shut behind them, closing out the rest of Sydney—her mother, Tony and anyone else who might hassle her—Chloe could only hope the guest house Max had offered her was not somehow full of his powerful charisma…like his car.

The driveway was paved with grey stones. It bisected perfectly manicured green lawns. Some spectacular trees had been planted artistically along the wall and towards the side of the house—like a lovely frame for the house itself. There were no gardens to distract the eye from it.

The three-storey redbrick mansion was quite stunning in its beautiful symmetry. The wings at either end featured white gables. The main entrance in the middle also had a white gable held up by Doric columns. The long white many-paned windows on the second storey were perfectly aligned with the attic windows protruding from the grey roof. On the ground floor there were rows of matching glass doors that surely flooded the rooms behind them with sunlight.

Chloe instantly fell in love with Hill House. If she could have afforded to buy it she would have without hesitation. Envy and curiosity drove her to ask, 'Why did you buy this place, Max?'

He flicked her a sharp glance, making a swift assessment of her reaction to the house, then smiled to himself as he answered, 'It called to me.'

His words surprised her, yet she completely understood the feeling behind them. 'You don't intend to sell it then?'

'Never.'

The need to know more about him prompted her to ask, 'Why does it call to you?'

'Everything about it pleases me. It welcomes me home every time I come through the gates.'

The deep satisfaction in his voice vibrated through her mind, stirring the memory of an article written about his rise from rags to riches. He'd been brought up by a single mother who'd died of a drug overdose when he was sixteen. Where he'd lived with her and under what conditions was not mentioned, but Chloe thought it likely he'd never had a sense of home in those early formative years.

'It's beautiful,' she murmured appreciatively. 'I can feel what you mean about welcoming. It makes you want to be drawn into it.'

'And stay there,' he said dryly. 'I virtually inherited the butler, the cook and the gardener from Miss Elizabeth, the last member of the Hill family. Although they had bequests from her will and could have retired on what they were given, they didn't want to leave. It was home to them, too.'

It was a curious arrangement for a man who undoubtedly made his own choices. 'Are you glad you kept them on?'

'Yes. They belong here. In a strange kind of way, they've become family. The three E's.' He flashed her a grin. 'Edgar is the butler. His wife, Elaine, is the cook. Eric is the head gardener. They have their own live-in apartments on the top floor. Eric hires help as he needs it and both

Edgar and Elaine supervise the cleaners who come in. They run the place to such a standard of perfection I'd be a fool to hire anyone else.'

He parked the Audi in the wide stone-paved courtyard in front of the house, switched off the engine and turned to her. 'You'll be meeting Edgar in a moment. He likes to be very formal but you'll find him friendly. He'll show you to the guest house and give you a rundown on how everything works.'

It was a relief to know *he* would not be accompanying her there. She gave him a grateful smile. 'Thank you again for coming to my rescue.'

'No problem,' he answered dismissively.

Even as he escorted her to the gabled porch, the front door was opened by a tall, slightly portly man who held himself with straight-backed dignity. He was dressed in a black suit, grey-and-white striped shirt with white collar and cuffs and a grey silk tie. His hair was iron-grey, his eyes a light blue, his face surprisingly smooth for a man who looked to be about sixty. Possibly he didn't smile much, Chloe thought, preferring to carry an air of gravitas.

'Good afternoon, sir,' he intoned with a nod of respect.

'Edgar, this is Miss Chloe Rollins.'

She received a half-bow. 'A pleasure to welcome you to Hill House, Miss Rollins.'

'Thank you,' she replied, smiling warmly at him.

'I'll garage the car, then I'll be in the library, Edgar. Some business I have to do,' Max informed him. 'You'll take care of Miss Rollins?'

'Of course, sir.' He moved his arm in a slow gracious wave. 'If you'll accompany me, Miss Rollins, I'll escort you to the guest house.'

A wonderful butler, Chloe thought, as she fell into step beside him, walking down a wide hallway dominated by a magnificent staircase that curved up to a balcony on the second floor—wonderful for making an entrance to greet incoming guests. The floor and stairs were carpeted in jade green bordered by a pattern of gold scrolls. The walls were panelled in western red cedar, matching the banister. The effect was very rich but not ostentatiously so.

There were paintings on the walls—framed in gold and seemingly all of birds—but Chloe didn't have time for more than a glance at them. They bypassed the staircase and she realised the hallway bisected the mansion and they were walking towards a set of double doors at the end of it, the upper half of them pannelled in a gloriously colourful pattern of parrots in stained glass. Other doors on either side of them were closed and Chloe would have loved to know what kind of rooms were behind them but didn't feel free to ask, given that she wasn't a guest in the mansion.

Edgar ushered her outside to a stunning terrace running the length of the house. The other three sides of it were semi-enclosed by an arched white pergola held up by the same Doric columns supporting the gable over the front doors. In the centre of the terrace was a sparkling swimming pool.

Luxurious green vines grew over the pergola providing shade for sun-loungers and tables and chairs made of white iron lace, and pots of flowers provided vivid colour at the foot of every column. The terrace itself was paved with slate, which had streaks of blue and green in what was mostly grey. Beyond it and through the open arches was a spectacular view of the harbour.

'The guest house is situated on the next terrace,' Edgar informed her, leading the way around the pool to the far left-hand corner of the pergola. 'It used to be the children's house in the old days.'

'The children's house?' Chloe quizzed. 'Didn't they live in the mansion?'

'Oh, yes, but they played down here during the day, supervised by their nanny. It was convenient for giving them lunch and snacks, putting the little ones down for afternoon naps. Miss Elizabeth said they loved having a place of their own. She kept it just the way it was until she died, often coming down here to relive memories of happy times.'

'Is it still the same?' She wanted it to be, charmed by the idea of a children's play house.

Edgar actually allowed himself a benevolent little smile at her eagerness. 'Not quite, no, though Mr Hart did retain the cottage style when he had it refurbished. The old pot-belly stove, the doll house, the bookshelves and the games cupboards still remain in the living room, with the addition of a television set and a DVD player. However, the kitchenette and bathroom had to be modernised. I'm sure you'll find it very comfortable, Miss Rollins.'

She sighed, wishing she could have seen it—felt it—in its original state, yet understanding the need for some modern conveniences in a guest house.

A flight of stone steps led down to the playground terrace—lush green lawn edged by a thickly grown hedge. The house was at one end of it—red brick with white windows and doors, just like the mansion in miniature. As they descended the steps, Chloe saw there was another terrace below this one, ending in a rock wall, which obviously formed a breakwater against encroachment from the harbour. A wharf ran out from it and beside the wharf was a boathouse.

Neither of these levels had been visible from the pool terrace. Access to them was by flights of steps, as well as a rather steep driveway from top to bottom just inside the security wall on the left-hand side, mainly used, Chloe imagined, by Eric driving a mini-tractor carrying garden tools up and down.

Edgar unlocked the door to the guest house, handed her the key and with a rather grandiloquent gesture, waved her in. Chloe walked into a delightfully cosy living area, which ran the full width of the small house. To her left were two rockers and a sofa upholstered in rose-patterned chintz. A large bow window had a cushioned window seat where one could curl up and read or idly watch the traffic on the harbour. A thick cream mat covered the parquet floor in front of the pot-belly stove, perfect for lying on near the heat in winter. An entrancing doll house stood in one corner near the bow window, a television set in the other. Cupboards lined the bottom half of the wall next to the front door, bookshelves the upper half.

To her right was a country-style round table with six chairs, and behind it a kitchenette, also designed in a country style—varnished wood cupboards and a white sink, no stainless steel visible anywhere. Edgar showed her the pantry cupboard, saying, ' My wife, Elaine, has stocked it with the usual staples, but if there's something else you'd particularly like, just press the kitchen button on the telephone and ask her for it.'

He also opened the refrigerator, which was similarly stocked with staples plus a chicken casserole ready to slide into the oven for her dinner tonight. 'Please thank Elaine for me,' Chloe said gratefully. 'This is so good of her.'

Another small benevolent smile. 'Let me show you the rest of the house.'

There were two bedrooms and a bathroom in between. The old bath, Edgar told her, had been replaced by a shower stall to leave room enough for the addition of the washing machine and clothes dryer. What had once been designated the boys' room held two single beds. The girls' room held one—queen-size. All of them had beautiful patchwork quilts. Both rooms had wall-length storage cupboards, plenty of room to hold all her personal things, although Chloe didn't intend to unpack everything, just enough for her immediate needs.

Edgar checked his watch. 'It's just on a quarter past three o'clock now. The removalist company gave their estimated arrival time here at four-thirty. Eric, Mr Hart's gardener and handyman, will conduct the transport of boxes to you, Miss Rollins, help you open them and remove those you wish to unpack after they've been emptied. Others can remain stored in the boys' room. In the meantime, if there's anything else…?'

'No, thank you, Edgar. I'll enjoy myself exploring everything I have here.'

'You're very welcome, Miss Rollins,' he said and bowed himself out of the house.

Chloe made herself a cup of coffee, sipping it as she checked out the contents of the bookshelves. There was a stack of CDs providing a range of classical and popular music, several shelves of modern books—most she recognised as bestsellers in both fiction and non-fiction. However, her interest was mainly drawn by the old books; Dickens, Robert Louis Stevenson, Edgar Allan Poe, the whole series of *Anne of Green Gables* and *Pollyanna*, an ancient set of Encyclopedia Britannica, a book containing drawings of birds—not photographs—a history of ships, a guide for all sorts of fancy needlework.

Her imagination conjured up the nanny teaching the girls how to sew, the boys identifying birds from the book, scenes of a happy childhood she had never known but which leapt vividly into her mind. She felt a strong wave of empathy with Miss Elizabeth, sitting in this room, opening these books to leaf through them again, reliving her memories.

The cupboards held more old treasures; a slightly tattered but still intact game of Monopoly, boards for snakes and ladders with coloured discs and dice for playing and Chinese checkers with sets of pegs, a chess set made of marble, packs of cards, boxes of jigsaws from very simple to very challenging. Chloe decided to start one of them tonight. It would be much more fun than watching television.

She finished her coffee and moved on to the most entrancing piece from the past—the doll house. It was made of wood and was double-storeyed. Its roof was hinged so it could be lifted up to rearrange the rooms on the second floor— the bedrooms amazingly well-furnished, cup-boards, chairs, dressing-tables with mirrors, even little patchwork quilts on the beds. The bathroom had a miniature china tub with iron claw feet, a washstand, a tiny china toilet.

All the windows and doors could be opened and shut. The ground floor was just as amazing. A central hallway held a staircase to the upper floor. A fully fitted-out dining room and kitchen were situated on one side of it, on the other an ex-quisitely furnished sitting room and behind it a utility room with laundry tubs.

Chloe was sitting on the floor, one finger stroking the silk brocade on a miniature sofa, when a loud tapping startled her out of her enthralment with the little masterpiece. Her head jerked around. Her heart kicked as her gaze met the dark brilliant eyes of Maximilian Hart looking straight at her through the multi-paned glass door. A hot flush zoomed into her cheeks as she scrambled to her feet, feeling hopelessly disarmed at being caught out doing something so childish.

She worked hard at regathering her composure as she crossed the living room and managed a rueful little smile when she opened the door. 'I didn't have a doll's house when I was a little girl,' she said, shrugging away her absorption in it.

'Were you ever allowed to be a little girl, Chloe?' he asked with a flash of sympathy.

She grimaced. 'It wasn't an ordinary life. My mother...' Her voice trailed off, her mind instinctively shutting out thoughts of her mother.

'Mine wasn't ordinary, either,' he said with a touch of black irony, then with a quizzical look, asked, 'Do you have the sense of something very different in this children's house?'

'Yes. Yes, I do,' she answered eagerly. 'I love the feel of it, Max.'

He nodded, and there was something in his eyes—a recognition of all she had missed out on, perhaps an echo of his own lost boyhood. It tugged at her heart, making it flip into a faster beat. Then it was gone, replaced by an intensity of purpose, which left her floundering in an emotional morass.

'May I come in?'

Embarrassment increased the floundering. She'd left him standing on the doorstep instead of inviting him in. 'Of course. Please…' She quickly stepped back, giving him plenty of room to enter, every nerve in her body quivering from the magnetic force field he brought with him.

'Leave the door open,' he instructed. 'I just wanted a private word with you before introducing the bodyguard who's waiting outside.'

'Bodyguard!' Shock galvanised her attention.

'I've employed him to drive you to and fro from the set at Fox Studios, or anywhere else you wish to go. He'll stay close to you while ever you're away from this property, ensure you're not harassed by anyone. It's simply a safeguard, Chloe, nothing for you to worry about. You can dispense with his services later on, but I think to begin with, you'll feel more secure having him around.' He made an apologetic grimace. 'Unfortunately, I have other calls on my time and can't always be on hand to protect you.'

'No. I wouldn't expect it of you,' she swiftly

assured him, acutely conscious of the time he'd already spent on her.

'I'd like you to accept the bodyguard, if only to make me feel I've covered every contingency for avoiding problems you might be faced with. I do hate failure,' he said in a self-mocking tone.

Considering all he had done for her, Chloe felt it was impossible not to oblige him on this point, though she thought a bodyguard was excessive. 'All right. If you really think it's necessary,' she said uncertainly.

'I do.'

No uncertainty in his mind. He immediately walked back outside and beckoned to someone who must have been waiting at the foot of the stone steps. Chloe imagined some big, burly hunk of a man, like a bouncer at a nightclub. It was a relief to see almost a fatherly figure, conservatively dressed in a grey suit, his salt-and-pepper hair and the lines of experience on his face suggesting he was in his fifties. He was as tall as Max, broad-shouldered, barrel-chested, and Chloe had no doubt he had a strong enough physique to impose his will on others, but he didn't look like a bully-boy, more a mature man who wore a confident air of authority and the muscle to impose it if needed.

Max performed the introductions. 'Miss Chloe Rollins, Gerry Anderson.'

A strong hand briefly pressed the one she offered. 'At your service, Miss Rollins. I'm Gerry to everyone so please feel free to use the name,' he invited in a deep, pleasant voice.

'Thank you. I hope I'm no real trouble to you,' she said sincerely.

'I'll be taking care of any that comes your way, Miss Rollins,' he assured her, taking a slim mobile telephone from his coat pocket. 'I'll be here six o'clock Monday morning to take you to work. If you want to go out anywhere before then, contact me with this and we'll make arrangements.' He showed her his stored contact number, then gave her the phone, satisfied she knew how to work it.

It was Saturday afternoon. She would probably be busy unpacking most of Sunday and there was plenty of food here to keep her going. 'Thank you, but I won't be going anywhere tomorrow,' she said decisively.

'Keep it with you. I'm on call anytime, day and night.'

'Okay,' she agreed.

'Thank you, Gerry,' Max said in dismissal.

The older man raised a hand in salute to both of them and made a prompt exit, leaving Chloe alone with Max again. The dark eyes bored into hers, as though tunnelling a path to her heart, which instantly started a nervous pounding.

'Since you have a good feeling in this house, Chloe, I suggest you stay here until the current twelve episodes of the show have been completed. It will be easier for you, no disruptive tensions to interfere with your work, and I can house any guests I wish to invite in the mansion, so it will not present any problem to me.'

Two months living here…it was so seductive.

But two months in close proximity to him…

'Think about it,' he commanded in a soft, persuasive tone. 'I just want you to know you're welcome to stay.'

'Thank you,' she managed to say, hoping he couldn't see her inner turmoil.

'And please feel free to use the swimming pool at any time,' he went on with a smile that put flutters in her stomach. 'They've forecast a very hot day tomorrow.'

'Thank you,' she said again, and wondered if she sounded like a parrot mimicking words that really meant nothing.

'Relax, Chloe.' His eyes turned to a soothing chocolate velvet and he reached out and gently stroked her cheek. 'Be happy here.'

It was the lightest feather touch, yet it left a hot tingling that Chloe felt for several minutes after he was gone. She didn't accompany him to the door. He walked out himself while she stood in a mesmerised trance, her own hand automatically lifting to cover the highly sensitised cheek, whether to hold on to the feeling or make it go away, she didn't know.

What she did know with utter certainty was that Maximilian Hart affected her as no other man had…deeply…and while it frightened her, it also excited her, as though he was opening doors she wanted to go through…with him.

# CHAPTER FIVE

MAX occupied one of the sun-loungers under the eastern pergola, idly doing the Sudoku puzzles from one of the Sunday newspapers. From time to time he glanced to the far northern corner of the terrace, expecting Chloe to appear at the top of the flight of steps, coming to the pool for a swim. It was a hot morning, so hot that a storm would probably brew up this afternoon. The shade of the vines and the light breeze from the harbour made his waiting tolerable.

He'd done all the groundwork to achieve what he wanted. He was sure Chloe would accept his invitation to stay, just as he was sure of the sexual chemistry at work between them. Restraint had to be kept for a while. A delicate hand had to be played, no pushing too hard, too soon. Any sense of being dominated by him had to be avoided.

She'd had that with her mother and having made the break from Stephanie's overbearing control, she would shy from falling into a similar situation. He had to make her feel whatever she did from now on was her own choice, but he'd be leading her to wanting him every step of the way—wanting him as much as he wanted her.

The strength of his desire surprised him. It wasn't his usual style to get so involved with a woman. All his relationships in the past had revolved around having regular sex with women he liked—an urge he took pleasure in satisfying. He could have had it last night with Shannah. She'd invited him to even after he'd told her their affair was over—a final farewell in bed—yet he'd been totally disinterested in anything physical with her. She'd accepted his dry, goodbye kiss on the cheek with wry grace—still friends, despite his moving on.

Chloe had been on his mind. It had been difficult to even focus his attention on Shannah. Thoughts of what Chloe might be doing in the children's house kept intruding, plans for how best to draw *her* into sharing his bed.

Her husband was history but Max didn't feel right about storming her into an affair with him. She was too vulnerable right now. It would be like taking advantage of a wounded creature. He had to wait, but the mental force to keep his desire in check needed considerable bolstering when he looked up and saw her moving towards the pool.

She wore a simple turquoise maillot, cut high on the leg and with a low enough V-neckline to reveal the swell of her breasts. Every lovely feminine curve of her body was on display and he instantly felt a tightening in his groin. It took an act of will to relax again and simply watch her.

She was unaware of his presence. The glare of bright sunlight made him virtually invisible in the shade of the pergola. She dropped the towel she'd been carrying by the edge of the pool, removed her sandals and waded in via the steps, which ran its width at the shallow end. The water was solar-heated to a temperature that kept it refreshing without being chilly. She smiled her pleasure as she slowly lowered herself into it and made soft waves with her arms. Max found the dimples in her cheeks strangely endearing, childlike, and he smiled himself, feeling a wave of indulgence towards her.

She didn't break into a swim. She pushed off from the steps and glided, rolling her body over and over, wallowing in the water, floating, her wet hair drifting around her like a golden halo. He could have remained watching her for much longer, enjoying her uninhibited pleasure, but when she started swimming, splashing, the noise made his own silence questionable. He rose from the lounger and moved to his end of the pool ready to greet her when she reached it.

* * *

'Good morning.'

Chloe was so startled by the greeting, she almost lost her grip on the ledge, which formed a seat at the deep end. Her head jerked up. She'd thought there was no-one on the terrace, that she had the pool to herself, but it was Max's voice. Max was here. He stood barely a metre away, and her heart started hammering as her stunned mind registered the fantastic body of the man—naked but for a brief black swimming costume that left very little to the imagination.

He had the physique of an Olympic swimmer, broad shoulders and chest, strong arms, every male muscle impressively delineated, lean waist and hips, powerful thighs and calves, and his tanned skin gleamed as though it was polished. It was all so in her face, she couldn't find the breath to speak.

He smiled apologetically. 'Sorry to startle you. I was reading the newspapers under the pergola.' He waved to where he'd been sitting. 'When I heard you swimming, I thought I'd refresh myself, as well. Mind if I join you?'

'No. No, of course not,' she gabbled. It was his pool.

'Did you sleep well?'

'Yes. Like a baby.' She grimaced at the phrase,

reminded of the baby Laura would have, the baby she had been denied.

He saw the grimace and frowned. 'Everything all right for you in the guest house?'

'Perfect,' she assured him, smiling to wipe out his concern.

'Good!' He grinned. 'Let's swim.'

He dived into the pool, barely making a splash and broke surface almost halfway down it, moving straight into a classic crawl. Chloe hitched herself onto the underwater seat and watched him as he swam the length and back again, using the few minutes trying to stop her heart from racing and her mind from dwelling on the fact that Maximilian Hart left every other man for dead when it came to physical attraction.

Tony's physique was well-proportioned but it didn't have that much male power. Amazingly, her mind hadn't been churning over Tony and Laura since she'd been here. It was as though they had drifted off to a far distance and she was already immersed in an existence without them. Was it because Max put himself between her and them, blotting them out with his overwhelming presence, or was it the effect of the children's house, giving her such pleasant distraction?

Both had played their part.

She was safe from the others if she stayed here,

safe from horrible, hurtful arguments with Tony, safe from the pressure her mother would apply with every bit of emotional blackmail she could concoct.

But was she safe with a shark?

The thought popped into her mind as Max finished cutting through the water and hauled himself onto the seat beside her, his dark brilliant eyes teasing as he asked, 'Did I scare you off swimming?'

She laughed to hide the tension triggered by his nearness. 'No way could I keep up with you.'

'I'll go slow,' he promised.

'A very leisurely pace.'

'You've got it.'

She plunged into the water ahead of him, wanting the activity to calm her down, soothe her twitching nerve ends. Max wasn't coming onto her. He was just being himself. Besides, he had Shannah Lian. Of course she was safe with him.

They swam several lengths of the pool together. It was impossible not to be acutely aware of the man beside her, but Chloe managed to put the situation in enough perspective to feel reasonably comfortable with his company when she called a halt at the shallow end where she'd left her towel.

'Enough?' he asked.

'For now,' she answered, walking up the steps, so conscious of her own body under his gaze, she quickly snatched up her towel and wrapped it around her.

'I hate to put a dampener on the day, but I think you should see what Lisa Cox has written in the entertainment section of her Sunday newspaper,' he said as he followed her out of the pool.

She swung around in dismay. 'Is it bad?'

'Somewhat sensational,' he answered sardonically, waving towards the eastern pergola. 'Come and read it for yourself. I'll pour you a cool drink that might make it more palatable.'

She fell into step with him as he headed back to where he'd sat, anxiety and apprehension over-riding most of her awareness of his almost naked state. Nevertheless, when they reached the welcome shade of the pergola, she was relieved that he picked up a towel from one of the loungers and tucked it around his waist.

The newspapers were on a nearby table, which also held a tray with some long glasses and a cooler bag, obviously containing a pitcher of whatever liquid Max was going to serve her. He moved to the table, drew out one of the chairs for her, then tapped the top newspaper as he reached for the cooler bag.

'This one. Take a seat, Chloe.' He busied himself opening the bag and removing a large jug of fruit juice while he talked. 'Apparently Tony broke the story. Out of spite, I should think, after the removalists had left to transport your personal possessions here. He'd demanded what authority they had and they'd shown him the fax, giving this address.'

Maximilian Hart's mansion at Vaucluse…it was a big step up from the apartment at Randwick, while Tony was out in the cold, fired from the script-writing team, and powerless to stop what was happening. Chloe could see him wanting to do something spiteful, yet how could he exonerate his own behaviour?

'Lisa Cox telephoned me late yesterday afternoon to get confirmation of your presence on my property and my comment on it,' Max went on. 'She wanted to speak to you, as well, but I'd left you reasonably happy in the children's house and didn't think you'd want to be stirred up by nasty innuendos, so I told her you were unavailable.'

He poured the juice into two glasses and sat one in front of her, a flash of inquisitive appeal in his eyes. 'I hope you don't mind my running interference for you with Lisa.'

She shook her head. 'I'm sure you handled the situation better than I would have.'

He shrugged and took the chair opposite hers, the

expression in his eyes changing to a hard, ruthless gleam as he flatly stated, 'I told her the truth.' His mouth twisted cynically and his voice took on a mocking tone. 'Tony had reported that you'd left him for me, omitting the salient facts like his infidelity and impregnating your personal assistant. I laid them out and apparently your mother has confirmed them, while hitting out at me for taking you away when you should be with her, being comforted as only a mother can comfort in such stressful circumstances. She made no mention of having her services as your agent terminated.'

Chloe grimaced at his summary of Tony's and her mother's spin on what had happened. 'I'm sorry, Max. I did warn you there'd be a backlash to protecting me as you have.'

'Makes me more determined to keep doing so.' His eyes flashed intensity of purpose at her. 'You need a complete break from them, Chloe. Best that you stay here the two months, avoid all aggravation. As I said, it's no problem for me if you do, and it will hold you clear of them so you can work out your own future.'

He liked being in charge of a battle zone, Chloe thought. A born warrior. And she liked being protected by him. Probably too much. But she could learn how best to stand up for herself from him.

'I'd better read the whole thing,' she muttered,

opening up the newspaper and lifting out the entertainment section.

The story was headlined Maximilian Hart's Star Hit by Scandal. It held much more detail than Max had given; rantings from Tony about Max taking her over, using his power to alienate her from their marriage; her mother taking a similar stance, saying Max had inserted himself between mother and daughter with no regard for what was appropriate or what was in Chloe's best interests. They more or less painted him as a ruthless manipulator, which wasn't the truth at all.

Max had stated the truth—that she'd been deeply shocked and distressed by the disclosure at the launch party that her husband had been having an affair with her trusted personal assistant who was now pregnant to him, and she hadn't wanted to go home to either her husband or her mother, so he'd offered her his guest house as a ready refuge where she was welcome to stay as long as she liked. The story ended, saying Chloe Rollins had not been available for comment.

'You could sue them for slander over the things they've said about you,' she murmured fretfully.

'Irrelevant,' he said carelessly, then shot her an ironic smile. 'Much better not to give them a stage to star on. Let them fade into insignificance as the show moves on.'

Chloe returned some irony of her own. 'You know what the most sickening part is? Both my mother and Tony talked me out of having a baby because starring in your show was more important.'

His gaze dropped from hers as he frowned over this new information.

'I guess you wouldn't have wanted me if I had been pregnant,' she put to him, interpreting his frown as confirmation that her mother and Tony had been right about that.

He shook his head. 'Nothing would have changed my determination to star you in that particular vehicle.' His eyes targeted hers again with their riveting power. 'If you had been pregnant, Chloe, I would have had the storyline altered to accommodate it.'

'Really?'

His mouth twitched with amusement at her wide-eyed wonderment. 'Really.'

'Then they were wrong.' It was weird how much satisfaction that gave her, as though it totally vindicated her current course of action. 'Not that it matters,' she added. 'It would be a worse mess now if I had got pregnant, with Tony fooling around with Laura behind my back. And I bet my mother knew about it, too. Nothing escapes her eye.'

'I'd say that was a fair assumption,' Max dryly

commented. 'She showed no outrage or disgust over their behaviour when I confronted them at the hotel. Only anger over the boat being rocked.'

Anger… Chloe winced, having been belittled by it too many times. And she'd always hated the strident way her mother dealt with other people, even with the man sitting opposite her, making sure she saw and covered all the angles. It was an agent's job, but the manner in which it was done… Chloe imagined Max had quite enjoyed severing the business connection with her mother. It was a huge relief to feel free of it herself.

She sipped her drink, noticing that Max seemed to have drifted into a private reverie, gazing out across the pool, his eyes narrowed as though he was thinking through a problem, assessing its effects, how to deal with it. After a few minutes, he turned to her with a curious, inquisitive look.

'Tell me…you're only twenty-seven, Chloe… are you desperate for a baby?'

She flushed, embarrassed at having babbled on about having one, knowing many women waited until their early thirties before starting a family. 'Not desperate, no,' she quickly denied, then with a rueful little shrug, confessed, 'I just wanted to have something I knew was real in my life. My mother would twist things around. Tony did, too.

But a baby…well, there's nothing more honest about a baby, is there?'

'Honest,' he repeated musingly.

'I'm glad it didn't happen,' she blurted out. 'It would have chained me to Tony for the rest of my life.'

'Yes. At least this way you can put him behind you.'

She grimaced. 'Except for the divorce.'

'That can all be done through lawyers,' he said dismissively. 'There's no need for you to meet. I was just wondering if you had the urge to rush into bed with someone else and get yourself pregnant.'

It shocked her into a vehement denial. 'I'm not that stupid, Max!'

He shook his head. 'I don't think you're stupid, Chloe, but people often don't react sensibly to a traumatic change in their lives.'

'I have a big enough problem sorting out my own life,' she insisted. 'I wouldn't add a baby to it.'

He smiled, satisfied that she was not about to run madly off the rails and ruin this chance to get herself straight on a lot of things. Yet she sensed something more in his satisfaction—something sharkish. A little quiver ran down her spine.

'I'm hungry,' he said. 'It's lunch-time.'

Chloe breathed a sigh of relief. The something

sharkish had nothing to do with wanting a bite out of her.

He picked up a mobile phone, which had lain behind the tray. 'I'll call Edgar to bring it out here. Shall I say lunch for two? It won't be any trouble to Elaine. I ordered salad and she always keeps enough provisions for an army.'

The invitation was irresistible. Despite the occasionally disturbing undercurrent of strong physical attraction she couldn't quite ignore, she liked talking to him, liked hearing his view of her situation, liked the way it clarified things in her own mind. She didn't want to end this encounter by the pool. Besides, having eaten the scrumptious chicken casserole last night, the offer of another meal prepared by Elaine was an extra temptation.

'Thank you. I'd like that.'

Max watched her smile, the sweet curve of her lips, the dimples appearing in her cheeks, the warm pleasure sparkling in her lovely blue eyes, and thought how artlessly beautiful she was. She wore no make-up. Her hair was drying in natural waves around her face—tighter than if she'd used a blow dryer. Her skin glowed, not a blemish on it anywhere.

He wanted to touch her, taste her, but now was

not the time. He called Edgar and ordered lunch for two by the pool, knowing he had to keep this encounter a casual one, relaxing, enjoyable, trouble-free, building the case for her to stay the two months.

The baby issue had been a snag in his plans. It was a relief to have it dismissed. Though, for a few moments, that something special about Chloe had actually had him wondering how life would be if they filled the children's house together. A brief flight of fancy. Not really feasible, given the jet-setting life he enjoyed, winning the challenges that added to his success in the battlefield he'd chosen.

They spent another two hours by the pool, sharing a leisurely lunch, chatting about the tele-vision business. He kept the conversation imper-sonal—safe—drawing Chloe out on how she saw and felt about the show, her part in it, her view of the other cast members and how they were dealing with their roles.

'You know, Max, I don't have a special gift for tapping into emotion on cue,' she said at one point. 'It's not like some magic I was born with. When I get a part to play, I make up the whole life behind the character so I know everything about her in my mind, why she is doing or feeling the way she does in various situations. When I'm on camera, I am her. It's real. I show it. That's all.'

He respected the work she put into adopting a character, but she was wrong about not having a special gift. It was innate. The play of emotion was on her face all the time in her own life. He didn't have to study her to read her feelings. They were mirrored in her expressions.

He'd first noticed her in a coming-of-age soap opera that had run for years. She outshone everyone else in the cast. He'd learnt that she'd been on television all her life—commercials featuring a baby, then a toddler, children's shows, teenage shows. He kept her in mind, waiting to acquire a storyline that would showcase her special talent, and she certainly wasn't disappointing him now that he had it.

By all accounts, her father had also been a very gifted actor. There were still people around who deplored his early death—suicide, in the grip of depression. He couldn't imagine Stephanie doing anything to help him out of it, more like driving him into it with her self-serving demands.

He didn't want Chloe falling into a depression, unable to put it aside to play her part in the show—a very solid reason for her to be here with him, out of her mother's reach. She looked happy at the moment. Nevertheless, he couldn't control her mood when she was alone.

An idea came to him. She'd wanted a baby.

He'd give her a puppy or a kitten, something for her to look after and pet, another attraction for staying in the children's house and it should lessen any loneliness she felt.

As it turned out, he didn't need to add another attraction.

Edgar had been and gone with his tray-mobile, clearing the table and leaving them with coffee and a selection of Elaine's petit fours. It more or less marked the end of lunch and Max knew he shouldn't press Chloe into staying longer with him if she made a move to go. She finished her coffee and faced him with an air of decision.

'I will stay the two months, Max.'

She said a lot more, expressing her gratitude for his offer, etc, etc, but he barely heard it, his mind buzzing with elation.

He'd won.

And he'd win all he wanted with Chloe Rollins before she left the children's house.

She was his for the taking.

# CHAPTER SIX

CHLOE was glad she had accepted Gerry Anderson's services on Monday morning, glad that Max had instructed him to use the black Audi Quattro sedan with tinted windows for transporting her wherever she wanted to go. Paparazzi were camped outside the gates of the Vaucluse mansion. They were also at the entrance to the studios. Interest in the scandal was obviously running hot.

Once they were safely inside the grounds of the studio, she asked Gerry to stop the car and summon the security guard so she could speak to him. She rolled down her window as the man approached.

'Miss Rollins?' He tipped his cap to her.

She smiled. 'Good morning. I just wanted you to know that my mother, Stephanie Rollins, is no longer my agent and I would not welcome her on the set.'

He nodded. 'Mr Hart has already given instructions to that effect. Covers Mr Lipton and Miss Farrell, as well. Don't be worrying they'll be let in, Miss Rollins. They won't.'

'Thank you.'

'No problem,' he assured her with a friendly salute.

Max…one step ahead of her. He thought of everything. But at least she had acted decisively for herself this time and Chloe felt good about that. She was never going to allow anyone to make decisions for her again, or be talked into anything she didn't want to do.

The whole day on the set felt better without her mother sitting in on everything, watching, criticising, coaching, fussing. No-one there was unaware of her situation, and at first the other cast members and the crew treated her with a kind of wary sympathy. Only after she had demonstrated that she was still on top of her role and determined to carry through every scene to be shot did they become more relaxed with her. Chloe felt her own confidence growing as she followed the director's instructions without a hitch.

Sympathy gave way to curiosity. She wasn't acting like a traumatised woman. Had she left her unfaithful husband and plunged into an affair with Maximilian Hart? No-one put it into words but Chloe read the speculation in their eyes. Oddly enough, she wasn't embarrassed by it. While it wasn't the truth, she sensed that people wouldn't blame her for it if she had. In fact, during the break for lunch, there was envy in some of the women's eyes when one guy brashly asked her if Max's guest house matched his mansion.

'It's much smaller,' she answered dryly, and her quelling look put an immediate stop to any further questions touching on her private life. She didn't want to describe how special the children's house was, nor reveal her decision to stay on there for two months. It was no-one else's business but hers and Max's.

However, she inadvertantly broke the confidentiality of their arrangement later that afternoon. After leaving the studios, she asked Gerry to drive her to her favourite green-grocer's market at Kensington, wanting to stock up with fruit and vegetables and be relatively independent of Elaine's provisions for the guest house. Gerry insisted on accompanying her into the market, saying the car had been followed, although not into the parking station, which allowed some room for doubt as to whether the pursuit had been coincidental or deliberate.

Coincidental, Chloe thought. The tinted windows of the car had frustrated the paparazzi this morning. Why waste their time following her again? Max was the better target and she wasn't with him.

But it was deliberate.

Chloe had only been shopping for a few minutes when an all too familiar voice cracked at her like a whip with stinging force.

'It's a shameful state of affairs when a mother is reduced to chasing a car to make contact with her daughter!'

The lettuce she'd been holding spilled from her hand. Her heart jumped and so did the rest of her body as she spun to face the oncoming attack. Her mother was livid with anger, her steel-blue eyes shooting furious arrows of accusation, her hands already lifting like talons to grab Chloe's shoulders and shake her. The old instinct to cringe swept through her but this time Chloe fought it. She was not a child to be shaken into submission and her mother did not *own* her anymore. Her spine stiffened and she stood her ground, although her stomach cramped and her legs started to tremble.

Gerry Anderson stepped between them and her chest almost caved in with relief at being shielded by him.

'Get out of the way! She's my daughter!' her mother hissed, grabbing his arm, trying to pull him aside.

'Miss Rollins?' Gerry was looking to her for direction.

He would strong-arm her mother away and swiftly escort her out of here if she gave the word. The temptation to flee quivered through her mind, but she'd been weak for far too long, letting her mother run her life. Running away from her now meant she still had power over her, would always have power over her. It had to stop if she was ever to forge an independent life.

She shook her head. 'I'll talk to her but stay near, Gerry.' She turned to her mother, eyes flashing determination. 'If you create any more of a scene, my bodyguard will step in and we'll go. Is that clear, Mother?'

'*Your* bodyguard,' she savagely mocked as Gerry stepped aside for the two women to face each other. 'Max Hart's, you mean. He's taking you over, lock, stock and barrel and you're too blindly naive to see it.'

'He is simply protecting me from the kind of harassment you're dealing out right now.'

'And why is he doing it, Chloe? Have you asked yourself that?'

'I don't care why. I'm out of the mess of my

marriage, which you hid from me so I'd keep on working and bringing in the money. I'm not so blindly naive that I can't see that, Mother.'

'You've been working today to bring in the money for Max Hart.'

'*He* didn't deceive me.'

'It was for your own good,' she snapped defensively. 'The affair would have blown over without any pain for you if Laura hadn't got herself pregnant.'

'I don't like your judgement of what is good for me. I'm not going to take it anymore.'

'You need me, Chloe,' she bored in. 'You'll be lost without me. I've handled everything for you for so long...'

'I'll learn to do it myself.'

'You think that can be done in a day?' she jeered.

'No. I expect it will take a while.'

'Making a host of *bad* judgements. For a start, where do you intend to live?'

Chloe hesitated, not having thought that far yet.

'You can't stay in Max's guest house forever,' her mother pushed, mocking Chloe's indecision.

'No, of course not.'

Maybe her lack of any urgent concern over where to live gave the situation away.

Her mother pounced. 'He's invited you to stay on, hasn't he? How long?'

'This is none of your business!' Chloe retorted defensively.

'Longer than a few days. Longer than a week for you to think you don't need me. A month? Two months?' Speculation turned to triumphant certainty. 'Yes. Two months. Until shooting all the episodes for the show is over. That would suit him very nicely. And you're so gullible you got sucked right in.'

'It suits me, too,' Chloe hotly insisted, hating how her mother twisted everything.

Her claim was dismissed with a derisive snort. 'Out of the frying pan into the fire!'

'What's that supposed to mean?'

Her eyes glittered with contempt for Chloe's intelligence. 'Max Hart is worse than Tony, flitting from woman to woman. He's setting you up for when he gets rid of Shannah Lian. Which will be very soon. Mark my words! You won't have two months free of him. I'll bet the bank on that.'

Dangerous…the undertow of physical attraction…impossible to ignore yet she hated her mother's interpretation of the situation.

'You'll end up in a bigger mess than you have now,' she went on in her disparaging voice. 'You need me, Chloe. *I'm* the one who's always protected you. Max Hart is a shark. He'll eat you up and when you've satisfied his sexual appetite…'

'That's enough!' Chloe cried. 'I don't have to listen to this and I won't! Gerry...' She turned to him in urgent appeal. 'I want to go now.'

He immediately hooked one arm around hers, holding the other one out in a warding-off gesture. 'Excuse us, Mrs Rollins,' he said politely, starting to move Chloe along the shopping aisle towards the exit.

'When you know I'm right, come home to me,' her mother sliced at her. 'I'll look after you.'

Chloe maintained a stony face, looking straight ahead, refusing to acknowledge the claim that she couldn't look after herself.

She would.

As for the rest, Max wouldn't force her into anything she didn't want.

All along he had given her choices.

*Not* like her mother, who dictated what was to be done.

And *not* like Tony, who cheated on women, playing two at once.

At least she could be her own person with Max. She liked that. It was a positive step. She was never, never going to take the backward step of running home to her mother for help. For anything!

'Would you like me to drive you to another shopping mall?' Gerry asked as he saw her settled in the car.

She had forgotten the trolley containing the few pieces of fruit she had selected. They had walked out, leaving it standing in the aisle. 'Tomorrow afternoon,' she said, in too much emotional turmoil to think of food and knowing she could make do with what was available in the kitchenette. 'Let's go straight home, please, Gerry.'

He nodded and took the driver's seat without comment.

*Home*...tears pricked her eyes at that slip of the tongue. The children's house was not her home, yet it felt more like one than any of the places she'd lived in with her mother. Even the Randwick apartment that she and Tony had furnished had been more to his taste than hers— wanting to please him. He'd probably insist on keeping it as part of the divorce settlement. Chloe decided she didn't care. Sometime in the next two months she would find a place of her own and please herself with the furnishings.

It was difficult to keep blinking away the tears. Her chest was tight with them. Max had made it possible for her to put the past with her mother at a distance since Friday night, but meeting her face to face...she felt both physically and mentally drained by the effort of standing up to her, standing up for herself. She had run away from the confrontation in the end, with the help of the bodyguard Max had had the foresight to hire. Would she have managed otherwise?

She wasn't sure. The old sense of helplessness had welled up in her although she'd fought it as hard as she could. It wasn't easy to shed a lifetime of being dominated, being told what to do and torn up emotionally if she resisted, giving in because she couldn't bear the many manifestations of her mother's anger. She needed the refuge Max had given her, needed the time to build up her own strength of purpose. Yet was her mother right? Did Max have a personal as well as a professional motive for helping her? Was she hopelessly gullible? What was the truth?

The tears spilled over. She tried desperately to mop them up and regain some composure as they arrived at Max's mansion. Gerry opened the passenger door for her and she kept her head down while alighting from the car. 'Thank you,' she choked out, swallowing hard before adding, 'I'll see you in the morning, Gerry.'

'Have a good night, Miss Rollins,' he replied.

'You, too,' she mumbled and bolted for the children's house, wanting its cosy comfort to embrace her and close out all the horrid feelings aroused by the meeting with her mother.

* * *

Max felt his jaw tightening with anger as he listened to Gerry Anderson's report. Stephanie Rollins was obviously going to be relentless in her drive to get her cash-cow daughter back in her clutches. She was a shrewd operator, sowing doubts, fears and seeds of suspicion in Chloe's mind—everything possible to undermine trust in him. It was good that Chloe had defied her, but at what cost?

'The mother's a very nasty piece of work,' Gerry summed up. 'I'd say there's been physical as well as mental abuse in their relationship. I'm not into hitting women but I sure wanted to thump that one.'

'While I sympathise with the urge, be warned that she'd sue you for assault and manipulate the situation her way,' Max advised.

'Miss Rollins...' He shook his head. 'Something about her gets to me. You did good to rescue her from that woman.'

Doubts about his motives had been seeded in the bodyguard's mind, too. Max read them in the eyes scanning his, asking if he was going to be good for Chloe Rollins in the long run. Which was none of Gerry Anderson's business, and he knew it, so it wasn't put into words. But he cared—that *something* about Chloe would inspire it in most men—and the caring made him say,

'She was crying in the car. Don't know if there's anything you can do about it....'

'I can provide a distraction,' Max said with a reassuring smile. 'You may well be looking after a puppy at the studios tomorrow whenever Miss Rollins is required on set.'

The bodyguard's concern was swallowed up by a wide grin. 'No problem, Mr Hart. Got a dog of my own. Always liked them.'

The report over, they both stood and shook hands. The bodyguard made his exit from the library. Max sat back down on the chair behind his desk and thought about where he was going with Chloe Rollins. There was no question in his mind that he'd done her a good service by separating her from her mother. But would he be good for her in the long run?

He'd never asked that question of himself in his pursuit of other women. They'd always known the score with him and he hadn't ever felt responsible for the choice they made. But Chloe was different. She was very, very vulnerable. He had to take that into account or he might find it difficult to live with himself afterwards.

Chloe cringed at the knock on her door. She'd cleaned up her tear-blotched face, had a long, hot shower to ease the tension in her body, wrapped herself in the silk kimono she favoured for lounging around after working all day, and was curled up on the window seat in the living room, trying to empty her mind by watching the traffic on the harbour. She didn't want to see or talk to anyone, didn't want to think.

The knock was repeated.

Several times.

Becoming more insistent.

It forced her to realise that whoever it was probably knew she was home and would be concerned if she didn't appear. With a reluctant sigh, she uncurled herself, swung her feet onto the floor and headed for the door. Eric's weather-beaten face was almost pressed against one of the glass panes, relief replacing worry when he caught sight of her approach.

Chloe made a rueful grimace, indicating she wasn't dressed for receiving visitors, though she didn't mind speaking to the kindly old handyman who'd helped her move in here, opening and disposing of the boxes brought by the removalist. He was in his seventies, wiry in build and still surprisingly strong, his skin deeply tanned from working outdoors, though he always wore a cap to protect his bald head from getting sunburnt.

He smiled encouragingly at her, showing the yellowed teeth that had been discoloured from too

many years of pipe-smoking. He was carrying a
basket, loaded with bags—probably something
he wanted to deliver to her. It wasn't until she was
almost at the door that she saw he wasn't alone.
A few paces behind him stood the unmistakable
figure of Max Hart, his back turned to her, his
head slightly bent as though he was studying the
lawn.

Her heart instantly leapt into a faster beat, her
hand lifting in agitation to the loose edges of the
kimono gown near her breasts. *Her bare breasts.*
She felt her nipples hardening as alarm jagged
through her mind. If her mother was right about
what Max wanted with her, she couldn't let him
see her so readily naked in this gown. He might
take it as an invitation. Besides, even though her
body was covered, just his presence made her too
acutely aware of it, too aware of his dynamic
sexuality and how it affected her.

She gestured to Eric to wait and fled to her
bedroom. Off with the robe, underclothes on,
slacks, top, a quick brush through her hair and she
was reasonably presentable. No make-up but that
was good. It meant she wasn't trying to look
attractive. She paused long enough to take several
deep breaths, needing to calm herself, then went
back to the front door, opening it without hesitation, speaking in an apologetic rush.

'Sorry to keep you waiting. I wasn't expecting anyone to call on me and…'

'Not to worry, Miss Chloe,' Eric assured her, grinning from ear to ear. 'We've brought you a little homecoming present.'

'A homecoming…?'

Eric stepped aside as Max turned to face her, and Chloe's bewilderment faded into a gasp of surprise at the sight of the tiny black-and-white puppy cradled in his arms.

'He's a miniature fox terrier,' Max said, smiling indulgently at the pup who was licking his hand. 'He looked at me through the pet shop window and his eyes said he needed someone to love him.' His gaze lifted from the pup, the dark brilliant eyes boring straight into Chloe's heart. 'I thought of you…saying yesterday you wanted something real in your life…'

'You bought him for me?' Delight was mixed with shame over letting her mother poison her thoughts about this man…her wonderful white knight providing her with everything she needed… never mind any dark side he might have.

'Do you want him?'

'Please…' She eagerly held out her arms and the adorable pup was quickly bundled into them. 'I wasn't ever allowed to have a pet. I'll love him to death, Max. Thank you so, so much!'

She hugged the squirming little body up against her shoulder and laughed as she felt her neck being licked.

'Got everything he needs here,' Eric said. 'Sleeping basket, food, bowls for water and food, collar and leash, dog shampoo…the whole works. Okay if I bring it in and show you everything?'

'Yes, please do.'

She stepped back inside to give him room to enter, expecting Max to follow. But he didn't. He stood in the doorway for a few moments, watching her petting the puppy, the sheer magnetism of the man making her pulse race and trapping her breath in her chest, and when he smiled directly at her, her mind felt positively giddy.

'Seeing your pleasure is my reward,' he said softly. 'I'll leave you to it, Chloe.'

He didn't wait for her to reply, striding away before she could find breath enough to speak. She told herself she had already thanked him anyway, but his departure and his wonderfully thoughtful gift left her feeling even more ashamed of letting her mother tarnish the image of him fighting her dragons.

She lifted the pup down from her shoulder to look into the eyes that had appealed to Max in the pet shop, asking to be loved. She saw the same expression in them and smiled. 'This is your home. With me,' she promised him.

And in that sweet moment of bonding with the beautiful little dog, she felt a huge welling of love for the man who had given her so much of what she'd needed, without demanding any more of her than fulfilling her contract with him as best she could.

# CHAPTER SEVEN

THE rest of the working week passed without any upsetting incident. Chloe felt nervous about doing another shopping trip but she refused to be deterred from it, telling herself that would mean her mother was still dominating her life. She stocked up on her favourite foods and settled happily in the children's house each night, loving the company of her darling little dog. She saw nothing of Max, which made her even more comfortable with the situation, feeling it proved her mother was totally wrong about his motives for taking her under his protective wing.

Saturday was a glorious day, tempting her outside as soon as she'd done her washing and tidied the house. It was great fun taking her dog for a frolicking walk down to the lower terrace. He had to stop and sniff at everything, yapped wildly at finding a frog, and generally leapt around with the sheer joy of living. Chloe laughed at his antics, vastly amused when he'd tumble over, then quickly stand on stiff legs, looking around suspiciously as though to ask, 'What did that to me?' before bounding off again.

She ended up rolling on the grass with him, much to his dancing excitement, and that was how Max came upon them on his way to the boatshed.

'Hi, there!' he called, startling Chloe into sitting bolt upright, which caused him to hastily add, 'Don't get up. It's good to see you looking so relaxed and I'm just passing by. It's such a perfect morning, I thought I'd take the catamaran out on the harbour.'

Like herself, he was wearing shorts and a T-shirt, and once again Chloe was struck by his awesome physique, her heart skittering, flutters in her stomach. He crouched down, his hands outstretched in open welcome as the puppy bounced across the grass to sniff him.

'Hi, little fella.' One hand was licked and Max used the other to scratch behind the dog's ear, smiling at Chloe as he did so. 'What did you call him?'

'Luther.'

'Luther,' he repeated in surprise, raising a quizzical eyebrow. 'That's a serious name for a playful pup.'

'It has dignity. He's only ever going to be little but he thinks he has dignity and I'm giving it to him.'

'Right!' Max grinned, highly amused by the idea. 'I can see that's important.'

'And he also reminded me of Martin Luther King.'

Both eyebrows shot up this time and Chloe grinned back at him as she explained, 'He's black and white and Martin Luther King fought for desegregation, wanting to bring blacks and whites together.'

'Ah! You've clearly given it a lot of thought.'

'A name deserves a lot of thought. You're loaded with it all your life.' She grimaced. 'I've always hated mine.'

He looked slightly bemused by this and asked, 'Why?'

She shook her head, not wanting to tell him it was how her mother made such a harsh gutteral sound of it when she was angry. 'I just don't like it.'

'You could have it changed,' he advised her.

She shrugged. 'Too late for that. It's a career name now.'

'It's never too late to make changes,' he said seriously, straightening up and strolling towards her, Luther prancing around his feet. 'What name would you prefer for yourself?' he asked curiously.

'Maria.' It was soft and had a loving sound to it. 'Ever since I saw the musical *West Side Story*, I've wished it was mine, though I guess it wouldn't go so well with Rollins. Not as distinctive as Chloe.'

'Maria…' he repeated whimsically.

'And I ended up marrying a Tony,' she said with bitter irony. 'Just goes to show how dreams can lead you astray.'

'Well, you've woken up from that dream now, and Luther will give you more real devotion than your husband did.' He dropped down on his haunches to pet the pup again. 'Won't you, little fella?'

He was right about that. Nothing about Tony's devotion had been real. But that was behind her now, no point in dwelling on it. She had to look ahead. If she ever married again, she would make sure it was to a man of substance like…

Her gaze fastened on Max, who sprawled back on the grass, laughingly pretending that Luther had knocked him over. The pup leapt onto his chest and madly licked his chin. 'Save me! Call him off!' Max appealed to Chloe.

'Luther, come here!' she said firmly, and the little dog raced over to her, tail wagging like a windmill. She cuddled him on her lap, settling him down, eyeing Max with amusement as he rolled onto his side, propping himself up on his elbow. 'I don't think you needed to be rescued from a miniature fox terrier.'

His dark eyes twinkled teasingly. 'He was getting a taste for me. He might have gobbled me up.'

She laughed.

He smiled, and this close to her, his smile set off a fountain of buzzing female hormones inside Chloe. He was so attractive, for one wild moment, she fiercely envied Shannah Lian's intimate relationship with him, wishing she could experience him as a lover. Her mind instantly clamped down on the shockingly wayward thought and sought some normal distraction from it.

'Did you have a dog when you were a boy, Max?'

The smile turned into a sardonic grimace as he shook his head. 'The circumstances I lived in then…it wouldn't have been fair on a dog.'

Not fair on him, either, she thought. A drug-addicted mother would not have given him a stable life.

'I had a job on Sunday mornings for a while,' he said reminiscently. 'Pulling a barrow of news-papers around the neighbourhood, blowing a whistle for people to come out and buy. Their dogs always came out and I made friends with them. They'd follow me down the street until their owners called them back. I always enjoyed doing that paper run.'

'You've come a long way since then,' Chloe murmured.

'Yes. And still too much on the move to acquire a dog.'

*Or a wife.*

She wondered if those early years with his mother had taught him not to get attached to anyone or anything, to count only on himself. But this place had called to him.

'You have a home now,' she said.

'A home to come home to. I travel a lot, Chloe.'

'Do you ever get tired of it…the travelling?' she asked curiously.

'The flights can be tedious. Australia is a long way from anywhere else. But I like having the world as my playground. Not being limited.'

She sighed. 'You make me realise how limited my world has been. I haven't even been outside this country. My mother always had more work lined up for me, hardly ever a break.'

'You can change that, too.'

Yes, she could. Freedom was a powerful thing if she learnt to use it wisely.

'Have you ever been sailing, Chloe?'

'No.'

'Then come out on the catamaran with me,' he invited, his dark eyes challenging her to take on a new experience. 'We'll only be gone an hour or two and Eric will mind Luther. He's up on your terrace trimming the hedge.'

Max watched temptation war with caution. She wanted to accept, but undoubtedly her mother had fed her fears about being alone with the big, bad shark. The dog had made this little encounter safe, put her at ease, but without Luther...

She turned her gaze to the harbour. Her chin lifted slightly. Then with an air of self-determination, she looked back at him and said, 'You'll have to tell me what to do.'

'You don't have to do anything except sit or lie on the deck and enjoy skimming across the water,' he assured her, smiling as he pushed himself onto his feet. 'While you fix Luther up with Eric, I'll take the catamaran out to the wharf, ready for you to board.'

There was eager delight on her face as she scrambled up from the grass. 'I'll be as quick as I can.'

'No hurry. Get a hat, too, and put on some sunblock cream.'

'Okay.'

Max felt a zing of triumphant satisfaction as he headed down to the boatshed. Stephanie Rollins was fast losing her influence on Chloe. Which was all to the good. He wanted her to feel free, to make choices for herself, and she'd just chosen to be with him, despite the witch's warnings.

Once they were out in the harbour, Max realised winning had its downside. He had the exhilarating pleasure of watching Chloe's uninhibited joy in the speedy ride across the water, her laughter when waves splashed over the hull, leaving them both dripping wet. She didn't care about how she looked. She simply loved all the sensations of sailing. And it stoked Max's desire for her to the point of severe physical discomfort.

Several times he had to turn away from her, focus fiercely on manipulating the sail, changing the cat's direction, waiting until the tension in his groin eased. His baggy shorts gave him some cover but not enough after they'd got wet, and it certainly didn't help that Chloe's damp clothes clung to every luscious curve of her body.

He couldn't remember ever being on fire for a woman to this extent. He wanted to lick the salt water from her beautiful face, taste her laughter, peel off her clothes, bury his face in her breasts, suck the nipples that were poking out at him so teasingly, bury himself so deeply inside her nothing else would matter—all-consuming sex, devouring all the reasons why they shouldn't have it.

He knew she wasn't immune to his sexual attraction. The occasional sharp intake of breath, the quick look away, the self-conscious curling up of her long, bare legs—all revealing little actions. The big question was—would she fight what she wanted with him, or welcome it?

Risky business.

Rushing into it might break her trust in him.

But it was damned difficult to hold himself back.

At least another week, he told himself. Keep building the chemistry between them, breaking down the mental barriers, issuing tempting invitations, which would seem simply companionable, no reason to refuse—no reasonable reason.

'Had fun?' he asked as he brought the catamaran in beside the wharf, grabbing the ladder to hold the craft steady for Chloe to get off.

She glowed at him. 'It was brilliant, Max. Thank you so much.'

He grinned. 'Hungry work, sailing. Like to join me for lunch by the pool after you've cleaned up?'

Again the hesitation.

He pushed, teasingly adding, 'We can feed Luther tit-bits under the table.'

Including the dog sealed it.

She laughed. 'He loves chicken.'

'I'll ask Elaine to make us chicken caesar salads.'

'That would be great. You'll have two eager guests.'

'Glad to have the company.'

Chloe told herself it was stupid to deny herself the pleasure of *his* company. He was a brilliant, fascinating man. The powerful tug of his strong masculinity would affect any woman. It wasn't special to her. She just had to learn to deflect it, concentrate on their conversation. This was a chance to learn more about him and his life and she wanted to know how he'd managed the journey he'd taken to here, what it took to become the man he was.

It was the right decision to go. The lunch was delicious. Max was totally relaxed, enjoying Luther's appetite for chicken as well as his own. Chloe had tied a sarong over her swimming costume, and relieved of being over-conscious of her body in his presence, she relaxed, too. Max had already been in the pool for a swim when she'd arrived and had a towel tucked around his waist—a decent enough covering to allay the unsettling awareness of *his* body.

Luther curled up on one of the lounges and

went to sleep while they lingered at the table, finishing off the bottle of wine Edgar had brought with their lunch. Chloe screwed up her courage to do some probing into Max's background, telling herself it was okay if he rebuffed her. He had a right to his privacy. She could apologise and backtrack into neutral subjects.

'Max, I know your mother died of a drug overdose when you were sixteen. You must have been through worse things than me in your growing up years,' she started off, her eyes earnestly appealing for his forbearance when she saw the shutting down of all expression on his face. 'I just want to know how you moved past it.'

He turned his gaze away from her, eyelids lowered to half-mast. For several tense moments, Chloe sensed him brooding over whether to answer her or not, his mind travelling back to the past, sifting through it, weighing up whether he was prepared to reveal anything. When he finally spoke, it was in a very dry, dismissive tone.

'When you have nothing, you have nothing to lose. You move on because there's no alternative.' He looked back at her, his eyes very dark and intense. 'You have the harder road to travel, Chloe. You know there's someone you can retreat to if you find it too difficult. That may weaken your resolve to move on.'

'I'll never go back to my mother,' she said vehemently, knowing she had been weak not to make the break before this. The feeling of being hopelessly trapped in a relentless cycle of demands was gone now, thanks to Max.

He smiled. 'I hope not. Today I've seen a vitality in you that was missing when you were yourself, not playing a role for the camera.'

*He* made her feel more alive than she'd ever been. This wasn't make-believe, escaping from reality. It was how she actually felt here and now. 'Did you daydream as a kid, Max?'—escaping his realities?

'No. I watched television. I absorbed television. I didn't have a normal bed-time and it blocked out my mother's crazy stuff. I'd sit there working out why one show had more popular appeal than another. Was it the storyline? Was it the actors? Was it the camera work? What would I do to make it better?' His eyes twinkled in mocking amusement at having turned a bad time into something good. 'Probably the best preparation for what I do now—judging what viewers will like and what they won't, getting the right cast and the right crew to give a show optimum appeal.'

'But you didn't start off in television,' Chloe remarked, puzzled that he hadn't headed straight for it, given his intense interest.

He shook his head. 'I didn't want to be an odd-job boy at a television studio, which was all I could have been in that industry at sixteen.'

'You might have been cast in a show if you'd tried out for one.' He certainly had the male x-factor that was very marketable in television.

'I didn't want to be an actor. I wanted to run the show, Chloe, be in control.'

Master of his own fate, she thought. Had the drive for control been born in him or was it a reaction to the out-of-control life his mother had led? Her own life had been so overwhelmingly controlled, any overt rebellion crushed by abusive tirades, she'd lost the spirit to even try for any control. Until Max had stepped in. She fiercely resolved to be mistress of her own fate after she left here.

'Getting a job at a publishing house was a stepping stone to the big picture,' he went on. 'It was the same field—selling stories, appealing to what people wanted whether it was fiction or non-fiction. I made it to marketing manager by the time I was eighteen. Which opened doors for me to get where I wanted to be.'

Chloe didn't know his exact age—somewhere in his late thirties. It was an amazing accomplishment to have risen from nothing to a billionaire television baron. 'It must give you a tremendous sense of satisfaction, having achieved the wealth and power to choose what shows you want to produce,' she remarked admiringly.

'Mmm…' Ruthless purpose flashed into his eyes. '*My* way.'

'Like getting me for the lead role in this show,' she murmured, remembering what he'd told her. 'You didn't care how much my mother haggled over the contract.'

His mouth quirked and the expression in his eyes simmered into something else—something that made her heart skip and sent tingles along every nerve. 'I wanted you,' he said.

On the surface it was a professional comment but it didn't feel like one. She quickly lowered her gaze and covered her inner confusion by picking up her almost empty glass of wine and slowly finishing it off. Was she hearing what she wanted to hear, seeing what she wanted to see? Max was in a relationship with another woman—a stunningly beautiful woman who was probably as self-assured as he was. Why would a man like him find a lame duck like herself desirable?

Apart from which, she shouldn't be excited by the idea that the attraction she felt with him was returned. It made her situation here perilously close to her mother's nasty reading of it. Although

Max had made no move on her. Not even the suggestion of a move. They were just talking. Which was what she should be doing instead of thinking.

'What was your favourite show when you were a boy, Max?' she asked, forcing herself to look at him with curious interest.

'M*A*S*H,' he answered without hesitation. 'The script was brilliant, the cast of characters was brilliantly balanced, the acting was superb, and it could make you laugh and cry and tug at every emotion in between. I loved that show.'

Love…she could hear it in his voice and wondered if he'd ever loved a woman with the same fervour, loving everything about her.

'Did it get to you, too?' he asked.

Chloe had to drag her mind back to the conversation. She shook her head. 'I've never seen it. My mother dictated what I watched.'

He grimaced, then looked consideringly at her. 'Would you like to see some of it? I have the whole collection of M*A*S*H in my library. I could give you the first season's episodes to watch and if you enjoy them…'

'Yes, please.' Chloe jumped up eagerly, seizing the opportunity to end the foolish meandering in her mind. 'Could we go and get the discs now, Max? The activity this morning and the wine over lunch… I'm feeling drowsy so I want to head off for an afternoon nap. But I'd love to see what you saw in *M\*A\*S\*H* when I wake up.'

He nodded agreeably, rising from his chair, and she quickly collected Luther, who was still asleep. The excursion to Max's library only took ten minutes. It was an amazing library, the shelves more stocked with CD discs of movies and television shows than books, although there were stacks of them, as well. Max moved straight to the *M\*A\*S\*H* collection, handed her a set of discs and invited her to exchange them for others anytime she liked. Chloe thanked him and quickly took her leave.

She *was* tired and she did go to sleep, driving off the madly mixed-up thoughts of Max by reading a book until her eyelids drooped. Luther's yapping woke her, the insistent noise bringing her slowly out of deep slumber. She rolled over on the bed, intending to scoop the dog up to cuddle him back into silence, then realised the yapping was coming from the living room.

Frowning over what might have disturbed the little dog, she pushed herself off the bed, automatically re-covering herself with the silk kimono she'd donned for her afternoon siesta and tying the belt securely as she walked out of the bedroom.

And stopped dead.

A face was peering through the glass panes of the front door, a face she never wanted to see again—the face of Tony Lipton!

# CHAPTER EIGHT

As Chloe stared at him in stunned disbelief, Tony caught sight of her and with an air of triumphant satisfaction, stepped back, his hand reaching for the door-knob, which turned because she hadn't switched on the locking mechanism. It had completely slipped her mind—being with Max, thinking of Max. Apart from which, she was supposed to be safe on Max's property.

The door opened and Tony was in before Chloe could do or say anything to stop him. 'I wasn't sure I had the right place with that damned dog here,' he said, casting a malevolent look at Luther, who was still yapping and jumping at his legs as though to drive him out again.

Good dog, Chloe thought, wishing she had the physical strength to evict her highly unwelcome husband. 'You have no right to be in this house, Tony,' she threw at him in bitter resentment.

He glowered at her. 'You're still my wife, and

Maxa-million-bucks Hart has no right to come between us.'

'You didn't mind Laura Farrell coming between us.'

He waved a sharply dismissive hand. 'That was nothing.'

'I don't call a baby nothing.'

He rearranged his expression to apologetic appeal. 'If you'll just hear me out, Chloe…'

'I don't want to listen to another pack of lies from you. Which is why I took up Max's offer of this house. What I would like to know is how you got past his security.'

He smirked. 'I came by boat, snuck under his wharf to avoid triggering any alarm, climbed up the rock breakwater and beat his bloody security.'

'Then I'd advise you to leave the same way or I'll call the main house and you'll get charged with trespassing.'

'You won't call anyone, Chloe.' He moved quickly to stand between her and the telephone, which he must have spotted on the kitchen bench. He held up both hands in a non-threatening gesture. 'I just want to talk with you. Given the years we've had together, I think I deserve the chance to…'

'No!' she cut in decisively, determined not to be moved by any persuasion he tried. 'Our marriage is over, Tony. I won't change my mind about that no matter what you say.'

The hands turned palm out in appeal. 'I know you're upset and you have good reason to be, but…' He huffed and frowned down at Luther, who'd ceased yapping to sink his teeth into one of Tony's trouser legs and was trying to tug him towards the door. 'Will you call this son of a bitch off? He's ruining my trousers.'

'I do not appreciate your calling my dog nasty names. He's simply doing his best to protect me from an intruder and I don't give a damn about your trousers,' she said, folding her arms belligerently. 'It's you who should call this off and go, Tony.'

'*Your* dog?' He looked sharply at her. 'Since when did you acquire a dog?'

'Since I walked away from the people who didn't want me to have a pet. Namely you and my mother.'

'It's not practical for you to have a pet,' he argued.

'Not practical for me to have a baby, either.'

Recognising that appeasement was his only favourable course in the face of proven infidelity, he backed down, hands lifted in surrender this time. 'Okay…okay…' He tried one of his winning smiles. 'It's fine by me if you want to keep the dog. Look…I'll make friends with him. What's his name?'

Chloe did not back down. Nothing on earth would make her back down. 'You don't need to know his name. You're not going to be part of his life.'

Tony ignored this assertion and crouched down, arranging his face in an indulgent expression as he reached out to pat Luther. 'Hello, little guard-dog,' he crooned. 'You're doing a good job but you've got the wrong guy. I'm a friend.'

Luther had great instincts. He didn't believe Tony for a second. He growled at being touched by the enemy, released the trouser leg, snapped his head around and sunk his teeth into Tony's wrist.

'Bloody hell! He bit me!' It was a cry of angry outrage.

*Serve him right,* Chloe thought with vicious satisfaction, trying to fool a dog like he'd thought he'd fooled her throughout their marriage. The blinkers had fallen off her eyes long ago on that score. No way could Tony charm her into believing anything or *doing* anything for him anymore.

But it was she who cried out as he shook Luther off, grabbed the dog's wildly squirming body, strode to the door, yanked it open, hurled the little terrier outside and closed the door on him. She flew at Tony, fists beating at his chest as he stood in front of the door, preventing her from reversing his action.

'How dare you treat Luther like that, you rotten bully!' she yelled at him. 'Get out of my way! Get out of my life!'

'You've completely lost the plot, Chloe!' he fiercely retorted, grabbing her wrists to stop the pummelling. 'Calm down! All I want is a civilised conversation without a rabid dog distracting us and that's what we're going to have.'

'Let me go!' she screamed, struggling to pull out of his hold.

He forcibly hauled her over to the sofa and flung her onto it. 'Sit there and shut up!' he commanded, all primed to prevent her from moving, glaring down at her with meanly narrowed eyes.

Chloe obeyed, frightened he might do her worse violence if she tried to escape him. She sat still and retreated into grim silence, staring stonily at him as he pulled one of the rockers around so he could sit in face-to-face confrontation with her. Fear was pounding through her heart but she refused to show it. Tony's behaviour was utterly contemptible. Yet the sense of being trapped again was eating at her mind, and all she could think of was how much she needed to be rescued.

Luther was madly yapping outside.

Was Eric still working somewhere in the grounds?

Would he hear the little dog's distress and wonder?

But it wasn't Eric her mind fixed on. She wanted Max to come—Max, her white knight, who'd been standing between her and her dragons, keeping them away.

Max decided the only way to get rid of this continually niggling frustration over Chloe was with a burst of intense physical activity—swim twenty lengths of the pool without a pause. It might also cool down the long-simmering desire she hadn't wanted to know about. He kept remembering her reaction when he'd let her see it, the swift lowering of her eyes, the agitated reach for her glass of wine, then seizing the first reasonable opportunity to part from his company.

She wasn't ready for him and Max wasn't used to waiting. In the ordinary course of events, the women he connected with were only too eager to get into bed with him. No reservations at all. The problem was this situation was not ordinary. The connection *was* there with Chloe. He didn't doubt that for a second. But she clearly had emotional issues, which were making her shy away from acknowledging the sexual buzz between them, let alone showing pleasure in it.

Did it frighten her?

Did she think it was too soon after her husband's defection to be feeling anything towards another man?

Max didn't give a hoot how scandalous an affair between them might be, but it could be worrying Chloe. Though surely she realised he would look after her, and on a purely practical level, there were many advantages in being attached to him. It certainly wouldn't do her career any harm. He could find the best roles for her to play, take her places she'd never been, show her the world and show *her* to the world.

Unfortunately he suspected she didn't have a worldly streak in her, and she was certainly not driven by ambition, which made her very different to most of the women he met. He'd recognised that from the start and found it very appealing. She'd been *used*, and suffered so much from it she'd never use anyone else to push her own barrow. He couldn't change her feelings in that regard and didn't want to. He just wanted...*her*.

Too much.

Too soon.

He headed out to the pool. The heat of the day was lingering on. Maybe Chloe would feel hot after her nap and come up for a swim. He wanted her so badly even a *limited* encounter with her was better than nothing. He'd no sooner stepped out on the pool patio than he heard Luther yapping in frantic ferocity for a little dog.

Something was wrong. Max instantly broke into a fast stride under the columned pergola that led to the steps down to the next terrace. It had been a bad summer for snakes. Eric had spotted a few on the property—harmless green tree snakes—but it didn't mean there weren't any red-bellied black ones around. Or a deadly brown one. Terriers were renowned for going after snakes. If Luther got bitten...

But why wasn't Chloe calling him off? Surely she hadn't let the dog out alone. He was only a pup—eight weeks old. Yet there was no sound from her. This felt like a bad scene. Adrenaline was pumping through him as the guest house came into view. Luther was clawing at the front door in a desperate frenzy. No Chloe in sight.

Max bounded down the steps. Luther didn't even register his approach. The little dog's attention was totally fixed on whatever was going on inside the house. Had Chloe fainted, collapsed, knocked herself out somehow?

A sense of urgency drove him into running to the front door, hand reaching instantly for the knob, testing if it was locked. It wasn't. It turned. Both he and Luther burst into the living room, the dog belting straight for the man leaping up from one of the rocking chairs. Chloe was huddled on the far corner of the sofa, her face lighting with huge relief at seeing him.

The man turned, scowling at Luther, his expression sliding to angry defiance as he saw Max.

Tony Lipton!

With her husband distracted from her, Chloe pushed up from the sofa, ran around the chair he had occupied and threw herself at Max, who was only too happy to curl a protective arm around her and hold her close, so close he could feel the agitated rise and fall of her lovely soft breasts and the rapid thumping of her heart. He rubbed his cheek against her silky hair—too tempting not to— and glared at Tony Lipton over her head, hating him for having had an intimate relationship with Chloe and not even valuing it enough to care about her.

'How did you get here?' he demanded.

Chloe answered in a wild rush. 'He came by boat, Max, and he threw Luther out and forced me to sit down and listen to him. I tried to make him go, but…'

'*Forced?*' Anger surged, the urge to punch out Tony Lipton rising to flash-point.

Fear flickered in the other man's eyes. 'Oh, for God's sake! She's making a drama out of nothing. I just wanted to talk to her,' he jeered dismissively. 'I have a right to, as her husband.'

'No-one has the right to abuse someone else's rights,' Max shot back at him contemptuously, reining in the wildly violent streak this situation had tapped. Control had been the key to the life he had achieved for himself, gaining it, holding it, never letting it slip. That *something about Chloe* was affecting his judgement, stirring feelings that made him a stranger to himself— jealousy, hatred, savagery. He sternly checked himself and spoke with icy control. 'This is my property. Chloe is my guest. She wants you to leave and I will not have that wish disregarded.'

'A lot more than a guest by the look of it,' came the rash retort, his eyes raking over Max's almost naked body, belligerently ignoring the aggression he was inciting.

It was suddenly clear to Max that Tony wanted to goad him into a physical fight regardless of any injury to himself, wanted to make an accusation of assault, milk another sensational story out of the situation. No way was Max about to oblige him. He wouldn't lower himself to gutter behaviour no matter what the provocation.

'Get out, Tony. Get out while the going is still good. You can't stop me from calling the police and having you charged for trespass, and if you continue to stalk Chloe, I'll have a court order issued to legally prevent you from coming anywhere near her. It won't be her name or mine dragged through mud. It will be yours.'

Tony's hands clenched into fists. He glowered at Max, hating his power, wanting to somehow bring him down. 'Chloe is my wife,' he said as though that exonerated his behaviour.

Chloe twisted around to hurl her own response at him. 'I told you our marriage is over. I'm never coming back to you. Never!'

'Because *he's* filled your head with other options,' he yelled back at her, shaking an accusing finger at Max. 'You're a fool to trust him, Chloe. Once he's had what he wants from you, he'll dump you like he dumps all his women.'

'I don't care!' she snapped. 'He gives me what I need, and even if it is only a short-term thing, I'd rather be with him than you.'

Elation spilled through Max's mind. She had just made an active choice. He'd won. All he had to do now was get rid of the hanging-on husband.

'Give it up, Tony,' he tersely advised. 'You're in a no-win situation. Leave now or I'll call the police.'

Luther, who'd lined himself up with Max and Chloe, growled his own warning.

Tony turned his vitriol onto him. 'Bloody dog!'

Luther charged, teeth bared to take a chunk of the enemy. Tony kicked him viciously right across the room. Chloe screamed and ran to check the little dog for injury.

Max's control snapped. With Chloe's scream reverberating through his head and outrage at the callous cruelty to a little pup pumping through his heart, he took one step forward and king-hit Tony Lipton on the jaw. The sight of him, sprawled on the floor near the door, still despoiling the children's house that should have been a safe refuge, could not be borne. Max grabbed the back of his shirt collar and dragged him outside, dropping him on the lawn before quickly returning to the living room to see how Luther was.

'Do we need to call a vet?' he asked Chloe, who was cradling the little dog on her lap.

'I don't think anything's broken,' she answered anxiously. 'I think he just tumbled, Max.'

'I'll look him over as soon as I get back from dumping Tony in his boat.'

'You needn't dump him gently,' she said with vehement feeling.

A fierce exhilaration zinged through Max as he headed back to her decisively *ex*-husband, who had managed to draw himself up on his hands and knees, shaking his head dazedly. It might not have been a wise move, punching out Tony Lipton, but he couldn't bring himself to regret it. Justice had been served, albeit in a primitive fashion, and he'd certainly not damaged himself in Chloe's eyes.

He grabbed Tony's collar again and the waistband of his trousers, lifted him onto his feet, and began frog-marching him across the lawn to the steps leading to the bottom terrace.

'Let me go! Let me go!' he gurgled, arms flailing as he tried to balance himself.

'You used force on Chloe and force on her dog. Have a taste of it yourself,' Max said, using unrelenting strength to push him along.

'I'll get you for this! You've broken my jaw.'

'No witnesses,' Max mocked.

'Chloe…'

'Will not testify on your behalf. You kicked her dog.'

They reached the steps and Tony struggled against Max's grip. 'All right! All right! I'm going! Just get your hands off me.'

'Okay. But try anything stupid and I'll throw you down the entire flight.'

Max let him stumble down the steps by himself, following to ensure Tony did, in fact, leave the property. He'd tied his boat to a pole at the base of the wharf—a small hired outboard motorboat—hidden by the rock breakwater. Max watched him clamber into it, untie the rope, start the motor and head out into the harbour. Neither man said goodbye.

Max waited until the boat was completely out of sight. He didn't think Tony Lipton would be returning in a hurry. Nevertheless, he made a mental note to have the security system tightened up on his harbour frontage. There should not have been a loophole for an intruder to scramble through. He'd failed Chloe on that count. If she now felt unsafe in the guest house, would she be willing to move into the mansion with him?

One step at a time, Max told himself. He had to get back to her now, seize whatever advantage he could from the positive flow of emotion towards him—ride the wave of opportunity.

He'd taken quite a few steps before it struck him he'd be breaking his own rules if he invited Chloe to share his own living quarters. In all his relationships with women, he'd never co-habited with any one of them, consciously avoiding any claim of a de facto wife partnership that could demand a financial settlement at the end of the affair. He hadn't wanted a wife, hadn't wanted a woman to fill that role in his life and he'd always made that quite clear.

That special something about Chloe was blurring all the rules that made his life what it had become. He'd just acted completely out of character. He should be appalled at his loss of control, not savouring the satisfaction it had given him. Life with his mother had been chaos and he'd hated it. Order, logic, a sane approach to everything…that was *his* safety net. He had to move with care where Chloe was concerned. Satisfying his desire for her was one thing, leading into an area of heavy commitment quite another.

But the only future he had to think of right now was this time with her and he was going to make the most of it.

# CHAPTER NINE

LUTHER curled up on her lap and went to sleep, probably a normal reaction to frantic activity and shock. Chloe hoped so. He was only a baby and slept a lot in the normal course of events. She kept stroking him lightly, wanting to soothe away any lingering trauma. Such a brave little dog, and his wild yapping had brought Max to her when she'd desperately needed some strong intervention.

Max, in his brief black swimming costume, looking like a Greek god with all his physical power on display—her saviour once again. She hadn't cared that he was almost naked. It hadn't worried her one bit having her body hugged against his. If she was honest with herself, she'd revelled in his muscular support and was savagely glad he'd hit Tony and hauled him away. If they were living in some primitive society, she would certainly want Max as her mate. In fact, she would be happy to share a cave with him in every sense.

But their lives weren't so simple. Hers, particularly, was complicated with a whole lot of issues, and she shouldn't keep leaning on Max to fix everything for her. Apart from which, he was currently attached to another woman, and she shouldn't be forgetting that relationship, either. Although she was feeling more and more connected to him on many levels, and the plain truth was she wanted him to want her, regardless of every other issue.

Was that weak and stupid?

She didn't know, didn't have time to sort it out. Max strode back into the children's house, filling it with his powerful presence, and her mind went to mush. He was a marvellous man—a dangerous, ruthless, infinitely desirable man—and she wanted to fling herself at him again, feel his arms around her, crushing her body against his, feel everything he could make her feel.

Did he see that wild, wanton desire in her eyes? For one heart-stopping moment, he paused, his dark riveting gaze holding hers, questioning, probing with an intensity that trapped the breath in her throat. Then he looked down at the little dog in her lap and moved forward, crouching down beside her.

'He seems to be breathing normally.'

Which was more than she could say for herself.

Her lungs relaxed back into action and she managed to speak normally. 'He whimpered for a while, but I couldn't feel anything broken.'

'I think Tony's foot went more under Luther's belly than connecting with his ribs, but if you'd like me to call a vet...'

She shook her head. 'I'll wait until he wakes up, see how he is then.'

'Where's his sleeping basket?'

'In the corner next to the doll house. He likes it there.'

'Don't get up. I'll fetch it and you can gently transfer him.'

Luther barely stirred as she lifted him into the basket, only opening his eyes to check all was as it should be then closing them again. Max carried the basket back to the corner as Chloe pushed up from the floor. Acutely conscious of her own nakedness underneath the silk kimono, she readjusted it to maximum modesty as Max moved the rocker Tony had occupied back to its correct position and closed the front door, scanning the room to see if anything else had been changed.

'Are you going to feel nervous staying here now, Chloe?' he asked with a look of sharp concern.

'No. I'm sure Tony won't come back.' She grimaced. 'It was my fault he got in. I forgot to lock the door before lying down for a nap.'

'It was not your fault,' he retorted vehemently. 'Tony had no right to do what he did.'

'I know. I know. I just meant…' She gestured apologetically. 'I was careless, Max. I'm sorry you had to come and rescue me again.'

'The fault is not yours,' he repeated, shaking his head as he walked over to her. 'You've been a victim for a long time, Chloe. You have to stop that kind of thinking and take a clear look at where you are and why.'

His hands curled around her shoulders, fingers gently kneading her tense muscles. His eyes blazed with a dark fire that seemed to sear her soul. 'You said you wanted to be with me,' he reminded her. 'Was that because I saved you or…?'

She didn't consciously lift her hands to his bare chest. They seemed to have been drawn there and she didn't want to pull them away from the warmth and strength of his intense masculinity. She wanted to go on touching him, feeling him, although she was quivering inside at her own boldness in making this physical contact with him. The look in his eyes was tugging at her, too, demanding a response with almost mesmerising power. Some part of her mind knew he wouldn't take unless she was willing to give, yet another part wanted him to take, removing all responsibility from her.

The weak part.

The victim part.

And with that awful recognition came a sudden surge of rebellious determination to be more assertive where her own wishes were concerned. 'It's not just gratitude I feel for you,' she said. 'And I don't want it to be just a protective thing you feel for me,' she added recklessly. 'I want…'

She couldn't bring herself to voice it out loud—all the wildly tumbling desires creating havoc inside her.

'This, Chloe?' he murmured, his eyes glittering knowingly as he slid one hand up her throat, his thumb tilting her chin up, his fingers stroking her cheek.

Her lips parted but not to speak, to draw in breath because she desperately needed it.

'This?' he repeated, his head bending towards hers.

*Yes, yes,* careened around her mind.

His lips brushed hers, raising a host of electric tingles, which were quickly soothed into softer, more seductive sensations as he moved into tasting them, tugging lightly on the sensitive inner tissues, sliding his tongue over them—a gentle, mesmerising kissing that held Chloe totally captivated, craving more.

Her hands slid up over his shoulders, around

his neck, fingers eagerly thrusting into his hair, clasping his head to keep it lowered to hers, blindly encouraging a deeper intimacy to feed the hungry desire racing through her veins, arousing needs that had never really been answered.

Almost instantly a strong arm encircled her waist, scooping her into full body contact with him, her breasts exulting in the hot pressure of his wonderfully masculine chest, her thighs revelling in the rocklike support of his, her stomach contracting excitedly at being furrowed by his sexual arousal, her mind lost in a tumultuous sea of elation at knowing that her own wanting was returned in full measure.

And his kiss was much deeper now, a marauding exploration of her mouth that incited her into invading his, their tongues tangling with a passionate intensity that shot wild excitement through her entire body. She couldn't get enough of him. A moan of gut-wrenching need dragged from her throat when his mouth broke from hers to draw in breath.

'Chloe…' It was a gasp, a groan, a sound he blew into her ear, making it tingle with an explosion of sensation.

She buried her face into the curve of his shoulder and neck, her lips grazing over his skin, tasting him, finding the pulse at the base of his throat, instinctively sucking on it, wanting his heart beating for her. His head jerked back. His hands clutched her bottom, squeezing her flesh closer to his, and just as she wished there was nothing preventing skin-to-skin contact, he growled and jackknifed forward, scooping her off her feet, whirling her up and into the bedroom, his chest heaving, his breathing harsh.

He stood her beside the bed, tugged the tie-belt of her kimono apart and slid the silk gown off her shoulders, following the glide of the fabric with his mouth, kissing the bared skin, making her shiver with delicious anticipation for what he might do to her when she was fully naked. As his hands drew the sleeves down her arms, his lips trailed a hot steamy path to her breasts, his tongue swirling around each stiffened peak, making them bullet-hard, shooting an arc of sweetly aching sensation to below her stomach.

She was barely conscious of the robe dropping to the floor, pooling around her feet. Her entire body was focused on what he was making her feel. Then his arms were around her, crushing her wet breasts to his chest, and one of his hands was thrusting up the curve of her spine to the nape of her neck, fingers threading through her hair. She lifted her face to his and his mouth crashed onto hers with swift devouring force, instantly inciting a passionate response.

Her arms wrapped themselves around his waist, hugging him tightly. The frenzied kissing stirred an intense frustration that he was not as naked as she was. Her hands dived down to hook her thumbs under the hip band of his swimming costume and drag them over the taut cheeks of his buttocks. She had to wrench her mouth from his to finish the task of peeling off this last barrier between them. Dropping into a crouch to pull the costume down his muscular thighs, she goggled at the size of his erection, fascinated by how much bigger it was than Tony's. *Everything* about Max was so different, so powerful, so incredibly exciting.

He lifted his feet for her to whip this last piece of clothing away. His hands were tangled in her hair, wanting to tug her upright again, but Chloe paused, drawn to do what Tony had always expected of her although with Max she really wanted to, swirling her tongue around the swollen head of his penis, encircling it with her lips, drawing it slowly into her mouth, savouring the tight, velvety skin.

'No, don't!' Max cried out, bending to grab her arms and haul her up to face him, his eyes glittering with agonised need.

Confused by his rejection of the intimacy, Chloe gabbled out, 'I'm sorry. I thought you'd like it. Tony…'

'I'm not Tony!' he said savagely. 'I don't want to be serviced by you, Chloe. I want *you*. And I'm so on fire for you, if I let you keep doing that…yes, I like it but not now. Not when I want all of you first.'

Again he crushed her to him, moving to the bed, kneeling over her as he lowered her onto it, passionate purpose blazing from his eyes. 'I want to feel all of you, taste all of you, know all of you, watch your face as we come together.'

Her mind reeled at the intensity of his desire for her. She felt it resonating through her in the ravaging depth of his kiss, in the way he set her on fire when he sucked on her breasts, her back arching to the intoxicating heat of his mouth, her flesh burning under his mouth as he moved it slowly, erotically, down her body, her stomach tightening with almost painful tension when he reached the apex of her thighs, parting her legs, stroking the soft hidden folds of her sex, kissing her *there*, licking her most sensitive place with delicate flicks of his tongue, an exquisite torture that she could hardly bear but didn't want stopped.

She lay with her hands clenched at her sides,

trying to hold on, feeling her insides quivering towards some cataclysmic meltdown. Her eyes were closed, every ounce of concentration focused on what was happening to her. She forgot to breathe until her chest grew so tight it threatened to burst and she sucked in quick little gusts of air. It had never been like this for her, never, never, never…so incredible, so agonisingly blissful.

She felt the last threads of her control starting to snap, tension breaking up, trembling on the edge of chaos, and her hands uncurled and flew into his hair, fingers scrabbling, pulling, wildly insistent words pouring from her mouth. 'Stop… please…you must… I need you to come into me now…now…' His strength filling her before she fell apart…his power making everything right…

He surged up, plucking her hands from his hair, slamming them into the pillow on either side of her head. 'Look at me, Chloe!' he commanded.

Her body was frantically poised for more direct action, her head threshing around in mindless need, but her eyes did snap open and she tried to focus on the face looming over hers—a harshly strained face, a darkly handsome face, with brilliant black eyes blazing down at her, demanding something from her, she didn't know what, couldn't think, but his name spilled from her lips in a husky cry of need.

'Max…'

'Yes…' It sounded like a rasp of satisfaction, then another command. 'Wrap your legs around me, Chloe. Take me as I take you.'

Her legs felt weak and shaky. Max released her hands and helped her, lifting her knees, and then it was easy, her ankles hooking together.

Holding him, having him encircled by her legs, actively offering the other more intimate encirclement…it felt wickedly wonderful, and she was dying to take him, all of him.

'Keep your eyes open,' he insisted.

She stared up at him, willing him to go on, desperate for him to give himself to her. A gasp fell from her lips as she felt his hard flesh push slowly into her slippery softness. Her inner muscles started convulsing, urgently wanting him deeper. Her heart was going crazy, heat racing through her veins, her face aglow with it, her whole body simmering, seething towards some unimaginable flash-point.

He went deeper. Her chest tightened up. She panted for breath. Her head felt as though it was splitting apart. Her eyes glazed over, losing their focus. And still he moved further inside her, deeper than she'd ever experienced, and it was so achingly sweet to be filled with him, so... Her head arched back and a cry tore from her throat as everything inside her seemed to erupt in an ecstatic fountain of exquisite pleasure. Her head swam into a blissfully dreamy state and she looked at Max, who had done this amazing thing, her eyes filled with awed wonder.

He smiled a slow benevolent smile, his dark brilliant eyes tenderly caressing her as he leaned down and filled her mouth with his in a long, delicious kiss that heightened the lovely sensations floating through her.

'Thank you,' she whispered as he drew back.

He shook his head, his eyes still smiling. 'It's not over.'

He started rocking back and forth inside her with a gentle rhythm, watching her face, and to Chloe's astonishment the floating sea of pleasure he had taken her to gathered waves that rolled through her, building up to one ecstatic peak after another, not as explosive as the first, but just as glorious in the intensity of feeling. And her heart swelled with love for him and what he was doing to her.

She watched his face as the surges inside her became more powerful, the rhythm faster, the smile swallowed up by tension, the need for release turning his eyes an opaque black. He threw his head back, too, and cried out as the shuddering spasms of climax sent their flood of pleasure through him.

His chest was heaving for breath as he collapsed forward, arms burrowing under her, rolling onto his back and carrying her with him, holding her in a fiercely possessive embrace. She lay with her head tucked under his chin, her hand spread over his thundering heart, her legs limply sprawled over his, and felt a strange wave of tenderness, wanting to soothe him into the same lovely sense of contentment he'd given her. Was it over now, she wondered, or was this the beginning of an intimacy that would move her life to a place she had never imagined?

Her mind drifted to the image she had once had of him—Maximilian Hart, the powerful, ruthless, intimidating mover and shaker who always got what he wanted. The master player. He'd moved her, shaken the whole foundations of her world, but what, in the end, did he want with her?

Right now, Chloe couldn't bring herself to care.

She loved being with him like this.

And she was going to revel in it as long as it lasted.

# CHAPTER TEN

MAX let himself bask in her soft ministrations, his mind still revelling in how she had responded to him—the excitement rippling through her body, the look of incredulous wonder on her face, the unequivocal seizures of intense pleasure. He had no doubt she'd never felt anything quite so climactic before, which gave him an enormous sense of satisfaction. Her rotten husband had obviously been a selfish lover—selfish in everything. It elated him that this sexual experience had been a revelation to her, that *he* had given her what she should have been given.

He wove his fingers through the silky tresses of her hair, loving the feel of it—soft like a baby's. Which reminded him. It had been totally reckless to go ahead without using a condom. The dog had brought him here. He hadn't come prepared for sex. But when he'd seen desire shining in Chloe's incredibly eloquent eyes, he hadn't cared about anything else, not even when it had flitted through his mind that she could fall pregnant. That cautionary bit of sanity had been crowded out by wild thoughts of taking care of her and the child, marrying her if need be—anything but putting her off having what he wanted, too.

He should check if there was any danger of pregnancy. He didn't really want that complication. It forced issues that shouldn't be forced. He didn't know how far he wanted to go with Chloe, but he knew the journey was better travelled free and clear of having to consider the life of an innocent child.

'Chloe…' His voice came out in a gravelly tone. He swallowed to clear his throat.

'Mmmh?' It was a contented hum, nothing fretting at her mind.

Which was good, Max told himself. 'I didn't plan this and I had no protection with me,' he said, unable to wipe all concern from his mind.

'S'okay,' she assured him dreamily.

'It's safe?' he persisted, needing that fact nailed down.

'Mmmh.' She sucked in a deep breath and explained, 'I'm in the middle of a month of contraceptive pills. Didn't think I should go off them until the end of the prescription. Just as well,' she added on a carefree sigh.

'Yes. Just as well,' he agreed, smiling wryly at his own lack of care.

Chloe wasn't the only one experiencing *a first* today. His lapse into physical violence, followed by this reckless plunge into intimacy…he'd never been so beyond normal control that he'd bypassed elementary protection from unwelcome consequences. The feelings she stirred kept pushing him to perform acts above and beyond the usual highly guarded parameters of his life. But now that she'd given herself to him, these aberrations should pass.

Her hand was gently fondling his penis as though she was fascinated with its size and shape and Max felt excitement rising in him again. 'You're playing with fire,' he warned.

'Good!' She lifted her head and threw him a wicked grin. 'I want to watch it grow.'

He laughed, surprised by her uninhibited comment. 'It can't be a mystery to you.'

She cocked her head on one side, eyeing him consideringly. 'I don't think women are a mystery to you, Max, but you wanted to watch me, so why wouldn't I want to watch you?'

Only with her had he felt compelled to see everything she was feeling with him. Whenever he'd had sex with other women he'd simply accepted they were both reaching for mutual satisfaction which invariably eventuated. The extraordinary circumstances had made this more important, he told himself. And the fascinating ability Chloe had to project so much emotion in her eyes, on her beautiful face...how could he not want to see?

'You're a very special woman, Chloe,' he said seriously. 'I didn't want to fail you in any way.'

It turned her serious. 'You don't. All the time you give me what I need, what I want. You never fail. And it's wonderful in one sense...' She paused, frowning slightly.

'But...?' he prompted.

She grimaced. 'It's like I'm being passive in all this and I don't want to be passive anymore.'

His mouth twitched with amusement. 'Believe me. You weren't passive. I wouldn't have completely lost my head if your response had not been so actively exciting.'

She eyed him curiously. 'You don't usually lose your head?'

'No.'

'Does that mean it was especially good for you?'

'Yes.'

She looked enormously pleased, her sky-blue eyes sparkling with joy, her smile so wide the dimples in her cheeks deepened in tantalising provocation and he reached out and placed a teasing finger in one of them. She laughed at his bemusement in her. 'Well, I'm glad I wasn't a failure to you. I would have shrivelled up and died. As it is, I don't feel at all bad about this, even though I should.'

'Why should you?' Surely she couldn't feel guilty about being unfaithful to a marriage that was dead and gone.

She winced. 'In a way, I've just acted like Laura Farrell, though at least you're not married to Shannah Lian.' Her eyes searched his worriedly. 'Did you forget about her, Max?'

It obviously troubled her that he might be in the same unfaithful class as her husband. *She* didn't owe loyalty to anyone, but he...there was empathy for Shannah's situation on her face. 'It's over between Shannah and me,' he quickly assured her. 'We parted friends. You haven't taken anything from her, Chloe. Nor have I cheated on her.'

He watched her process this information. The initial relief gave way to a narrow-eyed re-assessment of her own situation with him. He knew she was thinking of how her mother and husband had interpreted his actions on her behalf, that he was motivated by carnal desire, not keeping his television show on track. There was no more fondling. She drew her hand away from his groin and separated her body from his, sliding to one side, an elbow propping her up as she studied *his* face, her mind obviously whirling with questions.

They were still on an intimate footing, Max told himself. She hadn't flounced off the bed to grab her robe and cover herself. She didn't want to separate herself from him that far. Nevertheless, he knew the next words spoken could have a critical impact on where they went from here. He didn't try to pull her back to him, respecting the space she'd put between them. He didn't move at all but there was a shift inside himself, adrenaline pumping through him, relaxation obliterated by the growing tension of battle readiness.

He wasn't about to lose now.

Chloe decided she wanted the truth, whatever it was. There'd been no gossip about Max breaking up with Shannah Lian, so the break had to be very recent. The big question was *when*? The gorgeous redhead had not been with him at the launch party. Was that an indication the relationship had ended before then…before the revelation of Tony's and Laura's betrayal, which had made her so vulnerable to Max's escape route?

Chloe fiercely hoped so. She didn't want her

mother and Tony to be right about Max. He'd been so good to her…good *for* her. On the other hand, she couldn't bear to live with lies. Her whole life felt as though it had been false. Above all, she needed to get it straight now, not be fooled by anything anymore.

There was no guilt in Max's eyes. Not the slightest flicker of evasion, either. He was watching her intently, his dark brilliant gaze very steady and direct, waiting for her to tell him what was on her mind, why she had moved aside, breaking the intimate togetherness. There was waiting in his stillness, too, and the uneasy thought flashed across her mind that it was the stillness of a predator waiting for the right opening to attack.

He'd certainly seized the right opening at the launch party, moving in at the precise moment of absolute vulnerability, taking her into his keeping when she was too shell-shocked to be aware of it. But she wasn't shell-shocked now and she wasn't going to be weak, letting him steam-roll her into an affair that could distract her from what she should be doing.

Another question popped into her mind. She couldn't imagine any woman dumping Max, though it seemed relevant to the main issue so she asked, 'Did you end it or did Shannah?'

'I did.'

No surprise in that admission. Chloe couldn't see Max not being in charge of everything to do with his life. She had to ask the big question now. 'When, Max?'

'The day you came here. I had a dinner date with Shannah that night. I couldn't relate to her. I kept thinking of you.'

Relief swept through her. It sounded reasonable. Yet it didn't really answer the accusations made by her mother and Tony. 'Do you mean wanting me instead of her?'

'Yes.'

She took a deep breath and blurted out, 'Has everything you've done for me been about... about *wanting* me?'

His mouth quirked into an ironic little smile. 'Chloe, I doubt there's a man alive who wouldn't find you desirable, but if you're asking if it was lust driving me to take you into my protection that first night, no, it wasn't.'

A flush of embarrassment burned her cheeks. Of course, it was a ridiculous assumption. He'd whipped her away from a nasty scene because he hadn't wanted the whole focus of the launch party to be diverted into a gossip-fest that had nothing to do with the show.

'I spoke the truth to you,' he quietly assured her.

'Protecting the star of my show, ensuring its success was my top priority. I moved straight into damage control. And I'd have to say I quite enjoyed doing it.'

Going into battle, she thought, not attaching his relish for it to anything personal to her until he added, 'I've always liked you, Chloe. I didn't like the way your mother handled you. I didn't like your husband who was riding on your coat-tails. But that was none of my business until you gave me the go-ahead to act on your behalf to free you from both of them. Only then did I start thinking...she is now free to be with me.'

Having just reasoned away his actions, this statement came as a shock. Chloe didn't know what to think of it and Max moved, startling her into rolling onto her back as he propped himself on his side, his eyes glittering with dark, ruthless purpose, his hand reaching out to cup her cheek and keep her attention fixed on him.

'I wanted that, Chloe. I wanted that immediately. And proceeded to do everything possible to make it happen. For you to be with me,' he said without the slightest hint of apology. 'But it could only happen if you wanted it, too. If you chose to be with me.'

Choices...yes. All along he had presented her

with choices; tempting choices, seductive choices, reasonable choices, everything possible that would appeal to her state of mind. And heart. She couldn't call it a trap when she had walked into it willingly. Even though she had sensed that her white knight had a dark side, it hadn't stopped her going with him, wanting to be with him.

He hadn't interfered with her marriage. Tony had done that, not Max.

He hadn't *taken her over*, as her mother had put it, colouring him with her own *using* mentality.

Yes, he had dumped Shannah Lian for her, and Chloe was glad she was the more desirable woman to him and he had been honest about it, acting honourably, ending one relationship before pursuing another.

He had done nothing wrong.

And everything right for her.

What more could she ask of him?

The frantic pumping of her heart eased.

He smiled, as though he knew the cloud of troubling concerns had lifted from her mind. 'I think I'm good for you. Tell me if I'm not.'

The last of her inner tension dissolved in a gurgle of laughter. He was a beautiful man—an infinitely desirable man and she was enormously fortunate that he desired her. She raised her hands to cup his wickedly handsome face, smiling as she drew it down towards hers. 'I like how good you are for me, Max.'

He laughed, his eyes twinkling delight in her response. Their kiss started with a sense of mutual joy in each other but quickly escalated into passion. Excitement fizzed through her body, re-energising it into a wild craving for more intimacy with him. He was ready for it, too. She reached down and stroked him, marvelling again at how hard and powerful he felt, elated that she stirred such strong desire in this marvellous man.

'No more feeling passive,' he murmured against her lips, then lifted her to sit astride him as he rolled onto his back, grinning a wicked invitation as he said, 'Take me.'

She did, loving the sensation of slowly sinking down on him, feeling him filling her inside. Her grin back at him was pure blissful pleasure. He reached up and started caressing her breasts, his thumbs teasing her nipples, his dark eyes simmering a challenge for her to be as active as she liked. Chloe had never thought of herself as an exhibitionist, yet she revelled in rolling her hips, swaying her body in an intensely sensual and tantalising rhythm, watching him watching her, seeing the simmer in his eyes flare into a blaze of urgent need.

He whipped her onto her back, seizing control,

plunging fast and furiously, driving her excitement to the same shattering peak as before, both of them crying out as they climaxed together, both of them subsiding into a languorous state of sweet satiation afterwards. Chloe lay in his embrace, savouring a sense of perfect happiness. She didn't care if it was only ever going to be a temporary thing with Max. It was good. Better than anything she'd known in her entire life.

A questioning whine from the bedroom doorway snapped her head up from Max's chest. Luther! He was standing quite normally on his sturdy little legs, his eyes bright, his head cocked to one side, observing the fact there were two people on the bed instead of one and looking not too sure that he wouldn't get kicked again.

'It's okay, Luther,' Chloe promised him. 'See—' Max obligingly raised his head '—it's Max.'

'Come on, little fella. Want to join us?' Max crooned at him, throwing out a welcoming arm.

Luther happily scampered over to the bed and Max gently scooped him onto it, whereupon the little dog darted from one to the other, licking their faces in exuberant pleasure that all was well in their world. Clearly he'd suffered no damage from Tony's kick, and they finally settled him down between them, stroking him into blissful contentment.

'I'm glad I gave him to you,' Max said in a fond tone. 'If he hadn't been barking his head off this afternoon, alerting me to trouble, I'd still be wondering how long I'd have to wait before you felt comfortable about admitting the attraction between us.'

She sighed over the needless tension she'd put herself through. 'I thought I kept it hidden from you.'

He shook his head. 'You can't hide sexual chemistry, Chloe, and it's always been there between us. It was why you never felt comfortable in my presence. You clung to your mother or Tony, using them as safety barriers because you didn't feel safe with me.'

His perception shamed her in a way because she hadn't faced up to the truth in the past, her mind instinctively shying away from examining the feelings he stirred in her, labeling him dangerous—to be avoided whenever possible, kept at a distance when he was unavoidable. 'Well, I feel safe with you now,' she said decisively.

Although she wasn't safe from falling in love with him.

And he would move on from her, just as he'd moved on from Shannah Lian. That was his well-documented reputation with women, as her mother had pointed out. She couldn't expect it to turn out differently with her. She still had to keep Max at a distance…from her heart.

He frowned at her. 'What are you thinking?'

'I'm thinking I'll take all you want to give me of yourself for as long as you want me with you, but I mustn't get too addicted to it because it will come to an end sooner or later.'

Max instantly thought, *I might not want it to come to an end*, but he pulled himself back from saying it. He'd never held out even the suggestion of a lasting relationship to any woman and it would be wrong to plant the idea of it Chloe's mind. He didn't know the future. He knew this woman was different to the others who'd passed through his life, knew she evoked feelings that were not usually touched in him, but this was all very new and it was happening now. Next month…next year…sooner or later…the feelings might wane.

'All I want to give you of myself,' he repeated musingly, his eyes teasing hers. 'That's a sweeping statement, Chloe. You might want to draw limits. You can, you know. You're free to make whatever choices you like. I don't own you. I hope you won't ever let anyone own you again.'

It was good advice and he saw it sink in, saw her shedding the kind of ownership her mother and husband had inflicted on her, saw the realisation that her life was hers to shape any way she liked, saw the will to do it being born, saw her slipping away from him.

Which gave him the weird sense that he'd just cut his own throat and might end up bleeding to death from caring about her too much.

But it was still good advice and he wouldn't take it back.

He didn't want to be selfish with her.

She deserved to flower into the person she could be, freed from the suppression of her past life. He would enjoy watching her become that person—a survivor like him, moving forward, finding her own sunshine, opening up to it, seizing the opportunities that appealed to her. The husk of her mother's Chloe would be left behind and the Maria in her mind would emerge.

Maria…

Mary…

# CHAPTER ELEVEN

CHLOE did set limits. She would not go out in public with Max. First, it was bound to create a frenzy of gossip, bringing the paparazzi down on her like a cloud of bees, just when they'd lost interest since nothing juicy had eventuated from her move to Max's guest house. Second, the cast of the show would inevitably treat her differently. She'd already had a taste of that and decided that it would be much easier working with them if their suspicions about her relationship with Max were not confirmed. Third, she didn't want to give Tony any nasty ammunition to fire at her, nor give her mother the smug satisfaction that once again she'd known better than Chloe. Which she hadn't, but she'd think it.

'When we've finished shooting this season's episodes for the show, and I've moved to a place of my own, then I'll go out with you if you still want me to,' she'd said, being very firm on this point.

'Uh-huh,' Max had agreed, a gleam of wry amusement in his eyes. 'I can see that making an independent stand is important to you. But in the meantime, can we carry on in private?'

She'd laughed and hugged him. 'I'd be very disappointed if we didn't.'

'Then I shall attempt to make what time we have together as entertaining as I can.'

He did. For Chloe it was almost an idyllic existence, living in the children's house and being with Max. There were so many pleasures—making love, watching episodes of *M\*A\*S\*H* together, sailing, lazing by the pool, sharing the delicious dinners Elaine cooked for them in the big house, watching and discussing television shows Max was interested in acquiring.

At first she'd been a bit self-conscious about their new relationship where the three E's were concerned, but she needn't have worried about their reaction to it. Edgar maintained his air of deference at all times. Elaine, who was an avid fan of the show and loved how Chloe played her part in it, was only too happy to have a closer acquaintance with her and always welcomed Luther into her kitchen. Eric seemed to assume she was becoming a fixture at Hill House and took to asking her opinion of whatever he'd been doing around the grounds.

It would have been so easy to let everything else slide. Happiness was addictive. But the sense that she had to get her own life in order—apart from Max—could not be ignored. That had been her worst mistake in the past, letting things slide. She would not be guilty of it again.

Max gave her the name of a good divorce lawyer, whom she met, subsequently setting the ultimate separation from Tony in motion, listening very carefully to the legal issues involved so she could fully understand her position and make sensible decisions. The lawyer assured her he would negotiate a fair settlement with Tony, not allowing her husband to milk the divorce for more than he was entitled to.

She bought herself a little car, a white VW Beetle, which was cute and comfortable and easy to park in the city. Having acquired her own transport, as well as the confidence to handle her own problems, she dispensed with Gerry Anderson's services, thanking the security guard for having taken such good care of her and Luther.

'A pleasure, Miss Rollins. You have my card. Call me if you ever have a problem I can help you with,' he'd said with a touching sincerity, which left Chloe feeling she had a ready friend if she ever required a security guard again.

She needed the car in her hunt for suitable accommodation. Her choice was limited because most apartment complexes would not allow pets and no way was she going to part with Luther. She didn't want to commit herself to buying a property, not before her divorce was settled, so finding something right to rent was difficult. Saturday mornings were taken up with looking at places, none of which really fitted her requirements.

'I'd like something close to a park that I can take Luther to,' she remarked to Max after being disappointed in her search once again.

'There's no time pressure, Chloe. I'm perfectly happy for you to stay on here beyond the two months,' he assured her.

She gave him an arch look. 'I don't intend to hang on until it doesn't suit you, Max.'

He frowned. 'I wasn't suggesting you do.' The dark brilliant eyes sharply probed hers. 'I like what we have together, Chloe. It may suit me for a very long time.'

Her heart skipped a beat. She liked it, too. She loved it. But indulging in forever dreams with Max was not good for her. A long time might only mean a year or two.

Max watched the temptation to stay with him slip into uncertainty and the urge to do battle with her doubts was too insistent to deny. He liked coming home to her, more than he could ever have imagined coming home to anyone. He felt a buzz of joyful anticipation each time he drove through the gateway and it wasn't so much the welcoming sight of Hill House he looked forward to, but being with Chloe again. She delighted him in every sense.

'You're happy here,' he argued. 'Luther is happy here. Eric and Elaine are happy to mind him when you go out. When *we* go out. As we will as soon as your work on this season's episodes is done.'

They were in the children's house and he drew her into his embrace, deliberately reminding her of the ready intimacy they shared. He stroked her cheek as his eyes bored into hers, commanding her surrender to his will. 'You love this place,' he said with soft seductive persuasion. 'You have your own car, your independence. You can pay me rent if that will make you feel more right about staying on.' He moved his fingers to her lips, arousing sensitivity to his touch. 'I want you to stay, Chloe.'

He saw a multitude of emotions warring in her eyes—desire, hope, yearning, fear, panic…the latter jolting his drive to win what he wanted.

She pushed away from him, words tumbling

out in a desperate burst. 'I can't, Max. I can't. Don't ask me to.'

Her hands clapped her cheeks, smacking off the lingering influence of his touch. Her eyes begged him to understand. Max didn't but he stood still, instinctively knowing he had to wait for her to explain, not press for anything. It appalled him that he had struck fear in her. She was precious to him. Hurting her in any shape or form had never been his intention.

Her hands dropped from her face. She wrung them as she gulped in deep breaths, struggling for control of the agitation that had gripped her. Max was acutely aware of feeling more tension than he did in any critical business meeting. He'd always been prepared for them, confident of coming out on top, but he'd had no experience of what was happening here and now with Chloe.

She gathered herself to speak. 'All my life…' She stopped, swallowed hard, started again. 'For most of my life, I did what my mother wanted. I learned…she made me learn…it was easier to obey, easier not to resist, easier just to fall in with whatever she decided.'

Max saw the memories of punishment flit through her eyes and his jaw clenched at a surge of hatred for Stephanie Rollins. He'd been the victim of negligence, indifference, crazy outbursts of emotion from his own mother throughout his boyhood, but never cruelly pressured into performing to her will.

'Then when I married Tony and realised I was only a tool to him, too…someone he could use to get what he wanted…I took the easy path again, letting him do it because at least he made the process more pleasant than my mother did. He pretended to love me. I could live with that. He made it easy.'

The con man keeping his gravy train sweet, Max thought in blistering contempt. Yet a disturbing niggle of conscience started whispering he was doing a very similar thing.

'And it would be all too easy for me to stay on here with you, Max,' Chloe went on, nailing the tack he had used to keep her with him. 'But if I did that, I'd be slipping back into the same old pattern that I need to break, giving you control of my life instead of being in charge of it myself.'

'No!' he vehemently denied. 'I would not control your life, Chloe. You'd always have freedom of choice with me.'

Pained eyes looked back at him. 'I can't choose when you'll meet some other woman who sparks your interest, Max. Shannah Lian had no choice at all in the end, did she?'

*But it's different with you.*

The words burned to be said. He barely stopped them from exploding off his tongue. As true as it was, it didn't promise the kind of longevity that would mean they would never part. They were still in the honeymoon phase of their relationship. The deeply honed pragmatic part of his mind dictated a much longer period was required to test the depth of his feelings for her. Rushing into some rash declaration would not serve either of them well.

'I need a place of my own, Max,' she asserted with quiet conviction, her eyes pleading for his acceptance. No more argument. 'I don't ever want to feel again I have nowhere to go if...other things...start falling apart.' Her lips quivered into a wry little smile. 'It might not be so convenient for you...for either of us...'

'That's not important.' His hand sliced the air in sharp dismissal. 'Your sense of well-being is. I'm sorry. I wasn't thinking...just wanting to hold onto what we've been sharing.' He shook his head in mute apology as he moved to reassure her, his hands curling gently around her shoulders, his eyes projecting empathy with her feelings. 'When my mother died, the welfare people moved me to a hostel. I couldn't wait to leave school, earn enough money to get a place of my own. Do you want me to help you find one, Chloe?'

Relief and joy sparkled back at him as she wound her arms around his waist, pressing close to him. 'No. You've helped me enough, Max. I can't tell you how much I appreciate all you've done for me. Even when we're not lovers anymore, I'll always consider you the best friend I could ever have had.'

'Hmmm... I'm not ready to end the lovers part yet. Are you?'

'No.' She looked wickedly at him as she rubbed her lower body against his.

He laughed and scooped her up in his arms, needing to assuage the strong sense of possessiveness that he had to contain. Luther barked at the exuberant action and he smiled down at the dog. 'You get your fair share of her, little fella. This is my turn.'

Chloe laughed as he strode to the bedroom and kicked the door shut behind them. There was no sense of conflict between them as they made love. Chloe gave herself to him with uninhibited pleasure and Max revelled in the certainty that she would still be his woman, regardless of a change in residence.

Lying together afterwards, he felt a deep tenderness towards her, cuddling her close, softly stroking her hair and the lovely curve of her spine. 'You are safe with me, Chloe,' he murmured. 'I'm not out to exploit you in any way.'

She sighed, her breath drifting warmly across his chest. 'I know that, Max. You don't need to. You run your own race.'

Which she had not done up until now. He understood her need to take control, given the victimisation she had helplessly resigned herself to in the past. It was right for her to establish her own ground, her own space. Yet the simple truth she had just spoken made him think about the life he had made for himself—running his own race.

He'd had to as a child. His mother had been totally irresponsible. More times than not there was no food bought for him, her single mother's pension all spent on drugs. She'd slept in most mornings, not worrying about getting him off to school. He went because it was better than staying with her, trying to shut off her rants about whatever got stuck in her mind.

It had been a lonely life, looking after himself. Becoming self-sufficient had not been an easy journey but it had been the only way to survive in his mother's environment. He'd hated it when she had bursts of sentimentality, hugging him, rocking him in an excess of emotion as she raved on about how much she loved her little boy. Her so-called love was just some mushy thing that had no reality attached to it. Max remembered thinking he would be much better off without it.

And he had done very well without it—running his own race—not letting anything or anyone divert him from achieving the goals he set for himself.

But would he be content to keep it that way, having spent this brilliant time with Chloe, sharing more with her than he had with any other person—man or woman—enjoying everything about her? He'd never minded being alone. It had been an advantage, not having consideration for other people hold him back from what he chose to do. He'd consciously avoided emotional strings that might tie him down. Yet he knew he would miss Chloe's ready company when he came home.

He couldn't stop this private idyll from coming to an end. However, he didn't have to accept an uncrossable distance between them. The need to nail down some definite future with her was paramount. There was so much more he wanted to share with her, introduce her to.

'When you leave here, Chloe, keeping our relationship a secret will become untenable,' he said matter-of-factly. 'Someone will pick up on my visiting you. You will want me to visit, won't you?' he added confidently.

'Yes, of course,' she said without hesitation.

'Then I see no reason why we shouldn't appear in public together. Work on the show will have finished for the season. By the time we start the next set of episodes, the cast and crew will be used to the fact that we've linked up so our relationship will be taken for granted, not be a hot item for speculation. It shouldn't cause you any discomfort. Agreed?'

She didn't answer.

Max felt tension seizing him again as he waited. He couldn't force her to agree with him. She had to want to. He couldn't see her face, didn't know what was going through her mind. Her marriage was dead. She shouldn't be worrying about what Tony thought. Or what her mother thought. She now had her own life to do whatever she liked with it. Surely she would choose to spend as much time with him as they could arrange. No way would he accept remaining her secret lover! It was too limited!

Chloe's mind was in turmoil. It was a daunting prospect, being publicly linked to such a powerful man, being labelled his new paramour, which would inevitably raise speculation on how long this liaison would last, given Max's reputation for moving on. On top of that, despite the lapse of time since her separation from Tony, her relationship with Max could still be viewed as scandalous. The paparazzi would be all over every appearance they made together.

She shrank from having to face it, wishing they could still be lovers in private. These past two months had been heaven, so easy…

*Easy.*

The word mocked her, instantly accusing her of sliding back into her old mindset. She'd just made a stand with Max over not taking the easy path of staying with him here. Not only that, at the beginning of their affair, she'd insisted they not appear in public together until the show was wrapped up for this season and she had a place of her own. As he'd just pointed out, that time was almost up. Backtracking on her word, denying him what he wanted when he'd given her so much was simply not on. Besides, she knew she would crave his companionship, in every sense.

So what if it wasn't easy going public!

She'd have Max at her side.

That was more important to her than anything else.

Having him.

She lifted herself up from his chest to smile that assurance at him. 'I will be very pleased to go out with you, Max,' she said, secretly wanting far more from him than she could ever ask or expect—like having this amazingly wonderful man with her for the rest of her life.

'Good!' A smile of satisfaction spread across his face.

Chloe told herself to be satisfied, too. The experience of Max had already changed her life for the better. She would always be grateful he had stepped into it...even when he stepped out of it.

# CHAPTER TWELVE

ON the Saturday before the last week of shooting the show, Chloe finally found a place she was happy to rent. It was a small terrace house, situated on a street that ran parallel to Centennial Park. She didn't care that it was old and in need of some modernisation in the kitchen and bathroom. It was functional—two bedrooms upstairs, enough living space downstairs, with a small, enclosed backyard so that Luther didn't have to be kept inside all the time—and being right across the street from the park was ideal. It was also close to the shops she knew from living at Randwick.

It was a huge emotional wrench, leaving the children's house, saying goodbye to the three E's, who had contributed so much to her comfort while she was staying there, moving away from the daily intimacy with Max. She was glad to have Luther's company, staving off the loneliness she might have felt, though she occupied herself very busily during the first week after the move, arranging her belongings in her new accommodation, acquiring the furniture she needed, having a dog door inserted into the door to the backyard and teaching Luther how to use it.

Max dropped by most evenings to see how she was getting on, bringing her flowers and gourmet treats from Elaine's kitchen. They invariably ended up in bed together, which was the best treat of all to Chloe. He only had to look at her and her whole body started buzzing with anticipation for the sexual connection between them.

Sometimes they didn't make it upstairs to the bedroom. Like when he brought her a bunch of the most gloriously scented yellow roses and he took the one she'd held up to her nose and caressed her skin with it; her cheeks, her neck, down the V-neckline of her shirt, undoing the buttons, brushing it over the swell of her breasts…he'd hoisted her up on the kitchen bench and had incredibly erotic and exciting sex with her there.

He was a fantastic lover. Chloe had a losing battle on her hands, fighting to keep him at any distance from her heart. He made her feel so beautifully loved, so wonderfully cared for. Had he treated all the women in his life like this, or was she more special than the others? He'd said she was special. The tantalising question was *how* special? Enough to want her with him for the rest of their lives?

They started going out together. They went to parties, to charity functions, to the theatre, ballet, opera, walked the red carpet together at a film premiere. They were the talk of the town—the television baron coupled with the star of his latest hit show. Max handled the red-hot interest with practised ease. Chloe simply glowed her pleasure in his company. It wasn't difficult. She loved being with him and didn't care what anyone else thought.

However she did refuse one request from him, that she hostess a dinner party at Hill House. Somehow that was too much like being a pseudo-wife. Fulfilling that role was too close to her secret yearning to be his lifetime partner. She wouldn't let herself pretend. She was finished with pretence.

In fact, she shied away from returning to Hill House at all, knowing it would tug at her heart, make her wish it was her home. It had been hard enough to leave. She didn't want to feel that wrench over and over again.

Max grew frustrated by her turning down his invitations to join him there. 'You liked Hill House. You liked the three E's. They liked you. They miss you, Chloe,' he argued.

He didn't say *he* missed her. Max wasn't into revealing any weakness in himself. There were no cracks in his self-contained armour. She had to learn to be self-contained, too. 'It's *your* home, Max. I don't belong there,' she quietly asserted.

He frowned. 'You don't have to belong. What's wrong with visiting?'

She shook her head. 'I can't go back. I have to move on in my own way. You see me as much as you like, don't you? We go out a lot together. Doesn't that satisfy what you want from me in our relationship?'

He stared at the appeal in her eyes for long, nerve-tearing moments. 'Your choice,' he finally said with a grimace that seemed to mock himself.

Much to Chloe's relief, he didn't raise the issue again. He arranged dinner parties at restaurants. She didn't mind being his partner on these occasions. It was not the same as being his hostess at Hill House.

The rest period before shooting the next set of episodes for the show was almost up when Chloe received an unexpected and highly unwelcome visitor at her terrace house. It was a Monday morning and she'd just done a load of washing and was about to have a coffee break when the doorbell rang. Luther raced down the hallway, barking at the noise. Probably a delivery person,

Chloe thought—Max sending flowers. Nevertheless, she took the precaution of looking through the peephole in the door to check.

Her heart instantly contracted with shock.

Laura Farrell was on her front porch. She was standing side-on, the baby bump clearly visible, outlined by the form-fitting grey skirt and grey-and-white top she wore. Her long brown hair fell lankly forward, hiding much of her face. Her shoulders drooped. As Chloe was still coming to terms with the identity of her visitor, Laura turned, reaching out to press the doorbell again, her face devoid of make-up and her amber eyes leaking tears.

Chloe jerked back from the peephole, her mind reeling with confusion as well as shock. Why would a weeping Laura Farrell come to her doorstep? She couldn't possibly hope to be rehired as a personal assistant after such a flagrant betrayal of trust and the vicious verbal attack at the launch party. What on earth did she expect to gain by coming here? Forgive and forget?

Not in a million years, Chloe thought as the doorbell kept ringing, sending the message that Laura Farrell was not about to give up and go away. While part of her inwardly recoiled from facing the woman again, another part insisted on putting a decisive end to whatever was on Laura's mind—affirmative action. She was no longer the old Chloe who had been brainwashed into avoiding any form of confrontation. She'd learnt how to handle a lot of things since being with Max.

Luther was barking his head off. She bent and scooped him up in her arms to calm him down, then opened the door, intending to tell Laura she was not welcome in her home.

'Thank God you're here!' Laura cried in pathetic relief, her hands jerking into a trembling gesture of appeal. 'Please, Chloe, I have to talk to you. I have no-one else to turn to. Tony...' She broke into sobs, covering her face with her hands, shaking her head in anguish.

Chloe didn't want to be moved by the other woman's distress. What happened between Laura and Tony was their business, not hers, and she certainly didn't want to be involved in it. Yet it seemed too cruel and callous to send her away in this state.

'You'd better come in,' she said reluctantly, standing back to give her entry.

'Oh, thank you, thank you,' Laura babbled brokenly.

Luther barked at her as she stumbled into the hallway, instinctively picking up Chloe's dislike of the situation. He started to wriggle in her arms, wanting to get down and check out this visitor to his satisfaction, but Chloe held onto him until she saw Laura seated at the dining table and fetched a box of tissues for her to mop up the tears.

'Would you like a cup of tea?' she asked, knowing it was Laura's preferred drink.

A nod as she snuffled into a tissue.

'I'm letting my dog go now. He's sure to sniff around your feet. I'd advise you not to kick him,' she warned.

'Wouldn't do that,' Laura choked out.

Chloe released Luther, who instantly did as expected. Leaving the little terrier on guard duty, she went to the kitchen, made Laura a cup of tea and herself a coffee, and took them to the dining table. She sat across the table from her ex-personal assistant, who had assisted herself to her employer's husband, waiting for her to be composed enough to speak.

Laura finally raised a woebegone face and in a despairing voice, said, 'Tony has abandoned me. Even though I'm having his baby, he won't give me any support.'

Chloe was shocked to hear this. Despite his lies and infidelity and the nasty burst of temper that had lashed out at Luther, she hadn't thought him a complete and utter rotter.

'I can't get another job. No-one wants a

pregnant P.A.,' Laura wailed. 'I need help, Chloe. I can't manage having a baby without help.'

Lots of single mothers had to manage by themselves, Chloe thought, and Laura was definitely not a helpless kind of person, but maybe she was floundering in a trough of depression and couldn't see a way forward. 'Do you want me to speak to Tony about this?' she asked, thinking Laura had one hell of a hide to want that from the injured wife.

She shook her head. 'It's useless. He's furious that I told you, won't have anything to do with me. Or the baby.' Tears welled again. 'I'm sorry I told you the way I did, Chloe, but I was so upset, so madly in love with him, I was out of my mind that night. He was my baby's father and all I could think of was he had to break from you and marry me.'

Despite the offence to herself, Chloe couldn't help feeling a little tug of sympathy. The baby did make a difference. Although Laura shouldn't have been having an affair with Tony in the first place.

And she knew it, immediately trying to justify it, her whole body leaning forward in an appeal for understanding as she rattled on. 'I tried not to fall in love with him. He was your husband and on every moral ground he was out of bounds to me. I truly struggled against the attraction I felt,

Chloe, but he sensed it and played on it. I liked working for you. I didn't want to give up my job, but I was terribly drawn to Tony and one night when I'd had too much to drink, he seduced me into bed with him. I'm as much a victim of his charming ways as you are. I thought he really did love me and his marriage to you was just a sham to further his career. I'm terribly sorry you were hurt but at least now you've got Max Hart so you've moved on and up.'

'I've certainly moved on but divorce brings everyone down and having Max as a friend does not mean I'm up,' she sharply corrected her.

'More than a friend surely,' she snapped back, an envious flash in her eyes.

*Better value than Tony.*

She didn't say it but Chloe knew she was thinking it, and instantly started bridling against the mercenary aspect of Laura's outlook. She cut to the chase.

'Why have you come here, Laura?'

She gave an anguished shake of her head. Her hands fluttered in agitation. 'I'm out of work. I thought Tony would support me but he won't and I can't pay the rent on my apartment. I'm almost destitute, Chloe.' Her eyes begged for help. 'I don't have anyone to turn to. We used to be friends. If I hadn't been thrown so much into Tony's company because of working for you…'

Anger stirred. 'Are you saying your pregnancy is my fault?'

'No...no...but he did deceive both of us. I thought you might understand and forgive how it was, and for the sake of the baby...please, Chloe...if you could lend me some money to tide me over for a while...just bypass Tony and give me what he should be giving me. You could tell your lawyer what it's for and he could deduct it out of Tony's divorce settlement.'

*The cash cow*... Chloe couldn't forget that phrase. She wanted no part of this—none at all. Yet there was an innocent baby involved and she was appalled at Tony's callous dismissal of it. 'What sum of money do you have in mind?' she asked, careful not to commit herself to anything.

Triumph...greed...something glittered in the amber eyes that was at odds with Laura's supposed desperation, although the glitter was quickly swallowed up by another gush of tears. 'I hate asking this of you...' She blotted up the moisture with a tissue, blinked rapidly, took a deep breath and gabbled, 'Maybe a lump sum settlement would be best. I could go away, make a life for my child somewhere else, a more simple existence...'

'How much, Laura?' Chloe bored in, hating this scene.

She wrung her hands, looked distracted, then hesitantly, pleadingly answered, 'If you could write me a cheque for fifty thousand dollars…'

Fifty thousand!

The sheer boldness of it floored Chloe for a moment. Had she been such a walkover person in the past? Apply emotional pressure and she'd buckle to it every time? No mind of her own? Is that what Laura had been counting on?

However, there was still the baby to be considered.

'I won't hand out that amount of money, Laura,' she said decisively. 'I *will* talk to my lawyer about your situation and get him to talk to Tony's lawyer….'

'But that could take weeks…months…I'm down to the dregs of my bank account now,' she wailed.

'I assure you something will be done to persuade Tony into shouldering his responsibility within days,' Chloe said with steely resolve, rising from the dining table to put an end to the distasteful conversation.

'He won't…he won't,' she cried, remaining seated and burying her face in her hands.

Luther, who'd also sprung to his feet as Chloe had risen to hers, started barking at her to get up, too. Laura ignored him. Chloe sighed impatiently, shushed Luther and spoke very firmly, 'I promise you, something will be done about getting child support to you one way or another. There's no more to be said, Laura.'

'Oh, please, Chloe…' She stumbled up from her chair—a picture of wretched despair. 'Don't send me away with nothing. I don't know what I'll do.'

Was that a threat of suicide?

Luther started barking again, not liking whatever his instincts were picking up.

'If you could just give me a cheque for five thousand,' Laura begged.

Chloe didn't like it but she was troubled enough to go to her handbag and extract five hundred dollars from her purse. She held out the notes to Laura. 'That's all I have on hand. It should help enough until other money comes through for you.'

She took the money, though still pressing for more. 'I could cash a cheque…'

'No. I've promised to act on your behalf and I'll keep my word. That's it, Laura. I want you to leave now.'

Chloe headed off down the hallway to open the front door. Luther stayed behind to bark at Laura until she followed. Which she did, weeping so noisily, Chloe felt it was a deliber-ate attempt to weaken her resolve. Though it might not be. She hated this. It was churning her up, making it difficult to cling to her sense of rightness in how she had acted.

Laura paused in the doorway to start pleading pitifully again.

'No, stop!' Chloe cried, completely out of patience. 'Don't come here again, Laura. I won't be swayed into doing any more for you.'

Amazingly, her screwed-up face suddenly smoothed out. The leaking eyes flashed fury. She lashed out, not the slightest wobble in her voice. 'What are a few measly thousands to you when you're feathering your nest with Max Hart's billions? Next to nothing!' The vicious tone turned into wheedling. 'This is so bad of you, Chloe, sending me off with a pittance, not caring about the baby…'

Luther growled and jumped at Laura's legs, making her scuttle onto the porch away from him. Chloe immediately shut the door and locked it, breathing a grateful sigh of relief. She bent and scooped the little terrier up in her arms. 'Good dog, saving me again,' she crooned, petting him lovingly as she headed for the backyard, wanting as much distance as possible between her and Laura Farrell.

Her head was throbbing and her insides felt all twisted up. So many times in the past she had given in to whatever was being demanded of her, needing to end this awful inner turmoil, but she didn't feel bad about not giving in to Laura. This was Tony's fault, not hers. Tony's responsibility. Laura's, too. It was wrong that *she* should be expected to fix the situation.

Although she would call her lawyer and set up a meeting with Tony. One way or another, he had to be made to give his child appropriate support.

Max parked his Audi outside Chloe's terrace house at Centennial Park and wished once again she was still living with him at Vaucluse. He'd liked having her on hand, liked the sense of going home to her. He knew it was important to her to be independent of him, knew he should be pleased about it for her sake, but it didn't please him.

It pleased him even less when he went inside and listened to her account of Laura Farrell's visit and the outcome of it with Chloe involving herself with Tony Lipton again. It was pointless telling her she shouldn't have given any money to Laura. The baby was the big issue with Chloe. Max suspected it was always going to be a big issue—one that would inevitably separate them if he didn't rethink his life.

'Anyhow, I told my lawyer I wanted urgent

action on this and he's set up a meeting with Tony in his office tomorrow,' she finished with a grimace of distaste. 'It's going to be horrid but I can't just forget it, Max.'

'No,' he agreed. 'It will play on your mind until it's settled. But don't assume Laura told you the truth, Chloe. There's something very fishy about her story.'

Like a lot of emotional pressure for the big handout—a very clever piece of manipulation that Chloe might have fallen for a few months ago, the kind of manipulation Laura would undoubtedly have seen used on Chloe by both Stephanie Rollins and Tony.

She laughed. 'Luther didn't like the smell of it, either.'

Max smiled. 'I made a good choice, getting him for you. Worth his weight in gold.'

'Absolutely!' She wound her arms around his neck, her lovely face tilted up to his, eyes shining pleasure in his gift. 'You have a happy knack of getting everything right, Max.'

He slid his arms around her waist, drawing her closer. 'Would you like me to go with you tomorrow? Help sort things out with Tony?'

'No. This is something I should do myself.' Her mouth curled into an ironic smile. 'I can't expect you to protect me forever.'

The urge to do precisely that was very strong. Max found it difficult to back off from it. Probably his intense dislike of her ex-husband was driving it. He didn't want Chloe meeting with the slime. Yet the encounter with Laura Farrell had definitely demonstrated she could no longer be influenced into doing anything she didn't feel was right. She was no-one's fool anymore, and he had no right to fray her confidence in handling a situation which she saw as her business.

'Besides, I should be perfectly safe in my lawyer's office,' she insisted.

'True,' he conceded. 'I'm worried about when you leave it. If Tony turns nasty...' No mental strength could fight superior physical strength. Chloe *needed* him to protect her.

She frowned, fretting over the very real possibility that Tony could try physical force on her until a solution struck. 'I know. I'll call Gerry Anderson, ask him to take me to the lawyer's office and bring me home. Gerry's a very good security guard.'

An independent solution.

Little by little she was separating herself from him.

Soon she wouldn't need him at all, although wanting him was still strong. He made sure it would stay strong, pouring every bit of his sexual expertise into their love-making later in the evening. Afterwards she cuddled up to him with a satisfied sigh and murmured, 'You know, Max, I'm not with you because I want to feather my nest with your billions. You don't think that, do you?'

'No, I don't. Never would with you, Chloe.'

She snuggled down contentedly, accepting his word without question.

Max knew he couldn't buy her.

Wouldn't want to, either.

Her heart and mind were now geared to making the choices that felt right to her—running her own race.

To keep her he had to make himself *her* choice.

The hell of it was he wanted her to share everything with him, wanted to share everything with her. Running his own race into the future looked very empty without her at his side. Even Hill House felt empty without her there to come home to.

Max had never thought of his life as dark. A deep sense of purpose had driven it forward from nothing to everything he wanted. But Chloe lit him up inside with her lovely, shining, artless personality and all he had valued in the past—the brilliance of his achievements—lost its gloss compared to what she made him feel.

The plain truth was he didn't have everything he wanted.

Chloe was slipping away from him and he wanted more of her.

# CHAPTER THIRTEEN

DESPITE Chloe's determination to set things right, she felt very nervous about the confrontation with Tony. He was sure to be angry and spiteful, and although their respective lawyers would be at the meeting—hopefully keeping the situation calm and orderly—having to face her husband again was not a pleasant prospect.

'I can feel your tension, Miss Rollins,' Gerry Anderson remarked caringly as they set out on the drive into the city. 'Want to spell out the problem so I'll know what to watch out for?'

He was a nice man. She had always felt comfortable with him. It was easy to tell him what had happened with Laura Farrell and the purpose of this meeting with her husband.

'May I give you a piece of advice?' he said when she'd finished.

'Please do.'

'Miss Farrell was using every angle she could

to milk you. Sounds like a very practised con lady to me and I've had a lot of experience with that kind of person. Don't be surprised if she's already milked Mr Lipton for all she could get.'

'You mean she lied to me about Tony not giving her anything?' It was a stunning thought.

'I'm just saying it's a possibility. For my money, she was going after the cream with you.' He shot her a smile of approval. 'I'm glad you didn't fall for it.'

Chloe grimaced. 'I did give her five hundred dollars.'

'Not too bad a loss. And it made you feel better, which was fair enough. I think you'll probably have to accept it as a loss. I doubt you'll get it back from Mr Lipton. In fact, I think you should listen carefully to his side of the situation before accusing him of anything.' He glanced a quick appeal at her. 'Okay?'

'Yes. Thank you, Gerry,' she said thoughtfully. 'I really appreciate your advice.'

He smiled and nodded. 'Glad to be of assistance to you, Miss Rollins.'

'I'm glad I called you. I feel more…more prepared now.'

'I'll be right on hand if you run into any trouble,' he assured her.

'Thank you,' she said on a sigh of relief.

Having parked the car under the Opera House, Gerry escorted her up Castlereigh Street to her lawyer's chambers and settled himself in the legal secretary's office, right outside the door to the boardroom where the meeting was to be held. Tony and his lawyer were already there when hers walked her in.

The men were dressed in sober dark grey suits. She'd also worn a suit—a light pink linen—and after the preliminary formal greetings, Tony complimented her on it, smiling at her as though he was delighted to be in her company again.

'You look lovely, Chloe,' he said, throwing her into confusion with his charming manner.

She looked at the lawyers in agitated appeal. 'Let's get down to business, shall we?'

They sat at a long boardroom table, each party on opposite sides.

Tony leaned forward, hands outstretched in appeal as he earnestly stated, 'Laura lied to you, Chloe. She lied to me. She's not pregnant. Never was. It was all a lie.'

She'd been prepared for lies but not this. Nothing like this. Her mind reeled with shock. 'But…but I saw her. She had a baby bump. Four or five months…'

'Clever padding, I promise you,' Tony asserted. 'When the other guy she'd tricked contacted me,

I insisted that Laura accompany me to a doctor to have the pregnancy confirmed. She wouldn't do it, carrying on about me not trusting her, trying to get me to back off from having proof of pregnancy. No way. She's done this before. Blackmail and fraud.'

Chloe stared at him, barely able to take in what he was saying. She kept seeing Laura standing on her front porch in profile, her pregnancy on obvious show. Was Tony spinning a story to suit himself?

'What other guy?' she asked, finally homing in on his back-up proof for the accusation of blackmail and fraud.

'He'd read the story about our break-up in the newspapers. Laura Farrell's part in it. He thought about it for a while, then decided to contact me, said he didn't want another one of her suckers to suffer as he had, didn't want her to get away with it again.' Tony gestured to his lawyer. 'Show Chloe his statutory declaration.'

The lawyer opened a manila folder and passed her a sheaf of documents. On top was a statutory declaration, made by a John Dennis Flaherty with a Perth address, not anyone she knew or imagined Tony would know since he lived on the other side of Australia. Still, it was entirely possible that newspapers over there had picked up on a juicy celebrity scandal, so that part was credible.

She began reading.

According to John Flaherty, Laura Farrell had been his personal assistant four years ago. She had seductively maneuvred him into a sexual relationship although he loved his wife and had no intention of breaking up his marriage, which he'd made clear to Laura Farrell, who had apparently accepted this situation until she told him she had accidentally fallen pregnant, subsequently pressing him to leave his wife. He refused, ending the affair and offering only to pay support for their child. Laura Farrell went to his wife, begging her to dump him so they could be married. His wife divorced him. He had nothing more to do with Laura Farrell except to pay out a substantial settlement to get her out of his life. A year later he decided he wanted to see his child. He hired a private investigator to track down Laura Farrell. The investigator discovered there was no child and no medical record of there ever being a pregnancy let alone a birth.

Photocopies of the investigator's reports followed. On being questioned, Laura Farrell had declared the money was a personal gift—'a kiss-off'—and there was no proof of anything else. It was her word against his—the ex-wife would not testify on his behalf because he had admitted infidelity—so no legal action for fraud could be taken to recover the money.

It was a nasty story, making Chloe's spine crawl over how Laura had come to her—*the wife*—forcing the marriage break-up then playing on her sympathy, playing every emotional string she could, making herself out to be Tony's victim. Chloe wondered if the substantial settlement had been fifty thousand dollars—not a bad take for a bit of pregnancy padding.

'Laura didn't suck you in, did she?' Tony asked anxiously. 'You didn't shell out a lot of money to her?'

She slowly raised her gaze from the documents to look directly at him. 'No. I thought *you* should. Which is why we're here.'

His face sagged with relief. 'At least she didn't do us that damage.'

It sounded as though he was wiping all fault from himself and Chloe was not about to accept that, eyeing him coldly as she pointed out, 'You put us in this position, Tony. You gave her the power to play this game.'

'Do you think I haven't cursed myself a thousand times for falling into her trap?' he pleaded.

'Laura said you seduced her.'

'Well, she would say that to you, wouldn't she?' he scoffed. 'It served her purpose. Just as it served her purpose to hang out availability signals to me from day one of working for you. Flirtatious looks. Sexy double entendres. The occasional brush past. A whole stack of sly temptations. I laughed it off for months. I didn't want her.'

Again he leaned forward earnestly, his blue eyes begging her understanding. 'I had you, Chloe. I didn't want Laura Farrell. Even when she was doing it to me I told myself I should be stopping her, but I'd had too much to drink at the party and…' He raked his hands through his hair in an anguished manner. 'I tell you, Chloe, she's a female predator. I was coming out of the bathroom. She pushed me back in, had me unzipped in a flash, went down on me and…'

'Spare me the details!' Chloe snapped.

'I'm sorry…sorry… I'm just trying to explain how it was, how I never meant it to happen. I love *you*,' he cried emphatically.

Anger flared at the way he was twisting things again. Whether Laura had seduced him or the other way around didn't really matter because it hadn't stopped in that bathroom. Her eyes savagely mocked any excuse for his continued infidelity.

'Don't tell me this was a once only lapse on your part, Tony. I know it wasn't.'

'What did Laura tell you?' he quickly countered.

Chloe shot down any more lies before he could

come up with them. 'My mother told me. She dismissed the affair as unimportant. *The affair*, Tony. Not a one-night stand.'

Chloe could see him recalculating, knowing he was under the gun with Stephanie Rollins's sharp eyes never missing anything. It wouldn't suit her purpose to plead his cause so he had to give the affair a forgivable twist.

'All right,' he conceded with a self-deprecating grimace. 'Laura knew how to work sex to get to me and it did. Any man would have taken what she was giving out. I'm only human, Chloe. But it made me feel guilty as hell and in the end I did stop it because I cared about our marriage and didn't want her messing with it.'

She wondered if Max would have taken what Laura could do with sex. Obviously Tony had found it more exciting than what he'd had at home. Was sex more important to men than love? Perhaps the reason why Max had never married was because sex with the one woman got boring after a while, and he preferred to remain free to go after something new and exciting when the urge took him.

Like with her.

A wave of depression rolled through Chloe. She didn't want to listen to anymore. There was no need to fight for child support on Laura

Farrell's behalf. The business of this meeting was over. She looked bleakly at the man she had married with blind faith in love and spoke what she knew to be the truth.

'You didn't want to lose your cash cow, Tony.'

His face flushed an ugly red. 'Those are Laura's words, not mine. She was determined on alienating you from me, Chloe, but she's out of our lives now. No baby for her to hang onto me. That's all behind us.' Again his hands reached out in appeal. 'I'm begging you to forgive me. Give us another chance.'

She shook her head, pushed her chair back and stood up, turning to the two lawyers. 'Thank you for your services in clarifying the situation with Laura Farrell.'

All three men rose to their feet, Tony rushing into more urgent speech. 'Please think about it, Chloe. We had a good marriage before this. I know you wanted a baby and I put it off but I won't if you give us another chance. I promise you...'

Chloe had no doubt he would keep that promise. A baby was the best string of all to hold her to their marriage. But she vividly remembered how he'd treated Luther—a baby dog— and she couldn't see Tony as a good father. Nor as a good husband for her. He never had been.

'This meeting is over,' she stated flatly. 'It wasn't about us, Tony.'

'But surely you now realise I was Laura's victim, just as John Flaherty was,' he pleaded. 'You're letting her win, Chloe.'

'No. She didn't get anything out of this.' Except the five hundred dollars, which would have been peanuts in her overall scheme.

'She got the satisfaction of breaking us up,' Tony vehemently argued.

Oddly enough, Chloe now felt Laura Farrell had done her a favour—the catalyst for breaking up a lot of bad things in her life. 'I've moved on, Tony. There's no going back,' she said firmly.

An angry red flushed his face this time. 'I can forgive you Max Hart. He took advantage of the situation.'

She shook her head. 'I'm leaving now. I'd appreciate it—' she glanced at Tony's lawyer '—if you and your client remain in this boardroom until I've gone.'

The lawyer nodded. 'Understood, Miss Rollins.'

'Chloe…' Tony persisted pleadingly.

She turned away and her own lawyer escorted her to the door, opening it.

'Max Hart won't marry you,' Tony threw after her. 'He won't give you children. You'll end up on the scrap heap with the rest of the women he's had.'

She knew Max would move on as he always did and she knew it would hurt when he did. But he had been there for her at a critical time in her life, giving her what she needed, helping her to find the strength to become a person who could stand on her own feet and make her own choices. She fiercely resolved to remember the good he'd done after he moved on. It had to outweigh the hurt she would inevitably feel.

Her lawyer stepped back to usher her out of the boardroom. Chloe walked forward into the legal secretary's office.

'I'd give you a better life than Max Hart ever will,' Tony persisted in a last, heart-clawing plea. 'I swear you're the only woman for me. I'll never again even look at anyone else. And we'll have a family. As many children as you want. What we had was good before Laura mucked it up. Think about it, Chloe. Think about it. Call me....'

The door was closed behind her.

Gerry Anderson rose from his chair in the secretary's office.

Chloe thanked her lawyer.

She could leave now and she did.


Max checked his watch again, frowning over the time that had passed since Chloe's eleven o'clock meeting with the lawyers and Tony Lipton.

'What's got you so uptight, Max?' Angus Hilliard inquired, his bespectacled grey eyes glinting with sharp curiosity. 'That's the third time you've checked the time and frowned, apart from the fact you haven't been giving our business your undivided attention.'

Max grimaced at the head of his legal department who was too astute a man to let anything go unnoticed. 'Waiting on a call from Chloe. A bit of nasty stuff going on with Tony Lipton and Laura Farrell.'

'Ah! The pregnant P.A. making more waves? Anything I can do?'

'No. The divorce lawyers are handling it, Angus. What's worrying me is the meeting shouldn't have dragged on this long. I wanted to accompany Chloe to it….'

'Better you didn't, Max.'

'I know. I know. But I don't trust her husband to play anything straight. Anyhow, Chloe came up with the idea of having the security guy escort her to and from the meeting.'

'Gerry Anderson?'

'The same,' Max affirmed.

'He's one of the best,' Angus assured him, having vetted the security guard personally. 'Why not call him? Check out what's going on? I have his number here.' He opened the teledex on his desk.

'I'm not his client this time,' Max pointed out. 'And Chloe promised to call me.'

'You have his client's interests at heart,' Angus argued. 'I'm sure Anderson will appreciate that position.'

It smacked of going behind Chloe's back. Max didn't like it, yet he felt too uneasy not to make the call. The sense of Chloe separating herself from him was getting stronger. She should have contacted him by now. Unless something was very wrong.

He had to know.

He made the call.

Ten minutes later he was assured that Chloe was safely home, had been since shortly after midday. He'd also been informed of the fraudulent pregnancy—a con game Laura Farrell had played profitably before. The most disturbing news, however, was Gerry Anderson's report of what he'd overheard Tony Lipton say as Chloe was leaving the lawyer's office—the strikes against any hope of sharing a long-term future with him lined up against what her husband was offering. And the final plea...

*Call me.*

She hadn't made the promised call to him—the man whose lifestyle suggested she was only one link in a chain of many women, none of whom had locked him into marriage or having children.

Was she considering the self-serving promises her husband was holding out to her? Tony Lipton would have played the victim to the hilt, begging forgiveness, pleading for another chance to make a go of their marriage—cancel out his affair with Laura, cancel out her affair with Max, make a fresh start, have a family together...

'Max, you're wearing out my carpet.'

The dry comment jolted him into realising he was prowling around Angus's office like a fiercely frustrated tiger, wanting to lash out at the situation, yet hemmed in by bars he couldn't simply knock aside. Chloe was no longer living on his property, not so readily accessible, especially if she didn't choose to be. And she was still married to Tony Lipton, who was undoubtedly trying to capitilise on Laura Farrell's deceit.

He came to a halt in front of Angus's desk, who leaned back in his chair and held up his hands in mock fear of being shot down where he sat. 'Whoa! I'm not the target. I'm the negotiator, remember? Just point me in the direction you want to take....'

'She's mine!' The words snapped out in an explosive burst of feeling. His hand sliced the air as violently as a slashing sword. 'I don't want that worm of a husband wriggling back into her life!'

Angus shrugged, looking askance at Max as

though his behaviour was distinctly weird. 'Why would she take him back?' he queried in a tone of calm reasoning.

Max snarled back at him. 'Because the P.A.'s pregnancy has been proved fraudulent. Because Tony Lipton knows how to twist that to his advantage—an infidelity trade-off—plus all the forever promises of love, having a family.' He threw up his hands. 'That pregnancy was the breaking point because Chloe wanted a baby.'

'Then give her one, Max. Give her one.'

As though it was the simplest thing in the world!

Max rolled his eyes.

Angus proceeded to argue his strategy, the grey eyes glinting absolute certainty behind the frameless spectacles. 'If Chloe wants children, sooner or later you're going to lose her if you're not prepared to give her any. Basic instinct in most women. Given that you want to keep her, there's only one sure-fire *win* position for you to take, Max. Otherwise, you'd best start resigning yourself to letting her go.'

He couldn't bear the thought of letting her go. It would be totally intolerable to watch her walk away from him to share her life with someone else.

Angus wriggled his fingers in a weighing-up

gesture. 'You've never had a problem attracting beautiful women. I happen to think that Chloe Rollins has something very special, but…it's your life, Max. Your choice.'

Angus was right.

There was only one sure-fire way to *win*.

The only question was…would Chloe want to join him in the longest run that two people could ever take on together?

# CHAPTER FOURTEEN

CHLOE sat on the garden bench in the small backyard, feeding Luther pieces of ham as he frolicked around her feet. It was good to be outside in the open air, good to have the uncomplicated company of her darling little dog. She didn't feel like eating lunch herself yet. The meeting with Tony had left her with a sense of deep distaste. She didn't want to talk about it, either.

Her mobile telephone lay beside her on the bench, along with the mug of coffee she'd brought out to drink. Max would be expecting a call from her. She'd promised to let him know the outcome of the meeting. Dirty business, she thought, the whole thing so horribly grubby she didn't want to rehash it.

Especially the sex in the bathroom bit. Had Max ever had a similar experience while he was in one of his past relationships? Had he knocked it back or let it happen, enjoying the thrill of unplanned pleasure? How much had a woman ever really meant to him, beyond the sexual satisfaction he both took and gave?

She barely registered the distant ringing of the doorbell but Luther went streaking inside to bark at the caller behind the front door. Chloe didn't move, reluctant to see or talk to anyone. It rang a few more times. Luther kept barking. Chloe reasoned that both Gerry Anderson and Max had her mobile telephone number. They could call her to check if she was in or not. No-one else had the right to bother her.

Whoever was at the door eventually went away. Luther returned, looking triumphantly pleased with himself for having driven off what was obviously an unwelcome visitor. He trotted over to her to be petted and she smiled at him, leaning down to pick him up and set him on her lap, where he curled up contentedly as she patted him.

'I'm glad I've got you, Luther,' she murmured—the something *real* Max had given her as a substitute for a baby.

A thoughtful gift.

A caring gift.

But also a stop-gap gift because Max had no intention of giving her a baby.

She realised now why he had commented on

her relatively young age—only twenty-seven, not old enough to be desperate about the biological clock. He obviously hadn't wanted to feel guilty about holding up her need for motherhood. Parenthood was not in Max's plans. Lust was a temporary thing in his life, not to be encumbered with any lasting commitment. He'd acted with integrity, but also with self-interest. Which was fair enough, Chloe told herself. It wasn't his fault that she wanted so much more from him.

Luther stirred, his head lifting, ears pricking up, a low growl rumbling in his throat as he stared at the back fence, which closed off the property from a narrow alley between the rows of terrace houses. The gate allowing access to the alley started rattling. Luther leapt off her lap and raced down the yard, barking his head off.

Chloe was stirred to action herself. The gate was bolted so no-one could gain easy entry, but someone intent on burgling might scale the two-metre fence. Since the front doorbell hadn't been answered, the assumption might well have been made that no-one was home. Breaking in from the backyard was nowhere near as public as from the street along Centennial Park.

She picked up the mobile phone and quickly followed Luther down to the fence. 'I'm calling the police if you don't quit shoving at my gate,' she yelled out. 'Just go away or I'll hit triple zero right now!'

'Chloe!' It sounded like a cry of relief. 'It's me…your mother. I was worried about you. Let me in, for God's sake!'

Chloe was too stunned to reply. Her mother! Here! Who had told her this address? Laura Farrell had tracked it down so it probably wasn't incredible that another determined person could and her mother was nothing if not determined.

'Chloe!' The demanding tone was back in force. 'Let me in!'

'No, I don't think I will,' she answered, bridling against her mother's relentless will-power. 'There's no need to worry about me. I'm perfectly okay.'

'I don't believe it,' her mother snapped. 'You always hid when you were upset about things and that's what you're doing—hiding in there. I can help straighten everything out for you, Chloe. Just open the gate….'

'I don't want your help, Mother. Please go and leave me alone.'

'I know all about the Laura Farrell fraud. I know what went on in your meeting with Tony this morning. He desperately wants you back, Chloe….'

'Have you come as his ambassador?'

'No, of course not! Though I'd have to say he'd

be more devoted to you from now on than Max Hart ever will be, but it's you that I care about. What's best for *you*.'

'I can work that out for myself, thank you.'

'No, you can't. You have no idea. You're a babe in the woods in this business. Max Hart will exploit you for as long as you're starry-eyed with him. You have to understand his interest in you won't last, and if I'm not at your side to make sure there's no fallout damage, you could sink without a trace. If you're clued in you can use this affair with him as a stepping stone. You've got to learn how to use your head, baby! I can teach you, show you how to work the angles…'

Revulsion created waves of nausea through Chloe's empty stomach. The strident voice went on, spelling out how she could *use* Max to advance her career, to extract as much as she could from him while the affair was still running hot, because it would end…

It would end…

'Stop it!' she screamed, unable to bear hearing any more.

'Chloe, this is why you need me,' her mother argued. 'Let me in, baby, so we can talk it through. I'm your mother. I'll always be here for you. You need me.'

'No!' Chloe clapped her hands over her ears.

'I'm going inside now. Leave me be, Mother, or I *will* call the police.'

The voice kept trying to beat at her mind as she bolted away from the fence, almost tripping over Luther, who was scampering around her, distressed at her distress. It was a relief to reach the door into the kitchen, even more of a relief to close herself inside the house. She pelted up the stairs to her bedroom, stripped off her clothes, crawled into bed, buried her face in the pillow and dragged the bed-covers over her head, shutting out the rest of the world and everyone in it.

She didn't care if it was hiding.

Sometimes hiding was the only way to fend off the unbearable.

Max waited for Chloe's call all afternoon, growing more and more tense as the silence from her continued. It wasn't in her nature to break a promise. Had the meeting with Tony stirred such deep mental and emotional turmoil that contacting him felt wrong to her? Whatever was going on, Max couldn't shake the feeling that he was on the losing end of it.

By five o'clock he was determined on confronting the situation. He drove to her house. She didn't answer the doorbell. Luther didn't bark at it, either. It suggested she had gone out and taken the dog with her, possibly for a walk in the park. He crossed the street. It took him half an hour of criss-crossing Centennial Park to assure himself she wasn't there. Totally frustrated at this point, Max whipped out his mobile phone and called her, only to be frustrated further by finding hers was switched off.

He returned to the house, rang the doorbell again. No answer. Chloe had given him a key for his convenience if she was occupied when he arrived at her door. This was not an expected visit and Max was reluctant to use it without her implicit permission. Invasion of privacy did not sit well with him, yet the possibility that something might be badly wrong inside could not be ignored. More accidents occurred in the home than anywhere else.

He unlocked the front door, opened it. As he stepped into the hallway, a low growl alerted him to Luther's presence. He looked up. The dog stood at the top of the stairs, stiff-legged and bristling, ready to leap into attack until he recognised Max. Then he relaxed and trotted off in the direction of Chloe's bedroom.

Was she asleep? At this hour of the day? Sick? Too ill to move?

Max closed and relocked the door, moved quickly and quietly to the staircase. Conscious of his heart beating much faster than normal, he mounted the stairs two at a time, anxious to check out the situation, do whatever was needed to be done.

She was in bed. Clothes were strewn carelessly around the floor as though getting them off had been her one thought. Only the top of her blonde silky hair was visible above the bed-covers. Her body was tightly curled up beneath them. Luther had nestled himself on the pillow next to hers, obviously intent on being as close as he could, waiting for her face to emerge as well as guarding against her being disturbed.

Max stood beside them for a while, listening to Chloe's breathing. As far as he could tell it was normal. He resisted the urge to strip off his own clothes and join her in bed, not for sex, simply to hold her close and assure himself everything was still right between them. But he knew it wasn't right. She had shut him out. Whether it was a deliberate act or an emotionally fraught one he had no idea. Either way he intended to fight the decision.

He pulled up a chair and sat beside the bed—man and dog both waiting for the most important person in their lives to stir, to respond to them again.

Chloe moved sluggishly towards consciousness. Her eyelids felt too heavy to lift. It was easier to leave them closed. She might slide back into oblivion again. The memory of crying herself to sleep made a blank nothingness more desirable than having her mind recall the reasons for her misery, starting up another tormenting treadmill of thoughts. Better to keep them blocked out.

She took a deep breath and wriggled into a different position, frowning as she realised there was other movement on the bed. Then a small wet tongue licked her forehead. Luther! Had she slept a long time, missing on giving him dinner? It was wrong to keep indulging herself if he was hungry. He'd been such a good guard dog.

She dragged an arm up, pushed the bed-covers away from her head and affectionately ruffled the fur behind Luther's ears. 'It's okay. Mummy's waking up, baby,' she mumbled, slowly forcing her eyes open.

'I'm here, too.'

Max's voice—deep and gravelly, wanting his presence known and acknowledged.

Her eyelids flew up.

He was sitting on a chair beside the bed, leaning forward, elbows on his knees, his dark riveting eyes scanning hers anxiously. 'I was worried about you, Chloe, so I let myself in.'

She grimaced, remembering her promise to call him. 'Sorry. Should have phoned. My mother came and…'

'She came here?'

His sharp concern brought back the whole horrible barrage of advice. 'I won't do it,' she muttered fiercely.

'Do what?'

She hauled herself up to a sitting position, hugging her knees as she viewed the man she loved with rueful eyes, answering his question with blunt honesty. 'Screw all I can get out of you while you're still enjoying a relationship with me.'

He straightened up in his chair, his face tightening with grimly held anger. 'You shouldn't have let her in, Chloe. Shouldn't have listened to her.'

'I didn't let her in. But it's a bit hard not to hear her when she's shouting at you over the back fence.'

'Persistent harridan!' he grated out, rising to his feet, his hand flying out in a furious, cutting-off gesture. 'You can't stay here, Chloe. She's going to keep pestering you now that she knows where you're living. And she'll tell Tony this address, have him camping on your doorstep next, use him to help muddy your mind against me, get you back with her. And him.'

It was strange seeing Max so disturbed and edgy. He'd always been the man in absolute control of himself and the situation. She watched him stalk around her bedroom, aggression pouring from him as he talked through what was on his mind.

'No doubt in the world that Tony won't try to get you back, use Laura Farrell's fraud to plead malevolent manipulation on her part, grovel for forgiveness...'

Surprise spilled into an instant query. 'You know about that?'

He whirled to face her, throwing up his hands in wild dismissal. 'I was worried about you not contacting me. I called Gerry Anderson, and before you say it wasn't my business to ask him what was happening with you, I couldn't stand not knowing if you were in some kind of trouble. Which is also why I used the key you gave me to enter this house when there was no response from you. And Luther showed me where you were because he understands I care about you,' he finished vehemently, his eyes blazing a fierce refusal to accept any protest about his actions.

At the mention of his name, Luther leapt up from his pillow and trotted down to the end of the bed for Max to pat him in approval. Which he did, eyeing Chloe with determined purpose. 'I'm taking you and Luther home with me. No argument.' He took out his mobile phone. 'I'll call

Edgar, tell him we're coming, ask Elaine to do dinner for two…'

'No, Max.' She shook her head at him. It was strange how calm she felt, probably from having spent all her emotion before falling asleep this afternoon. 'I'm not going to run away from my life again.'

He frowned. 'You're better off with me. I can protect you, ensure that…'

'For how long, Max?' she wryly inserted.

'As long as need be,' he retorted, his strength of purpose sharp and strong.

She sighed, looking at him with sadly resigned eyes. 'Eventually it will end…whatever you feel for me. And if I let myself become dependent on you, it will be even harder to manage on my own. Today was—' she winced '—difficult…nasty… and I just wanted to shut it out, but I have to face other things that come up, Max, not expect you to always rescue me.'

His mouth thinned in frustration. His eyes burned with the need to override her opposition. 'I don't like it,' burst from him with explosive feeling. 'I don't like you being on your own. You belong with me.'

*Belong…?*

Her heart flipped at his use of that word. It was the first time he had expressed such a possessive connection—the deep caring it carried. She stared at him, her breathing completely suspended, hopes and fears tumbling through her mind as her need and love for him beat through them, demanding the chance for real fulfilment.

Yet there was one question she wanted answered and it spilled out in a wild rush. 'Would you have had sex with her, Max?'

'What?' He looked stunned, confused.

'Laura Farrell...' A flood of heat burned her cheeks as she explained what she needed to know. 'If she had come onto you in a bathroom...like unzipping you...and...and being aggressively available...'

His grimace held an appalled distaste, wiping the horrid image from her mind even before he spoke a vehement denial. 'Never! I would have knocked her back so fast...' He shook his head, frowning over her need to ask. 'I've been targeted by women like that many times, Chloe. I've always turned them away. They're not only trouble, they're not my choice.'

The relief of absolute certainty was sweet. Of course, Max wouldn't take on anything he didn't choose himself. She should have known that. The formidable drive of the man was based on pursuing *his* will. The master of control. Although he didn't seem so absolutely in control of himself right now.

'Is that how Tony excused his infidelity?' he shot at her, brows beetling down over a dark blaze of anger in his eyes.

'It doesn't matter, Max.'

'It matters to me if you think I'd act like that.'

'No.' She offered an apologetic smile. 'I realise now you wouldn't. I'm sorry for bringing it up.'

'I'm not like Tony, Chloe,' he stated fiercely.

'I know.' She heaved a sigh. 'This whole messy business muddled up my mind.'

'Which is why I want you free of it.' A few quick strides and he was sitting at her side on the bed, one arm curled around her shoulder, turning her towards him, his other hand tenderly caressing her tumbled hair away from her face, his eyes intensely commanding surrender to his will. 'Come home with me, at least for tonight, Chloe. You've had more than enough to deal with today. Let me take you back to Hill House. Let Elaine pamper you with a fine dinner. Give yourself this time to relax and not be hassled by anything.'

He kissed her forehead, as though imprinting his words on her mind. 'Say you will,' he murmured, drawing back enough to give her a self-mocking little smile. 'If only to save me from worrying about you.'

She couldn't help smiling back. 'Well, that's something I can rescue *you* from. So yes, I will.

Go ahead and call Edgar while I have a shower and get dressed.'

It was an easy decision to make. Max did care about her and she loved his caring, wanting to bask in it as long as she could. And maybe he would want her to belong with him forever. She had to give it a chance. It was impossible to imagine ever meeting another man as wonderful as him—a man in a million, Maximilian Hart.

# CHAPTER FIFTEEN

CHLOE stood under the shower, growing slightly uneasy about her impulsive decision to go with Max to Hill House. It began to feel too much like the beginning of their relationship when she'd taken refuge with him, letting him keep her safe from the same three people who had once again caused her distress. Though she had stood up to them this time—turned them all away from the life she was making for herself. It was really their references to her relationship with Max that had upset her.

But they were wrong about him only wanting her for sexual pleasure. Max cared about her. He'd helped her develop into the more confident person she had become under his guidance—capable of managing by herself, choosing what answered her needs. There was nothing selfish about that. And he worried about her well-being, which surely meant she was much more to him than a throw-away woman who merely served the purpose of satisfying him for a while.

*You belong with me now.*

Chloe hugged those fiercely spoken words to her heart as she stepped out of the shower, dried herself, and began to get dressed. They felt as though they held a promise that Max would never throw her away. If that was true, letting him take her home with him was okay—a step into a future she hadn't allowed herself to envisage before. Although maybe she was hoping for too much.

Anyway, it was only for one night. The chance that it might mean what she yearned for was worth taking, even though it was going to hurt if it came to nothing apart from removing Max's concern for her.

It wasn't until she automatically checked her appearance in the mirror that she realised her hands had chosen the same blue-and-white polka dot dress she had worn to Hill House the first time Max had taken her there. It shook her for a moment. Was it some psychological slip back into the past?

Then she remembered feeling that electric connection between them when Max had walked into the hotel room and seen her dressed in it. Perhaps it had been more than an unspoken mutual sexual attraction—possibly a subconscious recognition that they would become deeply significant in each other's lives. Chloe wanted to believe that. She kept the dress on, wanting it to be a good omen for the future she couldn't help hoping for.

Having brushed her hair and livened up her face with some make-up, she took a deep breath to settle the nervous flutters in her stomach and walked out of her bedroom to the top of the staircase. Max was in the hallway below, in the act of carrying Luther's transportation basket to the front door, ready to go.

'We don't have to take Luther with us, Max,' she called out. 'He's used to staying here alone when we go to functions.'

He swung around, looking up at her, his dark eyes blazing with determined purpose, battle-tension making his strong, male face all hard angles. 'This isn't a function,' he asserted. Then as he took in her appearance, his expression changed, softening, warming into a smile of pleasure, his eyes transmitting an intense satisfaction that shot a bolt of happiness through Chloe. Clearly she looked *right* to him. Maybe he was even thinking she was right *for* him.

'Luther will be happier with us, Chloe,' he said.

*With us*…the two of them…the three of them together.

'I've promised him chicken for dinner,' he added persuasively. 'Elaine is already cooking it for him. You know how he loves chicken.'

She laughed, needing some outlet for the bubble of bliss that had bounced around her mind. 'Okay. I can't do him out of that treat,' she replied, telling herself not to attach too much meaning to everything. It would be too big a letdown if she wove a fantasy that had nothing to do with reality.

He watched her walk down the stairs, making her acutely aware of his physical effect on her—the tug that grew stronger with every step she took towards him. He told her he'd locked up the house apart from the front door, which he proceeded to open, ushering her outside. Once they were in his car and on their way, he reached over and took her hand, interlacing his fingers with hers in a strong grip.

Warmth flooded up her arm and tingled through her heart. He wanted connection with her. It definitely wasn't just sexual. She stared down at the physical link he'd just made, not a seductive, sensual one but powerfully possessive, reinforcing those wonderfully sweet words—*you belong with me.*

Please let it be true, Chloe wished, her whole being aching for it to be so. What she had once felt with Tony—being in love—had been such a fluffy, insubstantial thing compared to the depth of her love for Max. She knew there could never be another man to replace him in her life. If he didn't love her as she loved him…but she didn't want to think about that tonight. She simply wanted to soak up all Max's caring for her—caring she'd never had from her mother or Tony.

They arrived at the gates to his property at Vaucluse. He released her hand to operate the remote control to open them. As they drove in and Hill House came into view, a sense of homecoming seared her soul. This was why she had stayed away. It was a magical house with its classical perfection, promising a happy life inside its stately walls. Max had shared it with her. She had loved being here with him.

He parked the car in the courtyard adjacent to the front entrance of the mansion. He didn't immediately alight from the driver's seat, turning to her instead, taking her hand again and studying her face intently as though he needed to see every shade of her response as he said, 'It wasn't only the three E's who've missed having you here, Chloe. I've missed you, too. I hope you feel right about coming back tonight. It feels very right to me.'

For a moment she felt too choked up to speak. His fingers were dragging on the flesh of her hand as though wanting to dig inside her, feel what was going on in her mind and heart and soul. It was impossible to hide how much his words meant to her. She tried not to answer him too fervently.

'Yes, it does feel good, Max. Thank you for…'

'No need to thank me.' He smiled, happy with her reply, his happiness sending hers zooming to giddy heights. 'This house is waiting for you to light it up with your presence. Let's not make it wait any longer.'

She could hardly believe Max saying such a romantic thing to her but she glowed with pleasure at the lovely fantasy that she lit up his home. And he'd missed her being here. Max always spoke the truth. He wasn't into deception. There was no reason not to believe him.

Luther had fallen asleep in his transportation basket. Max lifted it out before collecting her from the passenger seat, offering his arm for the walk up the porch steps. The front door was opened by Edgar before they reached it, the portly butler half-bowing to Max as he stood back to give them entry.

'Good evening, Mr Hart.' Then he actually broke his air of great dignity to smile at Chloe. 'Welcome home, Miss Rollins. We are all delighted to be of service to you again.'

Her heart swelled with a huge rush of emotion. It was so good to be with people who truly liked you and wished you well, no rotten agendas for using you. Her own smile beamed delight back at him. 'Thank you, Edgar. I've missed you, too.

And Elaine and Eric. It's lovely to be…here with you all once more,' she finished in a rush.

It had been on the tip of her tongue to say *home*, but as much as she wanted it to be, it wasn't really hers. Not yet. Maybe not ever.

Nevertheless, the three E's went out of their way to make her feel at home. When she and Max took Luther to the kitchen, Elaine fussed over her as though she was a long-lost daughter, Eric was all smiles, saying he'd planted her favourite flowers in pots outside the children's house. Luther woke up and Eric took him out of the basket to give him a cuddle—with much face-licking—exclaiming over how much the little fella had grown and what a good dog he was, great company for when he was working in the grounds.

Edgar served them dinner in the dining room with more panache than usual, encouraging Chloe's appetite by describing in detail the courses Elaine had prepared and informing Max he'd taken the liberty of opening a bottle of his finest wine, which Max instantly approved as entirely appropriate.

Amazingly, Chloe completely relaxed over dinner, basking in the flow of benevolence towards her and the caring implicit in everything Max said and did. The food was superb, the wine divine, and she felt beautifully pampered as though she was very special to everyone at Hill House. And Max's eyes kept telling she was. Which fed the hope that he really meant this to be her home, as well as his.

Not a refuge.

A real home.

For always.

After dinner, he suggested they stroll down to the children's house to check out Eric's flower pots. Daylight saving was still in force so it was only twilight, not too dark to see. She happily agreed, linking her arm with his, loving the feeling of being close to this very special man, wanting the complete sense of intimacy with him.

Max also seemed content to simply have her at his side, remaining silent as they walked around the pool patio. It was a beautiful evening. Stars were appearing in the violet sky. The air was scented with the jasmine that covered some of the pergola. With the northern side of the city lighting up beyond the harbour, it was like looking at a sparkling fairyland over the water.

She smiled to herself, remembering how nervous and wary she'd felt in Max's presence when she'd first come here, disturbed by the sexual magnetism of the man, fearful of his motives for taking her into his protection. He truly cared about her, cared for the person she was and the person she wanted to be. No-one could have looked after her as well as he had, keeping her safe, leading her into thinking for herself, making decisions, acting on them.

She hugged his arm and leaned her head against his shoulder as they descended the flight of steps to the children's terrace. 'Thank you for being the man you are, Max,' she said.

'I'm no longer who I was,' he answered in a wry tone. 'I should be thanking you for the woman you are, Chloe. You've changed the way I've viewed life, made me aware there's far more to be had than what I'd aimed for…settled for…'

'Like what?' she asked, curious to know and understand the effect she'd had on him.

He was slow to reply, and when he did it was as though he was musing to himself, thinking back through the distance of years. 'I guess I learnt emotional detachment from a very early age…the art of a survivor, looking out for myself, not letting other people get to me deeply enough to hurt, not being dependent on anyone for anything. I made myself self-sufficient. That's not to say I haven't enjoyed the company of many people—men and women—but I never let the connection turn into a need for it, because that would have given them a kind of power over me, influencing what I considered the successful operation of my life.'

'Well, no-one could argue with how successful that's been, Max,' she said, her heart catapulting wildly around her chest at the hope he was leading up to saying it was different with her, that the connection between them was so deep, he couldn't bear to live without it.

'Successful as far as ambition and material gain are concerned,' he said mockingly. 'So successful I was blinded to what I was missing.'

They reached the bottom of the steps and started along the path to the children's house. Chloe wanted to ask what he was missing but Max kept talking and it was more important to listen than to interrupt.

'Even when my instincts were sliding past my mental shield, whispering thoughts that were alien to my usual thinking, I reasoned them away as foolish fantasies.' He shook his head. 'They weren't foolish. Deep down in my heart they were the truth of what I wanted with you, Chloe.'

He stopped her on the doorstep, turned her to face him, his expression gravely intent, his eyes searing hers with a blaze of need. He lifted a hand to her cheek, cupping her face as though it was infinitely precious to him. 'You *are* my Mary.'

Mary? Confusion rolled through Chloe's mind.

He'd spoken that name before, when he'd returned to the hotel suite after severing the agency ties with her mother…those few moments of electric stillness as he'd looked at her…then dismissing his use of the name, saying she reminded him of someone.

Anguish twisted through her heart. Had he lost a Mary? She didn't want to be linked to some other woman who'd been dear to him. She needed to be wanted for herself.

'That's not my name, Max,' she whispered hoarsely, her throat having gone completely dry.

'It's *my* name for you. Chloe doesn't suit you. I renamed you Mary in my mind even before there was any chance of our coming together. Not Chloe Rollins. Mary Hart.'

'Hart?' She was so stunned, it was all she could do to mutter, 'But that's your name.'

'Yes. And I'm asking you to take it. Be my wife. Share the rest of your life with me,' he said with a passionate intensity that completely rocked her. 'I know we can't marry until after your divorce but I can't wait another day for us to be together, live together.' He sucked in a deep breath and the words she most yearned to hear burst from his lips. 'I love you, Chloe. I love everything about you. And I want nothing more than for you to be yourself with me.'

'Oh, Max!' The words spilled from her lips on a breath of pure bliss. She wound her arms around his neck, her eyes shining with all the love that didn't have to be hidden anymore. 'I want to be with you, too. All the days of my life. I had to force myself to leave here because I thought there'd be a time limit on our relationship and I had to prepare myself for a separation, even though I knew I'd never love anyone as much as I do you.'

'I hated the separation. We'll never be separated again,' he declared vehemently. 'We'll give each other all we've missed out on in the lives we've had up until now. We'll make the best of all possible futures together, Chloe.'

And he sealed that promise to her in a kiss that made her believe it, the whole indomitable power of the man pouring through her—filling her heart, her mind, her body and soul with absolute trust in him, making her certain that they did belong with each other and always would.

They would have a wonderful future together.

When Maximilian Hart set out to make something happen, he made it happen.

# EPILOGUE

VERY shortly after Chloe had accepted Max's proposal of marriage, he informed her that her mother had moved to Los Angeles and would undoubtedly contrive to set up as an actors' agent there. The ruthless gleam in his dark eyes told her the master player had been at work, ensuring that the woman he loved would not be stressed by Stephanie Rollins ever again. Chloe didn't question him about it, simply accepting with huge relief that her mother had been cut completely out of her life and would never re-enter it.

She learnt from her lawyer that Tony had also moved away from Sydney, setting himself up at Byron Bay on the far north coast of New South Wales where there was a community of writers. Apparently he fancied the idea of writing a book. Chloe thought it more likely that was an image he would use to pass himself off as someone worth knowing while he bummed around on her money.

Not that she cared. It was worth the divorce settlement to have him out of sight and out of mind. She wondered if Max had forcefully suggested the move to him but he only muttered, 'Good riddance!' when she passed on the news. The divorce went through without any further meeting with Tony and that, also, was a relief.

Chloe did not worry about being confronted by Laura Farrell again. Her ex-P.A. would have known her fraud would be uncovered as soon as Tony was contacted about child support, making it certain there was no profit in making another approach. She was, in fact, arrested some months later, for trying to blackmail a prominent businessman, and Chloe was glad that someone had put an end to her evil mischief.

She and Max were married as soon as it was legally possible.

Gerry Anderson became a permanent fixture in their lives, accompanying Chloe whenever Max could not be at her side, and watching out for their children's safety as the years went on.

Max moved on to producing movies, which always starred his wife and were invariably box-office successes because he never chose to bring anything but satisfying stories to the big screen. The two of them became legends in the movie world, renowned not only for having the golden touch, but for being a golden couple, their obvious love for each other never losing its shine.

They had four children, two boys and two girls, all of whom travelled with them wherever they went. They had residences in New York and London, villas in France and Italy, but these were only places for their family to live when work demanded they be in other countries. Hill House was always home to them.

The children loved having their own little house to play in and it was kept for their exclusive use. Guests were housed in the mansion. The three E's stayed on, keeping everything as it should be for the rest of their lives, training and supervising their replacements as they grew too old to carry on their roles themselves. They were like grandparents, enjoying and taking a caring interest in the children, minding Luther when the family was away.

Luther lived to the grand old age of eighteen. He was buried beside the children's house with a gravestone that read Here lies Luther, the best guard dog in the world, and much loved pet of the Hart family.

The question Max had once asked of himself—would he be good for Chloe Rollins in the long run?—lost all significance in the future they made together. He took immense pleasure in watching her face show everything she felt and those feelings invariably lifted his own heart. He was not only good for her, she was good for him.

He didn't know that in her eyes he was her wonderful white knight.

Not one bit dark.

He'd banished all the darkness for her, just as she had for him.

In their private life they became known as Max and Mary to all those close to them.

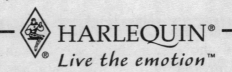